NINE LIVES

The Douglas Files: Book Ten

Volume III

by

Nathan Birr

Published by BEACON BOOKS, LLC

Cover Images Copyright ©
vichie81/Shutterstock.com
okimo/Shutterstock.com
Konstanttin/Shutterstock.com

Scriptures taken from the Holy Bible, New International Version®, NIV®. Copyright © 1973, 1978, 1984, 2011 by Biblica, Inc.™ Used by permission of Zondervan. All rights reserved worldwide. www.zondervan.com The "NIV" and "New International Version" are trademarks registered in the United States Patent and Trademark Office by Biblica, Inc.™

ISBN: 978-1-7374270-4-9 (hc)
ISBN: 978-1-7374270-5-6 (sc)

This novel is a work of fiction. Names, characters, businesses, places, events, and incidents are either the products of the author's imagination or used in a fictitious manner. Any resemblance to actual persons, living or dead, or actual events is purely coincidental.

www.nathanbirr.com

Also by Nathan Birr

The Douglas Files
Overnight Delivery
Three's a Crowd
All an Illusion
Shot List
Chasing the Wind
Blood and Treasure
One Life to Lose
Golden Key

Douglas Files Shorts
Black Male
WinterKill
Short Sail
As Good As Dead

Last Resort Series
Fire & Ice
Broken Trust
The Fountain

**Standalone Novels
& Novellas**
*God, Girls, Golf & the Gridiron
(Not Always in That Order) . . . A
Love Story*

All is Calm? – A Christmas Novella

The Book of Levi

Augusta Whispers

Non-Fiction
*Rights or Wrong?
Examining the Declaration of
Independence in the Light of Scripture*

www.nathanbirr.com

To everyone who played a part—
large or small—in Jackson's story,
or in mine . . .

Previously in
Nine Lives . . .

Thursday, May 15, 2014
7:04 p.m.
St. Thomas, U.S. Virgin Islands

"YOU'RE QUIET," JACKSON observed as he and Reggie walked into town—Charlotte Amalie—for dinner.

"Just thinking through all this, J."

"Any particular part?"

"You gonna pull the trigger?" There was enough light left in the sky for Reggie to look Jackson in the eye. "You gonna execute these dudes?"

"If this was my dad, and he'd tracked them down, he wouldn't have batted an eye to call in a drone strike. Would have pressed the button himself."

"I'm not questioning the legitimacy, J. You got me, these guys are terrorists. I'm asking about you, man. Can you live with being the one to press that button?"

"I've pressed it before."

"Not to be indelicate, J, but it hasn't exactly done your psyche a world of good."

"Yeah, well, the guy who picks up roadkill probably doesn't smell too good when he comes home at night either, but somebody's got to do it."

Reggie nodded.

"You not convinced?"

"Just wondering if you are."

"I'll let you know in a couple days."

THEY HEADED down to the beach again, walking far enough apart that it wasn't weird in the moonlight. Then they found seats on the beach, at the far end of the resort, where they could talk freely. For the second time that day, Jackson ran through the particulars of Operation: Patriot. By nine-thirty, they called it a night, both wanting a good night's sleep before "D-Day."

They took the steps to the second floor, where Jackson branched off. Not before Reggie slapped his hand. "We gonna do this, J."

"Yeah."

"And you and I are going to fire up those cigars, like Will Smith and Jeff Goldblum."

"I'm clearly Will Smith, the cool one, in the *Independence Day* reference."

"Yeah, you keep telling yourself that."

They squeezed hands to end the handshake. Jackson nodded. Reggie winked. And they headed for their separate rooms. Jackson took his time with his brief evening routine, then stretched out on his queen bed. It took a long time for his brain to quiet down, in part because he was trying to pray and couldn't find the words to express what he wanted to. Finally he trusted that God knew his heart and knew what he was asking.

He only wished he could be as certain that God, knowing his heart, approved of what was in it.

His mind going a mile a minute, Jackson tossed and turned and got up to get some air and returned to bed to toss and turn some more. Finally, at close to midnight, he succumbed to sleep.

Part Five

Chapter One Hundred Twenty-Three

Three months later . . .
Monday, August 18, 2014
5:33 a.m. (Hawaii Standard Time)
Honolulu, Hawaii

JACKSON'S BREATHING WAS heavy, and his muscles ached. He kept going, his eyes on the back of Maggie's legs in front of him. There was now enough ambient light that he didn't need a flashlight to follow in her steps, even as her pace became harder and harder to match. Then again, she wasn't relearning how to walk.

Her legs were tan, darker than the hiking boots she wore, and contrasted nicely with a pair of white shorts. They complimented the "Huskers" scrawl on the red tank top she wore, in honor of Reggie. Jackson's nod to the big man was tucked in the front pocket of his shirt, which was proving to be too much clothing, even before dawn, even with the sleeves rolled up to the elbow.

When he couldn't take it any longer, Jackson stepped to the side of the trail, called out a halt to those ahead, and clumsily unscrewed the cap on a bottle of water that was half gone. He gulped half of what remained, then reached down to massage a pain that wasn't really there. His left leg, below the knee, was carbon fiber, incapable of feeling anything. Tell that to his neurons.

He looked at Hillary, who was bringing up the rear of the group, as she approached. The exertion required to climb over five hundred feet of zigzagging pathways was played out in a stoic, marble-like expression. In other words, she looked the same. She was dressed similarly to Maggie, albeit in different colors and with an extra shirt tied around her waist. Yet somehow, she looked not like a hiker but an L.L. Bean catalog model, right down to the designer rucksack over her shoulders.

"You want me to carry . . . it?" Jackson asked.

"No," she said, stopping beside him. He extended the water toward her, which elicited a small smile. But instead of taking it, she reached for her own in one of the compartments of the backpack. She gracefully took a drink, then capped it. "Thank you, Jackson."

"For?"

"Inviting me along. I know this was your dream."

"You're family, Hillary," he said, glancing at the diamond—appropriately—ring on her finger.

She reached up and touched his bearded face, the kindest gesture she'd ever made toward him.

"You two ready to keep going?" David called from the front of the pack. Thinner, clearly older and grayer, he had otherwise not changed much. Still a mirthful smile just beneath the surface, still as easy-going as could be, still easily able to set the pace for people half his age.

"Ready," Jackson called.

Hillary nodded for him to resume his place in line, and they continued to climb, closer and closer to the summit of Diamond Head Crater. Sunrise was just after six, and the optimal experience included not just the fiery orb peeking over the horizon, but the gradual warming of the sky. Already, its black had faded to blue, and all but the brightest stars had disappeared.

They continued on the trail, through tall tufts of grass and native plants, then climbed grated metal staircases. Jackson was still working out the mechanics of walking with a prosthetic leg, and his gait was unorthodox to say the least. His physical therapist had advised against the trip to Hawaii and, particularly, against the hike to the top of Diamond Head. But as Jackson had proven over and over again, he was not to be deterred.

Finally, they ascended to the top, where an observation deck provided panoramic, three-sixty views of Oahu. From the ridges of the Ko'olau Range that split the island to Koko Head at the eastern tip of the island, then all the way back around to Waikiki, Pearl Harbor, and the Wai'anae Range in the distance. Beneath them, the dark Pacific was split by the caps of waves breaking on the reefs and beaches, and it was spectacular.

As Jackson leaned on a railing, catching his breath, David Douglas put his arm around his son's shoulders. "I never thought this day would come, Son."

"Neither did I, Dad."

His father's eyes scanned the western horizon, toward the naval base where much of his career had been spent. "I only wish your mother was up for travel, but for whatever reason, leaving home just seems to set her off."

"Maybe next time," Jackson said.

"Yeah, maybe so."

Jackson turned his eyes back to the sky. Already, it was becoming evident where along the eastern horizon the sun would appear. Then he turned his eyes to the right, where billowing clouds were half lit by the hidden orb. They were growing quickly, and he hoped they wouldn't block out the sunrise.

Maggie stepped up behind him, resting her chin on his shoulder. She gave him a peck on the cheek, and he turned to face her. She tipped her head to the side, and he gently reached the index finger of his good hand to her chin and tipped it back. Then he reached it up to lift her dark, wavy hair off her cheek. Her eyes looked up to meet his before he looked to his finger, gently tracing the three-inch scar that ran from beside her eye to her jaw. She tipped her head again to the side, now resting her cheek in his palm, and smiled contentedly at him.

The sky grew lighter, at the same time illuminating the clouds that continued to grow, continued to plume higher into the sky. Jackson checked his watch, saw that it was just minutes before sunrise. Beside Maggie, Hillary had shrugged the backpack off her shoulders. It sat at her feet, as she solemnly stared out at the eastern horizon.

There were a few other hikers who had made the pre-dawn trek, but the Douglas family was largely alone. So Jackson reached into his shirt pocket and withdrew a Churchill cigar. He bit off the tip and spat it over the railing, then fumbled in his pocket for a lighter. Maggie ultimately helped him light it, and he inhaled several deep breaths, not just of cigar smoke but also the brilliant morning. The stillness of dawn was incredible, and Jackson could almost hear the sun rising.

He exhaled a cloud of smoke and watched it waft into the heavens. He'd shed his tears already, and now the memories of Reggie brought a smile to his face. As did the thought that Reggie would shake his head at something so silly as Jackson smoking a cigar in his memory.

"Shall I?" Hillary asked.

David and Jackson both nodded, and she reached into the backpack and lifted out a plain, silver canister. With trembling hands she unscrewed the lid, then briefly clutched it to her breast. With a deep breath, she extended the canister over the railing, then tipped it and released Grant's remains into the breeze.

Beside Jackson, David bowed his head, and Jackson reached a hand to his father's back. David in turn placed his hand on the back of his son's neck, his face like granite. Hillary dropped the canister with a small sob, then turned into Maggie's waiting arms. After several minutes, the foursome embraced each other side by side, just as the burning orange ball appeared over the ocean.

Then it disappeared behind the clouds. They were now towering in the sky, exploding out so that their mushroomed tops were directly overhead. As if instigated by the disappearance of the sun, a stiff wind swept over the summit, causing both women to shiver.

"I think we should start down," David said.

Maggie hoisted the backpack for Hillary, and the foursome started back along the trail to the interior of Diamond Head. They had only made it a few dozen paces when giant drops of rain began to pelt them. They were accompanied by rumbles of thunder, and then a jagged bolt of lightning knifed across the sky.

"We should get off this metal," Jackson said, taking the grated steps down as fast as he could. He was last in line, and as such saw Hillary slip a moment later on the wet stair. Her backside landed with a clang, and her arm banged against the side.

"Hillary," Maggie said, turning back to help her to her feet before Jackson could get to her. "Are you all right?"

She took a few breaths. "Yeah."

"Your arm," Jackson said, looking at a gash above her elbow. The rain was now falling heavily, fast enough that it washed the blood away before it could run down her arm.

"We need to keep moving," David said, not indelicately.

Lightning flashed to light up the recently darkened sky, and the immediate clap of thunder shook the mountain. Rain and wind now combined to make the footing on the trail treacherous, and threatened to blow them off the slope. With his prosthetic leg, Jackson hurried to keep up, but kept losing pace. He was some thirty-five feet behind Hillary when he saw a piece of metal railing tear loose.

"Look out!" he shouted, but his words were caught up in the breeze. The section of railing flew into Hillary's back, knocking her off balance. She stumbled into the rock wall beside her, banged her head, and collapsed to the ground.

"Hillary!" he shouted, at the same time that David turned around. Hillary's body rolled and slid toward the rocky cliff side, catching on a railing support for a moment, before the eddy of water racing down the paved walkway carried her over the side.

"No!" David yelled, lunging out for her. He managed to grab just an ankle, jerking Hillary's body back and into the cliff. Despite the wind and rain, Jackson could hear her head crack against the rock. The torrent of water running down the path splashed David in the face, and he coughed and gagged against it, reflexively losing his grip on Hillary. She plunged down a chasm, and with another cry, David extended in a desperate attempt to grab her. He missed, but the effort took him off balance and he too plummeted over the side.

Jackson screamed in horror—or tried to—but words wouldn't come as he watched Maggie make a desperate lunge to save his father. The image of her bright white shorts and bright red shirt, backed by the gray and black of the roiling clouds and the streaks of rain across the interior of the crater, etched itself in his brain. She swiped for David as he fell, but missed, and herself slid down the path, flailing at the railing to stop her momentum.

Jackson could do nothing, unable to compel his legs to move. Then the water carried Maggie toward the railing support, and her head banged against the metal. A flash of lightning nearly seared Jackson's eyes, and when he was able to see again, he caught just a flicker of red and white, as Maggie's limp body disappeared from view around the bend in the trail and likely over the side.

"No!" he wailed, tipping his head back and nearly drowning in the deluge from above.

"No!" he shouted again, then sat upright.

Everything was dark. Sweat poured off his head. The bedsheet over his legs was soaked. He panted several huge breaths, looking around, gathering his bearings.

The Emerald Beach Resort. St. Thomas.

He exhaled a few more times, wiping a damp arm across his face and forehead.

He turned for the clock. 5:40.

It was May 16, a.k.a. "D-Day."

He tore the sweaty sheet off him, swung his legs over the edge of the bed, and looked down at them. There were two, both flesh. He looked at his left hand, fully normal and functional. He realized the pounding sound he heard was his heart. He stood, wobbled, and walked into the bathroom, where he splashed cold water on his face, then his chest to jolt his body. He raised his head and looked in the mirror.

For a good five minutes, he stared at himself, wondering if this was all a mistake. What if he failed, and those he loved didn't make it through, or were physically or emotionally or mentally scarred when they did? Could he live with getting Grant or Reggie killed, with Maggie being disfigured, with Hillary being abandoned again? Was his nightmare a warning, a vision from God, like in biblical times? Or was it nothing more than fear, than his subconscious trying to weasel out?

He began to shake his head back and forth, the look on his face turning into a snarl.

No, he wasn't going to be scared away. Not now.

The shake turned to a nod.

He'd planned and prepared meticulously. He had assembled the best team possible. He was on the cusp of achieving a goal a year in the making, and eliminating a global terror threat.

George Washington and Thomas Jefferson and Benjamin Franklin probably had nightmares too. But that hadn't stopped them, and it wouldn't stop him.

He turned away from the mirror with a look of defiance in his eyes.

It was go time.

Chapter One Hundred Twenty-Four

Friday, May 16
5:52 a.m. (Atlantic Standard Time)
St. Thomas, U.S. Virgin Islands

JACKSON TOOK A cup of coffee onto the balcony and watched the sunrise play out on the bay and the hills beyond it. The sky was clear with only a few tufts of cloud quickly losing their color as day broke. The breeze was steady but pleasant and the air was already warming. Just another perfect morning in the tropics.

The dream turned nightmare was quickly fading, but Jackson couldn't shake the fear that it had been some kind of forewarning or omen—even though he didn't believe in such things. Nor did he believe God would call him off from Operation: Patriot in such a fashion. Yet it was hard to shake the thought of Grant dying though his role seemed safe, Reggie not making it home, Hannah being stricken by sadness so that she became a shell of herself, or future tragedy befalling the Douglas family. At least Sam hadn't appeared in the dream, floating in the heavens with angel wings, sending down the lightning bolts.

In the old days, Jackson had tried to pray his anxieties away. So over a refill of coffee, he did it again. He asked God to bless his mission with success—for David and Hannah's sake, and for the sake of everyone GrayStar would unjustly hurt if they weren't stopped. More importantly, he prayed that none of the people working for him would get hurt, that if anyone had to bear the consequences, it would be him. There was no guarantee of that prayer being answered either, but he felt better anyhow.

The second cup finished, Jackson turned on the TV, wondering if they got ESPN in the U.S. Virgin Islands. They did, and he listened to *Mike & Mike* as background noise and a distraction as he showered, shaved around the edges of his beard and brushed a hint of gray dye into it, then dressed. He and Reggie had most of the day with nothing to do, so he wore a T-shirt and a pair of shorts. The Patriot would be decked a little differently later on.

It was 6:45, and he called Reggie. No answer. Either the big guy was in the shower or had taken up yoga in the last nine months and was downward dogging on the beach somewhere. Or GrayStar had tracked him and taken him out overnight, but Jackson wasn't going to worry about that for at least a quarter of an hour.

He turned the TV to The Weather Channel. Sure enough, Anthony had become a hurricane overnight. With sustained winds of eighty-two miles per hour, it was still moving west northwest at thirteen miles per hour. Its eyewall had become much more defined overnight, per the satellite and radar images, and was currently located thirty miles west of St. Vincent. Jackson watched for fifteen minutes, long enough to see the damage—minor—on Barbados as well as a host of forecasts. The spaghetti models were all over the map, literally. The National Hurricane Center's projection cone was as wide as it was long. Even the talking heads didn't agree as to what would happen. That said, the general consensus was that it would continue heading on a somewhat northwest track, passing over Puerto Rico, Hispaniola, or Jamaica before possibly making landfall in the States. That meant it would skirt St. Charles by a couple hundred miles, and even so, wasn't going to pass by the northernmost Caribbean islands until midday Saturday at least. The outlook for the party was still good.

Reggie called back just after seven, said he was ready to roll, and the duo met up for breakfast. "How'd you sleep?" Reggie asked over a feast of eggs, bacon, pancakes, and orange juice.

"Dreadfully."

Reggie raised an eyebrow.

"Pre-game jitters."

"You wanna run through the playbook again?"

"Not here," Jackson said, nodding at half a dozen vacationers also having breakfast at the Emerald Beach Café.

"You talk to Maggie yet this morning?"

"I told her I'd call around nine."

"And when do we have to be at the airport?"

"Departure is eight o'clock, so we should be there by seven-thirty."

"Gives us a day to kill."

"I told you," Jackson said as he reached for his orange juice.

"Yeah, I just didn't figure this much. Got a plan?"

"I was thinking of worrying and biting my nails down to the third knuckle."

"Sounds like a good time."

"Watch some TV, go for a run later, hit the plan a few times."

"Kind of late to make adjustments now, ain't it?" Reggie bit off half a strip of bacon.

"Better late than never."

"Man, I forgot you were such a cliché machine."

Jackson was contemplating a retort—and coming up empty—when his phone buzzed. He checked the display, then frowned at Reggie. "Maggie," he said, then accepted the call. "Hey, Maggie. What's—"

"Jack, we've got a problem."

"What's that?"

"Robbie."

His heart sank. She'd pulled one of her routines, sold them out for a few million dollars, and now was Wendy Knight, a soccer mom from Tulsa who doubled as a Serbian sleeper agent. Or Lola Spring, a diamond thief who made back-channel connections between foreign governments.

Maggie cut him off mid-speculation. "She woke up sicker than a dog."

"Sicker than a dog?"

"Puking, diarrhea, achy, feverish."

"I'm getting sick myself." He sighed. "When she come down with it?"

"Middle of the night."

"Twenty-four hours puts us . . ."

"Too late. She's sleeping now, or trying to, and still plans on working tonight, and her second-in-command will run the kitchen—she's already called her and she's on the way. But we need to consider a backup for Robbie's part tonight."

"Let me think for a while. I'll call you at nine as scheduled."

"Okay."

"Anything else?"

"No."

"How's the weather?"

"Sunny, breezy, beautiful."

"I'll call you," he said, then briefed Reggie.

"Got any ideas?"

"A guy like you stay afloat?"

"I can get by. Why?"

"Well, if Robbie can't go by tonight . . ." He looked around, then lowered his voice. "You may need to take out whoever's on the boat."

"I thought I was your bodyguard," Reggie said, leaning forward to speak in hushed tones.

"If everything goes right, I don't need the bodyguard at the end," Jackson said. "Just the threat of him."

Reggie raised his eyebrows.

"It's that or sending Blackshear into the fray."

"Um-hmm."

They finished eating and returned to Jackson's room, where they spent the next hour and a quarter going over the plan and Reggie's part in it again. By nine o'clock, Jackson was convinced his pal knew exactly what he needed to do. Jackson had never doubted it, but Reggie's quick study encouraged him. Now if only he didn't have to call a last-second audible.

Jackson called Maggie at 9:02, putting the phone on speaker. "How goes the war, Mags?"

"Um . . . okay."

"Awesome."

"Several of the kitchen staff arrived at eight, including Robbie's understudy, so they're busy getting things prepped. I don't have any concerns about us being able to serve up to two hundred people."

"How is Robbie?"

"Sleeping."

"I guess that's something," Reggie said.

"But we may have another problem."

"Oh?"

"Hurricane Anthony."

"What now?"

"The NHC will be issuing its next advisory at ten local, but in the last hour or so, it's made a pretty sharp turn north. Could be just another bobble, or it could be headed our way."

"Isn't Anthony a couple hundred miles south?" Reggie asked.

"Yeah. West of St. Lucia."

"No way it gets there by tonight, is there?"

"No. Not until late Saturday or Sunday, if it comes here. But the way it's growing in size, they're speculating that some of the outer rain bands and the wind especially could impact us by tonight."

Jackson dropped his head and sighed. "Rain isn't ideal."

"No."

"But it doesn't ruin our plans."

"Rain and wind could mess with Grant's aim," Reggie said.

"And close down a beach party and keep guests away."

"Eli's running out to get another generator, in addition to the ones we already have, as a precaution," Maggie said. "Latest forecast for tonight says breezy and a chance of rain."

"Not much we can do about it," Reggie said.

"Any last-minute guest notifications?" Jackson asked.

"A couple, but nothing relevant. How are you doing, Jack?"

"Fine."

"Reggie?"

"He's his usual self."

"Good. So the next wave of kitchen staff is set to arrive at one, including Armando Martínez."

"Who we think is GrayStar?" Reggie said.

"Right. I was going to say, want to touch base around twelve-thirty? That will give us a few more weather updates, and hopefully we'll know more about Robbie's status."

"Sounds good," Jackson.

"I'll call you."

"Okay, Mags. You're doing good."

"Bye, Maggie," Reggie said.

She said goodbye and ended the call.

Jackson stood. "I'm going to go for a walk."

"You want some company?"

"No, I wanna think. Or not think, actually. No."

Reggie nodded.

"I won't be long."

"I'll be here, J."

"You always are."

*   *   *

11:03 a.m.

REGGIE LAY sprawled on one of the beds in Jackson's room, watching Hurricane Anthony coverage. The storm was still several days to a week from impacting the U.S., so The Weather Channel was only giving it half their time. Jackson, meanwhile, had been sitting on the balcony, staring at a notepad for the better part of an hour. He'd been trying to write a letter to Leroy, an "if you're reading this then I'm dead" sort of goodbye letter. He couldn't find the words, and had scribbled only a few lines thus far. Needing to stretch his legs, he entered the room and sat on the corner of the other bed. "What's the word?"

"Not much change."

Jackson nodded. As of ten o'clock, the National Hurricane Center had issued more hurricane warnings and watches, the latter of which included St. Charles, starting at midnight. The earlier turn north had been confirmed, and instead of moving west northwest, the storm was now moving north northwest. It was also growing in size, and in intensity, and the projection cone now was almost useless. Some models thought it would curve back to the east and spin out into the Atlantic while some projected it would resume to the west eventually. Either way, while it wouldn't get to St. Charles until sometime Saturday if at all, the chance of inclement weather that evening seemed to be growing.

When the anchors switched to a pending drought in California, Reggie turned the channel. *Back to the Future Part III* was just starting on a cable network, and it provided a good distraction. Jackson sprawled on the other bed, trying to take his mind off things, off contingencies, off a compulsion to run one more time through the plan he knew better than the back of his hand already.

The distraction lasted all of five minutes before his phone buzzed. He looked down and saw it was Grant's number. Motioning to Reggie to mute the TV, he sat upright, then stood as he answered the call. "Hey?"

"Jack, we've got trouble."

"What trouble?"

"You been watching the news, about the hurricane?"

"Yeah, it's a long ways off."

"Not for a cruise ship. The captain just announced that due to the expected rough weather, our itinerary has changed. The *Explorer of the Seas* is no longer visiting St. Charles."

Chapter One Hundred Twenty-Five

11:19 a.m.

"EXCUSE MY HEBREW," Eli said after his first response to Jackson's announcement that Grant wouldn't make it to St. Charles.

"Do we have any other options?" Maggie asked. She, Eli, Tori, and Blackshear were conferenced with Jackson and Reggie.

"Options?" Jackson asked.

"For getting him here. Choppers can land on cruise ships, right?"

"You got a chopper?" Eli asked.

"Gonna raise some eyebrows if you do," Reggie said.

"Yeah, he's right," Jackson said. "We have to assume GrayStar's watching for anything unorthodox today. And that would be unorthodox."

"So what do we do without Grant?" Blackshear asked.

"Two options," Jackson said. "A, we let Blye go and take him when we take the pilot. Or B, we put Eli in the sniper position."

"Then who goes in Eli's position?"

"Depends. How's Robbie?"

"She's still sleeping," Maggie said.

"What's your take?"

"Fifty-fifty."

"Eli?"

"Sixty-forty that she'll be available."

"For the record," Tori said, "I'd be surprised if she can walk on her own tonight."

Jackson sighed.

"Does no one care about my opinion?" Blackshear asked.

"Not really," Eli said.

"If Robbie can rally, maybe Reggie can split off and cover Eli's role," Jackson said. "But if she's down, then he has to do her job on the yacht."

"Which leaves me to take out Andretti and possibly Walkie," Maggie said.

There was silence for a moment.

"I can do it."

"As a contingency," Jackson said. "We've got some time. Let's see how Robbie is in a few hours. In the meantime, Hoss, we'll walk through each potential plan. And Maggie, think this through."

"There's nothing to think through, Jack. We need me to do it."

He sighed again. "Okay. Let's see where we are in a couple hours. Check in at three?"

They all agreed.

"Maggie, hang on a second."

Everyone else said goodbye, and Jackson took the phone off speaker as Reggie went to "get some air."

"Maggie, just you?"

"Just me."

"You don't have to do this."

"We covered this, didn't we?"

"I don't want to turn you into a killer to accomplish my pur . . . poses."

"What is it?"

"I just realized, that's the speech that old white-haired guy gave Higgy's girlfriend in 'Tropical Madness.'"

"'Tropical Madness'?"

"Possibly the greatest episode of *Magnum, P.I.* ever."

"Is that all you can think about anymore, which movie or TV speech what one of just said sounds like?"

"You wanted me on my game, didn't you?"

"Your game, not Shawn Spencer's game."

"Come on, son."

"Should we get back on point here?"

"Yeah. Point is, what we do here, we're going to have to live with for the rest of our lives. I've made my decision, but—"

"So have I. Jack, I've been with you on this since I came to Lincoln."

"Taking a life is different, Maggie."

"I know, Jack. Anecdotally, anyhow. But I'm with you, whatever you need me to do."

"Okay. Let's get Robbie up to speed, make her some soup or something."

"Yeah, sure. Oh, wait, Eli wants to talk to you again."

"All right."

"Here he is."

"Jack?"

"Yeah, what's up?"

"There's another option, a C."

"What's that?"

"We go after Blye in person."

"In person?"

"Instead of hiding a sniper in the hotel, we send somebody up to Perigon Point. The danger is he could see that person coming, but the upside is it wouldn't have to be someone with sniper skills. In fact, the person could even be there waiting."

Jackson exhaled. "You have a recommendation?"

"No. That's the other problem, is everybody else needs to be on site."

"Yeah. Good idea, though."

"I'll keep thinking. If there's A, B, and C, maybe there's a D."

"Yeah. Maybe."

"Don't worry, Jack. We'll figure this out."

"Thanks, Eli."

He ended the call, took a deep breath, and texted Grant to let him know he could go ahead and enjoy the rest of his cruise. Then he went back onto the balcony to try to write a goodbye letter to his grandpa.

*　　　　　　*　　　　　　*

4:14 p.m.

AS JACKSON'S phone chirped, Reggie muted the TV.

Jackson tapped his phone to answer the call and again to put it on speaker. "Yeah?"

"We're all here," Maggie said. "Except Walker's hidden away in her den."

"Okay, what's first?" Jackson asked.

"I'm here," Robbie said.

"How you feeling?"

"Dead."

"Are you up for tonight?"

"Not to be rude," Reggie said.

"I feel like crap, but I'm up for it."

"Are you sure?"

"Eli gave me some Israeli home remedy. A kick in the pants to give me energy."

"And you feel dead?"

"Should have seen me before the remedy." She sighed. "I'm out of things to puke or poop, and I didn't come this far to lay in bed while you all take these guys down. Emma is covering for me with prep, but by show time, I'm in."

"Okay," Jackson said. "What's the forecast?"

Their call had been delayed seventy-five minutes, at Eli's suggestion. Hurricane Anthony had been heading north and growing as of three o'clock, so they'd decided to wait for their final check-in until after the four p.m. NHC briefing . . . and the talking heads' breakdown thereof. But the St. Charles forecast was another matter.

"Worse and getting worse," Eli said.

"It's actually raining now," Tori said. "Formed out of nowhere."

"We've tasked her to monitor the weather since she can't do much else from the pool house," Maggie said.

"Raining hard?"

"Just a shower," Tori said. "More of the same for tonight. Off and on showers, possibly heavy at times, winds could get gusty."

"Define gusty."

"Thirty to forty."

"Radar didn't look like there was much of a band of rain anywhere close," Jackson said.

"They figure it will fill in, from what the local outlets are saying."

"So do we go ahead with the outside plans?"

"I think we go ahead with everything as planned until we can't," Eli said.

"Me too," Maggie said.

Reggie nodded for Jackson to see.

"Okay. As planned until we can't. Rain and wind don't kill us. Inconvenience, but that's it. So let's talk roles. Anything better than Eli being the sniper?"

He was greeted with silence.

"Okay, Eli, you're on sniper duty."

"When do you want me there?"

"Think you can get in the car with Benny without being spotted?"

"Should be able to make that work."

"He can drop you on his decoy run to the airport. Should give you plenty of time."

"Leaves me stranded there."

"You want to take the Jeep?"

"Might be more noticeable when I leave, which could be plausible. My not coming back, not so much."

"What if we stash the Jeep ahead of time?" Tori asked.

"We have to assume they have the estate surveilled," Jackson said.

"In a pinch, I can always find a vehicle," Eli said.

"All right, let's go with that." Jackson took a breath. "That leaves us with someone to take out whoever's on the yacht, someone to plant a device on the car, and someone to take out Walkie, Andretti, and whoever's left."

"I can still do the yacht," Robbie said.

"And I can plant the device," Maggie said.

"Otherwise I can," Robbie said. "Emma will be handling most of the cooking staff, and I'll have time if Maggie can get me the device somehow."

"Can't we stash it somewhere?" Tori asked.

"Too risky," Blackshear said. "Someone could find it, or someone could be in the room where we hide it."

"Can't she have it on her all day?"

"It is somewhat delicate," Blackshear answered. "Best not to have it hidden in her chef's coat all evening while she's banging about in the kitchen."

"Why don't I just plant it to begin with, like we originally planned?" Maggie asked.

"Because ideally you're monitoring Walkie, keeping an eye on the room with Blackshear—"

"And not seen skulking around," Robbie said, cutting off Eli.

"Then, after we release the gas," Jackson said, "I and maybe Reggie will be available to help you round up anybody who's left."

"And I can trigger the device remotely," Blackshear said.

"This work?" Jackson asked.

He got a chorus of yes votes.

"Anything we're missing?"

No one answered.

"Okay. That's it. Maggie, when are you briefing staff?"

"Quarter after six."

"Okay, comms have a six-hour battery life, give or take. Have them in by the time you're in position, whenever that is. Reggie and I will be on by the time we're in range, about ten miles out. I'll be in touch with Blackshear in case of emergency or if Anthony grows into a *Perfect Storm* situation. Otherwise, radio silence from here on out."

They all agreed.

"Anything else we need to cover?"

Nobody spoke.

"Okay. You all know your roles, you're all ready—with the possible exception of Robbie who may hurl or faint at any moment."

"Ha, ha."

"Let's get this done, everybody."

They all gave an affirmation of some kind, then ended the call.

"You ready to eat?" Jackson asked Reggie.

"Last meal of the condemned?" he said with a grin.

"Funny."

Reggie winked, and they headed out to find an early dinner.

*　　　　*　　　　*

6:29 p.m.
St. Charles

HAVING FINISHED her briefing of the staff—all but two of whom had arrived on time, despite on and off rain that had just ended—Maggie retreated to the office where Blackshear and Eli were waiting. She closed the door and turned to face them.

"How'd it go?" Eli asked.

"Good. We're down one valet and one server, nothing we can't handle."

"How's Robbie?" Blackshear asked.

"Tougher even than I knew. She said the sight and smell of food makes her want to heave, but she has nothing left to heave, and whatever you gave her, Eli, is doing the trick so far."

"Once adrenaline kicks in, she'll be good to go. After taking what I gave her, I once swam across the Sea of Galilee with dysentery."

"Show off," Blackshear said.

"All cameras functional?" Maggie asked.

The Brit nodded from behind a bank of monitors. "All systems go."

"Security staff?"

"All have reported for duty," Eli answered. "I just made the rounds at six, and I'll do so again every half hour until guests arrive."

"Okay. I've tasked Bram with handling the beach party, which is still a go. Julia's taking care of welcoming anyone who comes by boat, and Milan is in charge of the valets on the driveway, and they're all headed to their places now."

"How about Garçon?" Eli asked.

"I've caught him once or twice maybe snooping or maybe admiring the artwork," Blackshear said. "Seems to be keeping a low profile and working hard."

"Good," Maggie said. "Latest on Anthony?"

"Last forecast suggests we should be dry for at least a few hours, and might even see some clear skies," Tori chipped in remotely.

"Where's the eye?" Eli asked.

"A hundred and twenty-five miles south southwest of the island, and maybe starting to turn a little west."

"That's good."

"I think we've dodged a couple bullets with the storm and with Robbie," Maggie said.

"Let's hope we can dodge real bullets."

"I did just see a notification that St. Charles has canceled their fireworks for tonight," Blackshear said. "Or rather, postponed them."

"Not a huge loss," Eli said.

"Our hope was to keep the party going until at least midnight," Maggie said.

"We may have to increase the liquor dispensation."

"Yeah. Anything else?"

They shook their heads.

"I'm going to go put on my dress, and I told Robbie we'd do a comms check at quarter to."

Both men nodded.

"Otherwise, we're in character now, so this is our last little powwow."

"I'll miss them," Eli said.

Maggie smirked as she turned to leave.

*   *   *

7:14 p.m.
St. Thomas, U.S. Virgin Islands

BEFORE LEAVING his bathroom, Jackson took one last look in the mirror.

He wore a three-piece ivory suit with a black shirt underneath and a bright crimson tie. It was loose around the neck—not sloppy homicide cop at the end of a shift loose, but just enough to add a touch of casualness to his attire. Under the suit was a thin Kevlar vest. A Glock 19 was tucked in a holster on the back of his waist, under the suit vest. A backup gun, also a Glock, was in an ankle holster. So was a KA-BAR tactical knife. The satellite phone was in his breast pocket, and a spare magazine for the Glocks was in his vest pocket. A silver Rolex was on his left wrist. His hair was freshly slicked, wavy and dark to match the tapered beard.

The Patriot was ready to go.

Double- and triple-checking his room to make sure he had everything he needed, which included his wallet and earwig, Jackson carried everything else in a duffel bag, which he would toss in the hotel dumpster before they left. But he went up, instead of down, to Reggie's room.

The big man greeted him dressed head to toe in black. He too wore a Kevlar vest under his suit, and was carrying a pair of guns, a dozen zip ties, and a knife. He admitted Jackson, who tested him on several points to make sure he had everything he needed. Then he asked, "You got a free pocket?"

"Why?"

Jackson handed him three folded sheets of paper.

"This what you've been working on all day?"

"Letters, in case I don't make it."

"J, you gon—"

"Top one's for Grandpa. Next one's for Maggie. Last one's for Grant and my parents. If this succeeds but I don't make it, or if we fail but somehow they come in from the cold, see that they get it."

"You know I will, man."

"I was going to write you one too, but . . . I ran out of time."

"Don't worry about it, J."

"Reg, I can't do this without telling you how much you mean to me, man. Eight years ago when you rolled into that parking lot, I'd never have known that scary black dude blasting gangsta rap would have become my brother. And that's what you are, Hoss. You've always been there, always had my back, through the ups and downs. And there've been a lot more downs lately, but you never gave up on me, never let me down. And here you are now, risking your life for me . . . again. And you know how I hate to get all mushy, but you gotta know, I love you, brother."

Reggie slowly licked his lips, his stoic face fighting back emotion. It took several beats before he replied. "Right back at you, man. I know you don't see it, but you've done more for me than I ever have for you, J. You my boy, and I ain't gonna let nothing happen to you, man. Or your girl. We gonna get this done, get through this, and tell stories about it forever. 'Cause that's what brothers do, man."

They embraced, a manly hug with backslaps and everything.

"You ready?" Reggie asked.

Jackson held up his fist, Reggie bumped it firm enough to sting, and they headed out into the night.

Chapter One Hundred Twenty-Six

7:56 p.m.

THE PILOT WAS a skinny, young guy named Scott. He wore a white button-down shirt with sleeves rolled to the elbows, a tropical tie looser than Jackson's, and knee-length board shorts. Boat shoes and a San Antonio Spurs baseball cap completed the semi-professional look. He ran his own charter helicopter service, catering to more private clients than some of the others on the island. Jackson had booked the flight and Scott's service under the name "Jack," which had been sufficient for the reservation and sufficient for identifying himself to Scott. He'd paid $2,500 via a wire transaction ahead of time, which was double the fee for the round-trip flight. Whether it was the huge tip or just a perk of flying Scott's Charter Service, there were chilled bottles of water waiting for Jackson and Reggie when they arrived in the small office crowded with several others amid the hangars at the outskirts of Cyril E. King Airport.

After introductions, Scott finished his preflight check, then welcomed the duo onto his Bell 427 helicopter. It was black, sleek and spyish looking, and absolutely perfect for the situation.

"Headed to St. Charles," Scott said as they boarded. More chilled bottles of water were waiting for them, along with headsets that resembled those football coaches wore. "Hurricane Anthony's kicking up some pretty strong winds, even this far out. Could add about fifteen minutes to our flight time."

"That's fine," Jackson said.

"All right, we'll be airborne in just a couple minutes."

Both men sat in the back of the chopper, since it was dark and sightseeing wasn't a priority. Scott gave them a two-minute tutorial on turning off and on the headsets and changing the channels, so that Jackson and Reggie could talk freely to one another in private. Then, sharply at eight o'clock, he pulled up on the collective, and the Bell 427 floated into the sky.

Jackson thumbed a quick text to Blackshear, letting him know that they were departing on schedule. The hacker replied with a note that all was proceeding as planned at the estate, which Jackson relayed to Reggie. Then he sat back, briefly watching the lights of Charlotte Amalie below before closing his eyes and trying to calm himself before the grandest and most important act of his life.

His phone buzzed him from a reverie—somewhere between conscious dreaming and visualization. He looked down to see a message from Blackshear.

Chapman's yacht has arrived
40-footer very luxurious
two guests, both males
one might be Hayes
other unknown white male w short dark hair
running facial rec now

Jackson tipped the phone to Reggie, then typed a reply.

How confident on Hayes?

75% full beard and image is grainy

Have Maggie greet and confirm.

copy

Anyone else on the yacht?

not that I've seen
named Sterling Silver
running a check on it now

Keep me posted.

Jackson sat back. He looked out his window, seeing distant lights of some or other island—the British Virgin Islands, likely. So far, while the ride wasn't as smooth as sitting in his recliner at home, it wasn't topsy-turvy either. So far.

Blackshear texted back in a minute.

Maggie just welcomed two guests, man and woman
man is black, tallish, looks athletic
could very well be Carter
woman is 5-9, white, dark hair up,
blue gown athletic too

Jackson digested the information. If it was Carter, who was the woman? A beard? An independent contractor, like Mia? A female member of GrayStar? Did that change their numbers?

He tipped the phone to Reggie, who nodded, and then replied.

Keep an eye on them.

of course

They drive themselves?

negative. checked footage they came in a limo

Where's the driver?

remaining in vehicle for now

Location?

at bend in driveway due south of garage

Jackson exhaled. So far, so good. Then Scott signaled to get their attention, and they turned their headsets to his channel.

"Got a small rain band directly east of us. I'm going to detour a hair north and get around it."

"All right, thanks," Jackson said.

"Might add five minutes to our flight."

"Copy that."

He looked down to see another text.

Maggie confirms is Carter

woman is his date or playing same

moving to Hayes now

Jackson again showed Reggie, then acknowledged the remarks via text. He again sat back, closed his eyes, and forced himself to breathe normally.

*   *   *

9:27 p.m.

THE NEXT hour went by with little fanfare. Blackshear texted a few more times, once when Maggie confirmed to the best of her abilities that the man who'd gotten off the yacht was indeed Carleton Bryant Hayes II. He also messaged around nine to say the party was in full swing, albeit mostly inside, with what he estimated was a nearly full guest list. He updated Jackson again when Benny and Eli left, and when Eli announced that he was in position in room 1519 at the Royale Hotel. And he kept him in the loop regarding the weather on St. Charles. Windy at worst, so far. Then Jackson's phone lit up with a call, and he followed Scott's earlier instructions to patch it through to a secure channel on the headset.

"What's up?" he asked with Reggie listening in.

"Maggie just informed me that Carter and his date have asked to meet with The Patriot. Gave names of Jared Jefferson and Christy Rollins."

"You're sure it's Carter?"

"Maggie says yes and everything I've seen on camera matches Lexi's description to a T."

"Any clue on the woman?"

"Nothing. I wish there was. She's quite lovely, in a lethal sort of way."

"They say what they want to talk about?"

"A business transaction, Maggie said. She said she'd put them on the list."

"All right. Find anything on the yacht?"

"I believe it was chartered out of Gustavia this morning, by a Mr. Clive Chapman."

"Matches," Reggie said.

"Yes, quite. Dead end thereafter."

"We know it's Hayes, so we know it's them. Jared Jefferson equals J.J. Carter. Clive Chapman, probably Charles Collier. We figured he'd drive the boat or the car. See if you can find anything about a woman with initials C.R. anywhere in connection with GrayStar."

"Of course, I'll just comb through all our records while monitoring everything else."

"Anything you can find, G."

"Right. Oh, Robbie says to tell you she's A-OK."

"Good. Anything else?"

"Not at present."

"All right, I'll touch base when we're closing in."

He ended the call, and a moment later, Scott signaled for them again.

"What's up?" Jackson asked after adjusting the channel.

"We're about forty, forty-five minutes out. Radar shows a pretty heavy rain band moving over the island about that time. If I take us in direct instead of circling from the east, saves seven or eight minutes."

"We can spare the minutes," Jackson said. "And wet is wet."

"If you can keep this bird up in the rain," Reggie added.

"Depends on how heavy it gets, along with the wind. We'll stick to the plan for now," Scott said.

Jackson nodded. "Copy."

"Hang on, it might get bumpy."

It was about fifteen minutes later that Jackson began to feel the wind gusts rocking the chopper, and a couple minutes later that rain started splattering the windows. They passed just north of Anguilla, as evidenced by the GPS on Jackson's phone and the lights out Reggie's window, and Scott announced he was dropping down lower, where the wind was hopefully lighter. Jackson called up a radar on his phone, and saw a steady band had moved over St. Charles, and didn't appear to be going anywhere.

"Gonna mess up your hair, man," Reggie said, leaning over to look at the screen.

"Should we scrub the mission?"

Reggie grinned.

At ten o'clock, Scott said they were ten minutes west of St. Charles, but they were banking around to come from the east, a plan Jackson had implemented just in case GrayStar had somebody monitoring incoming choppers and decided to check who had taken off from the west in the last few hours. Even if they did, they were unlikely to be able to backtrack far enough to learn anything damaging in that time, but Jackson wasn't taking chances.

He felt the phone vibrate and looked down.

Maggie says to close tiki bar

too much rain and too few people using it

Jackson thought for a moment. If there was nobody down at the beach, anyone who saw Robbie heading down there might get suspicious. At the same time, her removing her chef's outfit wouldn't be noticed if no one was around.

Okay.

also Anthony now cat 2

Awesome.

Location?

100 miles west of Dominica

turning more west

Good.
We're 15-20 minutes out.

comms should be working soon

Any tech trouble with the storm?

none

Copy.

Jackson started to update Reggie when a boom echoed through the chopper. Jackson looked at Scott, then switched his headset channel. "What was that?"

"Thunder," Scott said. "I'm diverting."

"Diverting where?"

"I can get around it to Barbuda."

"I don't want to go to Barbuda."

"Depending on the storm, we can loop around to Antigua, but it's farther away."

"I need to be on St. Charles."

"I hear you, man, but it's not safe right now."

"I'll give you ten grand when you touch down," Jackson said.

"Doesn't do me much good if we get hit by lightning on the way in."

Jackson sighed. "Fifty grand. I'll set up the wire now, and the moment we're down, I send it via sat phone."

Scott sighed.

"Hundred grand. How much you want, man?"

He looked back. "A hundred grand?"

"Just get me down according to the plan."

"You've got a hundred grand?"

Jackson spent two minutes initiating a transfer on his phone, then turned it so Scott could see. "Hundred grand," he repeated.

"You're desperate to get on that island, aren't you?"

"I am."

"All right," Scott said. "For a hundred grand, you got it."

Jackson phone vibrated again.

fyi, St. Charles Intl just diverted
or canceled all incoming flights

Splendid.

Had to bribe our pilot to make landing.

Another bolt of lightning flashed off to Jackson's right, and he saw Reggie motioning toward him. They turned the channel on their headsets.

"Don't let the storm get you off your game, man."

"Copy that, Hoss."

They tapped fists again, and Jackson closed his eyes and breathed one final prayer as the chopper began to bank toward the south, toward St. Charles.

Chapter One Hundred Twenty-Seven

10:15 p.m.

HIS HEADSET ASKEW, Jackson put his hand to his ear, trying to block out as much of the chopper's noise as possible. Ahead of them, the lights of East Bay Resort were obscured by streaks of rain as they marked the eastern edge of St. Charles. The peaks of Mount Hudson and Vin Mountain were indistinguishable against the night sky. In the cockpit, Scott was all business, seemingly just able to keep his chopper airborne, but maybe he was putting on a show for his hundred grand. Either way, Jackson trusted the pilot and focused on his tasks.

"Freckles, this is Tom Terrific, how do you copy?"

"Still going with call signs, huh?" Maggie's voice came back. "What's your status?"

"We're over the island now."

"Bram's making sure there's a clear spot for landing, but there's nobody outside in this rain."

"Copy that. Mighty Man?"

"In position," Eli answered. "But I can't see anything on Perigon Point, much less have a clear shot, not in this weather."

"Let's hope it clears. We've got a couple hours. Chameleon?"

There was no answer. Jackson looked down at the lights of Williamsburg, blurry but visible between the darkness of the two mountains.

"Chameleon, you copy?" Jackson asked again.

Her reply was a mumble, indiscernible.

"Night Ram, you have Chameleon?"

"I'm here," Robbie said. "Just having a little trouble with the smell of devil—gulp—deviled eggs."

"Are you good?" Jackson asked.

"Five by five."

32

"Night Ram?"

"All cams up, most clear. All comms working. Security systems are go."

"Everything on schedule?" Jackson asked.

"As soon as you land, Tom Terrific," Maggie said. "We're all indoors, but the party isn't diminished and everyone seems to be enjoying themselves."

"Good copy. Sammich, you getting all this?" he asked, looking at Reggie.

"Sammich, really, that's what our relationship is to you?"

Jackson shrugged, then said, "On the ground in two."

Reggie grinned wide until the chopper jolted suddenly and something on the control panel started beeping. The muscles in Scott's forearm were visibly strained as he gripped the cyclic, fighting to keep the Bell 427 level. Both Jackson and Reggie braced themselves as up ahead a bolt of lightning disappeared behind the ridge of Vin Mountain. The rain was so heavy it drummed against the glass of the helicopter to drown out the rotors. Scott took them out over the water, then down, then left so that Millionaires' Row appeared out Jackson's window. They were maybe one hundred feet up, and dropping again, this time intentionally.

Another blast of rain smacked the window, and then the distinct lights of Vossenhol took shape. The tiki torches on the grounds were all out, and the floodlights and solar lights muted by the rain. Running lights on three yachts were still illuminated at the dock, and nearly every window in the house exuded a warm, yellow glow. And a pair of green flares sparked in the lawn, identifying the helicopter's landing spot.

"Hang on," Scott said.

They descended below the wildly flapping palm fronds, suffered one more brief jerk, and then were on the ground. Jackson tapped the button on his phone, initiating the transfer of one hundred thousand dollars to Scott's account. He showed the phone to the pilot, then reached out to shake his hand. "Nice work, Captain. Come in, enjoy the party, but don't tell anyone anything other than you flew us here."

"Okay."

"I mean it. You don't say the name I gave you, don't say when we left or where we came from. Nothing."

"For the money you pay, I'm whoever you want, man."

Jackson nodded, then looked at Reggie. "Ready, Hoss?"

"Let's do it."

Jackson removed the headset and placed it over a small hook beside him. Then he unlatched his door and swung it open, immediately greeted by a blast of rain and wind. Equally quickly, he was greeted by a young man with dark hair and a forced grin. He held an umbrella, a remarkably rigid one, which he extended over Jackson's head.

"Sir, my name is Bram," he yelled. "Welcome to St. Charles."

"Thank you, Bram." Jackson took a look to see Reggie circling the rear of the chopper, and nodded for Bram to lead the way. They hurried toward the cover of the master suite's balcony and paused just outside the double French doors leading into the music room. The wind revolving around Hurricane Anthony was out of the southeast, so they were sheltered from the elements.

"Katherine is waiting for you inside," Bram said. "She temporarily cleared the room so you have a moment to collect yourself."

Jackson shook his hand. "Thanks, Bram."

"Yes, sir."

Bram stepped aside while Reggie brushed a hand over his head and reached for the door handle. He looked at Jackson, who nodded, then opened the door.

The darkness and ferocity of the hurricane's outer bands were replaced by the soft glow of the music room's chandelier and the gentle strains of a string quartet. They were the only occupants of the music room, whereas beyond it, the solarium was filled with guests in tuxedos and fancy gowns, the hubbub of their conversations competing with the classical music. Jackson took a moment to adjust his jacket and tie and pat down his hair as he looked around the room. It seemed like months since he had been here, not a mere few days.

Reggie softly cleared his throat, and Jackson looked up at him, then followed his eyes.

Maggie stepped from the crowd in the solarium. She wore a burgundy, full-length halter-top dress, a cross between fun and formal. Her hair was down but partially swept back from her face and held by silver clips. They were matched by a silver diamond necklace, teardrop earrings, and several bracelets. She was stunning, and it had as much to do with a warm smile as she approached Jackson as it did her apparel.

Maggie extended a hand and offered a professional, "Good evening, sir," that belied the look in her brown-tinted eyes. "Welcome to St. Charles."

"Thank you, Katherine," Jackson said, shaking her hand.

"How was your flight?"

"Expensive."

"We're at ten . . . twenty-three," she said, consulting a wristwatch—also silver. "I told everyone to assemble in the living room at ten-thirty. You still want to meet in the office first?"

"Yeah, I can be fashionably late."

"Then let's go," Katherine said, flashing a smile and heading into the solarium. The crowd parted around her, and Jackson and Reggie followed closely on her heel. Jackson felt like a pro golfer walking to the next tee as he offered a few headshakes and smiles to those around him. Reggie played the role of bodyguard well and kept them moving, through the solarium and through half of the gallery, then into a hallway where they had privacy. Maggie used her thumbprint to unlock the office door, and the trio entered their sanctuary.

Reggie closed the door, and Maggie turned and wrapped her arms around Jackson. She gave him a quick kiss. "Good to see you again. You look like a drug lord."

"And you look like Miss St. Charles."

She grinned, then gave Reggie a hug. Then they entered the secret doorway into the control room where Blackshear was waiting for them. "Good to see you again, boss."

"You too, G. So where we at?"

"Crowded," the hacker answered, "but Robbie's keeping everyone sated and drinking."

"I've talked to several dozen people or groups," Maggie said. "And there are some VIPs who want to meet you."

"Besides Jefferson and Rollins, who else?"

"Governor van den Heuvel and his wife, the Minister of Tourism and his not wife, Carel Struycken from *The Addams Family*, and Caro Emerald. Sorry, no swimsuit models."

"What are you going to do? Caro who?"

"She's a Dutch jazz singer."

He nodded. "Okay. Well, I think we can stretch that out till eleven-thirty, especially if I mingle a little. We'll get to Jefferson and Rollins then. What have they been up to?"

"Same as everybody," Blackshear said. "Mingling."

"Hayes?"

"Doing the same. Mingling with no real purpose."

"Garçon?"

"I'm keeping him busy," Robbie said.

"We ID'd anyone else yet?"

"Negative," Blackshear said.

"Limo driver?"

"Still in the limo."

"Okay. Safe bet he'll stay there the whole time, which makes things easier. Mighty Man?"

"I can't even see the mountain right now."

"You have any sign that there's someone up there?"

"No. Couldn't get the drone up in this weather like we planned."

"Anything else we need to know about the storm?"

"You're seeing it out there," Tori chimed in from a computer monitor showing the pool house. "Might worsen after midnight, but the eye is moving westward again, so I don't anticipate it getting much worse."

"All right, then it sounds like we're on plan. Chameleon, you still up for taking out the yacht?"

No answer.

"Chameleon?"

"Yeah, sorry. Just locked myself in the pantry. I'm good."

"And she's planting the device?" Jackson asked Maggie.

"I'll slip into the office and get it after I introduce you to Jefferson and Rollins, and then I'll get it to her."

"How?"

"I'll hide it in my dress."

"G, see that thing doesn't blow early."

"Has to be activated first."

"If the weather lets up," Robbie said, "I'll take out some snacks to the drivers in their cars. There are a few. If not, I'll go stealth."

"Okay, I'll let the two of you work out getting the device passed. You're sure you can do that and get to the yacht?"

"Most of our work is done, and Emma can handle it."

"Okay. Raider, how you doing?"

"Yawn, yawn, yawn," Tori said.

"Just stay ready."

"I will."

"Good. Okay, I'll head upstairs and, Maggie, you can announce me at thirty-five after." He looked around the room. "We good?"

They all nodded.

"All right. On your mark, Maggie."

"Ten-twenty-nine now, so six minutes."

The group split. Jackson and Reggie headed up to the master suite via the staircase in the office. Maggie exited to the hallway, from whence she would go back into the living room and eventually up the stairs to the landing overlooking the living room and hallway. And Blackshear remained in the control room, eyes on everything.

"Man, this is some crib," Reggie said when he and Jackson were alone in the master suite.

"Funny what $37.5 million will buy."

Reggie whistled.

"Wait till you see the shower," Jackson said a nod over his head. While Reggie checked out the master bathroom, including a rain shower with windows on two sides, Jackson rehearsed his speech. What he said was only important in that he had to keep up his cover for another ninety minutes, but he still wanted to nail it.

Reggie whistled again. "How you have come up in the world, J."

"Yes, and at such little cost."

The big man put his hands on Jackson's shoulders. "Almost there, man."

Blackshear broke through on the earwigs. "I believe I've identified Walkie, white somewhat thinnish chap, late thirties, blah hair. He's on the move."

"Where's he headed?" Jackson asked.

"Not sure yet, but he was in position to see us all gather in the office, which clues him in as to where our control room might be."

"Keep an eye out."

"You know you don't really have to keep saying that."

"Yeah, okay."

"Heading for stairs now," Maggie said. "You ready?"

Jackson winked at Reggie as he said, "I was born ready."

Chapter One Hundred Twenty-Eight

10:35 p.m.

WITH REGGIE FOLLOWING, Jackson walked out into the loft, still hidden from view of guests down below. At the same time, Maggie climbed the stairs and stood at the semicircular railing looking down on the living room and entry hall, separated by the two-story fireplace. She held up her hands to get attention, which wasn't really necessary. The room quieted, and she said, "Ladies and gentlemen, thank you so much for coming this evening. And thank you for putting up with our efforts to deal with the effects of Hurricane Anthony. That said, I know you didn't come to hear me talk, so without further ado, it gives me great pleasure to introduce to you the man responsible for tonight's party and the man who owns this marvelous estate, and a man who will, in fact, finish introducing himself."

She stepped to the side and extended an arm toward where Jackson emerged from the darkness of the loft to a warm ovation. He greeted her with a quick nip on the cheek, a professional kiss if there was such a thing, and then took her place looking down on his patrons. He took a breath and launched into a well-rehearsed speech, doing his best to talk with a deep, booming voice.

"Thank you, Katherine, and thank you, everyone, for being my guests this evening. I am honored that you have chosen to kick off a weeklong celebration of St. Charles' independence here at Vossenhol. And I am particularly honored to have the governor of this great country, Governor Anders van den Heuvel here tonight," he said, gesturing toward him in the crowd. "And even more so to have his lovely wife, Sophie, here as well. Thank you so much," he said to polite applause. "I know we have other distinguished guests here, but at the risk of neglecting to mention someone— and because I made a promise to keep this short—I'll move along. But first, I need to correct something Katherine said. I'm not the person responsible for tonight; she is. She's the one who threw this party, who put everything together on short notice. So let's give her a round of applause."

He led it, feeling like a dork but knowing this was how the game was played. After thirty seconds, the clapping died out, and he got down to business.

"Now, it would be customary here to introduce myself, but that's more complicated than you might think. I've been known by numerous names and aliases throughout the years, only half of which I'll admit to."

He was rewarded, as he thought, with a few chuckles. He continued speaking, his eyes roaming over the guests, looking for Hayes, looking for Carter and his plus one.

"Many of you know me as 'The Patriot' and have an assortment of ideas about who I am, what I've done, how I've amassed my fortune. Some of those ideas are true, some are partially true, and some are quite flattering but nothing more. That said, all of that is in the past. Whatever I am and was, I am retiring. Many years ago, I was given the name Thomas, and so instead of picking your favorite alias or calling me 'The Patriot' as if I'm some sort of poorly named spy, you can simply call me Tom."

He settled on Hayes, standing in the far corner with a glass of champagne. A brunette in a strapless black gown may or may not have been with him. He made a mental note to have Blackshear check her out.

"And I hope you will get a chance to address me, because I have chosen this beautiful island as my primary home when I retire. From afar, I've fallen in love with St. Charles—its beaches and mountains, its people and culture. And while I regretfully have to leave shortly after this party—weather permitting—to tie up a few more loose ends in my business ventures, I eagerly look forward to returning and falling in love with this place and with all of you in person. To paraphrase the thirty-fifth president of the United States, John F. Kennedy, *Ik ben een Nederlander.*"

More polite applause. Jackson nodded and smiled, and spotted J.J. Carter, a.k.a. Jared Jefferson. He matched Lexi's description to a T, and stood on the opposite side of the room from Hayes. Without staring, Jackson quickly took in the dark-haired, sharply dressed woman next to him. Christy Rollins could have been cast as the stereotypical femme fatale, the beautiful and deadly assassin. On TV, they were alluring. In real life, sort of terrifying.

"I told you I wouldn't keep you long, and I won't. But before I conclude, I want to offer a toast." He turned to the side, where a glass of champagne was waiting for him on a small stand. He held it in between fingers from both hands. "In less than ninety minutes, it will be May 17th, twenty-five years to the day since St. Charles became an independent country. While being part of the Kingdom of the Netherlands in no way diminished her, this great place has only grown in the last twenty-five years. We've seen the island transformed economically, from being just another island in the Caribbean to a tourist hotspot. We have a new airport, a new cruise port, a revitalized entertainment district, cleaner parks and beaches, decreases in crime, improved education, and in 2012, we had the very first St. Charles native to compete in the Olympic Games, Daan Kelly."

He took a break for more applause. Blackshear was suddenly in Jackson's ear. "Walkie took the bait. They've got the cameras we want them to have."

"I could go on and on listing the virtues of St. Charles," Jackson said to the crowd, "but you all know them, and as I said, I wish to keep this brief. So to that toast," he said, lifting his glass in his right hand. "To St. Charles, her lovely people, her independence, her prosperity, and to twenty-five more years of each of them . . . and to home!" He extended the glass a touch farther, then brought it down to take a sip as others did the same.

"Now, please, enjoy the wonderful array of food, drinks, the music, and even if the official fireworks have been postponed, we'll see if we can't celebrate twenty-five years with a bang! Thank you, everyone."

He turned back to more applause, and had a brief conversation with Reggie and Maggie out of sight.

"You have something planned I don't know about?" Maggie asked.

"Huh?"

"Celebrate with a bang?"

"Keep people from leaving for another hour and a half."

"Aha."

"No offense, Freckles," Robbie said, "but she gets the credit for all the food while I'm fighting through the Spanish Flu in here?"

"We don't do it for the glory, Robbie."

"So much for code names," Reggie said.

"Speaking of, G, check out a brunette that was on Hayes' left during my speech. See if she's anybody."

"Yeah, seen her around. Don't think she's connected to them. People had to congregate somewhere."

"All right."

"Shall we meet the VIPs?" Maggie asked. "I told them to head for the solarium after your speech."

"Okay. Lead the way, Katherine."

*　　　　　*　　　　　*

11:27 p.m.

FOR THE next forty-some-odd minutes, everything went according to plan. Jackson had conversations with Governor van den Heuvel and his wife, the Minister of Tourism, Caro Emerald, and a local businessman named Levi Angela. Maggie introduced him each time, then drifted away and subtly returned several minutes later to whisk him off to the next VIP. Reggie, meanwhile, hovered a safe distance away, keeping his eye on things.

So did Blackshear. "Jefferson" and "Rollins" played the part of the couple, mingling and taking in the art in the gallery. Hayes did likewise, alone, with no interaction with the brunette in strapless black. Martínez continued to make his rounds, working dutifully, with no apparent interaction with any of the other GrayStar members. And Walkie spent an inordinate amount of time in the powder room off the hallway, directly across from the office. Blackshear speculated he was working on hacking the estate's communication system, which, the Brit assured everyone again, he couldn't. GrayStar would only see the cameras Blackshear allowed them to see, and would be unable to listen in on their communications. At best, they would be able to jam them— or rather, think they had jammed them.

Unless, of course, Walkie was better than Blackshear.

Daan Kelly was a distance runner who'd qualified for the 1500 meters in London two years earlier. He was wiry thin, borderline anemic, and he still looked fat compared to his supermodel girlfriend. Jackson had stereotypes of cross-country guys and models, but despite their looks, both belied those preconceptions, and his conversation with them was light and easy. He almost missed Maggie's cue, a clasping of her hands in front of her to signal he should wrap up the conversation and find his way to her.

She was standing by the opening from the solarium to the music room, and he was in the corner of the solarium, chatting with Kelly and his girlfriend. He put on his most convivial smile and tried to make his eyes twinkle. "I would love to continue this, but I'm afraid Katherine has a few more guests for me to meet," he said, very subtly pointing his finger at her. "Would you excuse me?"

"Of course," Kelly said. "We appreciate your time."

"And I yours," Jackson said, shaking his hand, then taking his girlfriend's and brushing it with his lips. "Enjoy your evening." He smiled wide again as they turned and headed for the bar. Then he made eye contact with Maggie. Hers contained the same spunk they always did. They also conveyed reassurance, something he'd noticed in recent weeks. But now there was also a trace of solemnity, indicating this was go time.

He took one step toward her and stopped. Two men moved into his path, naturally but intentionally. They were both tall and well-built, athletic types, both dressed in tuxes. One was blond, his hair wavy and his face baby smooth. The other, an inch or two shorter, had close-cropped dark hair and a five o'clock shadow. They stopped shoulder to shoulder, wide stances, directly between him and Maggie.

"Sir, we'd like to speak with you for a moment," the blond-haired one said. His English was tinged with an accent so subtle Jackson couldn't immediately place it.

"I'm afraid you'll have to check with Katherine," Jackson answered. "She's coordinating my schedule."

"It is very important," the dark-haired one said. "And urgent." His accent was thicker and more easily identifiable as Russian.

"It's about one of your employees," the blond one said. "Tess."

That's when Jackson knew they were the "Canadians" from next door, and that their presence here meant trouble.

Chapter One Hundred Twenty-Nine

11:29 p.m.

"COULD WE SPEAK someplace more private?" the dark-haired Russian said, continuing their tag-team. "In your office, perhaps?"

"Gentlemen, I do have other obligations . . ." Jackson said, making a show of checking his watch.

"At least in here?" the Russian asked, motioning toward the gallery.

Making quick eye contact with Maggie, Jackson turned and entered the gallery, and allowed himself to be guided to the less crowded east room of the gallery, where he planted his feet. They had as much privacy as could be possible at the party.

"We need to ask you some questions about Tess." It was the blond one again.

Jackson shook his head. "I need to ask some questions first. Who are you two, FSB, SVR?"

Dark-hair reached into his jacket pocket and withdrew a wallet. "Vyacheslav Turgenev," he said, saving Jackson from having to read the alphabet soup printed on the ID. "This is Erik Sidorov. We're with the Russian Foreign Intelligence Service."

"What's your interest in Tess?"

"For starters, we don't believe that's her real name," Sidorov answered.

"Then what is?"

"We're not sure. She has a lot of them."

"Look, gentlemen, I'm sorry, but this sounds like an HR problem, and this really isn't—"

"Whoever this woman is," Turgenev took over, "we have reason to believe she's in possession of an ancient Dutch Bible."

Jackson did his very best to keep a straight face. How had Russian agents—if they really were Russian agents, since nobody the previous January had been who they said they were—tracked Robbie to St. Charles? Was she the reason they had moved into the estate next door—was this really all a ploy to get the Bible and the spy secrets it allegedly contained? How was it that they had chosen *now*, of all nights, to make their move? And could any of this be a coincidence, the Russians coming for Robbie at the same time he was going after GrayStar?

None of those questions were able to dislodge the one foremost in his mind, however: How did he stall them for thirty more minutes?

"I'm afraid I'm not following," Jackson said after what felt like a terrible pause but had, in reality, been only a second or two.

"It's not just a Bible," Turgenev continued. "It contains information that, were it to get out in the open, would be very detrimental to Russian interests."

"And how does this tie to my head chef?"

"We think she has it."

"She has it?"

"That's right, sir."

"Well, gentlemen, I really am sorry, but I don't have time to get into what sounds like an international incident waiting to happen."

"We appreciate you're busy," Sidorov said, "but this is time-sensitive."

"I'm sorry, but I don't know anything about the woman. Like I said, this sounds like an HR issue. You should speak with Katherine, the majordomo here. But I doubt she can tell you much more than I can. Now, if you gentlemen will excuse me." For emphasis, he nodded at Reggie who had loosely trailed him and now stood several steps away, then took a step toward him before the Russians could object.

"Did you catch that?" Jackson asked.

"Just your half of it," Blackshear said. The downside of the team's earwigs was that they were so wired to block out ambient noise that they filtered out pretty much everything but the wearer's voice.

"They're headed for the parlor, by the way," Reggie said.

"Good."

"The convo?" Maggie asked.

"Somehow the Russkies are on to 'Tess's' Bible pilfering sixteen months ago and want to question her about it. Chameleon, keep your eyes out and, Freckles, I referred them to you, so after the intro, get lost in the crowd."

"Copy."

"Are we ready to go?"

"Yes."

Jackson had stopped in front of Reggie and appeared to be discussing something with his bodyguard. "Okay, laugh like I just told you a joke."

"Trying to relate to that experience."

Jackson gave him a quick glare, which brought a smirk to Reggie's face.

"Close enough," Jackson said, then turned for the solarium. He had no trouble spotting Maggie, who stood by the bar, having a conversation with an older woman with graying blond hair. Ostensibly catching Jackson out the corner of her eye, she excused herself and crossed the doorway to where Carter and the woman were posed with posture to repel chitchatters.

"Sorry for the delay," she said. "Tom is ready to see you now. Right this way." She gestured at Jackson with her eyes and led the duo toward him. "Sir, may I introduce Mr. Jared Jefferson and Ms. Christy Rollins?"

Jackson hesitated for just a second, realizing he was about to touch a man responsible for the pain he'd suffered the last three years. Yet he managed to plaster a smile on his face as he first reached for the woman's hand. It was delicate yet firm, which described her in general. She was beautiful, more Mary Ann than Ginger, with dark brown hair styled elegantly and a tight smile that was either flirtatious or devious. As he kissed her hand, he deftly ran his eyes over a stylish emerald green dress that fit her like a comfy T-shirt (while looking nothing like a T-shirt), looking for any sign that a weapon was concealed underneath it. He saw none, but if she was GrayStar, he wouldn't.

"Enchanted, Ms. Rollins," he said, standing upright. He looked her directly—thanks to her four-inch heels—in her brown eyes, and saw the same thing as in her smile. He concluded it wasn't flirtatiousness.

He turned to Carter/Jefferson and wondered what his role had been in the attack on the safe house in Argentina. He shook the man's hand, his grip firmer than Rollins' and his eyes just as intense. He was several inches taller, and filled out his tuxedo like a point guard.

"Mr. Jefferson, a pleasure."

"Likewise," he answered.

"I'm terribly sorry to make you wait."

"No trouble at all," Carter answered.

"What can I do for you?" Jackson asked, looking back and forth between them and maybe, just maybe, letting the corner of his mouth rise a fraction when looking at Rollins.

"We understand that you're the man to talk to for certain kinds of information."

"Your reputation precedes you," Rollins said, now with a little flirt in her smile.

"Like I said in my little speech, only some of that reputation is true."

*   *   *

11:36 p.m.

MAGGIE SLIPPED away and through the crowd in the solarium. She strode purposefully, hoping to head off any guests who wanted a moment of her time, and exited through the gallery into the hall leading to the living room. She didn't make it that far, stopping to try the knob on the powder room door.

"Walkie is still in there," Blackshear said into her earpiece. He'd separated the channels so that Maggie was no longer hearing Jackson, and vice versa.

She moved on to the mechanical room next door, used a thumbprint to unlock it, and slipped in unobtrusively. She took a breath, then reached into the bust of her dress and withdrew a small pouch. She unzipped the pouch and removed a tiny black device no larger than a 9-volt battery. She held it up, identified two hinges, and released them so that the device was as wide as a 9-volt but three times as long. And about a third as heavy.

"This thing can seriously blow up a car?" she asked.

"On the gas tank, yes," Blackshear said. "May not char the driver beyond recognition, but it will accomplish our purposes."

"Is I activated or is O?"

"I."

"Good." She carefully folded it back into its original shape, reinserted it into the pouch, and tucked the pouch back into her dress. "Chameleon, you ready?"

"Uh, negative. Hold on."

They held for nearly a minute before Robbie's voice sounded again, now somewhat out of breath. "I'm afraid Eli's magic elixir lost its potency."

"Sick again?" Maggie asked.

"Dry heaves and I can't see straight."

"You need me to plant it?"

"Just give me a couple minutes to rally my strength."

"Okay," Maggie said, suddenly not feeling so hot herself.

*   *   *

11:37 p.m.

JACKSON TURNED his head toward Carter. "What sort of information do you want?"

"One month ago," Carter said, "a U.S. Army Ranger was assassinated in South Beach. That same day, the bank accounts of an eight-year Navy vet were hacked. A month prior to that, the wife of an Air Force weapons specialist disappeared from her home in Denver and has never been found. We think the three events are connected, and the victims were targeted because of their—or their spouse's—military affiliations. I served in the Army myself for eight years, and Christy was in the Air Force. We want to find those responsible."

"And you think I can help with that?"

"Like she said, your reputation precedes you. If anyone might know who targeted them and why, it's—"

"A man with your connections," Rollins said, then took a sip of her champagne while looking at him all the while.

"We even heard that you may have been the source of the intel that led to the attacks," Carter said.

"Are you accusing me of something?" Jackson asked.

"No. I didn't mean to imply that. But we do think the intelligence could have originated with you."

"So I'm unwittingly responsible?"

"To be honest," Rollins said, "that's what we'd like to find out—for our sake, as well as yours. After all, I'm sure you wouldn't want someone to be pumping you for intelligence under false pretenses or using intel gleaned from you for something you disapprove of."

"Very true."

She shifted her weight very femininely. "Think we can make a deal?"

"A deal?"

"You provide us whatever intel you have, and we repay you commensurately."

Jackson slowly licked his lips. "What did you have in mind?"

"Diamonds," she said. "Five million dollars' worth."

He whistled. "That's a lot of money."

"We have the money, you have the intel."

He nodded, pursing his lips. "Why?"

"Why?"

"What makes these two so important to you? The bond between fellow servicemen—or women—isn't worth five million in diamonds."

"They were associates of ours," Carter said.

"And patriots," Rollins added.

Jackson acknowledged her with a brief half smile before asking Carter, "You're associates of Laurence Bosco and Charles Collier?"

Both of them noticeably flinched.

"Yeah, I know their names, although not this woman you mentioned. What I don't know is who you are."

"Five million doesn't buy secrecy?" Rollins asked.

"Like you said, Ms. Rollins, I'd hate for intel gleaned from me to be used for something I disapprove of."

"Would ten million change your mind?" Carter asked.

Jackson looked at him. "Are you suggesting I can be bought?"

"Every man has a price," Rollins said.

"And you think mine is ten million?"

"Ten million is the amount of diamonds we have . . . immediate access to," Carter said.

"And you're willing to pay ten million in diamonds for whatever intel I have that led to Bosco and Collier being targeted?"

"If it might also keep the same thing from happening to us, yes."

"Why would someone want to kill you or hack your bank accounts?"

"People have their reasons."

Jackson pursed his lips again. He paused.

"You are trying to arrange a meeting, aren't you?" Blackshear asked in his ear.

*   *   *

11:40 p.m.

ROBBIE'S RASPY breathing precipitated her voice in Maggie's ear. "I'm headed down."

"You okay—Down from where?"

"Upstairs bathroom. First one I could get to in a hurry."

"You sure you're okay to continue?"

"Yeah, I'm sure. And I don't have a choice."

"Okay, where should I meet you?"

"Front entry?"

"Negative," Blackshear said.

"Didn't know you were on this line," Robbie said.

"I'm on both lines. And I dare say the boss is getting close to making a deal."

"Why negative?" Maggie asked.

"Because Walkie just exited the powder room and turned into the hall. He's loitering and will see you."

Robbie sighed. "Okay, Freckles, head for the dining room, get an hors d'oeuvre, and I'll head for the kitchen, and we'll see where it's crowded and where it's not and we'll figure something out on the fly."

"Copy."

"Just fly quickly ladies," Blackshear said. "Clock is ticking."

*   *   *

11:41 p.m.

JACKSON TOOK a breath.

"You don't trust us?" Rollins asked demurely.

50

"Only because I can't figure out why you trust me. If you think the intel came from me, what makes you so sure I'm not behind what happened to your associates?"

"Because you have no reason to want Bosco dead or Collier destitute," Carter said. "Do you?"

"Can't say as that I do."

"So what do you say?" Rollins asked.

"For ten million in diamonds, I'll give you everything I have."

She grinned, like the cat who'd just clasped a mouse's tail in its paws. Carter nodded. "The diamonds are on our yacht. If you're willing to brave the elements, we can make it worth your while twice over."

"How's that?"

"Christy and I aren't a couple," he said, while her eyes practically undressed Jackson.

Jackson allowed a grin to begin emerging, and paused even longer as several patrons in the music room applauded the end of an upbeat number by the string quartet. He drew his eyes back to Carter and Rollins. "That's quite an offer, but I'm afraid my intelligence isn't something that can so easily be transported to a yacht."

Carter mostly hid a frown.

"We'll meet you in the pool house in . . ." Jackson raised his arm to check his watch. "Five minutes?"

"We?"

"The pool house?"

"Me, my shadow," he said with a brief nod toward Reggie, "and my intelligence—will meet you in the pool house. The doors are unlocked and it's a camera free zone, and I prefer to have certain . . . transactions," he said, looking at Rollins, "not be recorded. Go ahead and make yourselves comfortable, have a drink from the bar, and we'll conduct our business in a few minutes."

The duo looked at each other, then nodded.

Jackson turned to leave. Then stopped. "And bring your boss too."

With that, he turned and walked away.

Chapter One Hundred Thirty

11:43 p.m.

JACKSON MADE EYE contact with Reggie as he headed for the stairs. The big man deftly sidestepped several guests and followed him up to the second floor.

"All units, the hook is set," Jackson said.

"Not so fast," Maggie answered. "Still working to get the device to Rob—Chameleon."

"What's up?"

"Everything I've ever eaten," Robbie answered.

The loft was empty, so Jackson and Reggie clustered in the corner, out of sight of guests down below. "Do you need extra time?"

"Give us two minutes," Robbie said.

"Copy. G, where we at?"

"Walkie is in the front hall, just hanging about. Carter and Rollins are beneath you, headed for the living room. Garçon is in the dining room."

"Dangit," Robbie said.

"And Hayes is headed out into the bloody storm."

"Why dangit?" Jackson asked.

"We were headed to the dining room," Maggie said.

"He's been on the move constantly. Just give him a min . . ."

"G?" Jackson asked.

"Garçon just exited the dining room. He's outside."

"Headed for the pool house?"

"Maybe."

"Hayes headed for the yacht?"

"Looks like it."

"Mighty Man, what's your status?"

"No visual. Can't see the mountain."

"Okay, hang tight."

"Freckles, I'm in the hall outside the dining room," Robbie said.

"Headed in via lounge."

"All right, sounds like we're on plan," Jackson said. "G, keep updating us on GrayStar's movements."

"Roger."

The lights flickered once, twice, and then went out completely.

Immediately, several emergency lights around the house came on, keeping the guests from being in total darkness, but that didn't quell the murmuring of guests.

"G?" Jackson said.

"I've got all cameras and comms. GrayStar operatives seem surprised. Must be the storm."

"Freckles, how quickly can you get to the living room?"

"Two seconds."

"Get everyone's attention, let them know the generators will be up in a minute. They will be, right, G?"

"Should be just a minute."

"We need people not to panic," Jackson said.

"Generators work in here too?" Tori asked.

"Yeah, should," Blackshear answered, drawing out the word.

"What's that mean? Shhhooooould?"

"There's a chance some of our security measures may not draw enough juice. I wouldn't worry about it."

"Awesome."

"Headed into the living room now," Maggie said.

"Okay, we're coming down through the office," Jackson said, and nodded at Reggie to follow.

Seconds later, Maggie's voice came through the comms. "Everyone, ladies and gentlemen . . . Excuse me, everyone. It appears Hurricane Anthony has knocked out our main power, but we have generators that should be up and running momentarily, and will provide more than enough power for us to continue celebrating. So wait patiently for just a couple minutes. Thank you."

"Well done, Mags," Jackson said as he started down the secret stairs leading to the office. "G, any indication of what knocked down the power?"

"No, but it's out next door too. Both directions, in fact."

"All right. Let's—"

With another flicker, the lights came back on, just as bright as before. "We all good?" Jackson asked as he paused by the end of his desk.

"Looks on everywhere," Blackshear said.

"Where is everybody?"

"Hayes is climbing up from the beach. Carter and Rollins just exited the house, and Garçon is . . . I don't have him. Last I saw he was headed for the pool house."

"Walkie?"

"Hanging about still."

"All right. I'll give Hayes a minute or two. Freckles, you two good?"

"Heading to the—"

"Freckles?"

Silence.

"G, you have Maggie?"

"She's talking."

"Why can't I hear her?"

"Listening, more like."

"To who?"

"Um . . . uh-oh."

"What? What uh-oh?"

"Looks like your Russian friends."

"Dangit."

"They're taking her somewhere."

"What? Mags, can you hear me? Mags, what's going on?"

"She nodded, slightly, but they're escorting her toward the front of the house."

"Escorting. What do you mean escorting?"

"One on each side, walking her, trying to look relaxed. Might have a gun or knife hidden."

"Maggie, stay calm," Jackson said. He looked at Reggie.

"I got her. You get to the pool house. You're late."

Jackson nodded.

"Um, another problem," Blackshear said, his voice rising.

"What?"

"I've just lost the pool house."

"What?"

"My cameras in the pool house are gone."

"What do you mean, gone?"

"Blocked, jammed, something."

"How? Go," he said to Reggie, who was already at the door.

"I don't know how," Blackshear said.

"Raider, you copy?" Jackson asked.

Silence.

"Walker?"

More silence.

"Who's in the pool house, G?"

"Hayes, Carter, Rollins all inside, Garçon in the area. Walkie still anchored."

"I have to go in."

"You're going blind. And I'm blind."

"You still have access to the gas?"

"Yes, but no way to know when to use it."

"I'll clue you in."

"How?"

"I don't know, but you'll know it when I do."

"And if I lose your comms?"

"I'll take out the lights. You can see that from another camera, right?"

"Yeah."

"Jack, you sure about this?" Eli asked.

"Yeah. Reggie?"

"They're almost to the front door. I'm on it."

"Where do you want me?" Robbie asked. "Device or yacht?"

"Wait for Reggie's call. Hoss?"

"Copy."

"I'm headed for the pool house," Jackson said, pushing out into the living room. "G, can you reboot anything in the pool house?"

"Not a rebooting issue."

"They hack it?"

"I don't know."

"Okay." He dodged a couple people, shook a hand in passing, and opened the door onto the patio. The rain was light for the moment, but the wind whipped around the house, causing the palm fronds to gesticulate wildly and messing up Jackson's hair. Neither thing mattered. "Walker, you copy?"

Still nothing.

His heart pounding to match the distant thunder, Jackson squinted against the wind-driven rain and set out for the pool house.

*　　　　　*　　　　　*

11:47 p.m.

THE ADVANTAGE of being six-three and two-fifty was that, even when in formalwear, you were imposing. And while Reggie didn't make it a habit to intimidate people with his size, he had learned that when he put a certain look on his face, crowds would part before him. He put such a look on his face as he exited the hallway into the living room and turned the corner toward the front doors. He saw Maggie's burgundy dress for just a second before it disappeared out onto the veranda, and he quickened his pace.

"G, they just went outside."

"I've got them," Blackshear said. "Turning right."

"Copy that."

Reggie reached the doors in seconds, pulled open the right one, and was greeted by a blast of wind and rain. Why were they taking Maggie outside? To a car? Why hadn't she put up more of a fight? Did they have a gun or knife in her back? Did they have something else over her head? Not knowing, he squinted against the weather and turned to his right. The two men with Maggie between them had just turned, walking along the bedroom wing, under the U-shaped colonnade and partially out of the elements. The stone arches kept them in shadow and kept them from seeing Reggie as he hurried after them.

"Lost them," Blackshear said.

"I'm good, G," Reggie said softly, hoping the hacker could hear him despite the noise. He hurried to the corner and stopped behind the stonework, then peered around it. The trio turned around another corner, now headed south. Where were they going and what were they doing?

*　　　　　*　　　　　*

11:49 p.m.

"I STILL don't have anything in the pool house," Blackshear said.

Jackson could barely hear him over the wind and rain. He acknowledged briefly, then set his eyes on the pool house. The lights were on in the living room, as they should be, but outside, it was dark. No tiki torches, as had been planned. No floating lanterns in the pool. Virtually no illumination from solar lights around the property. No people milling about, just an angry hurricane.

Nothing was going according to plan. His bodyguard wasn't by his side. His girlfriend was perhaps being abducted. His yacht-sweeper was puking her guts out. His sniper was unable to get in place. His hitter was now his backup sniper, and was blind. Russian Bible thieves were trying their best to spoil things. And this was all taking place in a hurricane.

He tried to process what all the changes meant for the next few minutes. Reggie would save Maggie, and he or she could plant the device on the limo. Robbie, if she could keep from ralphing all over, could still get to the yacht and take out whoever was aboard. Eli would figure out some way to take out Blye, whether via sniper rifle or by waiting for him at the bottom of Vin Mountain. And he, with Blackshear's help, could still trigger the gas to take out Hayes, Carter, Rollins, and Martínez. They could still finish this.

They had to finish this.

*   *   *

11:50 p.m.

REGGIE WIPED blowing rain off his face and peeked around the corner of the house. The two Russians who had been talking to Jackson a few minutes ago now had Maggie backed up against the wall. They were shielded under the second-floor balcony and by a small copse of trees at the east end of the bedroom wing. And so far, they hadn't gotten physical, but it didn't look like it would be long.

Reggie didn't see any weapons. He was sure they were there, but at least not drawn. He reached for his SIG and thought about turning the corner, wasting the near guy, and then having the drop on the second. But he didn't know enough about these Russians, about who they were, to justify killing one of them in cold blood.

He also wasn't wild about the idea of spinning around the corner, yelling "Freeze!" and hoping they froze. It would be too easy for the far one to grab Maggie as a shield, or pull a gun on her. Even if he went with his first plan of shooting the first guy, he still ran the risk of not being able to get a clear shot at the second before he did something to Maggie.

They were standing just on the near side of the door exiting from the hallway, and on the near side of where the spiral staircase from the balcony landed. But by the time Reggie retreated inside and made his way to either the door or the spiral staircase, the Russians could do almost anything to Maggie. Not to mention, time was of the essence. Jackson would be at the pool house by now, and he needed backup. Somebody had to plant the device Maggie had on her person on GrayStar's getaway vehicle.

"Reggie, what's your status?"

It was Robbie, somebody else waiting on him, somebody else for whom time was of the essence. It was time to stop thinking and time to act.

"Hold one," he said.

"Copy."

Reggie tucked the gun back into its holster, took one more peek around the corner, then turned and charged forward in a full sprint.

Chapter One Hundred Thirty-One

11:50 p.m.

TAKING A DEEP breath, Jackson opened the door to the pool house and stepped inside. Christy Rollins stood straight ahead of him, her updo having survived the wind without looking like a rat's nest, and her dress having done a decent job of repelling water. Several feet to her right, beside the couch, was the mastermind of GrayStar, the man most responsible for ruining Jackson's life, Carleton Bryant Hayes II. He looked like a rugged James Bond, decked in a tux that was wet to match his head and hair. His face was handsome, his jaw bearded, his hair slightly disheveled. He wore a sober expression, emphasized by dark eyes that seemed to penetrate not only Jackson's disguise but his very soul.

Jackson cleared his throat, then said, "You must be Sergeant Major Hayes."

Hayes' eyes narrowed. He then extended a hand. "And you're The Patriot."

"Call me Tom," Jackson said, shaking his hand. "Mr. Carter isn't joining us?"

"He's waiting outside."

"He a frogman?"

Hayes faked a smile. "He's very dedicated. Shall we get down to business?" he asked, lifting the attaché case that was in his hand.

"By all means."

Without being cued, Rollins stepped forward. Hayes laid the case in her hands, spun a combination lock, and pressed on the clasps to unlock it. He lifted the lid and stepped back.

Jackson couldn't help but be impressed by the glittering gems set against a black display. There were dozens of them, ranging from quarter-inch to dime-size. Just as he'd planned, Jackson formed a crooked smile, then looked at Hayes. "Are they real?"

"They're real."

Jackson nodded.

So did Hayes, at Rollins, who shut the lid on the case, spun the dial, and grasped it by the handle at her side.

"Satisfied?" Hayes asked.

"I am," Jackson said. "And I trust you on the count."

Hayes bowed his head a fraction.

"My intelligence is in the bedroom."

"The bedroom?" Rollins said.

Jackson winked at her, staying in character. "Don't get any ideas." Then he turned to Hayes. "Follow me."

*   *   *

11:51 p.m.

A DECADE and change ago, Reggie had been an all-conference defensive end at the University of Nebraska, where he'd wreaked havoc on opposing quarterbacks, tying for the conference lead in sacks his senior season. More than good, he'd also been feared for the physical (sometimes penalty incurring) way he played. Now, as he bore down on the two Russians, he channeled his former self.

Lowering his shoulder, he aimed for the first man's chest. Both men and Maggie had turned their heads at the sound of Reggie's footsteps, and the near man had actually turned his entire body. It exposed him, and Reggie drilled him, shoulder to sternum. The man's feet went out from under him as Reggie went horizontal. Both of them crashed into the second Russian, who failed to get out of the way, and the trio tumbled onto the veranda's brick pavers.

At Nebraska, Reggie would have bounced up, slapping his helmet or crossing his arms beneath him as a gesture known to Cornhusker fans as "throwing the bones." Now, he avoided cracking his head on an arch support and rolled to the side. As he started to get up, he saw the first Russian was still down, holding his shoulder. The second had gotten to his feet, and lunged at Reggie with a knife he'd drawn with lightning speed.

Reggie heard the knife slice fabric as he ducked away from it, but felt nothing. He took a step back, dodging another thrust, and grabbed the knife hand as it passed. He pulled the man toward him and drilled him with his other hand, a hard jab that drew blood. The man swung his other fist, the one not held by Reggie, and landed a clumsy punch that did little. At the same time, he brought a knee up toward Reggie's groin. Reggie dodged it, but lost his grip on the man.

The Russian sliced with his knife again. Reggie jumped back, lost his balance, and fell through an archway into the railing of the staircase. Before the Russian could attack, Maggie swung a fist at the side of his head. It drew his attention, and he snapped back with an elbow that caught the side of her face and knocked her backward.

Reggie used the brief break to push off the stairs and send a haymaker at the Russian's jaw. It failed to connect perfectly, but knocked him slightly off balance. Reggie went old school, throwing a series of punches before the man could recover, and the Russian slumped back against the wall.

Reggie took a breath as he turned to check on Maggie. The other Russian had rallied, and when she'd been knocked backward, he had pounced, flipping her over and pushing her into the pavement. He had his knee in her back, and his hand holding her head down. He looked up as Reggie approached, just in time to get kicked in the shoulder and driven back off Maggie.

With no interest in another fight, Reggie drew his gun. He saw movement to his left, turned, and saw the Russian he thought he'd knocked out rising and brandishing the knife.

Reggie shot him twice, the echo of his pistol reverberating in the colonnade. The other man had gotten to his feet after the kick, but now slowly raised his hands.

"On the ground," Reggie said.

He dropped to his knees.

"Lay down, hands behind your back."

The shot Russian was moaning, slouched down, no longer a threat. Maggie had lifted herself up, and with his non-gun hand, Reggie helped her to her feet. "You okay?" he asked, noting a bruise forming on her cheek and a trickle of blood from her nose.

"Yeah."

He nodded and knelt over the second Russian, quickly using zip ties to bind his wrists and ankles. He stood, taking several deep breaths as he holstered his weapon. He looked past Maggie at the shot Russian, seeing his eyes shut and a pool of blood seeping out beneath him.

"Maggie's safe," he said to whoever was listening to his earpiece. "Two Russians down, one dead or dying. Anybody got the time?"

"Fifty-three," Blackshear said.

"Any eyes or ears on Jackson?"

"Negative."

"Robbie, you copy?"

"Copy."

"Get to the yacht. We'll take care of the device."

"Uh, Reggie," Maggie said through heavy breaths. She reached into the bust of her dress and removed the pouch and the device. It was mangled and bent and in several barely connected pieces, a result of being pushed into the pavement. "I don't think this is going to work anymore."

*   *   *

11:53 p.m.

FLICKING ON the lights in the den, Jackson led Hayes and Rollins toward the bedroom. He'd heard nothing on his earwig, and thus assumed Blackshear was still blind. He knew Reggie and Robbie would do everything they could, and had to trust them to complete their portion of the plan as he went ahead with his. And Walker had never really *needed* to be on comms, so he wasn't worried about her.

He cast his eyes over the den and the French doors leading to the patio, speculating that Carter and Martínez were waiting there, sheltered as much as possible from the elements. Then he turned to the bedroom doors. He pressed his thumb on a small sensor beside the doors and was rewarded with a soft click. He opened both doors and stepped inside.

The bedroom was already lit by a pair of lamps in the corners and a pale glow from a ceiling fan fixture, and looked like any in a tropical pool house, with beachy colors and themes. Blackout drapes covered four windows and the glass panels on yet more French doors, which opened to the patio. The room had all the standard furniture, including a queen bed with a frilly comforter, duvet, and an assortment of throw pillows. But it was empty.

Jackson stopped short of the credenza on the far wall. He tried to believe his eyes, and looked toward the closet. "Vicki?"

Had she hidden for some reason? Been unable to hold her water and gone to the bathroom, and was now there unsure how to make her entrance?

"Walker?" Jackson said, walking over to the closet. He opened the doors and saw the emptiness he expected. So where had she gone?

"Something wrong?" Hayes asked.

Jackson looked back, at the same time as the doors to the patio opened.

Martínez and Carter stepped through, each decked in dark camouflage and thoroughly drenched. Tori Walker stood between them, clad in a pair of silk pajamas, each arm in a firm grip. She was similarly soaked. Jackson's eyes went from her to Hayes, whose lips had curled into a wicked sneer.

"Now," he said, "let's talk business."

Chapter One Hundred Thirty-Two

11:54 p.m.

ROBBIE EXITED THE kitchen into a blast of wind and rain wrapped around the north side of the building. The original plan had been to head down to the beach in her chef's apparel, then remove it in the darkness. But now that there was no one on the patio or on the beach, she shrugged her way out of her chef's coat and peeled off the shirt she wore under it, leaving her in a black vest to match black pants. The vest was equipped with a holster containing a Beretta Nano and a sheath with a Casbah AUTO folding knife. There was also a pocket with an extra magazine for the Beretta and a second pocket with a screw-on suppressor. She quickly attached it to the gun, effectively silencing any shots she would take, then she set out across the patio.

There were windows all along the dining room and living room, but she counted on the lights inside reflecting off them and blocking anyone's view of her as she skirted the pool and headed for the stairs to the beach. She glanced at the pool house, the blinds of which were drawn, wondering what Jackson's status was. She realized she couldn't focus on that. She had her own mission to undertake.

The stairs leading to the beach were in two runs, with a landing between them. Robbie paused and crouched at the first landing, out of sight of anyone who happened to look out a window and spot her and now hopefully obscured from anyone aboard one of the vessels docked just offshore. She reached to yet another pocket on her vest and pulled out a pair of night-vision binoculars, which she held to her eyes. She ran them quickly over the dock and boats, spotting no one.

She toggled a switch on the side of the binoculars and they converted from night-vision to infrared, enabling her to pick up heat signatures. She went boat by boat and noticed only one signature, meaning one body. It was aboard *Sterling Silver,* the yacht belonging to GrayStar.

One person, particularly an unsuspecting person, would be easy. Robbie stood, ready to head for the yacht.

"Tess, what are you doing out here?"

*   *   *

11:54 p.m.

MAGGIE TOOK several deep breaths, still trying to calm her nerves after the last couple of minutes.

"G, the device is broken," Reggie said, looking at it in his palm.

"Broken?"

"Maggie got roughed up a little and it got smashed."

"They had some kind of jammer, too," she said. "I lost comms for a while."

"I sent Robbie to the yacht," Reggie said. "So that means I need to cover the car's exit, right?"

"No, I've got it," Maggie said.

He looked her in the eyes, one of which felt like it was swelling. "You sure?"

"Jack needs you." She placed her right leg on the stair and reached under her dress for a small gun, a Glock 43X, strapped to her thigh. "Gavin, if you can identify their car and let me know when it leaves, I'll do everything I can to stop it."

"Copy that."

She nodded at Reggie to reassure him, and he nodded back. "I'm headed to the valet station," she said.

"Freckles?"

It was Eli.

"Yeah?"

"You've been through the training and you know how to shoot. Steady yourself, and aim for the driver's-side windshield. One place you know there will be someone."

"Got it."

"Get going," Reggie said. "G, I'm on the move."

She nodded at him once more, swiped from her face wet hair that had come out of its clips in the fight from, and turned down the colonnade. When she reached the corner, she turned left, emerging onto the grass and out of the shelter of the colonnade itself as well as that of the trees. The force of the wind and rain almost knocked her over, but she blinked away the elements and lowered her head into the onslaught.

The valet station was a temporary structure built on the south side of the driveway, just past its turn to the west. Valets had been and were waiting for arriving guests by the front, where they took their keys and gave out a device they could use to signal when they were ready to have their car brought to the front gate again. In the meantime, valets waited in the small structure, situated amidst all the parked cars. It provided them a comfortable place to enjoy some food and drinks, and be centrally located. Or so had been the theory. With the onset of the storm, they had all relocated to the main house, meaning Maggie was alone when she reached the structure.

"I'm here," she said, ducking under its roof, which provided some relief from the storm. The size of a small garden shed, the structure consisted of a U-shaped seating area and a "counter" opposite it where all the keys would have been stored. Those too had been moved inside to another location, so all Maggie had was a rudimentary roof over her head.

"Maggie, GrayStar's limousine is parked right on the corner of the driveway, facing toward you. It's an Audi A8, black obviously. Only Audi on the curve."

"I've got it," she said, swiping more hair out of her face and behind her ears. She racked the slide on her pistol, checked the safety, and worked to steady her breathing and prepare to fire a gun at a human being for the first and hopefully only time in her life.

*   *   *

11:55 p.m.

"AND HERE I thought you'd deal in good faith," Jackson said, staring at Hayes.

"Like you did?" Hayes said.

"What are you talking about?"

"You had Bosco killed, financially ruined Collier."

"I did no such thing," he said, figuring he'd at least make an attempt at maintaining his cover while trying to figure a way out of this. "Not that you should talk, given your line of work."

"And what do you know about my line of work?"

"Why don't we go sit down," Jackson said, gesturing toward the door. "We can still make our deal."

"We can deal right here," Hayes said. "Why don't you start by explaining who she is."

"My intelligence, which I could have explained without these theatrics. How did you find her, by the way?"

"Infrared scanning of the pool house. How is she your intelligence?"

Jackson started toward the door, but Rollins raised a gun from behind her back.

"I was going to offer you a drink," Jackson said to Hayes.

"I'm not thirsty. Who is she?"

"Former CIA Officer Vicki Walker."

Hayes turned to Tori. "What was your security clearance level."

She hesitated for just a second, and Hayes backhanded her across the face.

"Hey!" Jackson said, stepping forward.

Hayes quickly drew a pistol and had it in Jackson's chest before he could cross the gap between them. Rollins still had her gun on Jackson, so Hayes turned his toward Tori, pushing it into her side, just under the arm held by Martínez. "I'll ask you again," he said, "and do not lie to me this time. Who is she?"

Jackson swallowed, and Hayes released the safety on his pistol. When Jackson didn't immediately speak, he nudged the pistol into Tori's side and began to curl his finger around the trigger.

*   *   *

11:56 p.m.

ROBBIE STOOD and whirled around to see Tanner and a woman. Both were dressed in black, he in pants and long sleeves, her in skin-tight shorts and a tankini top. Her dark hair was pulled back in a tight ponytail, a makeshift job that made Robbie think it had been down previously, and her outfit likely covered by a dress. Tanner's pants could have matched a suit jacket that had since been shed. None of that mattered terribly right now.

"Tanner," she said. "What . . ."

"We need to talk with you," he said.

"Tanner's there?" Blackshear asked in her ear.

"Yeah," she said to answer him. "I'm busy."

"We weren't asking," the woman said.

Robbie sized them up quickly, then slumped her shoulders. "Where?"

"How about at our place?" Tanner said, gesturing with his right hand.

Robbie turned her face that way, then struck her right hand out toward the woman's neck. She missed a direct blow, but still staggered the woman. So Robbie turned her attention to Tanner, who had reacted quickly and reached for a holster behind him. Before he got the chance, Robbie grabbed hold of the wood railing to her left and used it as a fulcrum to lift herself up and thrust her feet at Tanner. She caught him square in the chest, knocking him off balance as well.

"Robbie, you need help?" Reggie asked.

She didn't respond, instead moving toward the woman. They traded a few punches, all blocked or countered or flailing wide. Then Robbie was lifted off her feet backward by Tanner. She recoiled her legs and kicked out as the woman approached. One foot grazed the woman's shoulder, but the sole of the other shoe caught her flush in the jaw.

She dropped, and Robbie began launching elbows at Tanner's midsection and trying to kick his instep. She failed, and he pulled her into something of a headlock. Unable to get loose, she instead grabbed his arm with both of her hands, tucked her chin, looped her right leg behind his, then bent her knees and spun around, extending Tanner's arm. Using her leg as leverage, she pulled her arms across her body and flipped him to the ground. She performed the move with such violence that, after landing with a thud, he rolled all the way over beside the woman.

Robbie wasted no time, reaching into her holster for her knife. She stabbed toward Tanner's heart. He saw the blade coming and tried to roll out of the way, but was hindered by the woman's body beside him. Instead of hitting his heart, Robbie's knife slashed up his right pectoral muscle and between his shoulder and neck.

Tanner reached both hands to stem the flow of blood, and Robbie felt a moment of regret before sticking him again with the knife. Then she rolled him to the side, off the landing and into the sandy, grassy hillside. Then she turned to deal with the woman, who was out cold. The kick to the jaw had been flush.

Robbie stood and tucked the knife back into the sheath.

"Robbie, are you all right?" Blackshear asked.

"Peachy. Heading for the yacht."

"Reggie, where are you?"

"To the pool house. Anything on J?"

"Negative."

Robbie again pushed his predicament from her mind and raced down the second flight of stairs to the beach.

*   *   *

11:57 p.m.

REGGIE STOPPED at the French doors leading into the pool house. Without eyes inside, he didn't know if Jackson was on schedule, in trouble, or had just released the gas. And the sheer curtains covering the door windows kept him from seeing anything inside. The regular windows all had blinds, meaning Reggie had no choice but to enter blind. He decided to do so covertly, just in case, and eased the door open.

The living room was empty, and Reggie stepped through the door and quietly pulled it shut. He stood and listened, hearing voices but unable to make out what was said. He crept toward the doorway to the den and peeked his head through. The room was empty, which was not the plan. The doors to the bedroom were open, and Reggie spotted half a woman's body visible through it. She wore an emerald green dress, which matched what Christy Rollins had been wearing, and he doubted Tori Walker was dressed to the nines. But he couldn't see her face, and he didn't know the situation in the bedroom.

So he crept further into the den, crouching behind the end of the loveseat, underneath which were two gas masks. Reggie thought about releasing the gas now, but he didn't know how far it would carry—would it only knock out anyone in the den, or everyone in the pool house?

Reggie heard a slap, then Jackson's voice call out, "Hey!" He moved a few steps to the side, behind a chair, that offered him a better angle into the living room. It was Christy Rollins in the emerald green gown, and she held a pistol. Behind her, he saw several more people, including Hayes with a gun in Tori's side.

"I'll ask you again," Hayes said, "and do not lie to me this time. Who is she?"

Time was out, and Reggie had to do something. He scooted back to the loveseat, reached under it for a gas mask, and one-handedly slapped it over his head. At the same time, he stood and reached for the light switch just inside the doorway to the den. Hoping Blackshear was watching and still had access to the gas, he flicked it off and on several times, ending with it off.

Then he turned his attention to the bedroom, where several cries had rung out. A few emergency lights disguised as sconces provided enough light for him to see Rollins turn his way and take aim. He dove to the floor just before several bullets spat out of her gun.

Chapter One Hundred Thirty-Three

11:58 p.m.

INSTEAD OF RUNNING down the dock, Robbie cut into the wet sand. The dock was shaped like an upside down and inverted L. Their speedboat was anchored on the right, nearest the beach, and Robbie used it as a shield as she slowed her pace and waded into the water, removing her shoes in the process. When the water was waist high, she submerged and began swimming, first beside a thirty-two-foot flybridge yacht that infrared scanning had confirmed was empty.

Even on the leeward side of the island, sheltered from the brunt of Hurricane Anthony's fury, the water was choppy and the waves thunderous. That made swimming difficult, but Robbie circled the yacht and surfaced at the corner of the L, looking at the foot as it projected to the south. On its left, closer to shore, was moored a power cruiser that was rocking steadily despite being behind the dock. On its right, *Sterling Silver* was snugly secured to a pair of mooring bollards.

Robbie stroked to its stern platform and surfaced carefully. Her binoculars, which were waterproof, had survived the fight and swim, and she retrieved them and aimed them at the yacht again, verifying from close up the location of the heat signature. The binoculars again identified one body, so she hadn't seen two people close together from her previous vantage point. The one heat signature came from the bridge, looked like a man's body. He was sitting and . . . smoking or on fire.

Robbie lifted herself out of the water onto the stern platform, then stopped when she heard gunshots ring out.

* * *

11:58 p.m.

"WAIT. JUST wait," Jackson said. "Nobody needs to get shot. Can we please just go—"

The lights flicked off, then on, then off.

Jackson saw Hayes' eyes momentarily flit first to him, then toward the den. At that instant, Jackson lunged forward, hand outstretched to shove the gun away from Tori's side. His movement drew Hayes' head back around, but his focus now was on Jackson, not Tori, and instead of shooting her, he swung his elbow and gun hand at Jackson.

It was a grazing blow, the barrel of the gun swiping across Jackson's forehead, hard enough to hurt and likely draw blood, but not hard enough to cause significant damage. Still, it, and Jackson's efforts to dodge the blow, caused him to stumble backward. His right leg gave out and he fell to the floor at the foot of the bed.

Three muffled shots sounded, and Jackson saw as he fell that Rollins had turned and fired into the den. He also saw Tori struggling against the arms holding her and sending kicks toward knees and ankles. But Martínez and Carter held her tight.

Hayes turned his gun toward Jackson, but before he could fire, two more shots sounded. These weren't muffled, and Rollins recoiled behind the doorframe as one of the shots went into the wall behind Hayes and a second broke glass in the door. Martínez ducked, releasing Tori's arm in the process, and she turned and attacked Carter. She brought her foot up toward his groin, a kick that lacked oomph but still backed him off. It was the opening she needed to jerk free from his grip on her left arm and launch an uppercut toward his chin.

Jackson, meanwhile, scrambled backward and to his feet, at the same time reaching for his Glock. Hayes had turned his gun toward the den and squeezed off several suppressed shots, and now looked back to Jackson. Before he could do anything, a bullet hit him center mass, and he staggered back into the post of the doors leading to the patio. A second shot sailed wide, and then Rollins spun around the corner and unloaded a volley into the den.

Martínez had risen, and took two shots at Jackson, both of which missed when Jackson gained just enough balance to duck behind the credenza. At the same time, Rollins yelled something about gas. She squeezed several more shots off into the den.

"Echo One, Echo One," Hayes said, shaking off the bullet that had apparently hit a vest. He aimed at Jackson, who was unable to get his gun up to fire in time and instead dove behind the bed. He heard the bullets zip over his head, then turned on his back to aim over the corner of the bed.

He saw Martínez grab Tori again, pulling her back farther from attacking Carter. He dragged her like a child through the doors onto the patio, followed quickly by Hayes and Rollins. Carter, who had recovered from the effects of Tori's uppercut, was last out the door, just as Jackson pumped four slugs into the wall, door, and possibly his shoulder.

Then GrayStar was gone with a hostage.

*   *   *

11:59 p.m.

"GAVIN, WERE those gunshots?" Maggie asked, eyes wide.

"I've got nothing," he said.

"Robbie?" Maggie asked.

No answer.

"She's in the water," Blackshear said.

Two more shots echoed through the night. Or maybe it was thunder and wind playing tricks with Maggie.

"You have no idea what's going on?" she asked.

"Reggie entered the pool house two minutes ago. That's it."

"You have confirmed gunshots?" Eli asked.

"Sounds like it," Maggie said.

"I'm blind to the pool house and can't hear in here," Blackshear said.

"What are guests up to?" Eli asked.

"They're inside, with the music; they seem content."

"Where's Walkie?" Maggie asked.

"I lost him."

She bit off a growl.

"No, he's moving, headed through the living room."

"Is there any movement in or around the pool house?"

"I don't see anything."

"Eli, you still blind?"

"I am. Although . . ."

"What?"

"I think I just saw headlights."

"Headlights?"

"On Vin Mountain. Hard to tell, could have been another beam."

"Blye's leaving?"

"What was that?" Robbie's voice sounded.

"Did you hear gunshots?" Maggie asked.

"Yes."

"From the pool house?"

"Hard to tell."

"Where are you?"

"Stern of the *Sterling Silver*. There's one man on board. I'm going for him."

"Wait," Blackshear said. "I see . . ."

"Gavin," Maggie said.

"Walkie just exited to the patio. He's headed for the boat."

"Robbie, you copy?"

"Yeah, I copy. One at a time."

"And I've got two bodies coming around the pool house."

"Who?" Maggie asked.

"Carter and Rollins. They're headed east."

"Where are Hayes and Martínez? Where are our guys?"

"I don't know."

"What's going on?" Maggie asked.

"They're aborting," Eli said. "And making a break for it."

Chapter One Hundred Thirty-Four

Saturday, May 17
12:00 a.m.

JACKSON USED THE covers of the bed to pull himself to his feet. Covering his nose and mouth with his gun hand, he pulled open the door to the den that Rollins had shoved shut on her way out. He lowered his arm to shout, "Reg!"

He saw the big man getting to his feet behind the loveseat, a gas mask over his head. Jackson ducked back against the noxious odor, staggered toward the patio doors, and threw them open to inhale fresh air. Just that quick, Reggie was there, lifting him back to full height.

"You okay?" Jackson asked.

"No, I missed."

They squinted into the darkness, and Reggie pointed to the hillside beyond the pool, where a silhouette had just vanished.

"G, do you copy!" Jackson shouted.

"Loud and clear."

"They escaped with Walker, headed toward the boat."

"Two didn't. They're headed around the house."

"Robbie at the yacht?"

"Yes."

Jackson looked at Reggie. "Go, follow them."

"You sure?"

"Go," Jackson said, and took off toward where the silhouette had disappeared.

"Jack, Walkie just went down the stairs to the beach," Blackshear said. "That means you have three plus Walker, another on the yacht."

"Copy."

"Reggie, they're coming around the northeast corner."

Reggie's grunted acknowledgment came through the comms.

"Maggie, look alive."

"Roger."

"Robbie, you set?"

There was no answer as Jackson crested the ridge. He saw Hayes and Martínez pulling Tori across the beach, but with the wind, rain, uneven footing, and their movement, didn't like his chances taking the shot. So, now running at full speed, he jumped.

*   *   *

12:00 a.m.

HER GUN drawn, Robbie noiselessly slipped back into the water. Holding onto the dock, she edged over to the corner. Wrapping her legs around the pylon under water, she hid behind it as much as possible, peeking only her right eye and gun hand around it. She squinted against the rain and wind, both blowing directly into her face, and felt the muscles in her legs falter as she braced against the ebb and flow of the choppy ocean.

Then she saw movement at the base of the dock. A man in a tuxedo. It wasn't Jackson or Reggie, so Robbie fired two shots. As she did, her legs lost their balance and she slipped. Her gun came out of her hand when her elbow cracked on the dock, and she pitched backward into the water.

She floundered for a moment, then surfaced. The man in the tux was gone. She hadn't hit him, she was pretty sure. Before she could pan the entire beach, a bullet plugged into the pylon just inches from her. She made a flailing grab for her gun, snatched it, and ducked beneath the dock as she heard two more shots pierce the howl of the storm.

She did something between a float and a swim stroke to reach the bow of the flybridge yacht moored on the north side of the dock. With just her head above the water line, she continued along the dock, reaching her gun out at the place where the yacht's hull began to taper toward the bow.

There were now four bodies. The first man in a tuxedo was halfway to her along the dock. But as she bobbed in the water, she didn't dare fire. Because the two men behind her were directly in her line of fire, and they were half carrying, half dragging a kicking and struggling Tori.

*   *   *

12:01 a.m.

REGGIE CHARGED around the corner of the house and stopped. The twenty-five yards between the corner of the house and the corner of the garage were spanned by an arched colonnade that separated the driveway cul-de-sac from the lawn. He could see through the arches and down the driveway, but couldn't make out anyone running.

"G!" he shouted. "I lost 'em."

"They're running down the driveway."

Reggie frowned for a second, then took off. He squeezed through an arch and lost his footing on a slippery brick. He fell hard on his backside, but reacted quickly enough to avoid tipping back and cracking his head on the colonnade wall. He stood, took a step back under an arch to get out of the worst of the spray, and stared down the driveway. Gusts of wind caught bursts of rain, reflecting light to create a blinding sheen. Then it was gone, and Reggie could see through the veil.

A woman in a soggy emerald green dress climbed into the backseat on the near side of an Audi, parked half a football field away, on the corner of the driveway. A second later, a man got in the other side of the car. Then Reggie saw headlights and the Audi veered onto the driveway. Kicking up a spray of water, its tires skidded for a moment, then found purchase and shot the car forward. Before Reggie could raise his gun to fire, it was hurtling down the driveway and behind the cover of trees and the far corner of the garage.

"Maggie, on you!" he shouted, then gave chase on foot anyhow.

*   *   *

12:01 a.m.

JACKSON LANDED on his feet, but his momentum somersaulted him forward. He flipped head over heels through the sand and grass twice before rolling himself to the side and to a sitting position near the bottom of the cliff. He shook the cobwebs, then raised his gun. Before he could fire, he dove to the side as a spray of bullets came his way from the man holding Tori

When Jackson scrambled to his knees, Hayes and Martínez had reached the dock where it cut across the beach from the stairs to the water. Just ahead of them was a third man and, struggling between them, Tori. Even had she not been functioning as a human shield, the back of the speedboat blocked Jackson's line of fire. He stood and drove his legs through the wet sand toward the dock.

More shots exploded in the night, followed by a piercing scream. He leapt onto the dock, slipped but kept his footing, and turned to see Tori struggling against Martínez while Hayes and the other man pelted the water ahead of the flybridge yacht moored beyond the speedboat with bullets.

Jackson took aim at Hayes, who chose that moment to spin around. His gun already blazing, he fired several times at Jackson, who got off only one wild shot before diving to the side. His momentum carried him over the side of the dock and into the muck where the waves had been pummeling the sand. Before the next wave washed over him, he heard several more shots ring out.

*　　　　　*　　　　　*

12:02 a.m.

MAGGIE STEADIED herself, feet planted at shoulder width, arms braced on the counter of the valet station as the Audi started down the driveway. She took her support hand off her pistol to swipe hair out of her face. As she replaced it, she shook thoughts from her head about how Jackson would probably find her to be hot in a fancy gown, drenched from the storm, and toting a gun. The only thing crazier than her thinking about that now was that he would be too. Blinking as means of focus, she took aim and recalled Eli's advice as the Audi approached.

Her first shot sailed wide, but the second hit the windshield, causing spider webs to spread across it.

She kept shooting, bursting the windshield, then pinging into the hood, then missing, then exploding a side window. Almost to her, the Audi suddenly swerved to the side and crashed into another parked car.

Immediately, the back passenger door opened and a man poked his head out. Maggie saw his gun and realized he would get off a shot before she could get her gun around. She dived down behind the counter just before a cacophony of shots blasted into the wood, sending splinters flying.

The shots kept coming, not a barrage, but a steady crack, crack, crack, crack of explosions. The valet station was cheaply and quickly built, and Maggie knew it was only a matter of time before one of the bullets found its way through the wood to her. Or maybe the shooter was moving and would come around and shoot her through one of the side entrances.

On hands and knees, she crawled to her left, peeked around the edge of the counter, and recoiled as more shots hit the wood. She realized they were coming from the right and front of the structure, and continued crawling back around behind it, giving her another wall as protection.

As she turned the corner, she heard indistinguishable shouts, then renewed and increased gunfire. She didn't dare raise her head, but she also didn't dare let GrayStar get away on foot. So she carefully crawled to the far corner of the structure, peeking her head around. As she did, she was suddenly exposed by headlight beams, and ducked back just before more bullets plugged into the wood.

She scrambled back and around the previous corner, waiting for the piercing pain of a bullet wound. It never came, and she spun herself around as she slid behind the corner, just in time to see a black SUV turn the corner in the driveway and head for the exit.

Chapter One Hundred Thirty-Five

12:02 a.m.

ROBBIE BACKED INTO the hull of the yacht, treading water, waiting. When the lead guy was almost to her, she rose up and fired at him. She was virtually at point-blank range, yet with the wind, rain, and surging water, and with him running, it was almost impossible to take dead aim. Of three shots, she only confirmed that one hit him, and it appeared to be a grazing blow as he spun around and back against a pylon on the dock's other side, but didn't go down. Instead, he lifted his weapon and aimed at her.

Out the corner of her eye, Robbie saw one of the two men holding Tori let go and take aim as well. She inhaled a deep breath as she dove for the water. She plunged under the waves as a bevy of shots rang out, and felt something against her leg as she dived down until she touched sand with her hands.

She thought first about hiding under the dock, but didn't know if there was an air pocket there, nor if the wood would slow bullets enough if the men deduced where she was. Instead, she stroked for the yacht, knowing she still had a mission to complete, and there wasn't much hope of doing it bobbing in the water off the end of the dock.

*　　　　　*　　　　　*

12:02 a.m.

JACKSON GOT to all fours, then peeked over the dock. Tori had taken the opportunity of being held by only one person to resume struggling, and despite being outweighed by Martínez, was making a good fight of it. There was nothing Jackson could do from his vantage point, other than fire a few quick shots in the general direction of Hayes, keeping him from coming any closer toward him. But Hayes crouched, then fired, and Jackson had to duck into the muck again.

When he peeked back over the dock, Hayes had Walkie by the arm, leading him around the corner of the L. That left Tori alone with Martínez. She kept struggling and nearly got away, but he grabbed her by the hair and swung her around, right in Jackson's line of fire. He waited a second, allowing Hayes and Walkie to take a few steps south, then stood and fired like a crazed man. He got off six shots before Hayes ducked behind a pylon and returned fire, forcing Jackson to leap into the speedboat.

Three shots chased him, and then he dared a look. Hayes and Walkie were climbing aboard the yacht, while Martínez continued to drag Tori. She dug her heels in, flailed with her hands, and succeeded in tripping him. As he fell, she clawed at his hand and got loose.

Before she could stand, Hayes leaned over the gunwale of the yacht. Jackson stood, tipsy in the speedboat, and sailed his final three shots over the yacht so as not to hit Tori. But they served their purpose in keeping Hayes from shooting her. He ducked back at the sound, and Jackson jumped from the boat as Martínez abandoned his hostage and climbed over the side of the yacht with help from Hayes and Walkie.

Jackson dug his spare magazine from his vest pocket, loaded it, and started shooting again as he ran down the dock. He just missed Martínez as he was pulled aboard, and all three men ducked out of sight.

*   *   *

12:03 a.m.

REGGIE TURNED the corner of the driveway and saw a black man shooting at the valet station from the rear door of the Audi, which had crashed into a car on the left side of the driveway. Knowing Maggie was in the valet station, Reggie drew his aim on the man and squeezed the trigger.

Jackson had equipped him with the same gun he owned, a SIG Sauer P220. The only drawback, in Reggie's mind, was the limited capacity of just nine rounds. He expelled them all, then dived behind a parked car on his right as both the man and the woman who'd exited the other side of the Audi fired his way.

Seated behind the tire and bumper of a sports car, Reggie retrieved his backup weapon, also a P220. He racked the slide, then peeked around the car. Both the man and the woman had moved to the front of the Audi, and followed a third man toward a black SUV directly in front of the car the Audi had crashed into.

Reggie stood, using the sports car for cover, and sent them into a crouch with a hail of bullets. He ducked again as the woman returned fire, and when it stopped and he raised his head, the rear door of the SUV slammed shut. A second later, the engine turned over and the SUV accelerated onto the driveway.

Reggie chased it with some more shots, succeeding in blowing out the rear window but nothing more before it turned the corner and disappeared from view behind the tree line.

"Maggie!" he yelled.

She answered through the earpiece. "Reggie?"

"You okay?"

"No. They got away!"

*   *   *

12:03 a.m.

HER LUNGS about to burst, Robbie surfaced with a gasp. She was on the starboard side of the yacht, but with no apparent way to board it. She caught her breath and tread water, bracing herself against the hull as more gunshots rang out.

She debated between swimming back toward the stern and trying to get aboard, or going around the bow in an effort to cut off GrayStar as they boarded. Not knowing where they were, where Jackson was, how Tori might be in the line of fire, made both options risky. She could end up having no line of fire.

The hull vibrated as the yacht's engines revved, and Robbie knew it was now or never. She looked fore and aft again, then up, then back toward the bow. An ornamental rope was draped around the bow, and was just low enough that she could surge out of the water and reach it. Kicking hard, she lunged upward and snagged it with her left hand.

Gritting her teeth against the effort, Robbie hauled herself up, looping her gun hand around the rope. She braced her feet against the slick hull, unable to find purchase, and nearly tore her shoulder out of its socket and banged her head against the hull when she slipped. With renewed effort—and renewed teeth gritting—she tried again, this time clasping the railing with her left hand.

She once again lifted herself up, thankful for all the hours working out to strengthen her forearms. She balanced one foot on the ornamental rope and reached her gun hand for the railing. As she did, the yacht suddenly shook and started moving. It was pushing away from the dock, toward her, which caused her first to pitch forward, into the hull. That collision caused her to lose her hold on the railing and her footing, and she plunged backward and into the water with a loud slap.

All the while, the yacht continued on its course away from the dock, and now directly over the place where Robbie had fallen.

*　　　　　*　　　　　*

12:03 a.m.

WITH A deep rumble, the yacht edged away from the dock, its powerful engines churning out a wake. Jackson ran as fast as he could, now holding his fire. He skidded to a stop, sliding and grabbing onto a pylon to keep from plunging into the water. The yacht was at full throttle, already too far away from the dock for him to leap after it.

"Walker, you all right?"

She sat against the pylon, one hand reached out to help slow Jackson's momentum, the other gingerly holding her head.

"You okay?" he asked again.

"I'll live," she said, turning over her shoulder. "They're getting away."

He thought twice about jumping into the water anyhow, swimming for the stern, hoping the engines wouldn't suck him in or chew him up. But he realized the yacht was gaining speed quickly, and he'd never have a chance of catching it. He resorted to emptying his backup magazine into the stern in the hopes of hitting the pilot on the bridge or one of the engines.

With a sickening click, his gun stopped emitting bullets, and he unleashed a visceral growl.

GrayStar was about to escape.

Chapter One Hundred Thirty-Six

12:03 a.m.

ELI BURST THROUGH a fire door and out into the outer band of Hurricane Anthony. He turned away from the wind and rain and took several deep breaths, having just run down fifteen flights of stairs. Benny had dropped him off at the hotel, so he had no vehicle. But for a former Mossad agent, that wasn't a problem.

Parking at the luxury Royale Hotel was valet only, and the lot was beyond the "pool oasis" north of the hotel. The oasis was of course vacant, both because of the hurricane and the hour, and Eli wasted no time racing along its winding paths and through its alcoves. He emerged into the parking lot, did a quick scan for security cameras, and then began trying door handles. After finding the first four locked, he resorted to sending an elbow through the rear passenger side window of a black SUV.

No alarm sounded, and Eli quickly unlocked the car, then hurried around to the driver's side. There were no keys in the vehicle, so he leaned in under the dash and pried off the plastic panel. Ignoring the potential danger of hotwiring a car in the wind and rain, he focused on the process. Less than a minute after breaking the window, he had the SUV running.

Eli tore out of the parking lot, taking advantage of the absence of traffic as he headed south on Anne Frank Drive. He took the first left, onto Lagoon Drive. It would take him along the park beside Karaf Lagoon, then beside the base of Vin Mountain, and ultimately to a place where he could intercept Blye coming down from Perigon Point.

*　　　　　*　　　　　*

12:04 a.m.

MAGGIE WAS already on her feet by the time Reggie reached the valet station. Her hair was matted to her head, and her dress clung to her body, but her face was composed as she regarded Reggie. From that simple look, he knew she was physically okay and mentally dialed in. She proved that further when she approached the counter and began grabbing keychains off hooks.

"I thought the keys were inside," Reggie said.

"Most are. But they must have left some." She tossed several key fobs his way, then began pointing hers at various vehicles. Reggie did the same, then called her name when a Lexus just down the driveway blinked in response. He dropped the other fobs and pressed the unlock button on the one in his hand again, just to make sure. The sedan's lights blinked again.

"You drive," he said, tossing the keychain to Maggie. He paused a moment to check the rounds in his SIG, and saw he was down to one bullet.

"Here," Maggie said, handing him her Glock 43X.

He nodded and they hurried to the Lexus, an IS Sedan. Before Reggie had his door closed, Maggie had her foot on the accelerator, first spinning on the grass, then kicking up a spray of gravel. She nearly crashed into the trees in the corner of the driveway, instead skidding as she made the turn. Then she floored it again, while Reggie checked the magazine in her Glock. Four bullets. It wasn't much.

At the end of the driveway, Maggie slammed on the brakes, and they craned their eyes left and right.

"No tail lights right," Reggie said, eyeing the straight section of highway.

"They could be driving without."

"Not in this weather."

"And they wouldn't have stopped anywhere," she said, already cranking the wheel left. Once on paved ground, she again punched the gas, then looked at Reggie. Her eyes were filled with intensity, and he nodded back at her. Neither of them was willing to let Jackson down.

*　　　　　*　　　　　*

12:04 a.m.

ROBBIE KICKED away from the yacht, took a deep breath tinged with salt spray, and dove down as far as she could. She felt the draft of the yacht skim over her, and kicked as hard as she could toward the side, before its propellers could chew her up.

Everything was black, and she had no way to tell which way was up or down but by the feel of sand beneath her and the current of the yacht above her. She kicked a few more times, then pushed to the surface. She was almost out of breath, and made it with a huge gasp. Immediately, an incoming wave washed over her, and she submerged hacking and coughing on a mouthful of seawater.

She fought and clawed back to the surface, fighting to stay afloat and keep more water from entering her nose and mouth while coughing furiously to expel what had. Her nose and throat burned, and for several seconds, she was unaware of her surroundings. Then she saw the yacht chugging away and the dock two dozen feet ahead. Coughing again, she swam toward it.

Tori stood at the edge of the dock and reached down to pull Robbie up out of the water. She rolled over onto her back, gasping for air and getting a mouthful of rain instead.

"Are you okay?" Tori asked.

Robbie heaved a few deep breaths and sat up. "Yeah." She looked at the departing yacht, then Tori, then the empty dock. "Weren't there two people here a second ago?"

"Douglas," Tori answered as she helped Robbie up. "He ran to get keys for the speedboat."

*   *   *

12:04 a.m.

HEAVING HIS gun toward the nearest pylon and feeling a small amount of satisfaction as it cracked against the wood, Jackson turned and sprinted down the dock. He heard Tori yell something after him, but didn't slow. His snaffle loafers weren't ideal for running on wet wood, but he avoided slipping as he crossed over the beach, then up the stairs to the patio, giving no thought to the unconscious bodies he passed.

He was breathing hard, his heart pounding from the exertion and urgency. But it wasn't going nearly as fast as his brain, half of which was panicking as his opportunity to take down GrayStar slipped from his grasp, half of which was desperately searching for a way to achieve his mission, determined not to fail.

The noise of the gunshots had reached the people indoors, and several of them had spilled out onto the patio to see what was going on. Jackson ignored them, instead covering his ear to hear Blackshear as he asked for a SITREP.

"Reggie and Maggie are in pursuit of the SUV with Andretti, Carter, and Rollins."

"They're okay?"

"Yeah."

"Coming for the boat keys," Jackson said, turning for the doors into the living room.

"Copy that."

He entered and was besieged by confused looks, questions, murmurs, and gasps at what he surmised was a drowned appearance. He ignored everything and pushed through the crowd into the office. He tore himself loose from the restraint of his suit coat and hurried to the desk. He again used a thumb scan to open a secret drawer, from which he drew out another Glock 19 with fifteen rounds. Then he swiped the speedboat keys off a hook and dashed back into the living room.

Several more people called out to him and one even grabbed at his arm. He shook free and shoved through the doors back into the elements.

God, I don't know where You stand in all this . . . but give me a chance. Please.

He slipped on the wet concrete by the pool, but skidded back to his feet like a ballplayer sliding into second base. He took the steps down to the dock just slowly enough to keep his footing, then thudded down the dock.

Both Robbie and Tori met him as he reached the speedboat. Robbie was hunched over, her stomach's convulsing indicative of more dry heaves. As she raised her head to look at him, he saw both women had bruises and cuts and were soaked to the bone. But there was just enough light for Jackson to see grit in their eyes as they climbed into the speedboat.

"They're headed south," Tori shouted.

Jackson nodded as he cranked the engine. He took one glance to make sure both women were safely in the boat. He carefully edged around the flybridge yacht moored in front of him, then opened throttle and took off through the swells.

Chapter One Hundred Thirty-Seven

12:06 a.m.

"MAGS, YOU OKAY?" Reggie asked as they sped north away from Vossenhol.

"Why, am I bleeding?" She wrenched the wheel right and the sedan skidded for a moment before finding traction on the highway, which had curved along the cliff side.

"Not that I see. I just know what this sort of thing does to a person."

"Yeah, well, I don't have time for that."

He nodded, then braced himself as she made another correction to follow a dark road that was hard to discern from all the other darkness in the wind and rain. They were on a narrow shelf between the edge of Vin Mountain and the Atlantic Ocean, and as they came around another corner, the protection of the mountain was gone and the full force of the wind rocked the sedan. At the same time, the road straightened and began a slight descent into the valley. Maggie floored the gas pedal.

"You see anything?" she asked.

"No," Reggie said, peering through the rain-swept windshield in the hopes of spotting taillights. All he saw was black.

"They have to be headed for the airport, right?"

"Maybe. G, what's up with the yacht?"

Blackshear's voice crackled. "Hea— . . . —th."

"Say again, G."

"South!"

"Copy."

"So why'd the car go north?" Maggie said. "You think we miss—"

"Maggie, there," Reggie said as a flicker of red caught his eye to the right.

Maggie slammed on the brakes, but the sedan only fishtailed as it zoomed past a turnoff. "That them?" she asked, even as she fought to regain control and keep the vehicle on the road.

"Has to be."

Straightening out the car, she stepped on the gas again. "Usselincx Boulevard is less than a kilometer ahead. Cuts all the way to the other side of the island."

"So what'd we miss?"

"Shortcut," she said. "Eli, you hear me?"

"Maggie?"

"Where are you?"

"Uh . . . Lagoon and East."

"Cutting off Blye?"

"Copy."

"Keep eye out for a black SUV, might be headed your way."

"Copy."

Maggie slowed, even before an intersection appeared out of the sideways rain. "You got a phone on you?"

"Yeah," Reggie said.

"Give the police a call, let them know GrayStar's headed their way."

"Uh, you know the police number around here?"

"Same as at home," she said as she made an acute turn onto a two-lane southbound road. As Reggie reached for his phone and dialed 9-1-1, she swerved around half a fallen palm tree and accelerated again.

*   *   *

12:08 a.m.

"JACK, YOU'RE bleeding," Robbie said, shouting to be heard.

Jackson could barely acknowledge her remark, such was his concentration. The speedboat was barely cut out for ocean travel on a calm day, and the current choppy seas were beyond its capabilities. Thus he had to fight against every crest and swell. He had no target in sight, no sign of the yacht on the horizon. The rich folks along Millionaires' Row had generators, providing some lighting Jackson could use as navigation. What little mental effort he wasn't using to pilot the boat was dedicated to trying to remember the layout of the coastline, lest he run aground on a shallow point or crash the boat into the rocks.

Robbie touched his side, just under his ribs, not that far from where he'd been shot in Morocco. He felt no pain—likely due to adrenaline—even as she probed for the source of the blood. He strained his eyes against the rain—mercifully coming from behind his left shoulder—in an effort to see the yacht. If they weren't using running lights in this storm, the speedboat could be almost on top of them and he still wouldn't spot the craft. And the yacht had at least a three-minute head start, maybe closer to four. His only hope was that the speedboat could move faster.

"Looks like a flesh wound," Robbie said.

He quickly turned his head. "You okay?"

"I'll live."

"Walker?"

"She's okay."

He nodded.

"Where are we going?"

That was the question. He doubted GrayStar would make a getaway attempt aboard the yacht, not in this weather. Maybe they would try to cross the channel to Anguilla, Saint Martin, or Gustavia. But only half their members were aboard. More than likely, Hayes would direct them to a beach or pier where they either could pick up the rest of the crew or be picked up by them. Carter and Rollins had headed for the car, where their driver was waiting. And Blye was on his own, coming down from Perigon Point. Assuming a pilot aboard the yacht, GrayStar was split five on land and four on water. Would they make separate exfils? Would they rendezvous somewhere? Did they plan on hunkering down on the island instead? Whatever the answer to that question, the bigger question was where?

As they neared the pier at North Beach, Jackson veered a little closer to shore. The lights in the downtown hotels, casinos, and high-rises were all on, which gave him beacons to mark the shoreline. The cruise port was also lit, and he had to make a wide berth around it before swinging almost due south past the rocky West Point. He did so after straining toward the ocean, seeing nothing, and well aware that he could have easily missed the yacht on its westward course. Even so, he opened throttle, heading south, thinking some more.

The marina made the most sense, but would also take time. Maybe they'd run aground on Rainbow Beach, or go for the much smaller pier at its eastern end. Or would they dare try to find shelter in one of the small sandy inlets at the base of the cliffs by the airport? There was no way to scale them and reach the airport grounds, was there? That meant they had to be coming ashore, and if he wasn't there to see where, they would be gone forever. The throttle was already to the stops, but he pushed it anyhow, trying to coax a little more speed from the boat.

"Douglas!"

He glanced over his shoulder and saw Tori pointing ahead and to port. He followed her outstretched hand and saw nothing. He shook his head to clear water droplets away, then squinted into the rain that was now almost directly in his face but had relented considerably. Just visible in the darkness was the faintly lit white hull of the *Sterling Silver*.

With a resolute scowl, he eased the wheel left in pursuit.

*   *   *

12:09 a.m.

THE MEANDERING road that descended from Perigon Point ran straight east for several blocks before intersecting with Usselincx Boulevard. Before that, it intersected with the north-south Bodem Street. It provided the first point for someone coming down to get off the road, and as Eli coasted to a stop in a pitch-black neighborhood, he saw no signs of headlights coming out of the trees on the slope of Vin Mountain nor taillights headed down any of the streets.

He looked at his dashboard clock. It had been the stroke of midnight when he'd seen taillights on Perigon Point through his scope and thus determined Blye was fleeing. Eli knew from a test drive several days ago that it took roughly eight minutes to descend from Perigon Point if the driver pressed caution to the limit. In hurricane conditions, it had to take longer. But if caution was abandoned in the name of desperation . . .

"Blackshear, you copy?"

"Eli, I've got you."

"I'm at the base of Vin Mountain. No sign of Blye. What's everyone's status?"

"Jack, Robbie, and Walker are in the speedboat chasing the yacht. No word from them. Reggie and Maggie are chasing the GrayStar SUV."

"I talked to them a few minutes ago. Any update?"

"No."

"Maggie, you hear me now?"

"Yeah, Eli. Headed south on Usselincx."

"We have a destination?"

"The airport?" she said.

"Is it open?"

"Not commercially," Blackshear answered.

"Okay, I'll wait here for a few. You hear anything, let me know."

"Copy that."

Eli debated driving up toward Perigon Point for a minute or two. Problem was, if he didn't encounter Blye coming down, he'd know he'd already missed him and just be farther behind. And if the SUV Maggie had warned about came his way and he was out of position, it could blow any chance they had.

He watched another minute tick by on the clock, then pounded the steering wheel in frustration.

*   *   *

12:10 a.m.

THE BREAK in the weather didn't do much to lessen the rise and fall of the swells, especially now that they were on the exposed southern side of St. Charles. But at least Jackson had no trouble following the yacht as it curved around the southwestern promontory and chugged east, toward the entrance to the marina. Jackson was maybe half a mile behind it, and sought to make up the difference by plowing through a huge swell. He paid the price when the speedboat went airborne. He lost his footing and held firmly to the wheel with both hands to keep from flying out of the boat. When the craft thudded back into the ocean, he landed on his knees with a crack, and reflexively cranked the wheel left, nearly dumping the boat. He managed to straighten her out just as another wave nearly swamped it, instead washing seawater over the deck.

93

He shook and spat it away, then looked back to see Tori prone on a bench seat, grimacing as she held her back. She too spat out a mouthful of water, then grimaced again as she pushed off the bench and knelt down by Robbie, who had sustained a gash on the side of her head.

"Douglas," Tori said as he turned back to focus on steering the speedboat and avoiding any additional upheaval.

"How is she?"

"Hold on."

The next moment, the buttons on his vest popped as Tori yanked it off from behind, exposing the Kevlar vest he wore over a T-shirt. He steered into an oncoming wave with a slight reduction on the throttle, aimed for the entrance to the marina again, then looked back at Tori. She was holding the vest to Robbie's head to staunch the flow of blood, and Jackson had no idea how severe the wound was.

He did know the yacht had already passed through the rock jetties that formed a breakwater for the marina, and would be at a dock within a minute. If Blye or the other SUV had come to meet them there, he would be sunk. If it was the other way around, that the yacht was picking up passengers, he had fifteen rounds in the Glock from the office desk and whatever ammunition Robbie might have left in her weapon.

And quite possibly, he was the only one able to mount a fight against up to eight hostile combatants.

Chapter One Hundred Thirty-Eight

12:11 a.m.

THE ST. CHARLES Marina consisted of four separate piers extending south into the western terminus of Rainbow Bay. The two outside piers gave way to rock jetties that made ninety-degree turns to the southwest. The eastern pier's jetty, on the south, protected the entire marina from open water, and on the southwestern side of the marina, formed a hundred-foot-wide channel with the other jetty. That channel extended for the length of a football field, and its jetties were popular spots for fishing or hiking during the day. In the middle of a hurricane, they were empty.

Jackson aimed the speedboat into the heart of the channel at full throttle, crashing over one more swell and then reaching calmer water.

"On your left!" Tori shouted from behind him.

"I see it," he said, following the path of the yacht, which had turned into the channel between the farthest two piers and was currently in the process of drifting to the dock. There were enough other boats rocking in the calmer but still choppy marina water, and the rain and wind, while lessened, were still intense enough that he couldn't see more than its general shape. He certainly couldn't see if any dark-clad figures got off on the pier.

He heard a gagging sound, and briefly looked over his shoulder to see Robbie again doubled over, puking. How there was anything left in her was beyond him, nor how she managed to keep going. But she hurled while Tori held his blood-stained vest to her head, and Jackson turned back to piloting the boat.

He had to slow down considerably to make the turn, then goosed the throttle again. Beyond the piers was a parking lot, situated around the marina office. As Jackson drew closer, he was able to make out four people running off the end of the pier and into the parking lot. Seeing no empty slips, he eased the boat to the end of the channel, turning so that it bumped against the retaining wall with a soft thud. He took a glance back at the women, neither of whom were prepared to join in the fray. Then he unsheathed his backup Glock and, with the boat still idling, hauled himself over the retaining wall and onto the dock.

*   *   *

12:12 a.m.

MAGGIE RACED down Usselincx Boulevard as fast as she could. There was no other traffic—not even taillights of a fleeing SUV—but palm fronds, shingles, loose lawn and porch décor, and other small debris were in or blowing across the roadway. There was even a downed power pole, which required a brief detour on a side street. But the road had also opened to four lanes, meaning she could swerve around most obstructions easily.

"I've got nothing," Blackshear said into their earpieces. Reggie had asked him to try hacking any traffic cameras to give them a clue where GrayStar's vehicle was. Maggie didn't know if St. Charles didn't have traffic cams or the storm had knocked them out, but they were blind on that front.

She took her foot off the gas as they neared the five-way roundabout. Usselincx Boulevard bisected the city of Old Town, and particularly separated the poor sections of town from the rest of Williamsburg. They were to the east. East Street veered off from the roundabout and cut through Old Town toward the airport, making it the most likely direction for the SUV to take. But there was nothing but black down its length.

"You think they could be there already?" she asked.

"Maybe," Reggie said.

Maggie entered the roundabout, ready to follow East Street. It was separated from Usselincx Boulevard by a triangular-shaped, twelve-acre park that was shaded by hundreds of palms. Their wet, flapping branches reflected a pulsing red and blue light, and a second later, a police car made a sharp turn onto Usselincx Boulevard from the right.

"You think?"

"Uh-huh," Reggie said.

There was no traffic coming from the other two roads that entered the roundabout, heading east into Old Town or west toward the Parliament

Building, so Maggie took the circle on two wheels, then gunned the sedan again, following the police car south.

*   *   *

12:13 a.m.

ONLY A few vehicles occupied the parking lot. As Jackson had approached the retaining wall, then climbed over it, the four members of GrayStar had disappeared. He doubted they were hiding in one of the few cars on this half of the lot, so he raced on slick asphalt around the corner of the marina office. He was just in time to see a dark, emerald green piece of fabric disappear inside a silver four-door.

Jackson raised his gun, but before he could get off a shot, the sedan accelerated toward the parking lot exit, taking it behind a full-size van. Jackson resumed running, hoping to get an angle. By the time he was far enough around the van to shoot, the silver sedan was almost to King Willem Frederik Highway, a hundred yards away.

Stopping and crouching slightly, Jackson leveled his gun. But he didn't fire. Beyond King Willem Frederik Highway, more than a dozen hotels and condos, restaurants and casinos were in his potential field of fire. With his adrenaline coursing, with his lungs gasping for breath, with the elements around him, he knew he couldn't guarantee his bullets wouldn't go sailing wide or long. And he didn't have much chance of hitting the car's driver or tires anyhow.

So he watched only until he saw it turning right, then made a mad dash back to the boat to continue the chase.

*   *   *

12:13 a.m.

"BLYE HASN'T come down," Eli said. "I was too late. Where do you want me?"

"Best guess, head to the airport," Reggie said, bracing himself as Maggie swerved around a downed palm tree.

"Copy that."

They were following the police car a couple blocks back, knowing it could have been after looters or some joy-riding idiot. But in all likelihood, it had intercepted and taken up pursuit of GrayStar's SUV. Where it was remained a mystery.

Only for a second. Then a dark form shot across the street from the west and hopped the curb into the triangular park. A second police car followed close on its heels, and the one Reggie and Maggie were following had to slam on its brakes not to crash into it.

"What in the world . . . ?" Maggie asked.

The second police car also turned into the park in pursuit, but almost immediately ran aground on a small rise in terrain because of its slow speed.

"Keep going," Reggie said, and Maggie kept heading west of south on Usselincx Boulevard.

The park ran for five blocks, bound on the south by a street that dead-ended at East Street to the east and at Parliament Square to the west. Reggie motioned for Maggie to take it, and she did. Immediately, her headlights spotlighted an SUV coming their way.

"Maggie!" Reggie yelled as she aimed straight for it. At the same time, he raised his gun. She cranked the wheel hard left while stomping on the brakes in an effort to block the road. Reggie lowered his window and took aim, but before he could shoot, the SUV veered to its left. It clipped the bumper of the sedan, rocking it in place, as it raced past.

Maggie, acting far more like a tier-one operator instead of a journalist turned pundit, threw the gearshift into reverse and backed up a few car-lengths. As she shifted back into drive, Reggie wondered why the SUV was heading back west, instead of east toward the airport. He saw why as the second police car slalomed out of the trees and fishtailed on the road. Its headlights and pulsing red and blue roof lights illuminated another fallen telephone pole at the end of the street, blocking the path to East Street.

Then the sedan shot forward again, in hot pursuit.

Chapter One Hundred Thirty-Nine

12:15 a.m.

JACKSON LEAPT INTO the speedboat, almost overshooting it, and banging his shin on the port gunwale in the process. The crack was audible over the storm.

"Are you okay?" Tori asked.

He answered by grabbing the wheel, cranking it left, and also jamming the throttle to the stops as he shot down the channel.

Robbie stepped up beside him, leaning on the console, still holding the vest to her head. "What's up?"

He looked at her for a moment, pulled back the throttle to turn into the channel leading out of the marina, and then pushed it to the stops again. "GrayStar's in a car, heading east."

"Where are we heading?"

"East."

They were actually going west, for about two hundred yards total. As soon as they were past the southern jetty, Jackson cranked the wheel, made a one-eighty turn, and coaxed every ounce of speed out of the boat. He turned his eyes to port, toward the shore beyond Rainbow Bay. He saw two pair of taillights, headed east on King Willem Frederik Highway, one approaching the roundabout south of Parliament Park and one several blocks behind it.

"What's your plan?" Robbie asked.

"I don't know."

Several ideas raced through Jackson's head. If he could get in front of the sedan, could he come ashore, run up to the road and . . . open fire at the car when it came, hoping his fifteen bullets would not only stop the car but take out the five or more people inside? With enough speed, could he run the speedboat up the beach and onto the road to block it? He didn't know how far the boat would go on sand and grass, or if it would blow up like all the boats on TV did in such instances. Could he find one of the few sandy inlets south of the airport and free climb up the cliffs, then somehow sabotage GrayStar's airplane?

Ideas aplenty, but none of them good. And whether from being submerged or from the elements or from falling out, he had no communication with anyone else, no idea what had come of Reggie and Maggie or the rest of GrayStar.

*   *   *

12:16 a.m.

MAGGIE CAREENED back onto Usselincx Boulevard, the red taillights of the SUV now visible a block ahead as it headed for King Willem Frederik Highway. "What do I do, Reggie?" Maggie asked, glancing quickly at him. "I can't force them off the road."

"Just stay on their tail," the big man answered. "G, anything on Jack?"

Maggie heard Blackshear's reply in her earpiece. "Nothing from him, Robbie, or Walker. I think their comms are down."

"Copy that," Reggie said.

Maggie flitted her eyes to the rearview mirror, where the police car that had made it through the park was behind them. For a fraction of a second, her mind went to the legal ramifications of everything taking place, wondering how those chips would fall. She didn't have time to think about it, because they were almost to King Willem Frederik Highway, from which it was just a short drive to the airport. Despite Reggie's advice to stay on the SUV's tail, she didn't know what to do when they got to the airport. If they headed for an airplane, did she stop and let Reggie out? Plow into the SUV? Plow into the people getting out of it?

A sudden burst of rain blinded Maggie's view, and then she had to brake to avoid a trashcan lid that blew across the road. When she looked up again, she saw police lights flashing from the left, to the east on King Willem Frederik Highway. At the same time, headlights from the west announced an oncoming car. The SUV shot forward, trying to get around the police car. In an effort to turn before the oncoming car, it took the corner a little too fast, skidded, and tipped on its side.

The police car had already begun a sharp turn to the right, but skidded as well, its back end crashing into the bottom of the overturned SUV. A second later, another crash ensued as the oncoming car was unable to brake in time and plowed into the SUV.

Maggie was going too fast to stop in time, and instead cranked the wheel right. Her door just scraped by the back of the overturned SUV and then the rear bumper of the other car. Crossing King Willem Frederik Highway, she turned the wheel back the other way, trying to straighten out the car. But she had too much momentum and slid across the wet street.

With a thud, the car hit the curb. Something tore loose with a bang, and the car continued up onto the sidewalk and then the grass of Rainbow Park. Their momentum finally stopped with another crunch as the back corner of the car collided with a palm tree.

Then the airbag exploded in Maggie's face.

*   *   *

12:17 a.m.

THE SPEEDBOAT had passed the first of two cars paralleling the beach on King Willem Frederik Highway, a Jeep of some sort. Jackson still had no idea what to do, because the other car—GrayStar's silver four-door—would reach the end of the beach before he could intercept it, even if he had a reasonable way of doing so.

He could still head for the beach, jump ashore, run to the road, and carjack the Jeep. That timing was dubious, as was the plan, because it would take a couple of minutes, by which time GrayStar would be at the airport. He was leaning toward racing around the southern cliffs, finding an inlet, and attempting to scale the cliffs. Freehand, in the dark, in a hurricane, it was borderline suicidal, and would still put him on a runway facing off against a jet with nothing but a Glock pistol. But he had no other options.

Then he spotted flashing police lights coming from the east on King Willem Frederik Highway. He also saw headlights coming from the north on Usselincx Boulevard. As the boat continued to skip over the waves in the bay, he watched as the three vehicles approached the intersection at the same time. None of them slowed or gave way, and his eyes widened as the vehicle from the north tipped over and the other two crashed into it.

Beside him, Robbie said something that was lost in the wind, even as the sound of scraping metal cut through it. Then a fourth vehicle zoomed past the crash, spinning onto the beach and into a tree.

Jackson cranked the wheel hard left, setting the boat on a course just west of the small pier at the bay's eastern end. He looked at Robbie. "You got a gun on you?"

She nodded.

"Can I have it?"

"You empty?"

"Down to my backup."

She shook her head. "I need it."

Despite it all, he couldn't keep a smile from his lips as he eased back on the throttle.

"Here," Tori said, appearing on his left. She extended a flare gun to him. She shrugged. "Better than nothing."

He took it and pocketed it as the speedboat ran onto the beach with a soft thud, then knifed through several feet of sand before stopping almost entirely out of the water. Jackson killed the engine and hopped over the bow and onto the beach.

Fifty feet of sand was backed by fifty feet of grass, then the road. The car that had crashed into the tree was halfway up the grassy slope, facing toward the road. Jackson approached it from the rear. It was not GrayStar's Audi, but neither was the tipped over SUV. Had they taken another vehicle? Were Reggie and Maggie in one of them? Or was the silver four-door the only relevant casualty?

Speaking of, its doors were open, and people were scurrying toward its rear. At the same time, he saw movement on the top of the overturned SUV. He was too far away in the dark and rain to identify anyone, and he didn't want to risk shooting at GrayStar and hitting Reggie or Maggie by mistake. So he crept up on the sedan that had crashed into the palm tree, feeling Robbie's hand on his shoulder.

He was almost to the palm when the passenger door opened. Jackson raised his gun, but lowered it a second later when he saw a familiar black head emerge. "Reggie?"

The big man turned and looked his way. A flash of lightning revealed he had a bloodied nose but otherwise looked fine. Jackson immediately deduced that Maggie had been driving the car and circled it and the palm, arriving as she was extricating herself from her seatbelt.

"Maggie!"

He was answered by gunshots. He looked across the car's roof to see Robbie crouched behind the open door, firing at GrayStar's four-door and the overturned SUV. Trusting her lead, he reached for Maggie's hand, pushing her behind him as he used the driver's door for cover and took aim at two people on the roof of the four-door and two more on top of the flipped SUV.

But before he could fire, the Jeep that had been trailing GrayStar's four-door coasted to a stop to his left. Jackson turned his attention to it, wondering if there was a third GrayStar vehicle in play.

The driver quickly hopped out and ran to the front of the Jeep, then stopped when he realized Robbie and Reggie were shooting at the accident. And, as Jackson ducked down just in time, that several members of GrayStar were shooting back.

Crouched down, Jackson herded Maggie around behind the car, so she had its full body as protection and not just a door. Then he turned back around, and expelled several bullets as a duo disappeared from sight over the SUV.

Jackson panned left, through the shattered driver's door window, and saw a gunman approach the Jeep driver. He motioned with the gun, and the driver walked a few feet from the Jeep and stood with hands outstretched, forming a human shield. Jackson watched as two men ran from behind the four-door to the Jeep, and a second later dove into the front seat of the sedan as a hail of gunfire erupted from the Jeep and the front of the tipped SUV.

When the gunfire stopped a moment later, Jackson crawled backward, and shoved away the deflating airbag. As he stood, crumbles of windshield glass falling off him, he was just in time to see the rear of the Jeep disappear around the accident, headed east.

He quickly looked back at Maggie, who peeked out from behind the palm tree. She was fine. He looked over the hood at Reggie and Robbie, both okay. He looked at the Jeep's original driver, now splayed out on the pavement, apparently of his own choice.

So Jackson ran, following the Jeep's path into the westbound lane of King Willem Frederik Highway. He saw no signs of anyone still in the four-door. He came around the rear end of the SUV, saw the police car on fire, one officer slumped over the dash and blood staining the cracked windshield. And he saw a black Jeep peeling down the soaked highway, having apparently picked up the rest of GrayStar's members who had climbed over the SUV.

At that moment, a sudden gust of wind came up, and the rain intensified into a deluge. Jackson was nearly blown off his feet, took a few steps to steady himself, then fired at the rear of the Jeep.

The highway made a curve south, onto the promontory of land at the base of Mount Hudson, and several times he had to adjust his aim.

Then his gun clicked as the Jeep continued unhindered toward the airport.

With a visceral yell he slammed the gun into the pavement.

GrayStar had escaped.

Chapter One Hundred Forty

12:20 a.m.

THE LIFE WENT out of Jackson, and he fell to his knees. He rocked forward onto his forearms, his head touching the wet asphalt. It was over. He had failed. They may have wounded a few members of GrayStar, maybe scared them good, but they had failed to terminate them. They were minutes from the airport, from a private jet, from escaping St. Charles, Hurricane Anthony, and justice.

David and Hannah Douglas were stuck out in the cold. How long would it be before GrayStar figured out who had truly come after them? How long until Jackson or Maggie, Reggie or Tori or Grant, Leroy or Hillary became a target? And what would GrayStar, having survived an attack on their very existence, do to ensure it never happened again? What lengths would they take? How unstoppable might they become?

Jackson felt a hand on his back, then fingers under his Kevlar vest, lifting him. He turned to see Reggie, scratched in a few places, his lip red from a bleeding nose. His best friend's eyes were empty, reflecting what was in Jackson's own.

He turned his head to see Maggie coming around the accident scene, then Robbie checking on the driver of the police car. She shook her head as Maggie reached Jackson and embraced him in a sloppy, wet hug. He couldn't hug back. He had nothing left to give.

Nine months of preparation and work. Millions of dollars. Dozens of lives lost, most notably Lexi's. All of them casualties of his crusade, and if he'd done anything, he'd made the situation worse. All his precaution, all his careful planning, all his assurances to Grant that he was being careful, and now how much more work had to be done to keep GrayStar from finding those responsible? Was it even possible? Could he plausibly come back from a Mexican prison, from a death sentence? Could Maggie go back to her job after half a year off? Could Reggie let his face be seen again? Or Tori? It was what he'd told Maggie just a few days ago, if he swung at GrayStar and missed . . .

He looked at Robbie, who had slumped down beside the rear tire of the police car. He could barely utter words. "It's going to blow."

Reggie caught his meaning and went to help a sick, exhausted Robbie to her feet and to safety on the curb, while Maggie kept Jackson from falling over.

He turned again as headlights cut through the maelstrom, and a black SUV came around the accident, just as tongues of fire began to leap up the underside of the overturned SUV. The black SUV screeched to a halt, and Jackson squinted through the rain as the passenger window lowered.

"Did you get them?" Eli shouted.

"No," Maggie answered.

"Get in."

Jackson looked to Maggie. Her eyes were steely, and she gave a subtle nod. He had no idea why, but in that moment, he kissed her, hard and quick. Then he ran to the passenger door, arriving just before Reggie reached the back door. They jumped in, and Eli gunned the engine.

"How far ahead are they?"

"Couple minutes," Reggie said, shoving the magazine back into his gun. "Dark Jeep, have to be going to the airport. I've got seven rounds."

"Nines?"

"Yeah."

Driving at fifty miles per hour in a hurricane, Eli reached into a pocket and handed Reggie a spare magazine. "You?" he asked Jackson.

"Empty."

He handed him a Glock 19. "Fully loaded."

"No RPGs, huh?"

"Nope. Make 'em count, boys. They're all we have."

A moment later, he nearly tipped over the SUV turning right into the airport drive. They passed the backsides of two large hangars, then Eli took the first turn into an empty parking lot. Empty except for a pickup truck parked in the far corner, near the end of the terminal, where the control tower was, and a HUMMER parked by a chain-link fence on the near side of the tarmac. The fence was bent and bowed on either side of a gaping hole, revealing that the gate had been torn off its rollers, and in fact now lay a dozen yards away on the tarmac.

Two men in uniform were by the HUMMER, one leaning in through the open passenger door to speak on a radio and one, gun drawn, looking toward the hangars. Eli gave a quick blast on the horn and sped through the opening. He turned right on the tarmac, toward the hangars, and Jackson saw a white Learjet half obscured by the downpour. It was headed west, almost to the end of the runway, and as Eli mashed the accelerator, the plane began turning around.

"Can you intercept him?" Jackson asked.

Eli's answer was a look of grim determination.

They barreled down the tarmac, then slowed to make the turn to the short taxiway leading to the runway. As they did, the plane finished reversing course and immediately accelerated.

Aiming straight for the runway, Eli again stepped on the gas. The tires spun and spun, failing to find traction in what was tantamount to standing water. The runway had better drainage, and the Learjet had no trouble accelerating.

With a growl/yell, Eli eased slightly off the gas. The tires found purchase, the SUV shot forward, and he stepped on the gas again. The SUV had less ground to cover, but the Lear's powerful engines were firing at full speed, and the jet shot down the runway, its wing clearing the oncoming SUV by mere feet. Similarly, as the SUV shot onto the runway, it did so with almost no margin to spare behind the jet.

Eli slammed on the brakes, trying to slow and turn the SUV without running it off the runway. He failed, and the tires dipped down into soggy grass. He turned hard on the wheel, bringing it back onto the runway and over a runway light before straightening out. By then it was too late. The jet was nearing full speed, and they would never catch it in time.

Eli swore as the jet got farther and farther away and became more and more obscured by streaks of rain. And then it stopped getting farther and farther away.

"Why aren't they taking off?" Reggie asked.

"I don't know," Eli said. He handed Jackson another Glock, then threw open his door.

"Eli!"

He didn't answer, but instead took off running toward the hangars.

"What is he doing?"

Jackson didn't answer Reggie, but scrambled across the console to the driver's seat.

"What are you doing?"

"Chasing them."

"To what end?"

"About fifty bullets by my count," he said, handing the second Glock from Eli back to Reggie.

"You'd better shoot straight, J."

Jackson accelerated slowly on the runway. The jet was boxed in. For whatever reason—inability to get up to speed, too slick of runways, sudden realization that flying in a hurricane was a bad idea—the plane hadn't taken off. Now there was nowhere near enough runway for it to do so heading east, and if it reversed course, an SUV and fifty-some-odd bullets stood in its way.

The plane had reached the end of the runway, and turned left in an attempt to turn back around. But as Jackson got closer and saw through the rain, he realized the plane's front tire had gone off the runway, and the jet was now stuck. One hundred yards away, he pulled off to the side of the runway, turned to face the jet, and parked the SUV.

"Now what?" Reggie asked.

"Their backs are against the ocean. They have to come our way, and I don't think the plane will move."

"So we wait."

Jackson nodded.

"And hope they ain't armed to the teeth."

Wind rocked the SUV, and rain continued to pelt Jackson through the broken passenger window. He was so soaked that he was immune to it at this point, except for its blinding effect.

A couple minutes passed, which allowed Jackson's heartbeat to reduce to a jackhammer. He was so physically and mentally and emotionally spent that he couldn't think or feel anything. He just stared at the airplane, twice thinking he saw movement. Then Reggie tapped his shoulder, and he realized the airstairs behind the cockpit were coming down.

He opened his door, got out, and took aim, just as a head appeared at the top of the stairs. Jackson's bullets were wide, but forced the man to duck back. Jackson glanced to his right, and saw that Reggie had opened the back door of the SUV. He lowered the window and took aim through two open windows of two doors, adding protection. Jackson moved to do likewise, but ended up scurrying behind the body of the SUV as a torrent of gunfire erupted from the opening in the jet.

With Reggie firing away from the SUV's right side, Jackson took several shots, jerked open the back door on his side, and squeezed a few more shots between the door and the frame. Then he ducked back from another salvo, aware that bullets were now coming from two places aboard the plane, as they had apparently knocked out one of the windows.

Reggie squeezed a few shots, then Jackson stood to fire. But he was distracted by a blur to his left. He saw a giant truck rumbling down the runway. It was a refueling truck, no doubt driven by Eli, and the Israeli was taking dead aim for the Learjet's fuselage.

Chapter One Hundred Forty-One

12:31 a.m.

JACKSON COULDN'T BELIEVE it. Eli Haddad, former Mossad agent, borderline unscrupulous freelance operator, the man whose actions and tactics had sickened Jackson, was about to sacrifice himself by driving a truck full of fuel into the Learjet, creating a massive explosion, and incinerating GrayStar.

They sensed it too, because they turned their aim from the SUV to the truck.

"Reggie!"

The big man understood, and both he and Jackson unleashed a fusillade at the airplane, one last barrage to cover Eli's heroics. Jackson saw someone at the top of the airstairs duck back inside the plane, then his gun clicked.

The next second, his shock increased. Instead of ramming the Learjet, Eli must have wrenched the wheel almost off the column, because he tipped the truck on its side while spinning it one hundred degrees to the right. The large drum on the back of the truck slammed into the pavement and slid across it with a screech louder than the storm, coming to rest mere feet from the fuselage of the airplane.

"Was that on purpose?" Reggie asked.

"I don't know. Spare a clip?"

Reggie leaned through the open rear doors and tossed Jackson a magazine for the Glock. He hammered it home, then looked up with more astonishment as he saw the windshield of the fuel truck shake twice, then dislodge as Eli kicked it free.

"J!"

"I see it."

Jackson peppered the Learjet with bullets as Eli climbed out of the cab and began making a run for the SUV. With Reggie also providing cover, he made it halfway before a GrayStar bullet felled him.

Screaming in rage, Jackson emptied his magazine. Reggie had to be low on bullets too, and Jackson didn't dare ask for more from him. He looked desperately at the plane, which despite all their shooting, didn't seem to be running out of GrayStar members to peek out of openings with blazing guns. He looked at Eli, unmoving fifty yards from the fuel truck. Desperation again seized him.

Then he remembered the flare gun Tori had given him before he jumped out of the speedboat. He had no idea if TV was true, but it was worth a try. He opened the chamber, saw it held only one flare, and thus steadied himself on the door. He took aim for the fuel drum and fired.

True to its name, the flare streaked through the rain and wind, drifting because of it, and missed the drum entirely. It lodged into the fuselage of the airplane.

"Dangit!" Jackson screamed. He ducked down as several bullets raked the SUV, then looked toward Reggie, ready to ask for whatever ammo he had left so he could make one final charge at the plane. In the process, his eyes caught the sparks of the flare dropping to the pavement. They landed in a puddle on the concrete, a puddle not of water, but of fuel leaked from the overturned drum.

A moment later, the darkness was expelled by a fiery explosion. Huge, mushrooming balls of fire shot up from the fuel drum. The fuselage of the Learjet was broken in half, the middle ends being thrust into the air and the wings shearing off.

Jackson should have ducked down since the intensity of the explosion easily covered the hundred yards, warming the rain-chilled air. But he couldn't turn his eyes away. Then burning debris began raining down on the runway and surrounding grass, most of it being extinguished by the rain before landing, but some of it staying afire as it hit the ground. Jackson watched as several bodies jumped from the plane, which had been engulfed by flames. One of the bodies looked like a stuntman, waving his flaming arms, only without a fire-retardant suit. Another scrambled down the steps, and a third eschewed steps and jumped over them. He wasn't on fire, but landed in a heap of broken bones.

Jackson unsheathed the KA-BAR knife from its ankle holster, and took off running. At the same time, Reggie emerged from the other side of the SUV. Both ran toward Eli, who in addition to being shot was in danger of being burned or crushed by falling debris.

"Jack, duck!"

He instinctively dropped before a shot rang out. He heard a growl of pain, then two more shots. He looked left, where a man had crumpled to a heap, and then right, where Reggie had fallen, one hand on his leg, the other on his gun, with which he'd just saved Jackson's life.

"Reggie!" Jackson yelled, running toward him.

Instead of responding, Reggie pivoted on his backside and took two more shots toward the rear of the airplane, where a woman in emerald had opened a rear hatch. His gun clicked, empty, and the woman pitched out of the airplane, revealing the bottom half of the back of her dress had burned.

"Reg, how bad is it?"

"I'll live. Get Eli."

Jackson turned and scanned the devastation, the night now lit with an orange glow as the flames continued to lick up fuel on the runway and incinerate metal. For the moment, he saw no movement, and approached Eli. The Israeli had turned onto his side, propped up on one elbow. His hand was on his side, and both were soaked with blood.

"Eli. Eli."

"How . . . How many?"

"I don't know." Jackson knelt down beside him. "What can I do?"

"Make sure none of them got away."

Jackson looked into the Israeli's eyes, and they were hard and strong. He nodded. "Hang in there."

He turned, again surveying the scene. At first nothing, but then he saw movement, ahead of the cockpit, in the grass toward the fence at the north side of the airport. One man, running.

Jackson stood and planted his foot to run when Reggie called out. He turned to the big man, who had reclined onto his back so he could retrieve something from his waistband. As Jackson approached, he saw it was a gun, and Reggie underhanded it to him.

"Seven bullets."

"You gonna be all right?"

"Don't let him get away, J."

With a nod, Jackson turned and chased after the man. The runway was no more than a couple hundred feet from the chain-link fence surrounding the airport property, and it was less than a hundred feet from King Willem Frederik Highway. The total was a hundred yards, a football field, and the man was already at the fifty. Unlike in football, shooting in the butt wasn't a penalty.

As Jackson stepped onto the slick grass, he saw the man hop the fence, and nearly took a shot. But he waited, not sure if the man knew he was being followed, and not wanting to give himself away. So he kept running, temporarily stuffing the gun into his pocket as he too scaled the fence. When he landed on the other side, he saw the man was already to the road. He also saw red and blue lights coming from the left, from town.

Hope swelled in him, if he could convince the cops he was the good guy. Then hope disappeared when the man in front of him started firing at the police car. The driver slammed on the brakes, instinctively, instead of mowing down the shooter. A trio of shots plugged into the windshield, proving that to be a mistake. The horn began wailing, and the man fired again, this time at the passenger side of the windshield. Jackson was at the twenty-five and closing, and took several shots as the man rounded the car and headed for the driver's side.

Jackson had no cover in the open grass, and didn't want to give the man time to fire. So he squeezed off steady shots as he ran at the car, aiming just over the roof. He was almost to the roadway when his gun emptied. At the same time, he saw a head begin to rise over the driver's door. Out of bullets, Jackson did the only thing he could. His left foot landed on the gravel at the edge of the road, and his right found solid pavement beneath it. Pushing off, he hurtled himself up and over the roof.

In a movie, he would have displayed Olympic-caliber leaping ability and made a flying tackle. In reality, he landed in the middle of the roof, kicking the light bar and bruising his shin. Yet he managed to somersault and roll off the roof and into the man just as he stood to fire. They fell to the ground, and Jackson heard the clack of the man's gun hitting the pavement. As they scrambled to get the upper hand, Jackson tried to reach for his knife, which he had re-sheathed, but before he could, a bowling ball of a punch slammed into his midsection.

He reeled backward, rolling to his hands and knees. He turned as he started to get up, and saw two things. The first was the face of the man, backlit by the blaze. Even so, he still recognized him as the GrayStar leader, Carleton Bryant Hayes II.

The second thing he saw was the sole of a boot coming for his temple.

Then he blacked out.

Chapter One Hundred Forty-Two

12:37 a.m.

JACKSON FELT A weight on his shoulder and chest. He heard the crackling of the fire. He felt the rain pummeling his face. It washed away the coppery taste of blood.

He blinked open his eyes, seeing the inferno on the runway one hundred yards away, and not the police car that should have been in his field of vision. He tried to turn his head, and that's when he realized the weight on his shoulders was a body.

Jackson rolled the lifeless form off him, in the process sitting up. He turned his head, which caused pain to radiate through it, and saw taillights headed east. He thought about his gun, but remembered it was empty. He thought about the gun Hayes had dropped, but didn't see it.

He looked down at the body that he'd rolled out from under, a police officer, likely the driver. His chest and neck were soaked with blood, and his eyes were rolled back into his head. He was gone.

Jackson unholstered the officer's gun and stood on wobbly legs. The highway ran along the base of Mount Hudson, and just a hundred meters to the east, began to curve around the mountain's slope. Before he could shoot, the police car was around the corner.

His head pounding, his body heaving for breath, he looked around. No other cars. No other options. So he turned to the left and took off running.

As it curved to the north and hugged the rugged eastern slope of Mount Hudson, King Willem Frederik Highway actually climbed a couple hundred feet, making a pair of switchbacks before gradually descending to East Bay and the island's northern valley. The first switchback turned the road back south, and it traveled several hundred meters before reversing again to the north. On a slick, two-lane road (as King Willem Frederik Highway was east of the airport access) with hairpin turns and sharp drop-offs, not to mention during a hurricane, it would take Hayes a couple minutes to get to the second switchback. Then another thirty seconds to a minute heading north before he was out of sight from the switchback. That gave Jackson three minutes to run a quarter mile or so to get in position for one last desperate shot.

A quarter mile was not a long run, especially since Jackson was in good shape. But he was exhausted, possibly concussed from the boot Hayes had apparently been wearing all night, and wouldn't be running on a track, but up the side of a heavily forested mountain. But as long as there was even a remote chance of catching Hayes, he would take it.

Fueled by nothing but adrenaline and determination, Jackson plowed into the foliage. He had no idea what grew on the jungle-like slopes of St. Charles' tallest peak, nor what manner of wildlife occupied the wooded hillside. Leaves and branches slapped against him as he charged up muddy, slippery terrain, finding as many solid rocky surfaces with his knees and shins as with his feet. He was still wearing loafers, less than ideal for a jungle hike. But he charged on.

Working off memory of the island from maps, and with absolutely nothing other than an internal compass that was usually pretty sound, he did his best to maintain a due north course, zigzagging around tree trunks, thick undergrowth, and impassible steep ledges. The clock in his head was ticking, and he knew time was running out. He also knew he was getting higher and closer.

His lungs burning, his legs pleading for a break, he crested a steep rise, then turned a little left, having been driven off course. The tree canopy provided something of an echo chamber, and all he heard was his own breathing. And then a moment later, another sound. A car on wet pavement.

He found another gear and a further supply of resolve, and pushed on. He could hardly balance any longer, and nearly fell into a tree. He shoved off it and burst through thick fern bushes and felt the ground give way beneath him. He slid down a muddy embankment, feeling several rocks dig into his backside. He landed in a heap, but quickly stumbled to his feet.

Fifty yards ahead of him, headed north and climbing, was the police car. Its red and blue lights had ceased flashing, but Jackson could still make out their form atop the roof. Not that there would be any other cars out at this hour, but it removed any doubt about what he did next.

Standing and bracing himself, he rhythmically fired at the car. Several bullets hit the rear windshield or the trunk. Then a loud pop indicated he'd hit a tire, and immediately the car fishtailed right, toward the cliff to the right. A hard turn brought it back left, where it skidded into a rocky escarpment with a grinding crash.

Jackson lowered his gun and ran. He was on pavement now, moving fast, and the curves in the road were minimal enough that he was able to set a straight course and stay on pavement. He was still going uphill, and the muscles in his quads and calves were screaming. He pushed them on, his eyes on the driver's side door of the police car. Hayes had not yet shown signs of life.

That changed when Jackson was maybe twenty yards away. Suddenly the window burst and a trio of gunshots sounded. Jackson had no immediate cover, and instead dove to the ground. He rolled once, then leveled his gun. Hayes got out of the car, looking Jackson's way. Both fired a couple shots, neither accurate, and then Hayes scampered around the car, noticeably limping but still moving well.

Jackson stood to chase him, ducking as a few more shots sailed his way, then squeezing a few return shots over the police car, which shielded Hayes from him. By the time he reached the back corner and could use the car as his own shield, it was too late. He saw Hayes disappear into the foliage.

Jackson paused for just a second and checked his ammunition. Three rounds remaining. He hammered the magazine back home and thought about seeing if the other officer was still in the car and trying to lift his weapon off him. But he considered the very reason Hayes had taken a good thirty seconds to extricate himself from the car might have been that he was grabbing the weapon. Besides that, Jackson couldn't afford the time.

So he hurried to where he'd seen Hayes vanish and again charged into the trees and bushes. The slope was lesser here, and the going not so tough. Hayes had maybe twenty yards on Jackson, and the advantage of a dark jungle to hide him. But he was also limping, and Jackson was betting on the reverse of the old adage: he could run faster mad than Hayes could scared.

The question was, where was Hayes going? Had he been heading toward the East Bay resort and dock on purpose, or merely fleeing in the most convenient direction? And now that he was on foot, did that change?

Bits of tree bark pelted Jackson in the face as a bullet plugged into a tree a foot to his left. He immediately ducked as another bullet whizzed by him. When he stood again, Hayes was on him, flying out of the trees like a tiger. They fell to the ground and rolled, crushing small sticks and absorbing jagged rocks until they hit the trunk of a sturdy tree.

As he had back on the road, Hayes resorted to a series of punches aimed at Jackson's solar plexus. Jackson wriggled his body away from a few, at the same time trying to jab at Hayes' face. He realized he'd dropped the gun and that, as they struggled in the mud, he'd have to best the former Army Ranger and elite operator hand-to-hand.

A punch rattled Jackson's jaw, and he did the only thing he could; he rolled with it and away from another. Hayes had gotten the upper hand and upper position, and thrown a pair of haymakers. The momentum of the missed second punch, combined with Jackson rolling away, caused Hayes to lose his balance and slide away down the hill.

Jackson got to his knees, looking for any signs of the gun. He saw nothing, and instead reached for his knife. He stood and turned to face Hayes, but was driven off his feet before he saw him coming. He fell back, into the side of the hill, and only managed to get an arm up before Hayes dove for his neck. They grappled for a moment, then Hayes again got the upper hand and began to strangle Jackson. His flailing hands did little to stop the GrayStar general, and he feared his time was up.

Then his fingers founded a fallen branch, which he grabbed and swung. He couldn't get enough into the swing, being prone on his back, to do much damage. But he succeeded in freeing himself from the chokehold.

He swung again, left-handed again, but this time with a tight uppercut, as if trying to turn on an inside fastball. He still didn't have a lot of oomph in the swing, but the branch hit Hayes flush. It was only a couple inches thick, and dead wood, but it knocked Hayes back and off Jackson.

He stood, gripping the branch like a baseball bat for real now, and swung again. Hayes had rolled all the way onto his backside, half sitting, and Jackson's downward blow was thrown off by him slipping on the hillside, and cracked into Hayes' shoulder instead of his head. Even so, it was enough to knock him off balance.

He rolled twice, grabbed a low tree limb for balance, and stood. Jackson stepped forward, ready to park one in the cheap seats. But he swung and missed, and opened himself for a hard punch to the ribs that took the air out of him. He lost his grip on the branch, then stumbled to a knee. Before he knew it, Hayes had grabbed him by the hair. He pulled him back and then slammed him into a rock. Jackson was just able to get his arm up in time to protect his head, and it saved his life.

But maybe not for long. Hayes now had the branch, and moved on Jackson, who tried to get up. The branch came down on his back and shoulder instead of his head. He crumpled under the blow, then rolled out of the way of a downward chop. As he tried to scoot and sit up, Hayes struck again with lightning speed, a sideways uppercut that hit Jackson flush in the side of the head.

He saw stars as he rolled again, this time involuntarily. He also saw, with somewhat blurred vision, a polymer barrel that somehow found a tiny speck of ambient light to reflect. He desperately clutched it, rolling again, this time on purpose, several times until his legs hit a tree and he stopped. He now lay on his back, sideways on the hill, holding the officer's gun by the barrel. And somehow, he was in the rain again, getting pelted by water.

He blinked twice and saw Hayes standing ten feet away. He'd dropped the branch and drew a gun from his waistband. He aimed at Jackson, then squeezed the trigger.

Chapter One Hundred Forty-Three

12:45 a.m.

CLICK.

Hayes' gun didn't fire. Whether it jammed, was empty, or had gotten clogged with mud didn't matter. What did matter was that it didn't work.

Jackson's head was ringing and his vision was off either from rain or massive head trauma. But he was able to process that he was holding his gun, reorient it, and take a shot at Hayes. The GrayStar general had spent just a moment checking his empty gun, apparently unable to believe it was empty, and not believing Jackson was a threat. When he saw the gun, he scrambled up the hill to the cover of a tree, and Jackson's shot grazed the edge of his leg if anything.

He only fired once, knowing his ammo was limited, and not willing to risk another miss. He knew he had no chance in hand-to-hand combat, and Hayes had to know that. Which explained why he could be heard crashing through the jungle again, hoping to draw Jackson to waste the rest of his bullets.

Jackson rolled over and got up, spitting out a mix of rain and saliva, and maybe blood. He stood, wobbled once, then sucked in a deep breath to revive him. Hayes was headed off to Jackson's right, which he presumed was north based on the lay of the land.

He felt dizzy, one eye was blurred for sure, and his tank was past E. Yet he found some measure of willpower to keep going, pushing back into the jungle. He half expected a branch to come swinging for his head at any moment, but it didn't.

Jackson could hear Hayes just ahead. Even as he ran—and putting one leg in front of the other took about all his concentration—he wondered how far Hayes intended to run. How would he know how many bullets Jackson had left, and when it was safe to turn around and finish the fight? Or wasn't that his strategy after all?

Jackson slipped and slid, catching his foot on a tree trunk. When he stood, he now had a limp, and it caused him to slip again a moment later. He emerged into a driving rain and saw he was back on the road.

Hayes was only a few dozen paces to his left, north of him on the road. It made a slight turn back to the east, toward the coast, with a small turnout and parking area where motorists could enjoy the view. But Hayes wasn't enjoying anything. Whether it had been the accident or Jackson's shot had done more damage than he thought, the former Army Ranger was laboring, and seeing that gave Jackson renewed energy.

Now on solid ground, he ran. He was gaining on Hayes, and as they both neared the turnout, he stopped.

"Hayes."

He kept running.

Jackson fired at the pavement just wide of him.

"Hayes!" he screamed through the rain.

He stopped.

Jackson had yelled so loud the blood rushed to his head and he almost passed out. Or maybe that was something else. He willed himself to take several steps forward as Hayes slowly turned around.

"It's over," Jackson said, still practically yelling to be heard above the storm.

"What, are you going to shoot me in cold blood?"

"You could always surrender, come back with me to answer for your crimes."

"My crimes?" Hayes took a step forward. "I'm a patriot."

"You've killed and murdered indiscriminately, American citizens on American soil. You're a terrorist, and you will face justice."

"That's not going to happen."

"Then you don't give me much of an option."

"Thing is," Hayes said, taking another step, "I don't think you have it in you . . . Douglas."

Jackson did everything he could to keep the shock from showing on his face.

"Yeah, I know who you are. Although not for lack of effort. That was an impressive set up."

"How long?"

"Just tonight. Like I said, impressive setup."

"Well, if you know who I am, you know what I'm capable of."

"I do," Hayes said as he took another step. "You're a man of faith. At least, you were. You think Jesus would want you to kill me? Or your honorable father or dear sweet mother?"

"Too bad we can't ask them, seeing as how they were murdered."

"That was an accident. We wanted to capture him, not kill him."

"That supposed to console me?"

"No, I don't suppose so." He took another step. "Look, Doug—"

"Stop walking. You think I don't know what you're doing, inching closer until I'm in range? You think I'm coming out of another fight with you?"

Hayes smirked, and shuffled his foot forward.

"One more step, and I put a bullet between your eyes."

"Yeah, I think you would," Hayes said, leaning back, then actually taking a step back. "In self-defense. In a fair fight. But I'm unarmed." He shook his head. "But what if I just started to walk away?" He took a couple steps back. "You said it, you're not surviving another fight with me. And you wouldn't shoot me in the back, would you?" he asked, starting to turn.

"Hayes."

"Only a coward would shoot a man in the back," he said, then turned completely.

"Stop."

Hayes turned back with a smirk. "I'll see you around, Douglas." Then he turned and started walking again.

"Hayes."

He took another step.

"Hayes!" Jackson screamed, again to no answer. Hayes just kept walking up the road.

Jackson gritted his teeth and squinted through the rain. Then he took aim at the back of Hayes' head and squeezed the trigger.

Part Six

Chapter One Hundred Forty-Four

One week later . . .
Saturday, May 24
7:06 a.m. (Eastern Daylight Time)
Rehoboth Beach, Delaware

THE FOAM OF breaking waves glistened in the sun on what promised, despite the comfortable morning breeze, to be another hot day on the Atlantic Seaboard. Framed by dunes and seagrass that parted to provide an unencumbered view, the ocean—even if not the one he was used to—was just what Jackson needed after a restless night of sleep.

His lack of quality rest couldn't be blamed on the accommodations. He'd slept in a luxurious queen bed with sheets of an absurdly high thread count, his window cracked to hear the ocean and smell the salt air. The two-story beach house was set back from the road a hundred yards, on a driveway winding through the trees and the dunes, and the nearest house was at least that far up or down the beach, providing total privacy. No, it hadn't been physical issues that kept him awake until well past midnight, nor that roused him early and often before he finally gave up, had a shower, and descended to the deck to watch the sunrise.

One of the joists creaked, and he turned to see which of his three babysitters had joined him on the spacious deck. Good, the pretty one.

"Brought you a cup of coffee," Deputy U.S. Marshal Erin Kelly said. She made dark slacks and a light blue button-down look good. Or maybe it was the Glock .40 caliber strapped at her waist. More than anything, it was a handsome face, short-trimmed but cute dark hair, and the fact that she had treated Jackson like a person, not a profile. To wit, the mug of steaming coffee in her left hand.

He nodded as he reached for it, then said, "Thanks."

"Heard from Ross you mainlined the stuff. Thought you'd have a pot ready."

"Couldn't figure out how."

Kelly raised an eyebrow.

"Have a seat," Jackson said, gesturing toward another wood Adirondack chair beside him. "If that's permissible."

Kelly sat.

He sipped the coffee, which was somewhere between Folgers and the stuff he'd had in Switzerland. That was better than most coffee, so he had another sip.

"Can I ask you a question?" Kelly said.

He looked at her.

"Off the record."

"I'm supposed to believe that?"

For just a fraction, her face showed hurt. Then its smooth, tight features formed a mask. "Never mind."

"No, I'm sorry. Habit." He nodded. "Go ahead."

"You just engineered and orchestrated the takedown of a rogue special forces team, but you couldn't figure out how to make coffee?"

"They told you what this is about?"

Kelly nodded.

"So much for my government being tight-lipped about confidential matters."

"You blew up half an island, so not sure it's your government to blame."

"Touché," he said, then took a drink. Really good coffee.

Kelly raised an eyebrow, waiting.

"Right," he said. "My pot at home cost twenty bucks at Target. That . . . device in there has more buttons and levers than a small casino."

Kelly grinned, and it was quite pleasant.

Jackson took another sip and turned his eyes to the ocean.

"Forrester said he'd be here by eight-thirty. Ross is making breakfast. I say something wrong?" she said as he frowned.

"No. I think Forrester was one of the bad guys on *Mystery Science Theater*. The one who launched Mike or Joel or one of them into space."

"*Mystery Science Theater?*"

"*Three thous-and,*" he sang.

Kelly looked at him incredulously.

"What?"

"Can't make coffee, singing I have no idea what. You planning an insanity defense?"

"Am I going to need a defense?"

"Above my pay grade."

"*That's* above your pay grade?"

"Forrester is DNI, not DOJ."

"Fair point," he said, tipping his mug again, hoping Kelly had made a full pot. "Say, I've been meaning to ask about your pay grade, so to speak."

"How so?"

Jackson tugged on the pant leg of his oversized, government-issue khakis. He pointed with the hand holding the fabric toward his ankle. "The marshal who slapped that on wasn't too specific. But I take it if I wander where I shouldn't, I get a nice zap or alarms go off or something?"

Kelly's grin was bemused. "If you wander off the property, it will trigger an alert, yes. And it is GPS enabled, so we know where you are to within a foot."

"What if I try to swim to Atlantic City? Saltwater ruin it?"

"Nope."

"There goes the weekend."

"What does this have to do with my pay grade?"

"Well, I figured this thing was pretty high-tech, and if I tried to make a run for it, I wouldn't make it to the road. And yet there's three of you around the clock, dressed like it's nine o'clock Monday morning, game faces on, Glocks strapped. U.S. Marshals. Not here to keep me in custody but as some sort of modified WitSec, is that it?"

Kelly said nothing, but gave him a long look.

He slowly turned away and took another sip of his coffee.

"Kel, Duncan's on the line for you."

They both turned to see a dark-haired, middle-aged man sticking his head out the sliding glass doors from the dining room. Deputy Marshal Ross, who was handsome in his own right, and dressed like Kelly except for wearing his Glock in a shoulder holster.

"Me?" she asked.

"What he said."

She nodded, and Ross's head disappeared back inside.

Kelly stood. "You're wrong about Forrester. He's not a bad guy."

"I never said he was."

She pursed her lips and nodded.

"Thanks for the coffee," Jackson said, and she headed inside. Then he turned his eyes back to the ocean and the never-ending waves, figuring he should enjoy the peace and calm while it lasted.

*　　　　　*　　　　　*

8:30 a.m.

"GENTLEMEN, SHALL we get started?"

The voice belonged to the Principal Deputy Director of National Intelligence, Ronald Forrester. He was an imposing man without the title, tall and well built, with a touch of gray blending into a dark, full head of hair. The gray did nothing to detract from the vim and vigor of a stern, stony face, instead adding a scholarly air to the man. The previous two days, he'd worn a dark, tailored suit and power tie—today it was khakis and a light blue polo shirt with the DNI seal on the breast. He looked no less official.

The gentlemen in question were Jackson, one of Forrester's underlings—an assistant deputy director or assistant executive director or something like that—named Carsten, a lawyer (the first two days it had been a woman with a face of granite, and today it was a heavyset man spilling out of a suit with no tie), and two people whose job it was to do nothing but type on laptops all day. At Deputy Director Forrester's "suggestion," the six men took seats in a spacious living room around a glass-topped coffee table. A massive stone fireplace in the corner rose to the vaulted ceiling, and windows spanned the entire eastern wall, looking out at the beach and ocean. The living room was down a couple steps from the dining room, where three plates of varied pastries were set out, along with pitchers of water and the coffeemaker Jackson couldn't comprehend. Fortunately, whichever deputy marshal was assigned to keep eyes on Jackson—and thus be present with the group—also served as a butler. This morning it was Ross.

Forrester looked at one of the indeterminate people, who also had control of a small video camera on a tripod. He nodded back, and Forrester said, "Mr. Douglas, I want to again remind you that we are recording this conversation, but you are *not* under oath and you are *not* on the record. This is merely a fact-finding inquest."

"Yes, sir," Jackson said with zero faith that his words wouldn't come back to bite him if it served the government's interest to make them do so.

Forrester nodded. He had no notes today, nor had he the previous two days. And he didn't need them.

"I believe we concluded yesterday with the events at the airport and your pursuit of Bryant Hayes through the jungle."

"That's correct, sir," one of the typists said. Thursday had been spent covering Jackson's research on GrayStar, plans to go after them, his gathered intelligence. Short of revealing his sources, he'd given them everything he knew. Friday, the "panel" had gone into the events of May 16, not breaking until darkness started to fall over the marsh. There was no word if day three would be the end, or what the end game of this extensive Q&A was. But Jackson wasn't in a position to bargain.

"I want to circle back to that scene at a later point," Forrester said, "but for the moment, why don't you recap for us what happened next."

"Yes, sir," Jackson said. He cleared his throat and began. "I woke up several hours later in a hospital of sorts."

"Would you clarify 'of sorts'?" Forrester asked.

"The island was in the middle of a hurricane, and its resources were stretched. I was diagnosed with a moderate concussion and several 'flesh wounds,' which didn't qualify me for a hospital bed or room. I was in a hallway in the basement, as near as I could tell."

"I'm sorry," Carsten said, "but you said you woke up several hours later? What happened in those several hours?"

"Presumably I was asleep."

Forrester took in a sharp breath, and Carsten's hard gaze hardened more. Jackson quickly clarified. "I'm not being smart, gentlemen. I remember discharging the final round from the officer's pistol, and the next thing I know I was waking up in the hallway on a gurney. I don't know if I passed out, was knocked out, if either of those things happened immediately or after a while, if I was conscious at some point but don't recall. I just know the next thing, I was in the hospital."

"Go on," Forrester said.

"To be honest, I don't recall much of the next few hours after that either. I know several nurses stopped by to check on me, and then I was moved to a different hallway because water was leaking into the one I was in. I asked about my friends a couple of times, but I really can't account for every minute or tell you how much time elapsed before I was moved again."

"Moved again?" Carsten asked. He'd done that all day each of the last two days, prompting Jackson by repeating his last few words in question form. He also asked the accusatory questions whenever Jackson said something controversial, which, given his last nine months, was almost everything he said. That's why it had taken all morning, afternoon, and an hour after dinner Thursday to recount his hunt for GrayStar.

"A Detective Dekker came to question me and asked if I was well enough to leave the hospital and continue our questioning elsewhere. He said the police station was without power and all the generators were being dedicated to the hospital and some essential functions around town, so we went to a motel with vacancies." He took a breath. "And he questioned me for a while."

"What did you tell him?" Carsten asked.

"A condensed version of what I told you the last two days, less on the backstory and motivation and more on the events that took place on the island, in particular, on the sixteenth and seventeenth."

"What was his response?" Forrester asked.

"Initially, he was quite wary. He had three dead officers, another fighting for his life, an airport in ruins, a party involving the governor and other dignitaries that had been disrupted by a gun battle—including several dead or wounded Russians—and I was at the center of it. But he listened, and once I told him everything, he at least was considering the possibility that I wasn't the bad guy."

Forrester licked his lips.

"How long did he question you?" Carsten asked.

"Till about nine o'clock, when I asked to make a phone call."

"To inquire about your friends?"

"Uh, no, actually. Detective Dekker updated me when we arrived at the motel. Both Reggie and Eli had come out of surgery and were recovering, under guard. And Maggie was being kept under modified house arrest at another motel. He assured me they were okay, and I believed him. Dekker struck me as man of integrity."

"What about the other women, Tori Walker and Robyn Davis?"

"Walker was admitted to the hospital for a possible concussion and also held at a motel for further questioning. Davis had disappeared."

Forrester sat forward. "Disappeared?"

"Yes, sir. She, Maggie, and Walker were at the intersection of the King Will and Usselincx Boulevard at the crash, and from what Dekker told me, by the time the authorities arrived, Davis had disappeared."

"When did you make contact with her?"

"I haven't."

"Are you telling me Ms. Davis is still at large?"

"As far as I know, she disappeared in the confusion, without a word to Maggie or Walker, and hasn't been seen since."

Forrester frowned. Carsten did him one better, practically wincing. "Back to your phone call, Mr. Douglas. Who did you call?"

*   *   *

One week ago . . .
Saturday, May 17
9:02 a.m. (Atlantic Standard Time)
Williamsburg, St. Charles

FROM SEVERAL thousand miles away, the phone purred. Four times, before a sleepy but velvety voice answered. "Hello?"

"Hillary? It's Jackson."

There was a brief pause, then a far more lucid voice. "What's going on? Where's Grant?"

"He's fine."

"Is he with you?"

"No."

"Where is he? What's—"

"Hill, the hurricane kept him from ever getting here. He's probably at an all-day buffet right now, ten pounds heavy, but I need you to focus."

He felt a chill even through the phone.

"Hillary, I hate to ask this and start the cycle all over, but I need a favor."

"What did you do, Jackson?"

"A lot. I need you to come to St. Charles. It's in the Car—"

"I know where St. Charles is."

"I'm with a Detective Dekker right now, and he's fair, but I could use a lawyer. I know you probably don't have jurisdiction down here or license to practice or whatever, but any way you can come down here looking hot as a Georgia summer, throwing legalese around, and make sure I don't get railroaded? Or the rest of my crew? Just make sure we get a fair shake, everything gets done by the books? Especially Reggie, Maggie, and Walker?"

She was either still half asleep or could hear the urgency in Jackson's voice, because she didn't put up a fight. "I'll be there as soon as I can. I assume you're in jail?"

"I don't think the jail has power right now, so I'm in a crummy motel. Find Detective Dekker."

"What have you told him?"

"Everything."

"Did he read you your rights?"

"I don't think I'm under arrest yet."

"You don't think? Jackson, do not say another word until—"

"Hillary, I'm not hiding from what I've done."

"This isn't the time to be noble."

"This isn't about nobility. I did nothing wrong."

"Even if that's true, that doesn't mean you didn't do anything illegal, and it doesn't mean the authorities in St. Charles will see it that way. You want my help, you want me to get you and your friends out of trouble, you listen to my advice. Are we clear?"

"Crystal."

"Good. I'll get the first flight I can."

"Leave your hair down, Hill, and wear that red sundress you wore to dinner at Jillian's that one time."

"And if you make one more crack about my appearance, I will push for the death penalty."

Despite it all, he couldn't help but smile. "Thank you, Hillary."

"Not a word."

He ended the call, then opened the door to readmit Detective Dekker. He handed back the phone. "Thank you, Detective."

"You ready to continue or do you need a few minutes?"

Jackson exhaled. "Actually, my lawyer advised me not to say anything more until she arrives."

"Your lawyer?"

"Yeah."

Dekker bit down on his tongue.

"And Reggie, Maggie, and Walker's too."

The detective nodded into the room. "Get back inside."

Jackson took a step back, then had the door close in his face.

Chapter One Hundred Forty-Five

Saturday, May 24
9:48 a.m. (Eastern Daylight Time)
Rehoboth Beach, Delaware

"SO YOU REMAINED locked in your motel room for the rest of the day?" Carsten asked.

"Until about three o'clock that afternoon, when I was moved to a different building."

"Why were you moved?"

"According to Detective Dekker, they had been scrambling overnight to find room for hospital patients, petty criminals, 'potential terrorists,' and displaced tourists. Anthony delivered quite a bit more rain than was anticipated, so there were a few flash flooding incidents—particularly in the island's lower lying areas."

"And Dekker told you all this?"

"I picked it up in various conversations."

"Were you placed under guard at the new location?" Forrester asked.

"Yes, sir. I had an officer outside my door at all times."

"Forgive me, Mr. Douglas," Carsten said, "but one officer doesn't seem very much for someone of your . . . caliber."

"As I told you earlier, I believe Detective Dekker was a competent and fair man. I think he knew I wasn't a threat to anyone."

"Anymore?"

"Yes, sir."

"What about your associates?" Forrester asked.

"I was told Maggie and Walker were being kept in the same location. Reggie and Eli were still in the hospital. I had no update on anyone else's whereabouts."

"Did Detective Dekker attempt to question you further?"

"No, sir."

Forrester nodded for him to go on.

"I remained in the hotel room for the rest of the day and all the next. They brought me meals, a change of clothes, some personal items. From what I was told, the island's resources were stretched pretty thin cleaning up in the wake of the storm. I inquired about Miss McKenzie at one point, and was told the airport was still closed."

"Still closed because of the storm or because of the Learjet you detonated on the runway?" Carsten asked.

"I wasn't told, sir."

"Did anything else happen Sunday the eighteenth?" Forrester asked.

"No, sir. I sat in a hotel room all day without television. So I had no idea what was going on in the world—how bad the storm damage was, what the fallout was at Vossenhol from the events that took place there, whether or not all the members of GrayStar had been accounted for. Dekker was gracious enough to let me know that Reggie had been discharged and brought to the hotel Sunday afternoon, and he kept me up to date on Eli's progress. But he didn't allow us to see one another or give me any other information. My take was that since I wasn't talking to him without a lawyer, he wasn't talking to me."

Forrester nodded and glanced at his watch. "Let's take ten, everyone."

"Mind if I get some fresh air?" Jackson asked.

"You're free to move about the grounds as you wish, Mr. Douglas."

"Thank you, sir."

Whether it was Forrester's intimidating nature, the soberness of the proceedings, or the fact that Jackson had learned that Principal Deputy Director of National Intelligence Ronald Forrester had at one time been Lieutenant Colonel Ronald Forrester, U.S. Army, he felt sirs were appropriate. Besides, he'd been in this same mess a few years ago at an Air Force base outside Las Vegas. Then, he'd been before a tribunal of just about every agency known to man, evaluating his actions at a decommissioned Air Force base in the desert, where he'd killed twenty mercenaries to save Hillary's life, then captured and interrogated a U.S. senator before racing to Lake Mead to take out a few more baddies to again save Hillary's life. That panel had ultimately ruled in his favor, given the extreme mitigating circumstances and guilt of those he'd opposed—including the senator and several corrupt CIA agents. This panel, while smaller and without some of the service ribbons on the breast, scared him even more.

He exited onto the deck and leaned on the railing. Like the deck, it appeared to be made of old, weathered planks and boards, but was actually some synthetic material that would hold up far better to the elements. He wondered, as he stared out at the brilliant, sun-splashed ocean, what this house must go for over Memorial Day weekend. Or was it not a VRBO or Airbnb but a government safe house, maybe a time share for the powerbrokers in the nation's capital?

He wasn't sure exactly where they were. From his previous trips out east, he knew the highways around D.C. resembled an overturned bowl of spaghetti. But they had taken a familiar road toward Annapolis, crossed the bay, and then gone east through the low country toward the coast. He'd heard mention of Delaware and Rehoboth Beach, which were the reasons he knew he wasn't still in Maryland or maybe New Jersey. Pretty good with geography, he wasn't an expert on this part of the country. And didn't want to be. L.A.'s hustle and bustle wasn't any better than the gridlock out here— maybe even worse—but at least it was home.

Home.

Was that even a word that meant anything to him anymore? Did he have a home, besides an abandoned house to go back to? Would he be allowed to go anywhere, or was his modified house arrest the calm before the storm? Forrester and the panel had been vague, but he'd gotten the sense that, while what he said was off the record, it would count for a great deal when it came to determining his future. As he had in Vegas, with a few creative interpretations to protect those he cared about, he'd come clean. Speaking of those he cared about, their fate was still an unknown too—both currently and long-term. But he'd determined playing nice was the best way to get answers, and hopefully soon.

He sensed Deputy Marshal Kelly before he saw her. The deck wrapped around the north side of the house, and she emerged from the shade and leaned on the railing a few feet from him. "You mind some company?"

He looked at her. He didn't think she was coming on to him—certainly not in any real way. But she may have been playing good marshal, bad marshal, trying to buddy up to him. No, he didn't think that either. She and Ross and the other marshals seemed to be simply on security detail—to keep

Jackson on the grounds and to keep others off. Never mind for the moment who was out there to come after him, but the marshals weren't part of the interrogations and interviews. She wasn't out there to coax anything out of him—and why should she be? He'd told Forrester and gang everything.

Besides, he'd had a lot of time to himself sitting in the hotel rooms on St. Charles—time to ponder what he'd done, whether it had worked completely, whether his friends would be physically or mentally scarred or legally penalized for life because of it. Now, while he needed a break from the questioning and Forrester's panel, he was more than happy for some company.

"No," he said with a slight shake of his head. "I'd actually like it."

She took half a step closer. "How's it going in there?"

"I don't know. Feels more like they're asking questions they already know the answers to, to see if I'm being honest, than like they're asking to learn things they don't know."

"Well, they are with National Intelligence."

"DNI reports to POTUS, right?"

"He provides the daily intelligence briefing, yeah."

"So is it fair to say President Rutherford is the one asking questions, through the DNI, through the PDDNI?"

Kelly shrugged. "Maybe. Why?"

"Just trying to figure all this out. We're off the record in there, meaning these aren't legal proceedings. I'm wondering where all this is heading."

"You should ask Forrester."

"I'm scared of him."

Kelly smiled. Then she placed a hand on his arm, and he immediately questioned his conclusions about her motives. But instead of recoiling or moving his arm or giving her some smart comment, he smiled back. "Can I ask you something?"

"Um-hmm," she said, withdrawing her hand. She rested both arms on the railing, faced out toward the sea, but her head turned a little demurely to look at him.

"Have you been made aware of a specific threat against me?"

"I can't discuss that with you," she said, then slowly turned her head out toward the water.

"Come on, Erin, you—"

"Deputy Marshal Kelly."

So the arm touching was ancient history.

"Sorry, Deputy Marshal Kelly. You've watched the movies where the witness doesn't want to be in custody until they realize how dangerous it is out in the real world. Look who I'm talking to, you've probably lived it."

"Are you saying you'll be more cooperative if I level with you?"

"Yeah."

"You haven't been uncooperative."

"Feeling the ropes."

She nodded. "I can't tell you anything."

"Can you at least tell me if there is anything to tell?"

"No."

"What about my friends? Are they in danger? Are they being protected?"

"I should get back on patrol."

She backed away from the railing and headed south, to the stairs leading down to the beach. Jackson watched her go, wondering what she was up to. He'd always been pretty cool around the opposite sex, but lately, he couldn't read their signals or motives any better than he could read Russian poetry.

*   *   *

Monday, May 19
6:54 a.m. (Atlantic Standard Time)
Williamsburg, St. Charles

THUNDEROUS BANGING woke Jackson from a light but restful sleep. He rolled his head to look at the numbers on the bedside alarm clock, then blinked against the light making its way through the hotel's semi-opaque window shades. It was not a particularly bright light, and a second round of thunder—this the actual stuff—indicated why.

Jackson slowly sat up, pushing the sheets off him. "Yeah, give me—"

The initial banging sounded again.

"Yeah! Hold on."

He stepped out of bed, found yesterday's clothes and quickly pulled them on, then unlocked the door and opened it. A familiar but unnamed officer stood outside the door.

"Your lawyer is here to see you, sir."

"Where?"

"There's a small conference room at the end of the corridor."

Picturing his appearance, Jackson said, "Give me a couple minutes to freshen up."

The officer nodded.

Jackson shut the door, set his in-room coffeepot to brew the last package of coffee, then practically ran through a shower. He brushed his teeth, dressed, and tried to make his hair look reasonable. Hillary could be a stickler for appearances.

Eleven minutes after the officer had knocked, Jackson opened the door again, clad in shorts that weren't his style and a touristy T-shirt. His shoe choices were between the loafers he'd worn to the party or a pair of flip-flops likely purchased or commandeered with the other clothes, and he opted for neither. He just couldn't deal with dudes clopping around in flip-flops like a teenage girl or soccer mom.

"Ready, sir?" the same officer asked.

"Yeah."

"Follow me, please."

Rain was falling steadily but not heavily from a gray sheet of a sky as Jackson followed the officer down the external corridor of a hotel facing Karaf Lagoon. It was neither the island's best or worst hotel, but not uncomfortable, especially given the circumstances.

"Officer, when did my lawyer get here?"

"Last night, and she's been pestering Detective Dekker to see you ever since."

Jackson grinned.

So did the officer as he looked back over his shoulder. "I wish I could get a lawyer who looked like that to pester me," he said with a wink.

The corridor ended in a T, with another external corridor running right or left to more rooms. A little to the left, a set of stairs descended to the main floor, lobby, and parking lot. On either side of the stairs were two conference rooms, which surprised Jackson given the quality of hotel. But he didn't give it any more thought as the officer said, "In here," and opened the door for him.

It wasn't anything fancy, but the conference room had a long table, office chairs around it, a small credenza with a conference phone and room for drinks or snacks, and a window looking out at the street. A woman stood looking out the window, her hands loosely clasped behind her back. She was not Hillary, however, not unless Hillary had cut and died her hair (which would have been a national tragedy) and shrunk about six inches. The woman wore a white, straight, knee-length skirt and a Kelly green blouse, which nicely complemented her bob-cut auburn hair.

Jackson took a drink of his coffee, saying nothing, as the officer closed the door behind him. When it clicked, the woman turned around. Her mouth upturned in the smallest of grins. "Good to see you again, Jackson."

He dipped his head slightly to the side. "You as well, Lieutenant Paige."

Chapter One Hundred Forty-Six

7:08 a.m.

"YOU'RE NOT IN your Air Force blues," Jackson said, noting that JAG Corps Lieutenant Alison Paige looked quite nice in civilian clothes as well. Then again, the last time he'd seen her, she'd been dressed in civies too—and had looked very nice. That had been just before he'd been shot on New Year's Eve. Having represented him on behalf of the United States Air Force before the tribunal in Las Vegas, she'd come to visit him in Pacific Palisades to let him know his probation had been lifted. He had no idea why she was here now.

"That's because I'm not here on behalf of the Air Force," Paige said. She pulled out the chair at the end of the table and sat down. Jackson—because he was lonely, not because Paige was cute—walked down and took the seat next to her.

"Then why are you here, Lieutenant?"

"It's not Lieutenant anymore, either."

He frowned.

"I was promoted. I'm Captain Paige, as of the first of the year."

"Congratulations."

She smiled quickly. "It's like I told you last time, you can call me Alison."

"Okay, Alison. I'm guessing you didn't book a vacation rental on St. Charles for the weekend and happen to hear about my situation."

"No," she said, "I didn't."

"Then, as nice as it is to see you, you mind if I ask what's going on?" he said, then took a drink of his coffee. It was hot, but that was about it.

"I was briefed about your situation yesterday and asked to come down and keep an eye on things."

Jackson had a dozen questions. "Asked by whom?" came out first.

"The Judge Advocate General of the Air Force, on behalf of the Secretary of the Air Force, but I doubt the request originated with him. My guess is people pretty high up the totem pole have an interest in you."

"Higher up than the Secretary of the Air Force? Not much room left on the totem pole above him, is there?"

"No."

He narrowed his gaze. "Are you being coy with me, Alison, or do you not know?"

"I don't know. I was briefed—emphasis on brief—and asked to come down to make sure that you were treated fairly—and to see that you were . . . cooperative."

"Cooperative? What does that make me, the sacrificial lamb?"

"I wouldn't it put it that way."

Jackson sat back. "We may have a conflict of interest then."

"How so?"

"My lawyer advised me not to say a word."

"You have a lawyer?"

"Called her Saturday morning. She's on her way. Thought I was coming in here to meet her and found you instead."

"Miss McKenzie?"

Jackson nodded.

"Well, then you are in good hands."

"Depends if she's on my side."

Paige frowned.

"Our relationship is a unique one."

"I see." Her legs were crossed, stuck off to the side, and she smoothed her skirt. "I'm happy to represent you until she arrives. I got in last night on a Navy military flight bringing humanitarian aid, but I'm not sure when commercial flights might start arriving."

"Humanitarian aid? How bad is it here?"

"From what I was told, the valley between the two mountains doesn't drain water particularly well. A lot of displaced people."

"Hmm. Well, the detective in charge hasn't pushed since I told him I had a lawyer, but I appreciate it." He frowned.

"What?"

"If you were asked to see that I was cooperative, how are you going to represent me if I want to be uncooperative?"

"Why would you want to be uncooperative?"

"I'm not hiding from what happened, from what I did." He shook his head. "But I have no interest in playing Lee Majors."

"Who?"

"Lee Majors. *The Fall Guy*. He played a stuntman who doubled as a bounty hunter . . ."

Paige slowly shook her head.

He exhaled. "Like I told you in Vegas, I'm willing to take the rap for what I did, but not for anything more."

She sat forward. "I think you may have it wrong."

"How so?"

"I don't think Uncle Sam's asking you to fall on your sword."

"Then what?"

"You do have something of a reputation, Jackson," she said with a sly grin. "I don't know what's coming down the pike, but I gather Secretary Wittingham doesn't want you making any waves or stirring up any hornets' nests."

"Hmm."

"As I told you, I'm happy to represent you until Miss McKenzie arrives. Think about it," she said, leaning a little further forward, now resting her arm on the table. "Not only do I fulfill my obligation to SecAF—which is good for you—but, as your lawyer, I represent you and represent your interests. That works in your favor too."

"They okay with you representing me, officially, I mean?"

"They didn't give me too much in the way of specifics. I can sell that it was the prudent play."

He nodded.

"Either way, I can give you advice and suggestions, but I can do a lot better job of watching your six if I'm privy to more information and officially listed as your attorney. But it is your call."

Jackson nodded again. "Okay. You're hired. Which means everything I tell you is privileged, and can't be used against me if my government tries to nail me to the wall, correct?"

"Correct."

"Are they going to see it that way?"

"They'll have to."

"I like you Lieu—Captain."

She sat back and smiled, then raised her eyebrows. "Want to tell me what's going on?"

"How much do you know?"

"You were thought to be in a Mexican prison, but then showed up here posing as a wealthy man of mystery and staged *The Bourne Retribution* to stop a rogue special forces team. And that rogue team, by the way, is about as hush-hush as it gets in Washington."

"That is brief."

"I know a few more details, but the more you can tell me, the better." She narrowed one eye. "Have you had breakfast?"

"No."

She uncrossed her legs and stood. "Let me see about getting something to eat. Then we can talk."

"Okay."

"In the meantime," she said, reaching into a valise he hadn't seen previously, "this is a basic representation form. Your signature officially makes me your lawyer until such time as you choose. Always better to dot I's and cross T's."

He took the form from her. "This confidentiality business works even when you're off duty and not here in your official capacity?"

"It does."

"Even in a foreign country?"

"Even so," she said with a thin smile.

"All right."

"I'll see about some breakfast," she said, heading for the door.

"Hey, Alison?"

She turned on her heel.

Jackson shook his head to say, "Never mind," then gave the concept of déjà vu a few thoughts before skimming and signing Paige's form.

*   *   *

8:19 a.m.

"YOU STOLE two-hundred and fifty million dollars from a Columbian drug cartel?" Paige asked with mouth agape. She had finished a yogurt cup and a bagel already, so it wasn't impolite.

Jackson was halfway through his second bagel and nodded. He gulped the bite down. "I had help."

"Still. Were you crazy? You know the odds of pulling that off?"

"Between slim and none, but we were desperate."

She shook her head as a knock sounded on the door. The same officer as before opened it and stepped aside as Hillary walked in. By her standards, she was average—a loose-fitting blouse over blue jeans, flats, hair in a ponytail, not much jewelry or makeup. By comparison to most other women, she was still a ten. And that was without factoring in the aura that went with her, a combination of intelligence, confidence, and determination.

"Jackson, are you all right?" she asked, hurrying toward him and bending down to embrace him.

"Are you?" he asked into a tight hug.

She let go and stood. "I just talked to Reggie. He gave me a basic recap of what happened." Her eyes then settled on Paige.

"Captain Alison Paige, Air Force JAG lawyer and, at least for the moment, your co-counsel."

Paige stood and offered a hand. "You must be Hillary McKenzie. It's a pleasure to meet you."

Hillary forced a smile. "Likewise, Captain."

"You're supposed to salute," Jackson said.

"Shut up," she said to him.

"See," he said to Paige.

"Please, have a seat," Paige said, and she and Hillary both sat, flanking Jackson in a lawyer (and beauty) sandwich.

"How's Reggie?" Jackson asked.

"Like a wounded bear," Hillary answered. "He's fine, asking about you."

"What about Maggie or Walker or Eli?"

"Who's Eli?"

"Fellow patriot."

Hillary shook her head. "I only talked to Reggie, and briefly. You want to catch me up to speed? Have they charged you with anything yet?"

"No."

"All I know is what you told me on the phone and Reggie's five-minute recap. I'd like the unabridged version."

"Of course."

"No offense, Captain, but I'd like to speak with Jackson in private."

"I was actually in the midst of briefing her," Jackson said.

"Why is an Air Force JAG lawyer representing you?"

"She's here unofficially."

"Unofficially? As a friend or girlfriend or what?"

"The Secretary of the Air Force asked me to come down and make sure he behaved himself, make sure the wheels of justice didn't spin too quickly."

Paige hadn't mentioned that part to Jackson, but he let it go.

"Why is the Secretary of the Air Force concerned with Jackson's behavior?" Hillary asked. "Does he know him?"

"She's cute, isn't she?" Jackson said, gesturing at her with his thumb.

"As I told Jackson, I think the command came from higher up, and I don't know what it's all about. But my instructions were to see that he didn't make waves and get himself in any more trouble while they work out whatever they're working out."

"Isn't that why you wanted me here?" Hillary asked.

"Yeah, only I wasn't aware anyone in the U.S. government was aware of what was going on."

"How aware are they?" Hillary asked.

"I'm not sure," Paige said. "I'm on a need-to-know basis."

Hillary eyed her for a moment, then turned to Jackson. "Can you give Captain Paige and I a few minutes?"

"Now you want *me* to leave?"

"For a few minutes."

He took the last chunk of bagel and stood. "I'll hit the head." He walked from the room, almost able to feel the tension ease as he did. He didn't know what sort of basic training a JAG lawyer went through, but Paige was an officer in the United States Air Force, so there had to be some. He gave her at least a chance of being the one left standing when he returned.

*   *   *

8:42 a.m.

HILLARY AND Paige were alone for nearly twenty minutes before admitting Jackson back into the conference room. There was no indication on either of their faces that the discussion had been anything but civil. And there was no recap of it for Jackson. Instead, before he even sat down—now on the opposite side of the table instead of between the two lawyers—Hillary said, "Tell us everything."

Jackson took fifteen minutes to catch Hillary up to where he'd left off with Paige, then dove into greater detail recounting the creation of The Patriot legend, the purchase of Vossenhol, their arrival in St. Charles, and planning for the party and taking out GrayStar. They each asked a few questions, but mostly let him talk until he recounted his pursuit of Hayes that ended at the turnout on the east side of the island.

"You shot him in the back of the head?" Paige asked.

"I did."

Her eyebrow went up as she looked at Hillary. "Why?" she asked.

"Because it was that or let a terrorist get away. I had one bullet left, I was concussed, exhausted, unable to best him physically, and if he disappeared into the darkness, I—or Grant or Reggie or Maggie or you, Hillary, or Grandpa—would be dead before I saw him coming again. Or maybe he'd rebuild GrayStar with a new group and keep on killing innocent people. I shot him because that's what you do to terrorists."

"I wouldn't recommend telling that to a judge," Hillary said.

"What would you recommend?"

"I had a little time to do research while waiting for a flight that would come to the island, and I may be able to represent you, but it will take some doing. That's assuming the St. Charles AG charges you. Given everything you've told me and given Captain Paige's presence here, I think you could be facing much greater legal hurdles in a U.S. court."

"For an action that took place on foreign soil?"

"Hayes and his crew were Americans, weren't they?"

"Most of them, I think."

"An American kills other Americans overseas—I'm guessing they're working to have you extradited, and Captain Paige is here to keep you from 'making waves' so as you don't muck the deal."

"That would make sense," Paige said.

"So what do I do?" Jackson asked.

Hillary exhaled and stood. She paced to the end of the table. "You don't say a word. There is a huge legal quagmire here, way above my pay grade to sort out, and you're not going to explain it away. So it's not worth trying, especially because I'm not sure whose jurisdiction this will fall under—St. Charles, the U.S., the World Court. Until we know more, we say nothing."

Jackson looked to Paige.

"Miss McKenzie made it quite clear she is your lead attorney."

"Do you disagree?"

"I think, obviously, that you'd rather try and face the consequences— whatever they are—in the U.S. instead of here. Best way to do that is be cooperative, don't let the local authorities think you have anything to hide, and don't give them any reason to want to punish you themselves."

"Of course he wants to stand trial in the U.S.," Hillary said. "But you should let that get sorted out upstairs before you say anything further."

"He does that, he's going to look like he's guilty," Paige said.

"He is, at least in their eyes."

"That's why he should talk, to remove some of the stigma of guilt."

"Is that how you normally advise your clients?" Hillary asked.

"Are you suggesting I have an agenda here?"

"I'm saying I find it odd for a JAG lawyer to show up out of the blue and ask Jackson to throw away his rights and only leverage."

Paige exhaled. "I'm not asking him to throw away his rights. I'm merely suggesting a little cooperation may be in everyone's best interest."

There was another knock on the door, followed by Detective Dekker admitting himself. He held a cup of coffee and stood at the end of the table. "I see your lawyers have arrived, Mr. Douglas. Are you ready to answer some questions?"

"Detective, is Mr. Douglas under arrest?" Hillary asked.

He shook his head. "No."

"Then we're leaving. Jackson—"

"He's not under arrest, but our investigation is ongoing, and he is a prime suspect."

"Is it standard operating procedure to hold suspects captive in St. Charles?"

"That's not what's happening."

"Jackson, did you agree to place yourself in Detective Dekker's custody?"

"I honestly don't remember. I was concussed."

She shot a glare at Dekker.

"Miss McKenzie, it is very likely that we are going to bring some very serious charges against Mr. Douglas. Given the nature of those potential charges and, quite frankly, the events leading up to them, he is a major flight risk. For everyone's sake, we'd prefer not to level charges until everything has been sorted out."

"Then let him go."

"But we will if that's what's required. He's not in jail; he's in a hotel; his medical needs were treated; he's being given access to his lawyers."

"Detective, you can either arrest him or we're leaving. There's no middle ground."

He sighed. "All right. Mr. Douglas, you are under arr—"

"Wait, wait, wait. Detective, can you give me five more minutes with my lawyers, please?"

Dekker split his glare between Jackson and Hillary. Then he held up his palm. "Five," he said before backing out and closing the door.

"You both think our government is working to have me extradited?" Jackson asked when Hillary had had a few seconds to exhale.

They nodded.

"And you both think that is in my best interest?"

"Hard to say for sure, but yes," Hillary said.

Paige nodded again.

"Alison, you said SecAF didn't want the wheels spinning too quickly. So what are we talking, a couple days or a couple months?"

"Nobody in the government had a clue what you were doing, and thirty-six hours after it all goes down, I was already on the island. You tell me."

He looked to Hillary. "I say we give Dekker a little something to make him happy. In the spirit of cooperation, I'm willing to stay in his custody but not under arrest and give Uncle Sam a few days to work something out."

"He's not going to be content to have you sit in the hotel and watch cable. He'll want to question you."

"Cable's out. And I'll answer questions."

"No," Hillary said.

"With my lawyers by my side. I can be devious and clever. You could talk legal circles around a tenured professor at Harvard Law, much less a Dutch detective."

"What is that supposed to mean?"

"And we've got Captain Paige, her disarming smile, and the weight of the U.S. military on our side. I figure the three of us can answer at least a few of his questions to keep him pacified and stall for a little while without talking myself into never leaving this island. Keep everybody feeling like they're getting their way."

The two women looked at each other.

"And," Jackson added, "maybe just maybe if we butter Dekker up enough, he'll let me see everybody. And that's the other piece of this. I'll sign myself up for life in the worst of Dutch prisons if it means Reggie, Maggie, and the others go free."

"Captain Paige, will you—"

"Please, call me Alison."

"Very well, Alison, will you give us a couple minutes?"

"Sure," she said, standing and collecting her valise. "Can I get either of you a cup of coffee?"

"No, I'm good," Jackson said.

Hillary merely shook her head. When Paige was gone, she said, "Jackson, tell me you're not still running a game or a con or something."

"My game's over. Now I'm trying to get out of a mess."

She sighed. "Against my better judgment, I am willing to let you remain in Dekker's custody, on three conditions."

"What?"

"Number one, I am present for all questioning. Absolutely no exceptions."

"Done. Two?"

"Two, I'm the boss. You don't answer any question unless I okay it. I tell you to shut up, you shut up without finishing the syllable. And three, if you go off book even once, I'm packing up, going back to L.A. and you are on your own. Is that clear?"

"Perfectly."

She sighed again. "Okay."

Jackson reached out and placed a hand on her arm. "Thank you, Hillary."

Her face softened. "You're welcome. Just keep the smart-aleck comments and the games at bay and let me do what you asked me to do, okay?"

"Deal."

"And maybe let go of my arm?"

He released his grip. "Think we can invite Alison back in?"

She looked at him. "Is she going to be a problem?"

"A problem?"

"I've seen the way she looks at you."

"Is that just a thing women say all the time or what?"

"I don't trust her motives, Jackson, and I don't need a co-counsel."

"Alison's a good lawyer and a friend, and while you may not need a co-counsel, two heads are better than one. And I do trust her."

"And when we disagree?"

"You're the boss, Hill. She's a friend, but you're back to family-elect, from what I hear."

Hillary grinned. "Thanks to you, from what *I* hear."

"I'm pleading temporary insanity."

She stood. "I'll go tell Dekker." Then, just loud enough for him to hear, she muttered, "Temporary?"

Chapter One Hundred Forty-Seven

Tuesday, May 20
5:33 p.m. (Atlantic Standard Time)

MONDAY AFTERNOON DRAGGED on like a tax fraud case. Dekker peppered Jackson with questions, of which he answered maybe a third, and never without Hillary giving him a stern look or motioning for a brief whispered sidebar. By dinnertime, Dekker's tie was off, his hair was mussed, and he appeared ready to knuckle under. He finally closed his notepad, said they were done, and promised he would be in touch. He did not provide an update on Maggie, Reggie, or the others, and he didn't release Jackson despite more pressure from Hillary. She and Paige conferred with Jackson for another half hour, then headed out to their hotel rooms, Hillary with a promise to check in on everyone and Paige with a promise to reach out to her superiors to see what was going on, and also to find out about Jackson's friends and the U.S. government's interest in them.

Tuesday morning made Monday look like a picnic. There was no word from Dekker, either directly or through Hillary, who stopped by mid-morning to talk. She had garnered visits with Reggie, Maggie, Walker, and even with Eli, and was officially and at least temporarily representing them all. Nobody knew what that meant yet. Reggie and Eli were recovering well, and were in some sort of medical lockdown. Maggie and Walker were being kept isolated but treated well. Nobody had heard anything from Robbie.

Paige brought lunch for the three of them, and even something for the guard outside Jackson's room. Whatever sort of custody he was in, it was the opposite of *Cinco Picos Prisión*. Paige did not bring any word from Washington or the Secretary of the Air Force or anyone else. Her inquiries about the others had been stonewalled, but she promised to keep trying.

Early Tuesday afternoon, Dekker dropped by to say that Governor van den Heuvel had asked to speak to Jackson, one on one, no detectives or lawyers present. Hillary objected, but with the governor's promise that everything would be off the record, she finally relented. They sat down in the same conference room as Dekker had used, and talked for nearly two hours late Tuesday afternoon. Jackson told van den Heuvel everything, neither hiding nor sugarcoating. The governor listened carefully, asked tough but fair questions, and said little by way of conclusion. He merely shook Jackson's hand and thanked him for his forthrightness.

After an early dinner of cold-cut sandwiches, Hillary announced she was returning to L.A.

"Because I spoke to the governor against your advice?"

"No, because I'm useless down here."

He raised an eyebrow.

"I had a long talk with Alison while you were meeting with the governor. She's still not getting much from her bosses, but it sounds like they want her to stay down here for a while. And we're more or less on the same page, so there's no need for me to sit here and hold your hand when she can do it just fine, and you might even like it."

He didn't take the bait.

"I do have a job back home, and a wedding to prepare for, and I don't think the authorities here are a threat to you anyhow."

"No?"

"No. Dekker wrapped up his questions Monday, and then the governor wants to talk to you and hear your story? I think they're working with the U.S. on extradition, figuring out all the details, and the governor just wanted a face-to-face first. If that's true, I can accomplish more from the U.S. anyhow, and if I'm wrong and they do charge you, Paige is here and I can be back in a day."

He shrugged. "Okay. If you think that's best."

"I do."

He nodded.

"Oh, and I talked to Reggie again too."

"How is he?"

"Getting grouchy. He's still in custody, said Dekker questioned him for about an hour this afternoon."

"Without an attorney present?"

"He said he didn't need one to give name, rank, and serial number."

Jackson shook his head.

"Maggie and Tori have both been released. They're free but were asked not to leave the island without permission."

"Really?"

She nodded.

"Why them and not Reggie?"

"I don't know."

"Eli?"

"He's been released from the hospital, but he's still in custody too. He's not an American, so representing him might be a little trickier, but I at least got my foot in the door."

"Before you leave, can you tell Dekker I want to see him?"

"About?"

"Reggie and Eli. They did nothing but protect me and Maggie from attacks. All self-defense."

"I'll talk to him. And then I'm on the last flight out to Atlanta and catching the red-eye home."

"Okay. Thanks for everything, Hillary."

They hugged, for about the third time ever, and it was weird. And yet, not weird.

"Hang in there, Jackson. We're not going to abandon you."

"Thanks."

She stopped from turning away. "Oh, I've been meaning to ask you. What's your plan for reaching out to your mom and dad? That is the purpose of all this, isn't it?"

"That depends."

"On?"

"Confirmation that GrayStar has indeed been vanquished."

"You think some of them got away?"

"I think I didn't see them all die. I saw a plane explode, but—and speaking from personal experience here—I've known people to survive explosions."

"Even so, you know several of them died. You cut the head off the snake."

"I did. But I want to be sure before I call Mom and Dad out of hiding."

"Okay. You want me to tell Grant anything? Your grandpa?"

"Not yet."

She nodded. "I'll see you back in the States."

"From your lips to God's ears."

*   *   *

Saturday, May 24
4:16 p.m. (Eastern Standard Time)
Rehoboth Beach, Delaware

AFTER LUNCH, Forrester and Carsten's questions returned to Jackson's research on GrayStar. For a couple hours, they probed further details of what he'd learned, how he'd learned it, and if he'd been able to verify it. Judging by the looks on their faces, they found his intel thin in places, shocking in others, and generally conclusive overall. If nothing else, Jackson felt somewhat vindicated that the Primary Deputy Whatever of Something or Rather—after three days, the titles were mush in his brain—agreed that GrayStar was who he believed them to be.

At quarter after four, the gang started to pack their bags. "Before we head out, do you have any questions for us, Mr. Douglas?" Forrester asked.

Jackson managed to keep his eyebrows from racing up his forehead. Did he have questions? Only a million.

"Uh, actually, I do, sir."

Carsten sighed.

Forrester did not, but sat back into the couch. "Go ahead."

"For starters, sir, what exactly are you asking these questions for? What is all this headed toward?"

"We're trying to assess the situation."

Jackson hesitated, expecting more. When he didn't get it, he said, "Am I in legal trouble?"

"Not at this time."

Splendid.

"What about my friends?"

"What about them?"

"Will they be facing any legal charges?"

"I can't say at this time."

Jackson sighed. "What can you tell me about GrayStar and their . . . uh, demise?"

"You're asking us?" Carsten said. "You blew them up."

"I saw a plane explode and I shot one of them. Beyond that . . ."

Forrester licked his lips, and Jackson prepared himself for another brush-off. Then the PDDNI said, "Seven bodies were recovered from the wreckage of the Learjet or the near vicinity. Do you have the names?" he said, looking at Carsten.

"I don't. Lewis?"

One of the two men who sat and typed all day pecked away at his laptop for a moment. "First Sergeant Mark Barron, Sergeant First Class J.J. Carter, Chief Petty Officer Charles Collier, Second Lieutenant Vance Copperfield, Master Sergeant Armando Ramirez, Corporal Chelsea Rayburn, and Petty Officer Second Class Ahmad Salaam."

"And of course, Sergeant Major Bryant Hayes," Forrester added.

"All confirmed dead?" Jackson asked.

"That's right."

"That's eight." He frowned. "There should have been nine."

"Nine?"

"Unless one of them was the pilot. Has your research turned up anything further about other members of the team? Bayliss or Norman?"

"Our research is lagging behind yours, I'm afraid," Forrester said.

"Would it help if I had my, um . . . IT man send you our files—everything we've gathered?"

"None of it would be admissible," the lawyer said.

"According to Deputy Director Forrester, I'm not facing any legal charges at the moment, so I'd be supplying it merely for your information—to help you 'assess the situation.'"

The lawyer stammered for a moment.

"What Mr. Wilkens means," Carsten said, "is that it won't be admissible in court for your defense should charges be brought against you."

Wilkens winced out a smile.

"Either way, it's yours if you want it. I just want to know that this is over."

"I can appreciate that," Forrester said, "but all I can tell you is that it's being looked into."

"By top men?"

Forrester frowned.

"Never mind. Sorry."

Forrester reached into his pocket for a business card. He extended it to Jackson. "Have your 'IT man' send it to the e-mail on here. It's a secure link."

"Yes, sir."

"And if you should have any questions, please reach out to my office."

"Does that mean we're through here?"

"For the time being."

"Does that mean I'm free to go or will I be here for a while?"

"It will be a little while longer yet, at least."

Jackson nodded.

In five minutes, the entourage was gone and Jackson was left alone with the evening shift—Deputies Marshal Kingsford, Bostic, and Kwon. All males, all very by the book, all boring. Bostic ordered pizza for dinner, and Jackson ate while watching an Orioles game on TV. Oddly enough, it was a slice of normal, and it brought him a small measure of comfort. Halfway through the seventh, a phone line somewhere chirped. Jackson ignored it as the Orioles' shortstop drew a leadoff walk, then had a cordless phone handed to him by Deputy Marshal Kwon.

"For me? Who is it?"

The marshal cracked his first smile of the evening. "A woman."

*   *   *

Wednesday, May 21
4:31 a.m. (Atlantic Standard Time)
Williamsburg, St. Charles

THE BANGING on the door that woke Jackson was muted compared to Monday morning, but still enough to startle him awake. He looked at the clock, blinked away the grogginess that had distorted the numbers, then looked again only to see they hadn't changed. It was half past four in the morning. He groaned, feeling more tired knowing the time, and got out of bed.

An officer was waiting outside the door, one Jackson hadn't seen before. "Good morning, sir."

Jackson nodded in reply.

"Detective Dekker asked me to wake you and tell you to get dressed and be ready to leave as soon as possible."

"Leave for where?"

"I do not know, sir."

Jackson was too tired to think clearly about what might be going on, and too tired to care. He took the liberty of a shower, which helped him wake up a little, then dressed. Paige had been allowed to go to the estate the previous night and get some of Jackson's own clothes, so he dressed in his own blue jeans and a plain T-shirt. At five till five, he opened the door to see the same officer.

"Ready, sir?"

"I'm ready."

"Follow me."

It was still dark outside, and Jackson followed the officer down to the parking lot and a waiting squad car. The officer opened the back door for Jackson, and he got in to see Dekker sitting across from him.

Jackson frowned. "This the scene where you give me a buddy-to-buddy, one-last-chance talk before throwing me off a cliff or something?"

Dekker frowned. "Let's go, Martin."

The officer nodded from the driver's seat and started the car.

"Mind telling me where we're going?" Jackson asked.

"The airport."

"Why?"

Dekker only smirked and looked out the window.

The power was back on across the island, Jackson saw as they drove, and from the odd streetlamp and the faint dim of the oncoming morning, he could see that St. Charles looked in pretty good shape.

They passed the intersection where all the vehicles had crashed as Jackson ran the boat ashore, a memory that was foggy and felt ancient, despite having been just four days ago. Jackson remembered kissing Maggie before he'd darted off to chase GrayStar, and he wondered if it would be their last kiss. Or, for that matter, if he'd see her again.

He turned to Dekker. "Can you tell me about my friends? Are they all going . . . wherever I'm going too?"

The detective looked at him but said nothing.

Two minutes later, Martin turned the car onto the airport access road, then into the airport parking lot. They passed through the checkpoint and onto the tarmac, then made a right turn toward a twin-engine, high-wing cargo aircraft parked just outside the far hangar. They coasted to a stop next to an SUV parked adjacent to a flight of stairs leading to the fuselage. Martin got out and opened Jackson's door, and Dekker nodded for him to get out.

As he did, he saw a petty officer coming down the stairs. Dekker had also exited the car and circled the trunk to approach the petty officer. Curious, Jackson's eyes were torn away from them when the rear door of the SUV opened and a large black man in a Cornhuskers T-shirt stepped out, gingerly on one leg.

"Reggie!"

"Jack, man, you all right?"

He cast a quick glance at Dekker, who was holding out a sheet of paper to the petty officer, then to Martin who stood dutifully by the front of the car, before racing over and embracing his best friend in a tight hug.

"Are you okay, Hoss?"

"Nothing I won't be able to walk off," he said, looking down at his leg. He nodded at the plane. "You know what's going on?"

"Not a clue."

"I think you're being extradited," Paige said as she came around the front of the car. She was followed by Tori, and both of them gave Jackson a quick hug.

"Extradited? All of us?"

Paige nodded.

"You have the official word?"

"No, but I'm reading between the lines."

"What happened?" he asked, looking at Tori, then Reggie. "What did they say when they came to get you? Who came to get you? Alison, do you know anything?"

"Uh, J."

He turned to Reggie, then followed his gaze around the front of the SUV. Maggie stood in a pair of blue jeans and an orange Henley, hands in her pockets, a thin-lipped, straight smile on her face. She had never looked more beautiful.

They looked at each other for several seconds, then both hurried into a tight embrace.

Chapter One Hundred Forty-Eight

6:02 a.m.

JACKSON RATED THE folding seats in the C-2A Greyhound airplane somewhere between flying coach through turbulence and taking a ride in the dryer. Only the dryer would probably be quieter. He was seated sideways next to Maggie and Tori, with Reggie and Paige across the way, facing them. They were still ascending, and the few windows in the plane indicated the sun had risen—at least at altitude.

"So none of you know anything?" Jackson asked, practically shouting. "No idea what's going on?"

He was answered with headshakes.

"Where we're going?"

More headshakes.

"Where Eli is?"

Yet more shakes.

"What do you know? What's gone on the last three days?"

"A lot of cable, man," Reggie answered. "And that detective kept asking—"

"Wait, you got cable?"

"Basic. You didn't?"

Jackson shook his head. "What'd he ask?"

"Asked me to recap everything that happened, what I knew about GrayStar, all that."

"What'd you tell him?"

"Nothing."

"He give you any hint about where you stood legally?"

"Blustered a little when I didn't talk, but never even threatened an arrest."

"What about you two?" Jackson asked, looking from Maggie to Tori.

"He still thinks I'm Katherine Austin," Maggie said. "I stuck to the script, like you said I should."

"Never questioned me," Tori said.

"Alison, he say anything to you since yesterday?"

"No. I got a call from an Officer Kupp at four a.m."

"And nothing from Washington?"

She shook her head.

Jackson sighed, concluding he'd find out where they were going when they landed. "Any of you talk to Blackshear?"

"He was gone when we got back," Maggie answered. "And he or somebody left a mess in their wake."

"A mess?"

"Server room was destroyed. Machines torn apart, looked like somebody took a drill to the hard drives."

"Destroying physical evidence," Jackson said.

"He's in the wind," Reggie said.

"Yeah, but I need to get ahold of him."

"Why?"

"Because he thought he could hack into GrayStar's network through their hacking into ours."

"How would that work?" Tori asked.

"Beats me."

"You can still access the portal remotely, can't you?" Maggie asked.

"If they let me have a computer."

"Maybe he left you a message there."

"Or cleaned out our bank accounts and is never to be seen again."

"You think he would?" Reggie asked.

"No, but not the way I don't think you would."

"I'm touched."

"Mags, what's up with the estate?"

"I hired a local cleanup crew, a steward to manage the house, and lawyers to string red tape."

"String red tape?"

"I figured with all the shooting, the damage, the bodies—at a party involving major island bigwigs—there's bound to be a legal mess, and until we can figure out where we stand, it'd be prudent to have somebody keep too much from happening."

"Good work."

The door to the cockpit opened and the petty officer who'd been talking with Dekker emerged, clad in a flight suit. He was tall, black, relatively relaxed looking, for an on-duty petty officer. He even smiled. "You folks all doing all right?"

They nodded.

"We've got clear skies ahead. Should be about a three-and-a-half-hour flight. Sorry I can't offer you soft drinks or a tiny bag of peanuts. But there is a lavatory aft. And if you need anything, you can press that red button right there to speak to us in the cockpit."

"Thank you, Petty Officer," Paige said.

"Um, Petty Officer," Jackson said.

"Yes, sir?"

"Can you tell us where we're going?"

"You don't know?"

"No, sir."

"We're inbound for Pax River—That is, Naval Air Station Patuxent River, in southwest Maryland."

"D.C.," Jackson said.

"About fifty or sixty miles southeast of Washington, D.C., yes, sir."

Jackson nodded. "Thank you, Petty Officer."

"Yes, sir." He turned and headed back to the cockpit.

"If you're right and we're being extradited," Reggie said, "shouldn't we be under arrest?"

"Not if you haven't been charged," Paige said.

"Then what are we being extradited for?" Maggie asked.

"Potential charges." Paige shrugged. "It's a theory. Or maybe Uncle Sam bought your freedom and is ready to give Jackson a medal."

"I guess we'll know in about three and a half hours," Tori said.

The Q&A ended, and Jackson leaned his head back and tried to sleep. The drumming turbine engines made it hard. Then again, he hadn't slept well the last several days. His brain had been running nonstop, trying to figure out what his fate would be, how he could influence it, and, more importantly, what the fate of his friends would be and how he could influence that. He'd also been rerunning events of the previous few days back in his head, looking for a way to justify himself before this or that authority. Admittedly, these were all aspects of the plan that could have been laid out better, even with the contingency that the plan went sideways, as it pretty much had from the get-go on Saturday.

Combined with the draining of adrenaline, the physical fatigue and soreness, and the concern over how to verify GrayStar was absolutely wiped out and send word to his parents that the coast was clear, Jackson's brain hadn't had a spare minute in the last four days. And now, he felt like he should be having a joyous reunion—slapping Reggie on the back while telling war stories or making out with Maggie like it was V-E Day, but somehow, it didn't feel over yet.

The Marine corporal came back to check on them mid-flight, and then again to announce that they were beginning their descent into Pax River. Breakfast would be provided for them, seeing as how it was a little before eight o'clock in Maryland. The landing was a little turbulent, but they touched down without issue, then taxied for a couple of minutes. Soon the petty officer was back to help them out of their harnesses and welcome them to Naval Air Station Pax River.

Jackson was first out of the fuselage and down the stairs. He briefly surveyed flat, wooded terrain around the runways, before turning his eyes to the small entourage waiting at the bottom of the stairs. Several men and one woman were clustered together. They wore a combination of suits and military uniforms. Of the latter, one stood out, as did the man wearing it. Admiral Francis Sullivan was decked in his summer whites, and looked resplendent. He stepped forward and offered Jackson a hand.

"Admiral, is this your doing?" Jackson asked, shaking his head.

"I've had a hand. This isn't a great place to talk," he said, looking at the winding down propellers. "Will you come with me?"

Jackson nodded, gave a look to Reggie and Maggie, on his six, and followed the Admiral and the entourage toward an empty hangar. Once inside, the admiral introduced himself to everyone in Jackson's group, concluding with, "You must be Captain Paige."

"Yes, sir."

"A pleasure to meet you."

"Likewise, Admiral."

Sullivan stepped back. "I'm sure you all have a lot of questions, but unfortunately I'm not at liberty to answer many of them right now. We've arranged for you all to have something to eat at the Sea Wings Café here on base, and we can talk there."

"Admiral, are my clients under arrest?" Paige asked.

Jackson wasn't sure when the others had become her clients, but he wasn't of a mindset to quibble over legalities.

"No, but there are some people who have some questions, especially for you, Jackson."

"What sort of questions?" Paige asked.

"We'll talk at the café," Sullivan said. He looked to the group as a whole. "I imagine you folks are hungry. This way, please."

*   *   *

8:31 a.m. (Eastern Standard Time)
Naval Air Station Patuxent River

SULLIVAN WAS the highest ranked military member present, but Jackson had no idea who the suits were joining them at the Sea Wings Café, and thus didn't know who was ultimately calling the shots. At least for the little things—like letting Jackson, Reggie, Maggie, Tori, and Paige sit together and alone—Sullivan seemed to be the boss. And while he was cloaked in mystery and lack of liberty again, Jackson knew the man was an ally, and his presence here bode well for their future.

"You didn't cut a deal or something, did you?" Maggie asked.

"A deal?" Jackson asked, scooping up some scrambled eggs.

"Take the rap for all of us?"

"I just have more rap to take than all of you."

"That's not a no," Tori said.

"I don't think they'd let me if I tried."

"*That's* not a no," Reggie said.

"Aren't you the lawyer?" he asked Paige. "Not a no," he said before she could. "No, I didn't take the rap for all of you. He said people had questions for all of us."

"Should we get our stories straight?" Reggie asked.

"No innocent person has ever said that," Maggie said with a wary look.

"Tell the truth, Hoss. Don't shield me for a second."

"Shoot, you think I'm worried about you?"

Jackson scooped more eggs.

Sullivan let them finish eating, then sidled over to their table, a mug of coffee in his hand.

"This our last meal, sir?" Jackson asked.

The admiral grinned. "Not at all. But there are some people who have questions, like I said." He looked to Paige and cut her off before she could object. "None of you are under arrest, and you all have your rights. You won't be forced to talk. But, from everything I can glean, this is not a witch-hunt. I can't promise you that none of you will face any consequences for what happened, but my advice is, be forthright. I honestly believe your best bet is to come clean."

"All due respect, Admiral," Paige said, "but that sounds like what cops and district attorneys tell suspects to coerce a confession."

"I understand, but I'm neither a cop nor a district attorney. Some pretty hefty strings were pulled to get the four of you out of St. Charles, and I don't think it was done simply so the U.S. could be the ones to line you up in front of a firing squad." He held up a hand. "It's just advice; you're all welcome to do what you think is best and what your attorney recommends, but I believe in this case, the truth may just set you free."

"Can we have a few minutes to talk?" Paige asked.

The admiral checked his watch. "A few, but then we need to be going."

"Mind telling us where, Admiral?" Maggie asked.

"That I can't tell you, not specifically. You'll each be taken to a separate location for questioning. I'll give you a couple minutes."

Sullivan backed away, and the group huddled together.

"Name, rank, serial number?" Reggie asked.

"I don't like it," Paige said.

"I'll admit, it does have a certain 'and they were never seen again' quality to it," Tori said.

Maggie nodded at Jackson. "What do you say, Jack?"

He slowly rubbed his jaw. "I'm not going to tell any of you what to do or not do. But I'm not shying away from what happened. I'm coming clean and facing the consequences."

"Truth does have a way of finding the light of day whether you try to let it out or not," Reggie said.

"That, and I believe Sullivan."

"Do you trust the guys in the dark suits, the guys asking questions?" Paige asked.

"No. But my father trusted Sullivan implicitly, and so do I. And he wouldn't give the advice he gave if he wasn't convinced."

"That's good enough for me, man," Reggie said.

"Me too," Maggie said.

"What have I got to lose?" Tori said. "I barely know what happened anyhow."

"Besides, if all else fails, blame Eli."

"This is very noble," Paige said, "but I think we should still be careful."

"Absolutely," Jackson said. "I want you to play the lawyer card to the hilt. Pester and poke and make sure nobody's rights get trampled."

"With pleasure," Paige said with a grin.

The group stood, and Jackson motioned for Paige to join him privately. "When you get a chance, reach out to Hillary, let her know what's up."

She nodded.

"And make them your top priority."

"Jackson, I think the primary focus is going to be on you."

"I agree, but if things do turn sinister, they're likely to put pressure on one of my friends. I can handle myself. Watch out for them."

She nodded again. "You have my word."

Sullivan (or maybe it was the suits) permitted Jackson and his friends to say their goodbyes. After being reunited just hours ago at the airport in St. Charles, it was hard to part again. Especially not knowing what the future held for them. And yet, Jackson wasn't going to duck the consequences of his actions.

Several seamen joined the suits and took Reggie, Maggie, Tori, and Paige to a pair of dark SUVs parked outside the café. Jackson was given another handshake by Sullivan, then loaded into a third SUV with a Chief Petty Officer Nichols, a Seaman Hughes, and another man in a suit identified as Parker. Jackson sat in back with Seaman Hughes, a well-built man with a polite but firm face.

"We've got about a three-and-a-half-hour drive, Mr. Douglas," Nichols said. "If you need to stop for a restroom or get hungry, just let me know."

"Thank you."

They started north, then crossed the Patuxent River to the east. Jackson tried to do the math, wondering what was three and a half hours from NAS Pax River, which was itself maybe an hour southeast of D.C. Philadelphia, maybe? New York was too far. A secluded place in the middle of the Appalachians where shadowy CIA agents could waterboard him? He decided to sit back and wait.

They drove through a mix of woods, small towns, and rural settings. He wondered if maybe D.C. was the ultimate destination, and Nichols' time estimate had to do with Beltway traffic. Then they hit Annapolis and, instead of turning west, continued north and then east over the Chesapeake Bay Bridge. As they continued through more woods, marshes, and small communities—as well as a brief rain shower—Jackson grew more and more puzzled. Finally, after skirting some beach-community sprawl, they turned onto a meandering drive through a grove of trees and acres of seagrass.

The SUV stopped in front of a two story, gray-sided house with white trim that looked as beachy as possible. Two other SUVs were parked out front, and before Jackson's door was opened by Chief Petty Officer Nichols, a woman in a pair of dark slacks and a blue button-down shirt descended from the home's front stairs. Jackson was out of the vehicle in time to hear her introduce herself as U.S. Deputy Marshal Kara Walsh, and she signed a piece of paper on a clipboard handed her by Nichols. Then she looked at Jackson.

"Mr. Douglas, I'm Deputy Marshal Walsh with the U.S. Marshals Service. For the time being, you will be in our custody."

He looked up at the house, then across the dunes to the ocean beyond. So far, extradition wasn't too bad.

Chapter One Hundred Forty-Nine

"HELLO?" JACKSON SAID into the phone provided him by Deputy Marshal Kwon.

"Jack," Maggie said. "How are you?"

"Affirmative," he said.

"I think you can cut the cloak and dagger," she said. "They know who I am."

"How'd you get this number?"

"Thank Paige. She got it for me."

Jackson motioned toward the deck, and got a nod of approval from Kwon. He hurried out into the evening air.

"You there?" Maggie asked.

"Yeah, Mags, I'm here. What's up? How are you?"

"I'm fine. Just got back to L.A. this afternoon."

"L.A.? They let you go?"

"They let us go Wednesday afternoon."

"All of you?"

"Yep. Questioned us for a couple hours, then dropped us at Reagan, bought us tickets to wherever, and said we were free to go."

Jackson rubbed a hand over his forehead, trying to think. His brain was mush after everything he'd been through recently. "What . . . What'd they ask?"

"My guy just said, 'Tell us everything,' and so I did. Talked for an hour straight, answered another hour of follow-up questions, and got a nice smile in return."

"Who was it?"

"A guy named Howell."

"Military?"

"Spook."

"Reggie and Walker the same?"

"Variations on a theme."

"And you're in the clear?"

"As far as we know."

He sighed as he leaned back against the house. "That's great, Maggie." He frowned. "Why'd you just get back to L.A. today?"

"Reggie and I flew to Nebraska first to take care of everything there. Packed up the apartments, paid off the leases, everything."

"What'd you do with everything?"

"Reggie's bringing it with a U-Haul. Where are you, anyhow?" she asked as a cawing gull swooped past.

"Somewhere on the Atlantic. Rehoboam or Jeroboam Beach or somewhere."

"You're at the beach?"

"Yeah, and it's a nice place."

"To what end?"

"Same as you, only more in depth. I've spent the last couple days being questioned by the Principal Deputy Director of National Intelligence. Went over every jot and tittle of my life the last nine months."

"The Deputy DNI?"

"Yeah."

"He reports to the president, doesn't he?"

"The DNI does."

"That's promising," she said. "The president taking interest, I mean."

"Depends if Blackshear has anything. I told Forrester—the PDDNI—that I'd send him everything Blackshear had on GrayStar. I'm hoping it's more than we compiled."

"About that. I tried logging onto the portal the other day. It's gone."

"What?"

"Login didn't work, site couldn't be accessed. He must have taken it down."

Jackson muttered a, "Crap," under his breath and paced to the end of the deck.

"I figure it's fifty-fifty he's gone for good or is laying low and still loyal."

"You checked our bank accounts?" he asked.

"Everything's still there."

"Then he's loyal. He'll make contact when he can."

"So what's going down, any idea?"

"None."

"What should we do?"

"Get your old job back, if you can."

"I'm not abandoning you."

"I don't know, it's not bad here, and the food's good. Couple of the marshals are cute."

"Jack."

"I'm not asking you to abandon me. But whatever happens, you'll need a job or something to do. Plus, you can use your contacts to see what's going on. The government's involved, so I assume something's been leaked already."

"You think it's safe?"

"I think so."

"That was brimming with confidence."

"Forrester said there were seven bodies found in the Learjet wreckage, plus Hayes and Bosco. Our IDs were good on Carter and Blye, so the only GrayStar person we knew of who we haven't confirmed dead is Tyler Bayliss. Maybe he's at large, maybe he's retired—who knows?. Maybe don't take out an ad in the *Times* announcing you're back in L.A. just yet, but some phone calls from a burner should be safe."

"When do you think I can see you?"

"Ask Paige. She seems to be the gatekeeper."

"You haven't heard anything from her?"

"Haven't heard anything from anyone." He looked back where Kwon had stepped onto the deck and pointed at his wrist. "I think I've got to go, Maggie. I'll be in touch when I can."

"Okay."

"Any word on Walker?"

"She flew home. I'll be sure to let her know you asked."

Kwon was on his way over.

"Really gotta go. Love you, Mags."

"Love you too."

He ended the call and handed the phone to a stern-faced U.S. marshal. "Thank you."

Kwon nodded, and they headed back inside to watch the rest of the Orioles' game.

*   *   *

Sunday, May 25
1:24 p.m.

FOR THE first time in as long as he could remember, Jackson slept soundly Saturday night—and well into Sunday morning. He woke to fresh coffee and pancakes from a heretofore unseen deputy marshal, and ate on the deck while some morning clouds burned off. There were no interrogations scheduled, and yet no indication that Jackson was about to be released. It could be worse, he figured; he could be in Gitmo.

Jackson was not allowed to use the phone or the internet, so he scrounged Netflix for a few hours after eating. He chatted with Deputy Marshal Fielding, the pancake guy, and pried out of him their exact location, at a residence north of Rehoboth Beach, Delaware, itself just north of a string of beach communities. On Memorial Day Weekend, they would all be filled with tourists and beachgoers, which after months of seclusion and isolation, sounded appealing to Jackson. But he didn't bother asking permission to slip down to the boardwalk for some fair rides and cotton candy.

Lunch was the usual, cold cuts for sandwiches. He ate in front of another episode of *Love It or List It Too*, and was surprised to hear the doorbell ring shortly before it concluded. Anything different was exciting, so he paused the show and sat up, looking over his shoulder at the door.

Deputy Marshal Ross was back on duty and, after a word to the other two marshals via his earwig, approached the door. Hand on his holster, he inched it open, then pulled it back all the way. "Good morning, ma'am."

"Deputy Marshal," Paige said, folding closed her ID wallet. "I spoke to Deputy Marshal Walsh this morning."

"Yes, ma'am, she passed word on that you would be stopping by. Mr. Douglas is in the living room."

"Thank you," she said, then stepped past him and walked through the dining room to Jackson, who had stood.

"Alison, hi."

"Jackson, good to see you," she said, extending a hand.

He eyed her but responded to the formality.

She turned back to Ross. "Is it all right if we take a walk on the beach?"

"For a hundred yards in either direction."

"Is that really necessary?"

"Yes, ma'am."

She raised an eyebrow at Jackson, who tugged up his pant leg to show her. She turned back to Ross. "Very well."

They headed out onto the deck, and she dropped a pair of aviator sunglasses from her auburn hair down over her eyes. She wore a yellow cap-sleeved shirt and white Bermuda shorts, and couldn't have looked less military at the moment. Check that, she kicked off her flip-flops, leaving them on the bottom step of the deck, and she and Jackson wandered through the soft sand of the dunes to the open beach.

It was another hot day on the Atlantic coast, but a steady breeze kept it pleasant. They turned north, away from the more populated areas, even though they were only going a hundred yards. Paige walked on Jackson's right, closer to the ocean.

"So, you breaking me out?"

"Not exactly."

"Meaning kind of?"

"I'm here as your attorney."

"Well, I didn't figure they were allowing social visits."

"From my brief talk with Maggie, I understand that would be a no-go anyhow."

Jackson smiled in return.

So did Paige. "I have been asking every question I can, pushing every button I can, calling in every favor I can to try to figure out what's going on. I've also been in touch with Hillary, who I take it is doing the same in the private sector."

"I really appreciate that, Alison. I hope you're not expending personal capital on me."

"That's what I'm here about."

"Oh?"

"So far, as far as my superiors are concerned, I'm still working for them, making sure you play ball and don't rock the boat. That's presumably why I'm here, to check in on things."

"Presumably?"

"I received a phone call yesterday afternoon from a man identifying himself as Paul Rowe."

Jackson hesitated for a second. Paul Rowe, one of the aliases provided him by Crimson, eons ago—an alias with which he had bought his home security system, booked travel from Veracruz to Southampton, and contacted the Night Ram.

"Spoke with a British accent, said it would be in my and your interest to meet with him. Said if I wasn't sure, I should contact you."

"It's Blackshear."

"Your hacker?"

"Yeah. Rowe was an alias I used when first contacting him."

Paige nodded. "Then I'll meet with him."

"He say what he wanted?"

"Nothing more than I told you."

"If he's reaching out, he must have something. Maybe a data dump of everything we compiled on GrayStar, or maybe he hacked into their network and learned more. Maybe he knows if there's any of them left." He stopped and turned to face Paige. "What does this have to do with your personal capital?"

"Jackson, I believe every word you've said. I'm convinced you're telling the truth, and I'm willing to stick my neck out for you, if need be."

He nodded.

"And I seriously think someone very high up in the government—maybe President Rutherford himself—is trying to figure out what to do about this. I heard a rumor that they made a deal with the St. Charles government to get you and your friends out, a deal in the neighborhood of several million dollars' worth of aid packages and infrastructure improvements."

Jackson whistled.

"Like Admiral Sullivan said, I don't think they'd do that if their intent was to hang you, especially since I'm pretty sure the St. Charles government would have without intervention."

Jackson rubbed his neck.

Paige smirked for a second, then turned south—it'd been about a hundred yards—and started walking again. "That tells me they want to believe you were on the right side in all this. They know who you are, know who your father is and what he was doing, and have undoubtedly spoken to Admiral Sullivan."

"Then what's the hold up?"

"Evidence. Proof. If they're going to vindicate a person for killing several Americans—former U.S. service members, no less—they're going to need more than your word that they were bad guys. And they're going to need more than circumstantial evidence."

"Even if it's a mound of it?"

"I think so."

Jackson trudged a few paces.

"I'll meet with Blackshear, see what he wants, and if it's legitimate, that may be the thing to spring you."

"And if not?"

Paige shrugged. "I am still a Captain in the U.S. Air Force. At some point, they're going to want me back on official duty."

"At which time your ability to intercede for and help me will be gone."

She nodded. Then put a hand on his arm. "So if there's anything you've held back, any ace in the hole that you've been saving, this is the time to come out with it. I can be that conduit for you, whatever that means for my personal capital."

He exhaled. Then said, "My only ace in the hole would be anything Blackshear might have."

"Okay. I'll meet with him."

"Where?"

"He said I could pick the place, so long as it was private."

Jackson trudged on some more.

"What aren't you telling me?"

"It's nothing."

"It's clearly something," she said.

He sighed. "It depends if he was able to hack into their network and what he could find there."

"Why? What are you looking for?"

"This is nothing more than a hunch, mind you."

She nodded.

"From what I heard second- or third-hand, the knowledge of GrayStar has been passed down from president to president over the years. And I know how it is, every president has his baby, his legacy—ending a war, boosting the economy, whatever—and so every president can't fix every problem. But it sounded like when Rutherford took office, he made one of his objectives going after GrayStar. He was a Navy guy, and so somehow Sullivan and ONI got tabbed to head up the hunt, and Sullivan in turn recruited my dad. And yet somewhere between that moment and now, Rutherford has backed off." Jackson shrugged. "It could be as simple as it didn't work with Dad and ONI, and he thought there was no way to get them. It could be that the political climate in Washington changed and he focused his efforts and energy elsewhere. It could be that he started to see white supremacists as a greater threat than rogue special ops. But something changed."

"And you don't think it's any of those three," Paige said.

"I think it could be. But I also think it could be something else."

"Such as?"

"That's what I'm hoping Blackshear has found."

"You think GrayStar had their hooks into him?"

"I heard from a source I trust in Washington that there were rumors that somebody did."

"The rumors say who?"

"Everybody from Putin to the First Lady. And they were rumors, so maybe they're just that. But *if* somebody did, and *if* that somebody was GrayStar, it would explain why Rutherford lost steam in pursuing them."

Now it was Paige's turn to trudge in silence for a while. "*If* that's true," she said finally, "that's huge."

"Yeah."

"So your plan is to take possession of whatever GrayStar held over Rutherford and hold it over him yourself?"

He shook his head. "Well, I guess it depends what it is. If they have evidence he was getting cozy with Beijing, I know a certain reporter with some clout. If he got an intern pregnant while in the senate, I may just let a sleeping bear lie."

"You could be playing with fire, Jackson."

"I could be. That's why I want to see what Blackshear has, if anything. If it's too hot to handle, so be it."

"Like I said, I'll meet with him."

They turned back north again and chatted about other things on the return to the house. A dozen yards short of the path through the dunes back to it, Jackson stopped. Paige turned to him with a quizzical look on her face.

"I just wanted to say thank you, Alison. You've really gone out on a limb for me, and I appreciate it."

She smiled sweetly. "You're welcome, Jackson. I think you're worth it."

"You know," he said, starting slowly again. "We have quite a stash of cash left, if Blackshear didn't abscond with it all. If that limb should happen to break and you get drummed out of the Air Force or something, well, you won't go hungry."

"I'm not in the Air Force to pay the bills, Jackson. A JAG lawyer is who I am, not just what I do."

"I know, and I didn't mean to imply otherwise. But a girl does have to pay the bills."

"Keep your money." She winked at him. "Get Maggie a really big diamond."

Chapter One Hundred Fifty

THE SOUND WAS more of a thup than a thud, at least Jackson's somewhat sleepy brain told him. He'd been lying in his room, looking at the ceiling fan, listening to the ocean, trying to drift off. Today, his inability to sleep was blamed on a two-hour nap mid-afternoon. After all, there'd been nothing else to do. More Netflix, more watching the waves, more good food, and a little bonding with Deputy Marshal Ross watching the National Memorial Day Concert on PBS. There had been no word from anyone, friend or foe or fence-sitter.

Jackson lay alertly for a moment, trying to place the sound, trying to make sure he'd actually heard it and hadn't been semi-dreaming. He was pretty sure he'd been fully conscious, albeit drifting toward sleep. And he was pretty sure the sound had not come from in the house.

He waited, not hearing it again, then stood. He walked over to the open window, brushing aside the sheer drape that fluttered in the breeze. He peeked out at the darkness, everything an odd shade of blue thanks to a half moon high in the sky. He scanned the beach for nearly a minute, looking for signs of movement and seeing nothing.

He was about to turn back when he heard a hiss, then another thup, this time much louder and immediately to his left. After briefly recoiling, he turned to his left and saw a pair of small, suction darts stuck to the half of the window not open. They looked like Nerf toys, only a little larger and all black, and his first thought was to duck down out of the way of any further flying projectiles. But then he realized, anyone shooting Nerf suction darts didn't mean him harm.

So he unattached the screen, reached out, and removed the two darts from the window. At the same time, he kept his eyes on the beach, wondering who had shot them. Maggie, with a take on *Romeo and Juliet?* A bored deputy marshal out playing tricks? Or were these more than suction darts?

He examined one of them, found that the shaft unscrewed from the suction cup, and the inside of the shaft was hollow. Convinced this wasn't somebody playing with Nerf guns on the beach at quarter till midnight, he set the two pieces on the nightstand and unscrewed the other, which if he had them right in his head, was the second one. A small roll of paper fell out. He stooped to pick it up, then unrolled it to read a short note:

Come out to beach. –E

Jackson read it twice, then looked out at the beach. Nothing moving but the waves and seagrass.

He stuffed the darts and the paper inside his pillowcase, threw on a shirt and pair of shorts, and headed down the stairs with a fake yawn that spawned a real one. One of the three marshals was always awake, and in this case it was Deputy Marshal Bostic. He was watching CNN, and turned as Jackson's footfalls sounded on the stairs.

"Can't sleep," Jackson said. "Gonna get some air."

Bostic looked at him, then nodded.

"Not going to get shocked if I go stand on the beach, am I?"

"You don't get shocked at all. But you get in the water or go more than a hundred yards up and down the beach, you'll wake Ross and Gordon up, and they won't be happy."

"Got it."

Bostic stood, then led the way onto the deck. He spent a minute looking around, determined everything was satisfactory, and ducked back inside, leaving the door ajar. Jackson took his time, first taking in a few deep breaths while looking up at the sky, then slowly wandering off the deck and through the dunes to the beach. The dunes were tall enough that anyone standing on the beach was hidden from anyone on the deck, but there wasn't anyone standing on the beach.

There was, however, a man sitting on the dune to the left, smoking the last half of a cigarette. He wore a long-sleeved brown shirt and khaki pants, along with a baseball cap with a Nike logo on the front. The hat covered dark, medium-length hair and obscured the face until he looked up and blew a puff of smoke at Jackson.

Standing between a pair of dunes, and thus possibly visible from the deck or house, Jackson turned and took several steps toward him, then stretched out his arms. "You couldn't have called?" he said in a voice just above a whisper.

Eli Haddad stood with a half grin. He extended Jackson a hand, who shook it heartily. "How are you doing?"

"Healing. You in much trouble?"

"If you keep shooting darts at the window."

"They onto me?"

"Maybe a little suspicious that I needed some air. But keep blowing smoke, they might be."

Eli took one last drag, then tossed the butt into the sand and stepped on it.

"How in the world did you know where I was?"

"You insult me," Eli said.

"Even the right room?"

"Educated guess. And that's why the first dart was just a dart."

"Okay, so what's up?"

"I came to see what sort of trouble you're in and if I could help."

"I don't know yet," Jackson said, then briefly described his and everyone's situation. He concluded by saying, "I think—if Sullivan and Paige are right—things might be working in my favor."

"Well, you need anything—testimony to back your story, someone to break you out of federal prison—say the word."

"Thanks, Eli, I appreciate it."

The Israeli nodded.

"You in any trouble of your own?"

He shrugged. "Some flak from the Israeli government, I'm sure, but nothing I can't handle."

"Nothing with the people in St. Charles?"

"No. They released me rather unceremoniously, gave me a coach ticket to Miami, and told me to never return."

"Your government pull strings?"

"I don't think so."

Jackson raised an eyebrow.

"There is something else."

"What's that?" Jackson asked.

"I've been reaching out to all my contacts, exercising less discretion than before, and there's nothing to suggest there's any component of GrayStar we missed. We were nine for nine, counting Bosco."

"We expected ten with Bosco."

"We figured an extra pilot. Apparently not."

"They got airborne awfully fast if they all arrived just ahead of us."

"They were in a hurry."

Jackson pursed his lips.

"I also found out Tyler Bayliss bought it a couple years ago. He was the only loose end unaccounted for. So can I promise you with hundred percent certainty there's no threat left? No. But ninety-nine?" He nodded.

"I guess that's good. How'd Bayliss die?"

"Snapped neck. His body was found in the woods around a small lake outside Winnipeg."

"Hmm."

"I'm also checking on family members, known associates, wanting to be out ahead of any possible vengeance play. So far nothing, but I'll keep you posted."

"If they move me, I'll chalk my window."

Eli grinned.

"Anything else? I should get back in."

"No. You need to reach me, I'm still at the same number you originally called."

"Copy that. And, Eli, thanks. That stunt with the fuel truck, risking your life like that . . . I owe you forever."

This time he extended a hand, and Eli clasped it firmly.

"Take care of yourself," Eli said, dropping the grip. "I'll be in touch."

"You as well, my friend."

With a nod, Eli turned and started north up the beach.

Jackson waited a couple minutes, then turned and headed back inside, where Bostic was watching TV with a blank expression. "Want me to heat up some milk?" he asked as Jackson reentered.

"No, fresh air was the ticket, I think," Jackson said, yawning again. Then he hurried up the steps and back into bed, where he spent half an hour processing Eli's words and assurances before falling asleep, wondering if ninety-nine percent was certainty enough.

*   *   *

Tuesday, May 27
10:03 a.m.

JACKSON SLEPT in, then had a breakfast of leftover pancakes and fruit that was iffy after several days in the refrigerator. Then he had coffee on the deck with Deputy Marshal Fielding, who told Jackson some "war stories" about close calls the U.S. Marshals Service had encountered with people in WitSec. Unlike what TV and movies portrayed, the mob or cartel didn't always find the witness. In fact, the Marshals Service had never lost a witness, but there had been some tight spots over the years.

The sliding door opened and Jackson turned, expecting to see a replacement marshal. Instead, it was Paige, dressed today in a navy (technically probably Air Force) blue- and white-striped shirt, blue jeans cut at the mid-calf, and boat shoes. It was partly cloudy, and her sunglasses were pushed into her auburn hair.

Both men stood as Paige shut the door behind her.

"Gosh, I don't require such formality."

"Not like we saluted," Jackson said.

"All right if I talk with my client alone?" she asked with her head tipped to the side.

Fielding nodded. "Get you a cup of coffee, Captain?"

"No, I've been taking it intravenously all day. Thanks."

Fielding nodded again and left them alone on the deck.

"I didn't expect you back so soon," Jackson said.

"I met with Blackshear last night."

"Still, it's early in the day."

"Late in yesterday for me," she said. "I was up all night."

He frowned.

Paige walked to the railing, then hoisted herself up onto it. "Blackshear gave me a flash drive that he said contained all your research, conclusions— everything you had. I made a pair of copies, one of which I sent by courier to the PDDNI's office. I also e-mailed Forrester a summary, which it took me a few hours to put together."

"You couldn't e-mail the whole thing?"

"Way too big for an attachment."

Jackson nodded. "You think it's enough?"

"On its own, maybe. But Blackshear also got into GrayStar's network."

"He did?"

"He explained it to me, showing off I think, and I have no idea what he did. And I know my way around a network. Anyhow, he said it was a treasure trove."

Jackson leaned back against the railing beside her. "How so?"

"He told me he wasn't able to pull everything on the network, but he downloaded a ton of corroborating info—records of travel schedules, research into various victims, money trails, etcetera."

"Sounds circumstantial."

"Yes, but enough circumstantial evidence can be persuasive."

"You think it's enough?" he asked again.

"I'm not the one to ask."

"Come on, Alison, don't go all lawyer on me."

"I'm not going lawyer on you. I'm telling you, I'm biased. I already believe you," she said, leaning his way, bumping her arm into his shoulder. "You need to persuade a neutral party at best, and maybe a party who starts off thinking you're a terrorist."

"Super."

"That said, it is convincing. I think your chances are good."

He nodded.

Paige looked toward the windows and doors, then nodded toward the steps. "Come on, let's go for a walk."

"Still got my anklet."

"Gypsies wear anklets, Jackson."

"Can you say gypsies anymore?"

She nodded again. "Come on, a short walk."

He pushed off from the railing, extended a hand to Paige to help her down, then followed her down the steps. Both still in shoes, they crossed the dunes to the beach. Then Paige stopped.

"That was a short walk."

She reached into her pants pocket and pulled out a USB flash drive. She held it up.

"What's that, my copy?"

"Fire," she answered.

"Fire?"

"In case you want to play with it," she said, meeting his eyes with hers.

He frowned for just a moment. "You talking about what I think you're talking about?"

"Uh-huh."

He held out his palm, and she placed the USB flash drive in it.

"You want to tell me what's on here? I'm not sure I'll be able to talk my way into a laptop."

"I didn't look. Blackshear said it was for your eyes only."

He pocketed the drive. "I'll think of something. Blackshear give or tell you anything else?"

"Gave me a phone number, in case you need to reach him." She gave him the number, which he memorized, then asked her to reach out to Maggie with it as well. She said it was as good as done. Then he asked if she knew any more about the PDDNI's investigation. She didn't, but promised to look into it that afternoon—after a nap.

"I'd invite you to stay, catch forty in the hammock north of the house, but I don't think I'm allowed guests."

"I'll take Fielding up on that cup of coffee. Should get me back to D.C."

"I can't believe the Air Force still has you assigned to this."

Paige looked down, moving some sand around with the toe of her shoe. She looked up. "They kind of don't."

"How's that?"

She shrugged, sticking her hands into her pockets. "I had a talk with General Alberts, the Judge Advocate General of the Air Force. Secretary Wittingham was going to pull me off, which suggests they've arrived at something of a decision. Anyhow, I said I'd prefer to keep monitoring the situation. General Alberts is a lawyer too, don't forget, and he figured out I was working for you and told me if I was going to continue, it'd be on my time. So as of yesterday, I'm on temporary leave."

"Are you in trouble?"

She shrugged again and smiled. "Not yet."

"Alison, I can't ask you to do this, as much as I appreciate it."

She placed a hand on his arm. "You're on the right side on this, Jackson. And if I help make sure everyone knows that—or even help keep you up to date and at ease in the meantime—I'm happy to do it."

"Thank you."

"You're welcome."

"I don't know what I did to deserve the friends I got."

"You give just as well as you get, from what I hear." She licked her lips. "Besides, General Alberts gave me a wink-wink, nudge-nudge sort of look that made me think the bosses don't mind me still being in on things, getting the view from your perspective. This may work out in my favor after all."

"I hope so."

She smiled again, then said, "I should be going."

They walked back up to the house, where Deputy Marshal Fielding got her a cup of coffee to go. With a wave and another smile, she headed down to her car, and Jackson headed back to the deck where he watched the waves and tried to figure out how to get access to a laptop to see what was on the flash drive practically burning a hole in his pocket.

Chapter One Hundred Fifty-One

Thursday, May 29
10:57 a.m.
Arlington, Virginia

HE WAS THREE minutes early, which was practically unheard of.

Jackson and Deputies Marshal Walsh and Ross had been forty-five minutes early, having left Rehoboth Beach at seven to make sure they had enough time to navigate capital traffic. They'd given Jackson no word where they were taking him, this after a thoroughly uneventful Tuesday afternoon, evening, and all of Wednesday. They had told him to wear a tie, which Deputy Marshal Fielding had provided, and as they'd headed toward D.C., Jackson had started to believe he was going to meet someone awfully important. Like the Lord High Executioner.

They crossed the Anacostia River, then passed the Navy Yard, then continued west on the interstate. First the dome of the U.S. Capitol, then the Washington Monument, and finally the Jefferson Memorial appeared out Jackson's window, but the SUV bypassed them all and headed over the Potomac. Forget politicians, Jackson speculated he had an appointment with someone high-ranking in the Pentagon. But they drove past it too, flanking the Potomac until coming to a roundabout directly across the river from the Lincoln Memorial.

Jackson's curiosity as to where they were going and why was quickly dwarfed by the awe of Arlington National Cemetery. By flashing her badge, Walsh was permitted access to the narrow roads that curved through rows upon rows of small white tombstones. The morning was overcast, with heavy clouds hanging low, which only seemed to magnify the serenity of the tree-covered hillside. The cemetery seemed empty, another contributor to the somber atmosphere.

The SUV stopped at an intersection of sorts, where two men in suits were waiting for them. They had wired earpieces and talked into their sleeves, and carefully scrutinized IDs and badges, then wanded Jackson and the marshals. One of them then nodded toward a circular path, and Jackson looked at Walsh and Ross, who both stood by the SUV. Walsh nodded and said, "Go ahead."

So Jackson followed the circle to the left. Approximately one-third of the way around, where it widened into a small plaza rimmed by granite plaques on the right and a staircase on the left, another man in a suit stood at the base of the stairs, arms crossed, eyes hidden behind wraparound shades. He finally acknowledged Jackson when he was almost in front of him.

"You Douglas?"

"Yes."

The man briefly lifted his arm to look at his watch. "About forty-five minutes, Mr. Douglas."

Jackson didn't dare ask forty-five minutes until what, so he took in his surroundings. The small plaza was lined up perfectly with the entrance to Arlington National Cemetery, itself lined up perfectly with the bridge leading to D.C. and the Lincoln Memorial. He turned the other way, toward the steps, nodding at them. "May I?"

"Yes, sir."

There were three, ending in a landing with a sign in the middle that asked for silence and respect. Beyond that, eight more steps of marble. Jackson climbed them slowly and stood on a small marble terrace, and suddenly knew where he was.

In front of him, cordoned off by stanchions and chains, was a small stone garden. Set in it were four simple plaques, two large, two small. Beyond them, a nozzle emitted a faint but steady flame. Jackson watched it flicker for a moment, almost convinced he could smell the fuel amidst the magnolias flanking the gravesite. Then he turned his eyes to the left of the two larger plaques.

JOHN FITZGERALD KENNEDY

1917-1963

He turned to the plaque for Jacqueline Bouvier Kennedy Onassis, then the two smaller ones for the Kennedys' infant children. Whether it was due to the Kennedys' celebrity status or the fact that JFK had been the president or because of his assassination and the legend around it, standing in such a place felt almost like hallowed ground.

After a few minutes, Jackson's eyes drifted up the hill behind the gravesite to the ivory pillars of Arlington House, the Robert E. Lee Memorial. Originally, the home had belonged to the family of Lee's wife, Mary Anna Randolph Custis. When Lee joined the Confederacy, the Union took over the property after Lee's wife vacated the premises, and commissioned the use of the grounds as a cemetery. In doing so, they assured Lee would never move back to the house.

With time to kill, Jackson descended the steps and walked past the man in the suit and shades and over to the short wall of plaques marking the far end of the plaza. Each contained a portion of Kennedy's Inaugural Address.

Jackson had lost himself in something of reverie, eventually pacing back toward the Eternal Flame. He'd asked the man for the time, which had seemed borderline inappropriate given his response. But he'd announced the time as 10:56, and a minute later raised his sleeve to his mouth and uttered something Jackson couldn't hear.

A limousine following an SUV and a pair of motorcycles and trailed by another SUV and two more motorcycles had pulled up behind the SUV Jackson had arrived in. Three men were walking up the circular path from the limo. The two on the outside looked just like the one by Jackson. The other, very much, did not.

The 44th President of the United States stood six-three and filled out his dark blue suit without straining it. His black hair showed tinges of gray, and his face was somewhere between vigorous and venerable. His stride was purposeful, yet his posture indifferent, his head looking left and right across the grounds. When he reached the plaza, he made a motion to the two men beside him—Secret Service agents, the expert detective concluded—and approached Jackson.

"Miles, would you give us a moment," President Rutherford said. His voice, like when Jackson had heard it on TV, was both smooth and resonant.

"Yes, sir, Mr. President."

Miles nodded and stepped off to the side, leaving Jackson alone with the Leader of the Free World. Sort of made him wish he'd shaved in the last few days, had a haircut this year, and knotted his tie a little more crisply. He cleared his throat, which was suddenly dry, as Rutherford approached and stood beside him, both of them turning to face the Eternal Flame. But they stayed at the base of the steps.

"I've always felt a special connection to JFK," Rutherford said. "You know why?"

Jackson swallowed and managed to find a voice. "Because he was a Navy man like yourself, sir?"

The president nodded. "That's part of it, yes. John was a hero and a principled leader. I always admired the way he balanced his presidential duties with his faith. Are you a religious man, Mr. Douglas?"

"Yes, sir, I guess you could say that."

"Me too." He shook his head. "It's one of the hardest things I have to do as president, ordering an air strike that may take out innocent civilians or vetoing millions of dollars in an aid bill because of politically damaging riders. It's that way for any president, but some navigate it better than others—like JFK."

"Yes, sir."

"But, after all you've been through in recent days and weeks, I doubt you have any interest in listening to me wax poetic about a president who was dead before you were born. Nor, quite frankly, do I have the time for it."

"Yes, sir."

"Walk with me?" he said with a nod to his right.

"Yes, sir."

Rutherford turned to his right, and Jackson joined him, walking slowly across the plaza.

"I'll get down to business," Rutherford said. "The majority of your crimes—I'll use that word for the moment—were perpetrated against American citizens. Last week, my office negotiated with King Willem-Alexander of the Netherlands, Governor van den Heuvel of St. Charles, and Interpol, to have you extradited to the United States. So you will not face any charges from any foreign government body or any entity there within."

"Yes, sir."

They took several steps down from the plaza to the circular walkway. Jackson looked back briefly and saw one of the Secret Service agents trailing them casually. Another two stood amidst the tombstones ahead and to the right.

Rutherford continued. "Deputy Director Forrester briefed the Director of National Intelligence, Andrew Bernard, quite thoroughly on your testimony and the information you provided him. Director Bernard in turn briefed me yesterday morning, and I've given quite a lot of consideration to the matter." He pursed his lips. "Based on the recommendation of several advisors that mirrors my own conclusions, I've decided to issue you, Ms. Magstadt, Ms. Walker, and Mr. Cameron full pardons for all activities related to the termination of GrayStar."

Jackson went from barely being able to breathe to exhaling a huge breath that brought about the original condition again. He managed to utter a faltering, "Thank you, Mr. President."

"Officially, I cannot sanction you taking the law into your own hands like you did or some of the measures you took in your quest." He turned to look Jackson eye-to-eye. "Unofficially, you have the thanks of a grateful president. GrayStar was a terrorist organization that never should have been formed, and I'm glad they're gone."

Jackson swallowed.

"I'm going to sign your pardons tomorrow afternoon, and I assure you, the scope is broad and equal to all of you."

"Mr. President, I'm . . . not able to find words, which is unusual for me. Thank you very much, sir."

Rutherford nodded. "I wanted to tell you in person, and to unofficially express my thanks."

"Uh, it feels wrong to say it to you, Mr. President, but you're welcome."

The president nodded again. "Now, am I to understand that you believe your parents are still alive?"

"Yes, sir, I believe they are."

"But you don't know where?"

"No, sir."

"I've asked my press secretary to reach out to you. I can't promise you a declaration from the White House Rose Garden, but she obviously has an array of contacts who might be able to help you get the word out to your parents, or suggest conduits that could help you reach them, liaisons that could facilitate a connection, etcetera—wherever they are."

"I would greatly appreciate that."

Rutherford nodded again. They were halfway around the circle from the plaza to the road.

"Mr. President, at the risk of being too bold, may I say something?"

Rutherford stopped, stuck a hand in his pocket, and nodded.

"Maybe I got my wires crossed, but it was my understanding that you were the one who spearheaded the investigation into GrayStar originally, but that you also backed off that quest in recent years."

The most powerful man in the world bored his eyes into Jackson.

"Um, if I reach into my pocket, am I going to be tackled by four guys I can't even see right now?"

Rutherford shook his head.

Jackson reached for the flash drive Paige had passed him on the beach several days ago. He'd bartered with Deputy Marshal Kingsford for the privileges of using a laptop for a short while under the auspices of composing a letter and saving it to a flash drive. He'd been permitted half an hour with the Wi-Fi disabled, which had been more than enough time to verify the contents of the flash drive containing info from Blackshear, for his eyes only.

"This is for you, sir."

Rutherford took the flash drive. "What's this?"

"Pictures, sir, of the First Lady and an unofficial advisor to Muammar Gaddafi, apparently taken on your visit to Rome in late 2010, shortly before the outbreak of the Libyan Civil War. As far as I know, sir, they are the only copies in existence, procured off GrayStar's server and then erased. Mr. President, I want to be clear I'm not insinuating anything about your wife, sir, and the photos are nothing more than that. But a salacious journalist or a blogger could no doubt form any number of conclusions—conclusions that might seriously hinder a reelection campaign or curb your ability to govern."

"Mr. Douglas, are you suggesting that I was somehow compromised or negligent in my duties because of the existence of these photos?"

"No, sir, I am not. I'm only suggesting that if you *had* felt any pressure by knowledge of their existence, you needn't feel that pressure any longer." He shook his head. "And again, please forgive me if I'm out of line, but I thought you should have this."

Rutherford licked his lips. "Thank you." He pocketed the drive.

"Yes, sir."

They started walking. "Mr. Douglas, you're a free man. I wish you the best in your future endeavors. May I give you two pieces of advice?"

"Of course, sir."

"Number one, try to stay off my radar in the future."

"Yes, sir."

"Number two, if you have the time, stay here at Arlington a little while longer. Because of my presence here, the cemetery is mostly empty. Take the time to wander, to ponder, to contemplate. It's a life-changing experience, I assure you."

"Yes, sir."

Rutherford nodded. "I've instructed the Marshals Service to take you wherever you'd like, whenever you'd like—within reason."

"Yes, sir. Thank you."

Rutherford extended his hand, and Jackson—somewhat unbelievingly—shook it.

"Good luck, Mr. Douglas. I hope your parents are alive and well."

"Thank you, Mr. President, for everything."

Rutherford nodded one final time, then continued walking, more briskly now, back toward the limo. Jackson stood where he was, trying to figure out if the last five minutes had really happened. Five minutes later, the limo and all signs of the Secret Service's presence were gone, leaving just Jackson, Deputy Marshal Walsh, and Deputy Marshal Ross at the base of the John F. Kennedy Eternal Flame memorial.

Jackson slowly walked down to Walsh and Ross. "Do you mind giving me a few minutes to walk and think?"

"Take all the time you need," Walsh said and actually punctuated it with a smile.

Jackson nodded, then crossed the road and followed a narrow, curving drive through row after row after row of grave markers. He found a bench just in time, sat down, buried his head in his hands, and let a host of emotions surge out of him.

Chapter One Hundred Fifty-Two

2:38 p.m.

"CONGRESSWOMAN MASON."

"Heya, Becky."

"Jackson?"

"Guilty as charged. Although, not actually."

There was a slight pause on her end of the line. "What's going on? Where are you?"

"Just down the street and a few blocks north."

"What?"

"I'm in a suite at the Hay-Adams."

"Is this a joke?"

"No, fully legit."

"What are you doing at the Hay-Adams?"

"It was the only hotel I knew in D.C. Senior always stayed here."

"Who?"

"Anthony DiNozzo, Sr.—Robert Wagner . . . on *NCIS*. Although technically I think that was the Adams House Hotel, probably a rip-off—"

"Jackson, I do have a job."

"Sorry, but you asked. You happen to have an open dinner hour, or know of a good arcade in town?"

"I've got a dinner meeting tonight, actually. How long are you in town?"

"Through tomorrow."

"I'm flying back to Kansas tomorrow afternoon. Lunch?"

"Say when and where."

"Let me think. Call you in the morning?"

"This number. See you, Becky."

She went back to work, presumably, and he tried Maggie again. She hadn't answered his first call, but picked up right away this time.

"Jackson?"

"Hey . . ."

"Jack?"

"Sorry, just trying to think what to call you. Honey, baby, sugar, pookie, sweetie—none of them seem right."

"How about Maggie?"

"That works."

"How are you?" she asked. "What's up?"

"Well, I've got good news and bad news."

"What's the bad news?"

"I'm not going to be back for a while yet. At least a week."

"If *that's* the bad news, what's the good news?"

"I've been pardoned."

"What?"

"You, Reggie, and Walker too. Well, as of tomorrow."

"We've been pardoned? Are you sure?"

"POTUS told me himself."

"He told you—You talked to the president?"

"At Arlington. He said he pardoned us all and—off the record—thanked me for taking out GrayStar. Kind of feel bad not voting for him now."

"Oh my goodness. Jack, this is great!"

"I know."

"Baby, it's over."

He said nothing.

"Jack?"

"No, when you call me 'Baby' . . . I don't know, it feels weird, but it kind of works."

"Have you been celebratory drinking?"

"No, but maybe later. I hear the bar here is top-notch."

"Here?"

"I'm at the Hay-Adams. Walking onto my balcony now, looking at the White House, Washington Monument, America the beautiful."

"Jack, I can't believe this."

"Me either."

"So why aren't you coming back right away?"

"I'm going to rent a car and drive. I need some time—this is going to sound weird since I've been thinking nonstop for the last two weeks—but I need some time to think. Now that all the legal stuff is over, I need to process what's happened and what's next. How to get Mom and Dad back, how to re-acclimate to life, apologize to Grandpa for abandoning him for nine months and after his heart attack, come to grips with everything I've done. I've been on full-go mode for so long and I need to decompress."

"I get that."

"And I need to make a couple stops."

"Don't take too long, okay? I miss you."

"I miss you too, Maggie. I cannot wait to see you. I'm going to get you one of those little statues of the White House, and maybe a mug with Rutherford's mug on it."

"Would you, please?"

"I should go. I gotta call Reggie and Walker yet."

"Okay."

"I'll call you tomorrow night, once the pardon's in the bag."

"Okay. Be careful driving. I'd hate for you to survive everything of the last few months only to become the filling in a semi-sandwich on I-80."

"Me too. Thanks for that image."

"You'd do the same for me."

"I would. Okay, going for real this time."

"Right."

"I love you, Maggie."

"I love you too, Jack."

He ended the call and spent a few minutes smiling in the sunshine, drinking in the view, thinking about the future—for once with positivity.

Then he made a couple more joyous phone calls.

*   *   *

6:15 p.m.

JACKSON HAD the house burger at Off the Record, the famous bar at the Hay-Adams, then went for a walk. He wandered through Lafayette Square and spent a few minutes looking at the North Portico of the White House, still unable to believe that the president had taken the time to travel to Arlington National Cemetery solely to meet with *him*. Telling Reggie had made the big man speechless, and Tori had demanded proof before she'd believe it. He'd said wait for the pardon to come.

Looping around the Treasury Building, Jackson headed south on 15th Street, past the Old Ebbitt Grill, where he'd eaten with Becky on his previous visit to D.C. That had been a cold, November day, the exact opposite of the muggy, summer-like evening that was already causing him to sweat through his T-shirt.

He strolled leisurely through The Ellipse, past the Washington Monument, and through the World War II Memorial. It all drew him back to November, when he'd been in the early stages of plotting and researching. He'd never heard of St. Charles or Bryant Hayes or "The Patriot." He'd been alone then, without Maggie, having not met Lexi or teamed up with Eli.

He continued along the Reflecting Pool, reminiscing about all that he'd done and all that his family had been through in the last three years. As he reached the steps leading up to the Lincoln Memorial, his thoughts turned to what was next. How did he get word to his parents that all was clear? Nobody knew where they were, so he couldn't call a secret burn phone or send them a coded e-mail. Was it as simple as using his millions to make a few very public announcements? Would they see an ad in *USA Today*? Would they catch a spot on Fox News or CNN? Maybe he could hire skywriters to blanket all of South America?

He ascended the steps and lingered in the presence of Abraham Lincoln. The man who'd emancipated the slaves and kept the Union knitted together sat like a sage, looking down the mall at the Capitol, as if it was his job to oversee the nation's affairs in perpetuity. Jackson wondered what future generations would think of President Rutherford. Everything he knew about the man—or had known up until meeting him in person—said there wasn't anything remarkable one way the other about Rutherford or his presidency. Would the elimination of GrayStar under his watch—and, ultimately, because of a process he initiated—secure his place among the legends? Or would the world never know what had happened?

Jackson exited the Memorial and stood atop the steps, looking down the Mall, the Washington Monument and the U.S. Capitol glowing in the late-evening sun. He went down the steps, then followed the circular road around the Lincoln Memorial before taking another flight of steps down to the edge of the Potomac River.

The evening had grown hazy, and as the sun descended over Virginia across the river, it turned the sky orange. Traffic on Ohio Drive behind him and on the Arlington Memorial Bridge to his left was muted, as were the sirens in the background and the occasional jet descending along the path of the river to Reagan National. Everything seemed to blur into the background as he watched the river flowing lazily to the south, the tops of the trees on the far bank tinged with sunlight.

Jackson crossed the road and climbed a few steps, then sat and watched the sunset. As it dropped behind the office buildings of Rosslyn, Jackson's thoughts again drifted to his parents. This time, he wasn't thinking about how to notify them, but wondering what if he couldn't? What if they were so far off the grid that he couldn't reach them? What if he'd been wrong and they hadn't survived, or had but had died since? Or gone crazy? Or depressed beyond repair? What if he'd actually pulled off his one-in-a-million long shot, only to have it not pay out?

He couldn't think about that, he decided. He had to keep believing and hoping. And yet, he knew he had to do so with just a touch of restraint, in case his worst fears had come true.

Jackson waited until well after sunset, until darkness had fallen over the nation's capital. Then he retraced his steps back to the hotel, the various monuments and memorials now lit up as beacons to guide him home.

*   *   *

Friday, May 30
9:19 a.m.

JACKSON DREAMT he'd been carving a marble bust of Garrison Rutherford—head, shoulders, and chest on a base shaped like St. Charles so it could float up and down the Reflecting Pool. At least the pool hadn't been red with Maggie's blood while he and Sam played kissy-face in a rowboat following the bust.

He enjoyed a leisurely morning on his balcony, drinking coffee and reading the *Washington Post* to catch up on world affairs. They were largely as he'd left them last year—Russia being a pest while tensions were high in the Middle East, liberals and conservatives at odds over what constituted sex and marriage, and L.A. sports franchises struggling to keep up with their counterparts.

Becky called as he was refilling his cup. She recommended a place called We, the Pizza and asked if Jackson would pick up a pie to go and meet her at the Capitol. They settled on a time and exact place, and he killed half an hour working on the crossword puzzle. He also used a laptop he'd purchased the previous afternoon at a Best Buy (where he'd had Deputies Marshal Walsh and Ross drop him after Arlington) to check on his bank accounts. He had already reached out to the steward Maggie had hired to take care of Vossenhol about getting their stuff back. What to do with the estate—and how—was a decision for later. Right now, the steward and lawyers were sufficiently maintaining things.

A little after eleven, he headed out, taking a taxi to We, the Pizza. He ordered a large pepperoni and mushroom, then walked several blocks back to the Capitol grounds. Becky was waiting for him by the New Jersey Avenue crosswalk. She wore a navy blazer over a red blouse, knee-length skirt to match the blazer, pumps to match both. Her hair was cut shorter, just above the shoulders, which still looked good on her. As did her smile.

She embraced him tightly, forcing him to juggle the pizza. "I can't believe it, Jackson. I have to be honest, I thought I'd never see you again."

"I thought you wouldn't either," he said, nodding toward a bench in the shade. They walked over and sat down, Becky taking off the blazer first. Jackson balanced the pizza box on his lap and passed her napkins and a diet soda.

Becky took a bite, dabbed her lip, and then said, "Tell me everything."

Jackson gave her an abbreviated version, which only took twenty-five minutes. Her eyes kept widening as he went deeper and deeper into recent events, concluding with his last week with the marshals.

"And you're getting a full pardon?"

"I'm off the hook, Becky."

"Wow. You actually did it."

"In large thanks to you, and to Wade. If you hadn't given me that info from Senator Dennis, we may never have been able to do it."

"I owed you after all those air-hockey beatings."

"Yeah, yeah."

She took a final bite of her pizza, leaving the crust in the box with the other. She wiped her mouth again. "So what's next for you?"

"Getting my parents back."

"I meant after that. Once the Douglas Family reunion happens, then what?"

"I don't know."

"You and Maggie . . . ?" she asked with a smirk.

"Did I mention that?"

"Not overtly."

He nodded.

"I'm happy, Jackson. You're a good single guy, but I think you'd make a pretty good married guy too."

"Oh?"

"Anybody who'd do what you did for your family, yeah."

He nodded again.

"I hate to eat and run, but I've got a couple things I have to get done before flying out. It was good to see you, Jackson."

"You too, Becky. If you're ever in L.A. . . . . sneak into my garage and carjack me."

"That's right. I owe you another one."

"I really am sorry."

"I know."

They stood, hugged again, and looked at each other for several seconds. Jackson saw the same girl he'd first seen seven and a half years ago in Hawaii, when she'd been the cute daughter of an aide to a senator who meant nothing to Jackson. Now she was a married congresswoman whose small assist had been crucial in his taking down a band of terrorists and maybe reuniting him with his family. He and Becky had come full circle.

"Don't be a stranger, Jackson."

"You either."

They said goodbye. She lifted her blazer off the back of the bench, and with one last smile and wave, headed back toward the Capitol. Jackson watched her go, then called another cab, and sat down to eat another slice while waiting for it to come.

Chapter One Hundred Fifty-Three

Sunday, June 1
12:27 p.m. (Central Daylight Time)
Tuscaloosa, Alabama

THE CHURCH WAS small and warm, with ceiling fans unable to stir enough air cooled by a pair of window air conditioners in the foyer to mediate it much. And the service was long, nearly ninety minutes, a good half of that sermon. There was another fifteen minutes of prayer, led by a couple of deacons, and not just the simple fluffy, common prayers heard in so many churches. The deacons pleaded with and implored the Lord Almighty to move on behalf of their church, their community, their state, their nation, and the world. There were also a handful of hymns—familiar, unabridged hymns. It felt like the 1980s had come back as Jackson sat in one of the back pews—actual wood pews—and surveyed the congregation.

It was a mixture, maybe two-thirds white and one-third black. They weren't segregated, and from the few interactions he observed, skin color and hair color mattered about the same. Speaking of hair color, it was about two-thirds white as well. Several families or younger couples speckled the sanctuary, but of the sixty or seventy parishioners (that was the term in these parts, Jackson figured) a majority of them were senior citizens. Every last one of them was a stranger, which is what he had expected, and—oddly—both hoped for and against.

He waited patiently after the benediction, letting most of the people file out into the Alabama sunshine. The pastor had exited the sanctuary first, and stood by the front door—in the air-conditioning—to greet his parishioners and bid them a good and godly week. Jackson lingered until he was very nearly in the back of the line, only in front of the elderly pianist and two older but not old guys in blazers chatting about the weather, Alabama's chances in the SEC come fall, and a little politics from what he overheard. Then he approached the pastor.

He'd left D.C. bright and early the previous morning. Or rather, had tried to. After lunch with Becky, he'd taken a cab from the Capitol to a Hertz location, where he'd rented at great cost a Mercedes-Benz E-Class Cabriolet for a cross-country drive. After moving some money around—mere tens of millions—Friday afternoon and officially receiving notification of his pardon (by e-mail, of all things), he'd gone to bed early and checked the convertible out of the Hay-Adams' valet parking at six-thirty Saturday morning, after a light breakfast at The Lafayette. And then he'd navigated the mess of D.C. streets, half of which seemed cordoned off for something official and half of which were under construction. He'd finally gotten clear and exited the city via I-66.

For the first half hour, he'd monitored a Dodge Ram pickup that hung behind him, almost like a tail. He'd tried to convince himself it was paranoia, that no descendent of GrayStar had sought out a farm truck with a Hemi and was stalking him. When he'd switched freeways outside Strasburg, Virginia, and seen no further signs of a tail, he chalked it up to paranoia. His mind at ease, he'd journeyed southeast on I-81 through the Appalachians and parallel to the Blue Ridge Parkway through Roanoke, Knoxville, and Chattanooga before bisecting northeast Alabama. He'd spent the night on the outskirts of Birmingham, weary from the drive and from being alone with his thoughts for an entire day.

All his life, he'd struggled with wondering if the little voice in his head was the Holy Spirit, the devil, or the somewhat helter-skelter brain of Jackson Douglas. Christians were supposed to know, he'd often heard, which brought an entirely different set of concerns. But for the last couple of days, the voice had been giving him conflicting information.

On one hand, it said he'd murdered Bryant Hayes. Murdered him like a coward. Shot him in the back of the head when Hayes was walking away. He'd hunted down GrayStar like animals, baited them into a trap, and maybe even fired the shot that blew most of them to hell. He'd sanctioned—no, ordered—the hit on Laurence Bosco and practically been complicit in the death of Kim McMahon. He'd taken vengeance into his own hands and wielded it as the sword of death.

On the other hand, with McMahon being the possible exception, these men were terrorists. Everyone from Admiral Sullivan to Maggie to the President of the United States to his own father concurred. And while not officially part of an army at war with GrayStar, did one have to be an enlisted soldier to fight terrorism at home or abroad? The president apparently didn't think so. But did God?

Self-defense was always the old justifiable fallback position of Christians, one they could point to in Scripture. And while Jackson's life hadn't been in imminent danger when he'd targeted GrayStar or specifically when he'd shot Hayes, his and other lives had been spared by his actions. He was sure of that. Did that make it right? Did that justify it in God's sight?

He hadn't reached a conclusion on anything, and had spent half an hour coming out of the mountains praying for clarity. Then he'd drifted away to some country music on the Cabriolet's satellite radio.

Sunday morning, he'd been up early to shower and dress properly. He'd felt butterflies in his stomach for a variety of reasons, but was resolved in his heart that this was the right thing to do. He owed it to all parties involved.

"Good afternoon," the preacher said, extending his hand to Jackson. His face was tanned and hard. Maybe seasoned, was a better word for it. He wore something between a smile and a frown, his blue eyes twinkling as he regarded a stranger. His blond hair was longish, combed in a way that reminded Jackson of Robert Redford. He wore a short-sleeved dress shirt, no tie, and dark pants. The shoes looked a decade old. There was nothing fancy about this man of God, but after listening to him preach for three quarters of an hour, Jackson knew he was just that.

"Good afternoon," Jackson said shaking the firm hand. "I'm Jackson Douglas."

"Robert Lee Collins," he said, giving no indication that he was familiar with Jackson's name. "Your first time with us?"

"Yes, sir, it is."

"Well, we're always glad to welcome a new face."

"Thank you. Uh, Reverend Collins—"

"Please, call me Bob. Everyone else does."

"Yes, sir." Jackson took a breath. "I'm not sure if she mentioned it or not, but if you're the right Reverend Collins, I had the great pleasure of making your daughter's acquaintance last spring down in the Keys."

Collins' face beamed. "You knew Sawyer?"

The word "knew"—being past tense—hit Jackson like a bowling ball in the stomach. Collins seemed to sense it. He offered a quick handshake to the two chatty guys in blazers as they finally exited, then nodded for Jackson to take a few steps to the side with him.

Collins cleared his throat. "Sawyer died last fall."

Jackson swallowed hard.

"Pancreatic cancer, came on suddenly. Felt just awful one night, and we both thought she'd had too much pulled pork during the Tennessee game. It was much worse by morning, and we took her into the hospital. They ran a number of tests and panels, finally determined she had an aggressive tumor and . . . two weeks later, she was gone."

Collins kept a straight face as he said it, but Jackson had no idea how. He felt like his insides had been melted with a ray gun. He only managed to mutter, "I'm . . . so sorry for your loss," aware that Collins had also lost a wife to a drunk driver when Sawyer was very young.

"Thank you, Jackson. You know, there isn't a day goes by that I don't miss my little girl." He paused for a moment, hand over his mouth, composing himself. "The only thing that keeps me going, aside from my work and the knowledge that I'll see my baby again someday, is being grateful the good Lord allowed me all the days with her that He did. Every one of them was a treasure."

"I only knew Sawyer for a week or so, but I'd have to say the same is true. She was quite a woman."

Collins nodded, his eyes glistening. Then he smiled. "So, Jackson, what brings you to Tuscaloosa on this fine June day?"

"I was actually hoping to talk to you, sir, figuring Sawyer would be down in the Keys. If you don't have plans, could I buy you lunch?"

"I reckon that would do. There's a delicious barbecue shack just down the street a piece."

"That works for me."

Jackson waited for a few minutes while Collins made sure everyone had left and locked up the small church. Then they walked five minutes to a corner barbecue shack, which was being kind to the dilapidated old building. But the look didn't deter the customers. A three-hundred-pound black woman everyone called "Mom" served them up baskets of ribs, fries, and slaw, which they took along with sweating glasses of sweet tea over to a picnic table under the shade of a giant oak tree.

While they ate, Jackson explained how he and Sawyer had met, looking for their missing friend Ben, then for the pirate treasure they believed was responsible for his death. Or, more accurately, looking for the people hunting the pirate treasure. For whatever reason, Sawyer hadn't mentioned their adventures to her father, nor told him about meeting Jackson. Presumably, she also hadn't told him about the letter she'd written as means of a goodbye. So Jackson didn't either, instead recounting their time in Florida, New Orleans, and the Bahamas. The tale brought smiles, chuckles, and a few tears to Collins' eyes. As did Jackson's conclusion.

"She left me with all the gold, all but a single doubloon. She said she didn't want it. She liked her life the way it was, uncomplicated, without the trappings of wealth. She begged me not to track her down and try to give her money back."

"And yet, that's what you're doing?" Collins asked.

"In a manner of speaking." Jackson then gave the most succinct, sanitized account of the last year that he could, explaining how his parents and brother had been presumed dead but weren't actually, and how he had gone after GrayStar to free them and to rid the world of terrorists. Collins was a bit taken aback, but his eyes revealed belief, not skepticism.

"Everything we did to stop GrayStar and hopefully get my parents back, we were able to do because I had millions of dollars at my disposal. That treasure Sawyer and I found served as a . . . golden key that opened the door to possibility. Without it—without her—this wouldn't have been possible. And so I came here today, sir, because I wanted a chance to repay her."

"I thought you said you didn't think she'd be here."

"I didn't. Sawyer was the quintessential refined Southern woman, but she could be . . ."

"Stubborn?" Collins asked with a hint of a grin.

"I was looking for a different word, but that works. I thought maybe if I gave it to you instead, you'd see that she took it or at least directed it somewhere. I didn't expect she'd change her mind and suddenly take on the lifestyle of a millionaire, but I thought she might want a say in where some of that money goes. Half of what we found is still rightly hers."

Collins sat back and wiped his mouth with a napkin. He crumpled it in the empty basket. "In that case, I'm sorry you wasted a trip."

"Nothing's wasted. From what I knew of Sawyer, she inherited most of her character from you. So I don't expect you'll get wide-eyed at the thought of millions either. But I would be greatly honored, Bob, if you'd take Sawyer's 'cut.' We're going to be donating over one hundred million dollars to charity, and I'd like for you—in her stead—to decide where some of that goes. Buy central air or a new organ for your church, take care of the poor in the community, give Alabama football tickets to veterans—whatever you want to do. Whatever you think Sawyer would want to do."

"That's mighty generous, Jackson, but . . . I'm not sure I'd begin to know what to do with that much money. If you donated a couple hundred or couple thousand dollars in the offering plate, I'm sure our church could find a use for it. But you're talking a lot more zeroes."

"Would you think about it?" Jackson asked. "I'll give you my contact information, and if you decide yes, I'll send the money. Or if you don't want to handle it, send me a list of charities or needs, and I'll send the money."

Collins nodded. "I'll think about it."

"Thank you, sir."

The preacher took a long drink of tea, draining his glass. "You have someplace to stay in town?" he asked.

"I'm actually passing through. I have an appointment down in Baton Rouge this evening."

"Baton Rouge. Them's fightin' words around here."

"Yes, sir," Jackson said with a grin.

They took their empties back to the counter, then walked back to the church, where their cars were the only two left in the dirt lot beside the building. Collins again extended his hand. "It was a pleasure to meet you, Jackson."

"You as well, sir."

"If you're ever back down this way again, please stop by."

"I will. And please, don't hesitate to give me a call if you think of a use for that money."

Collins nodded in agreement. Then they said goodbye and headed their separate ways. For Jackson, that was back on the interstate, southeast toward Meridian, Mississippi. He still felt a sadness in his soul that Sawyer was gone.

Not for her. That rich, pure, Southern voice was singing with the angels now, and putting them to shame. Not even so much for her father, although that was part of it, since he seemed to be handling it and coping so well.

No, Jackson was sad for himself. Sad that another "piece" of him was gone. He'd been nervous about the possibility of running into Sawyer, because as much as he loved Maggie, he couldn't deny that there had been a draw to the dignified Southern woman who'd captured his heart if not his romantic affections last May. Part of him had hoped she would be there, so he could see her, his resolve could stand the test, and he could close the chapter on her for good. Turned out, that story was long over.

The sadness lifted as he crossed into the Magnolia State. Closure was a concept with which he'd never been too familiar, but he guessed this was it. Sawyer was gone, in a better place by far. And their relationship, platonic as it had been, was gone too. And he was in a better place, in so many ways.

But he had one more page still to turn.

Chapter One Hundred Fifty-Four

7:39 p.m.
Baton Rouge, Louisiana

THE AIR HUNG thick and oppressive over the Deep South. Humid didn't begin to describe it. Not a flutter of breeze stirred the leaves on magnolia trees in a grove to Jackson's right, and the Spanish moss cloaking the large oak to his left hung straight down. The evening sun was filtered by haze, but still fiery as it cast long shadows across the grounds.

He had driven from Tuscaloosa with just one stop, for gas and an ice cream cookie sandwich in Hattiesburg. Heading south on I-59, then west on I-12 through the toe of Louisiana, he'd thought about the various women who had entered his life and how they'd impacted him. Maggie was obvious, and they'd even discussed how her coming into his life had changed the course of his. And Sawyer, aside from helping him find his initial funding, had given him a morale boost just when he'd needed it most.

Sam, Ashley, Tori—all female friends bordering or drifting into more at times, each of whom had helped his career or molded his life. Becky, a brief, moderate crush turned congressional confidant who had been instrumental in his recent quest. Even Hillary, for all their bickering and backbiting, had come to his aid when he'd needed her. And Paige, her gentle belief and encouragement as valuable as her legal aid in a couple times of need.

Then there was the woman he was visiting now, so to speak, United States Marine Corporal Alexandra J. Hunter. Her grave marker wasn't any different from any of the others in the area, all plain and nondescript. The only difference was hers was newer, the grass around it a little greener. It'd been less than three months since she'd died, and Blackshear had confirmed just a few days ago—Jackson had no idea how—that her body had been recovered from Grenada and given a proper burial in the city where she and her late mom had been born, Baton Rouge. Jackson knew the body or the remains or whatever was left in the ground in front of him wasn't Lexi—her soul was gone. And he knew she couldn't hear anything he said. Yet there he was, standing alone in the cemetery, sweating through his T-shirt, clutching a small bouquet of purple and yellow flowers.

He still felt responsible for Lexi's death. He'd sought her out, and while he hadn't enlisted her, he'd gladly accepted her as part of his team. He hadn't dissuaded her from coming to Colombia, and hadn't protected her while there. He knew she wouldn't have let him take the blame, yet he felt he bore at least a share of it.

And yet, as he stood there looking at the *fleur-de-lis* etched onto her grave marker, he realized that Lexi, the former Marine, had died fighting for freedom, fighting for her "brothers." She'd lived bravely and died bravely, and without her—like without so many others—Jackson wouldn't be where he was now.

"I know you can't hear me, Lexi," he said after looking around to make sure he was alone, "and I know it's stupid to talk to a person who can't hear you. But for my sake, I need to get this off my chest." He swallowed and took a breath. "Thank you. Thank you for giving your life for me . . . for my family. We will never forget you."

He took a deep breath, then knelt down and placed the flowers by her tombstone. He'd already tasked Blackshear, to whom he'd given an extra million for his post-takedown work, to work with the lawyer he'd hired to maintain the trust in the U.S. Virgin Islands to find any living relative of Lexi's and give them her share of the money they'd taken from the *Pórtico Dorado* Cartel. That failing, he could give the money to some or other charity in her honor.

Jackson stood, looking at the flowers. From Tuscaloosa to Baton Rouge in an afternoon, from a dead Bama fan to a dead Tiger fan. What a strange world.

He lingered for a few moments in the tranquility of the cemetery, thinking how different it was than the one he'd been in a few days ago. Then he turned and walked for his car, hoping very much to never visit another cemetery ever again.

*　　　　　*　　　　　*

Monday, June 2
5:20 a.m.

JACKSON LEFT Baton Rouge before sunrise. He'd buried, figuratively, Sawyer and Lexi the night before, in part thanks to a talk with Maggie. It was like he'd told her before, had things played out differently, he may have fallen for one of them or Sam or some woman he'd never met. But no matter what stirrings or feelings he felt, every time he saw Maggie or talked to her, his doubts vanished.

They'd also kicked around some ideas for contacting David and Hannah. Then he'd called Grant, talking to him for the first time since Grant's quick update call from *The Explorer of the Seas*. The brothers caught up for a while and also talked about ways to reunite the family. Now, as Jackson crossed into Texas and began looking for a place to find fuel for both himself and his convertible, he did more of the same.

He gave long odds that President Rutherford's press secretary would actually call him, but certainly if she did, any ideas she had would be pushed to the top of the list. In the meantime, he planned to utilize Maggie. She was already reaching out to various contacts at Fox and from her days at the *L.A. Times*, and had garnered interest from Megyn Kelley and Jake Tapper, as well as several colleagues with the *Times*, and there had been a rumor about a possible appearance by Jackson as the "one lucky guy" on Fox's new midday hit, *Outnumbered*. While a press tour had some minor appeal, the real boon would be the chance to put his face on TV and announce that GrayStar was gone.

Jackson had also asked Maggie to look into using a few of his dollars to put out ads on TV stations and in major newspapers around the world. If David and Hannah were holed up in a mountain shack, it would do no good, but if they had access to any form of media, Jackson didn't want to risk missing an opportunity. And Maggie, being the media expert, knew more about that than he did. (Blackshear had offered to hack various newspapers and plant stories, but Jackson had decided to keep things aboveboard.)

He hit the Greater Houston Area around rush hour, and had to focus on traffic. Then he had a couple hours of Texas ranchland and farmland to once more ponder his options. He debated trying to reach out to Marcus Chase again, the man whose safe house David and Hannah had utilized in Argentina. But after being burned there, he doubted David would go back to Chase. Still, he kicked the idea around.

He blew through San Antonio around noon, but pressed on, stopping for lunch at a Sonic outside Junction, Texas. He stretched his legs for fifteen minutes, sweating through his T-shirt in the process. Then he continued west on I-10 through terrain that grew more barren by the mile. Under a wide, hazy, Texas sky, Jackson's thoughts again shifted to the moral question of what he'd done.

He didn't feel guilty, but felt like he should feel guilty. Was that a partially quenched Holy Spirit fighting to keep Jackson's pilot light going? Or was it years of being taught the rule without much focus on the rare exceptions?

He cruised into El Paso as the sun was setting, having put a thousand miles on the odometer in one day. He downed a burger at a restaurant next door to his motel, then sacked out and slept so soundly he didn't dream about Davy Crockett or John Wayne or the ladies on Fox's *Outnumbered*.

*   *   *

Tuesday, June 3
8:14 p.m. (Pacific Daylight Time)

JACKSON DEPARTED El Paso as the sun was rising on the Sun Bowl. He stopped three-quarters of an hour later to pick up breakfast in Las Cruces, then blasted west across the New Mexico desert. He followed the interstate into Tucson, then north to Phoenix, and grabbed lunch in the western suburbs. He had spent the morning reminiscing, and the two towns he'd used as landing spots on his scouting trip to Mexico only brought more memories to mind—memories from eight and nine months that felt like eight and nine years ago.

I-10 led across more barren desert, and Jackson stopped once near the state line to get gas and ice cream that melted before he got it back to the car. He drove through Blythe, a green valley in the midst of the desert, the town where his grandpa had been born. Thinking of Leroy both saddened him and filled him with hope. That hope was dimmed by uncertainty. Would he be able to get his family back? Would they be like the family of old, or would years and separation and the stress have changed David and Hannah forever? Would Leroy be his old self, or a frail version thereof post heart attack? And could Jackson, after having played a combination of Jason Bourne and Jack Bauer for the better part of a year, go back to being a smart-aleck P.I. with a pretty girl at his side?

The weirdness started when Jackson reached the sprawl of L.A.'s eastern suburbs—Redlands, San Bernardino, Ontario, Pomona, West Covina. After hours and hours and hours in the desert, city traffic felt foreign. But more than that, familiar places felt foreign. He'd left L.A. back in September, not knowing if he'd ever return. Now, to be driving back home—well, it was beyond surreal.

He stopped for something to eat, then cruised through downtown. Seeing such buildings as U.S. Bank Tower and Bank of America Plaza took the weirdness to a new level. Now he was on familiar turf, the Santa Monica Freeway. Exhausted and tired of sitting, he crossed the 405 and then was in Santa Monica, approaching the coast. I-10 became Highway 1 and turned north, and there was the Pacific Ocean, sparkling in the evening sun.

He thought about stopping at Cameron's, but he'd already eaten and was too tired for a reunion. Besides that, his emotions were suddenly out of whack, and he didn't feel like seeing anyone.

Jackson followed Chautauqua Boulevard into the hills of Pacific Palisades, and found his hands shaking as he turned onto Ridgeline Drive. The old neighborhood looked just the same as it always had—same neighbors out mowing their lawns, same cars parked beside the street, same trees casting shade across the road.

Then Connie's house was on the left. She was not outside, but would be sure to notice a bright blue Mercedes-Benz E-Class Cabriolet in his driveway. So he parked at the curb across the street, then collected his cup of watered down soda and a duffel bag with his basic belongings. He listened to the faraway whine of a lawnmower, the chirping of birds, a siren somewhere in the city as he crossed the street and approached his front door. He paused for a moment, unable to believe that this was really happening.

He entered the security code and applied his thumb to the automatic lock and opened the door, then stepped into his house.

After eight months and twenty-five days, Jackson was home.

Chapter One Hundred Fifty-Five

Wednesday, June 4
8:09 a.m. (Pacific Daylight Time)
Los Angeles, California

IT HADN'T BEEN late, but Jackson had been bushed. So after getting home the night before, he'd called Maggie to let her know he was home. They'd planned on getting together for brunch and to strategize at her new apartment, which he hadn't seen. Then he'd shaved the mess of beard off his face, showered, and crawled into his own bed to sleep as long as possible.

Wednesday's plans were blown a little after eight when Jackson's doorbell woke him from the most wonderful sleep he'd ever imagined. It took him several moments to wake up fully, then to stagger out of bed and look down to see if he was decent. He concluded not as the doorbell rang again, and threw on the first thing he found—yesterday's dirty clothes.

He took his time going down the steps as he debated the possibilities— Maggie surprising him with steaming hot coffee and a good-morning kiss; Reggie doing the same, sans kiss; someone from the Department of Justice to take back the pardon; Bryant Hayes' illegitimate son armed with a Spas-12.

It was a pan of sticky buns, still steaming, the aroma better than a good-morning kiss from anyone. The pan was held by a rotund woman in white skorts and a zebra-pattern blouse. Her hair was Lucille Ball red, and a clown troupe's worth of makeup was already starting to run as tears flooded her eyes.

"My goodness, I knew it was true!" Connie said. She stepped inside without being invited, flailing the pan around with one oven-mitted hand while grabbing Jackson with the other and engulfing him in a hug. "Boy, where have you been?"

"Hi, Connie. It's, uh . . . a long story."

She released him and headed through the living room toward his dining table.

"How did you know I was home?"

"I saw the lights last night and saw your new car. It wasn't Reggie's, and the women have stopped coming."

"How did you know I didn't sell the house?" he asked as he trailed her to the kitchen.

"There was no for-sale sign. Do you have coffee? I couldn't carry a thermos."

If he did, it was a year old, but he didn't tell her that as he entered the kitchen and opened the cupboard where he kept it. A small can of generic-brand coffee was sitting next to a new bag of filters. A Post-it note was stuck to the can:

Cheap crap, but figured your palette wouldn't know the difference. – Reg

Jackson grinned and set about brewing a pot while Connie found plates and forks and served up sticky buns. "So, where have you been, Jackson? I thought you were in a Mexican prison."

"I was."

"Then . . ." She looked out the window, as if it held an explanation. "How—I mean, where . . . ?"

"Have a seat, Connie. I'll explain everything. Just let me call Maggie first."

"Maggie? Why Maggie?"

"I'll explain."

Connie's eyes twinkled.

"Just let me call her first. This is going to take a while."

*   *   *

12:20 p.m.

"SO SHE just made a pan of sticky buns in case it was you?" Maggie asked.

"Well, baking to Connie is like waving to a neighbor for anyone else."

"You tell her everything?"

"Within reason."

"How'd she take it?"

"I think she's still in shock. Hopefully she'll bake as therapy; I have nothing in the house."

Maggie leaned forward, her chin on her hand. They were seated at a table at The Original Pantry Café on Figueroa, their brunch at her place transformed to a lunch out. "When are you going to talk to your grandpa?"

"Tonight, after Grant's shift."

"Is he back with LAPD?"

Jackson nodded, reaching for some fries. "He's bringing him to Cameron's."

"Does he know yet?"

"Yeah. Grant eased him into it."

"Had to be a shock," she said, then sat back with her milkshake. She took a slurp.

"Wait till we give him the full story that Mom and Dad might still be alive."

"Mm, speaking of," she said, sticking the shake back on the table. "I talked with an exec pretty high up at Fox this morning. "They really want you on *Outnumbered*. It'd be a great platform for you. But it's filmed in New York."

"Can't they remote me in?"

"Kind of loses the appeal when you're not sitting on the couch in the middle of the four women."

"Tell me about it."

She kicked him under the table.

"Anything else?"

"*USA Today* reached out about a multi-part feature about everything that happened, and there are a few people talking about a book deal for me, for you, for us. But that's not a right-now proposition. You hear anything from Cathy DeVane?"

"Who?"

"Rutherford's press secretary."

"No, not yet."

"What about Admiral Sullivan? Did you try talking to him?"

"No. That's not a bad idea, though."

"I also put in a couple calls to Bret Baier's people. They seemed to like me the few times I was on his show, so maybe I can get him to mention something."

"I still think an ad blitz might be the best idea. I mean, if I'm on Bret Baier or *Outnumbered*, there's a good chance Mom and Dad could miss things. But if I spend a quarter of a million dollars on full-page ads in a thousand newspapers . . ."

"You drop a quarter mil pretty easy."

"I'm rich now, remember?"

"That mean you won't be asking me to tip?"

"You're rich too."

She sighed. "How rich are we again?"

"That's what I like about you, Mags, so down to earth you don't even know how much you're worth. Like the knockout who doesn't know she's beautiful."

"*Like* the knockout?"

He shrugged. "You know you're beautiful."

This time he moved his shin before she could kick it.

"I wired ten mil to your account and another ten mil to mine. Then there's still ninety million in the St. Charles bank—assuming they haven't seized our assets—which will all go to charity. And then there's the diamonds GrayStar so thoughtfully left behind."

"What happened to them?"

"They must have dropped the briefcase somewhere in their flight. Blackshear found it the next morning and put them in a safe deposit box in the bank, where they still are."

"Whose are they?"

"I doubt we can figure out where GrayStar got them from, so my thoughts are to donate them to the people of St. Charles, as a thank you."

"You mean an 'I'm sorry'?"

"Either one."

Maggie reached for one of his fries. "I guess a quarter mil isn't a huge amount to part with."

"I'll give away every penny to get Mom and Dad back."

"You remember Jake at the *Times*?"

"Don't think we ever met."

"He's their political correspondent. He and I are meeting for coffee this afternoon, and I'll talk to him about ads."

"The political correspondent?"

"He's not in advertising, but can connect me. And he is the political guy. Plus he's someone at the *Times* who will take my calls."

"Hmm. Coffee with him. Should I be jealous?"

Maggie grinned. "No. Jake doesn't make anywhere near your kind of money."

*   *   *

5:41 p.m.

JACKSON PICKED up the silver convertible as he turned onto Chautauqua. It followed him when he turned onto the Pacific Coast Highway, then hung a few car-lengths back even though Jackson cruised along at the speed limit.

None of that meant anything. Lots of cars took Chautauqua to the PCH. Some of them went the speed limit. Even a few convertibles.

And yet, Jackson couldn't shake the thought that something was off.

So he kept driving and hung a left on the California Incline. The convertible followed, which wasn't all that unusual either. No more unusual than someone using a silver convertible for a tail job.

He tried not to panic. There was no reason to think anyone was following him, no reason to suspect a GrayStar orphan or another Mia was out there, plotting revenge. And if they were, they wouldn't tail him; they'd hide behind a bush and blow his head off one morning when he stepped outside. That thought didn't do much to mollify him.

He turned left on Ocean Avenue, since he had time to kill anyhow. After meeting with Maggie, he'd spent the afternoon taking care of errands—squaring his utilities accounts, stocking the fridge, and looking for a car since he couldn't drive a rental forever. He was due for dinner at six, but certainly didn't want to lead a tail there. So, since he had a few extra minutes, he decided to put his brain at ease.

He drove north on Ocean, with Palisades Park on the left and condos on the right. The convertible remained behind him, which didn't become weird until he kept going past Inspiration Point and curved east, and the convertible kept with him. He accelerated, and the convertible matched pace. At the next intersection, he was stopped at a red light, and finally got a good look at the driver of the convertible.

Well, sort of. It was a bearded man with sunglasses and a baseball cap with a logo he couldn't identify, meaning it could be anyone. Without staring, Jackson memorized the license plate number—it was a California plate. Then, as soon as the light turned, he peeled out.

He was now headed back toward the coast on West Channel Road, making a loop, and confirming the silver convertible was tailing him. Jackson had the wheels to try it, so he made a last-second right turn onto Sycamore and raced as fast as he dared through a residential neighborhood. When Sycamore dead ended, he made a left onto Rustic. Both times, the silver convertible hung with him, the driver no longer hiding the fact that he was on Jackson's tail.

Rustic emptied back onto West Channel Road, and Jackson made the turn with screeching tires and horns blaring at him, but still the convertible kept up. He thought about calling the cops, or calling Reggie to run interference, or maybe seeing if his convertible was faster. But he caught a break where Channel, Chautauqua, and the PCH all intersected. The light turned just as he arrived, and he raced through on a red arrow, very nearly causing an accident. The silver convertible was forced to stay behind, and, given the length of the light, Jackson had at least a two-minute head start.

He didn't waste it, speeding up for the three-quarter mile drive. He veered into the parking lot of Cameron's and found a parking spot where a large SUV shielded him from the highway. He took a minute to put the top up on the Cabriolet, then leaned over to peek through his passenger side-view mirror. He waited for several minutes until he saw the silver convertible cruise by on the PCH, showing no signs of slowing down.

Exhaling for the first time in a while, Jackson got out and headed inside. It was not paranoia; he was being followed. That didn't mean it was GrayStar, but it was definitely worth checking out. He pulled out his phone and sent a quick text to Blackshear, asking him to run the plates. In the old days, he'd have asked Mouse or Connie, but he hadn't talked to Mouse in months and Connie—well, that would be too many questions. And Blackshear was the best.

"Jackson!"

He turned to see a young woman with long, blond hair and a bright smile behind the hostess desk.

"I haven't seen you in ages!" she said, coming around to give him a hug. That was more of a greeting than they'd ever exchanged, but he didn't mind.

"Hi, Katie."

"You look good."

"So do you," he said, noting the black cocktail dress that gave her a beautiful yet professional look. "Your promotion fall through?"

"You heard about that?" she said, her smile widening.

He nodded.

"We've had a couple people call in sick today, so we're spread thin."

"Well, I always did think you had the perfect smile for the hostess desk."

"Thank you."

"And you'll do great as the big cheese. Congrats."

"Thanks," she said again. "Reggie's got the banquet room reserved. You remember where it is?" she asked, her grin now cockeyed.

"I'll find my way."

He gave her a wink, then climbed the stairs. Instead of entering the main dining room, he took the hall to the right to a private banquet room. The room was capable of seating up to forty or fifty people, depending on the arrangement, and was often rented out for parties. In this case, it had been reserved for a private dinner of three.

The room was empty, save for a single round table set as if at a fancy banquet. Jackson picked up one of several forks, tinked a glass with it for no reason, and then set it down and walked to the window. The view looked down on the beach and at the Pacific Ocean a hundred yards away. As always, the waves were mesmerizing.

A clearing throat drew Jackson's attention away from the ocean and to the door where Grant stood off to the side, dressed in his uniform, which likely meant he'd gotten off late. He looked like the old Grant—hair trimmed, face shaven, muscular and strong. He looked like a recruiting poster.

But Jackson's focus wasn't on his brother. It was on the seventy-six-year-old man who, while a little bit thinner than he remembered, looked just as spry and maybe a bit more ornery than he remembered. As usual, he wore a pair of jeans and a plain T-shirt, with a pocket on the breast—what passed for ornamentation. The hair was maybe a touch grayer, but the eyes were just as vivid as they regarded Jackson.

He felt his heart skip a beat, wondering what sort of response he'd get after nine months. Then all fears were removed when Leroy Douglas smiled wide and said, "Hey, bud."

Chapter One Hundred Fifty-Six

7:38 p.m.

AFTER HUGS AND backslaps and even a few tears, the three Douglas men had sat down to a feast of beef tenderloin, garlic mashed potatoes, and roasted green beans almondine. While they ate, the brothers told Leroy of their belief that David and Hannah were still alive and their reasons for keeping it quiet originally. He waved off their apologies, and then Jackson's when he expressed his regret at not being around during and after Leroy's heart attack, and for not having contact for so long. That had naturally led to Jackson recapping his adventures. Most of what he said was news to Grant too, and it was hard for Jackson to tell who was more shocked and amazed, his brother or his grandpa.

"So that's it?" Leroy asked as they were finishing decadent slices of cherry cheesecake. "You took out these GrayStar fellas, so now your mother and dad are free to come in from the cold?"

"Yeah," Jackson said.

"That lacked conviction."

He had been debating bringing up the silver convertible, but decided against it until he knew who the driver was and what his motive was. So he instead covered with an explanation of how he and Maggie were anticipating reaching out to them.

"They want you to sit on a couch with four women?" Leroy asked.

Jackson nodded.

"And you turned this down?"

"What can I say, Grandpa, I'm a one-woman man now."

"Um-hmm." He took a drink of coffee. He looked from Jackson to Grant, then back.

"Something on your mind, Grandpa?" Grant asked.

"To have it just be one thing."

"Right?" Jackson said.

"But foremost, I have a question, and I want you boys to level with me."

"Of course," Grant said as Jackson nodded.

"This a pipe dream, getting your folks back?"

"You think I did all this for a pipe dream?" Jackson asked.

"I think you would have, yeah."

Jackson raised his eyebrows. "Yeah, probably." He sighed. "I'm convinced they were alive, that they made it out of the tunnel."

"Me too," Grant said. "We had the DNA sample."

"But it's been a year," Jackson said. "And change. And we have no idea where they went from that tunnel, what shape they were in."

"What's your gut tell you?" Leroy asked.

"His gut?"

"He's always been pretty good with a hunch."

"My hunch is they're alive. Dad's savvy and determined, and Mom's tough and fierce in a loving wife and mother sort of way."

"I agree," Grant said.

"I was going to ask what your brain said."

"I think I'm hurt," Jackson said.

"For the reasons Jackson just said, yeah, I think they're alive."

Leroy nodded and reached for his coffee cup again. "Okay then."

"Your heart going to hold up if we knock on your door with Mom and Dad some night?" Jackson asked.

"I hope to find out."

"Me too."

Their waiter took that moment to drop back into the room. "You gents need anything else?" Reggie asked.

"Yeah," Leroy said. "You to pull up a chair."

"I'd love to, but we're still in the dinner rush."

"We're good, Hoss."

"Room's yours for the night, so stay as long as you want. And see me before you leave, J. I got something for you."

Jackson nodded, Reggie left, and the trio went back to catching up, this time on some of the minor details of Jackson's quest to hunt down GrayStar—details he'd left out the first time. He answered all of Leroy and

Grant's questions, then asked a few about their experiences the last nine months, especially Grant's return to LAPD and his re-courtship of Hillary.

Finally, a little after nine, Leroy subtly hinted that it was closing in on his bedtime. The trio headed out of the banquet room, planning to split up so Jackson could go find Reggie. But Katie met them at the door, coming out of the main dining room.

"Hey, you all have a good dinner?"

"Yes, ma'am."

"Good. I'll see if Reggie's free. He has a surprise for you," she said with a wink at Jackson.

"Sure about that one-woman man bit?" Leroy asked as she headed down the stairs.

"I was actually thinking she'd have made Grant a good match. Still time to change your mind, bro."

"She's more your type."

"All women are Jack's type," Leroy said.

"Just the good-looking ones."

"Same old Jackson," Grant said.

"Would you want anything different?" he asked, looking at his brother.

With a smile, Grant shook his head.

"You guys heading out?" Reggie asked as he climbed to the top of the stairs.

"Not until I get my surprise."

"This way."

Reggie led them downstairs and out to the parking lot, which had thinned. The SUV that had blocked Jackson's convertible from the road was long gone but, then again, so too was the silver convertible in all likelihood. They turned right, away from where Jackson had parked, and around the corner to the south side of the restaurant. Reggie stepped around to the side of a large sheet draped over a vehicle and yanked it off with a flourish.

Shining under the lights mounted to the side of the building was the candy-apple red paint of a 1976 Ford Granada. It was polished to look factory new. The tires *were* new, including radiant whitewalls. The chrome bumper and door handles sparkled. Even the white vinyl roof looked straight off the assembly line. And yet, one look at Reggie's face told Jackson this wasn't a car from a collector's showroom, but *his* Granada, last seen at the parking lot of *El Saguaro* in Ensenada. To top it off, he'd even replaced the long-lost nebulous hood ornament.

"How . . ." Jackson said. "Where did you find it?"

"Wasn't easy, J. But I had a few days while you were gallivanting across the country. I went down to Mexico, poked around a little, found it at a used car lot. Apparently Mexicans don't appreciate classic cars."

"Mexicans don't . . . Never mind." He finally looked up from the car. "Thanks, Hoss."

"I even got the engine tuned for you. Might be able to coax it to highway speeds."

"Maybe you can take that girl of yours to the picture show in that," Leroy said.

"Don't you find it odd to be cracking on the car you gave somebody?" Jackson asked.

"It was supposed to be a starter car, not a lifelong love."

"This car is memories, Grandpa. You, me, Grant, and Grandma driving to get ice cream; you and me just bumming around on a summer evening with Scully on the radio; hearing you say 'Cottonpickin thing,' whenever you'd burn your hand on the metal seatbelt. You can't put a price on that."

"You can," Reggie said. "Couple dozen thousand pesos."

"Seriously, Reg, this tears."

"You do for family, ain't that right, J?"

"Always."

Reggie nodded and tossed him the keys. "Take her for a spin?"

Jackson caught them with a wide grin, for the moment forgetting his nerves the last time he'd been behind the wheel.

*   *   *

Friday, June 6
8:20 p.m.

THE NEXT couple days were absolutely crazy.

White House Press Secretary Cathy DeVane woke Jackson up at eight-thirty on Thursday morning. It took him a moment to catch up and realize what was going on. DeVane was professionally quick yet friendly and gave

Jackson several ideas and contacts. He and Maggie, along with Jake La Canfora, the *Times* political correspondent, spent the afternoon making calls and arranging interviews. Jackson also utilized Blackshear to (legally) put ads in over a thousand newspapers around the world.

Speaking of Blackshear, he'd called back shortly after Jackson got home Wednesday night. The silver convertible's license plate traced back to a reporter for a local rag called the *City of Angels Weekly*. Conceivably, he had been trying to track down Jackson for a circulation-boosting interview. At any rate, unless the car had been stolen, Jackson's tail had not represented a threat from GrayStar. He'd slept much easier knowing that.

Friday, Jackson did several remote interviews on Fox News shows, as well as with Ronan Farrow from MSNBC and with *WGN Morning News*. Feeling out of place in a shirt and tie and intimidated by the camera in a small studio at KCBS, Jackson answered whatever questions the interviewers asked. In exchange, they each gave him a few seconds to issue a plea to his parents. "Mom and Dad, GrayStar has been neutralized and it's safe to come back. Wherever you are, please reach out. Herman the shark is dead." It varied marginally by network and host, but each let him make the plug. He had another interview scheduled Saturday on *Fox & Friends*, and a few more possibilities the next week, in case David and Hannah didn't happen to be in front of a TV on Friday.

The ads were full-pagers, color where possible, and contained the same basic message about Herman the shark, a nod to a *Magnum, P.I.* episode where, coincidentally enough, Magnum lamented his father's death. Jackson hoped it would prove to David that his message wasn't coerced or some sort of trap. The ads were scheduled to run in every other edition for two weeks, in the hopes that David would buy at least a weekly paper wherever he was living.

And, thanks to Jake and, more significantly, Cathy DeVane, the story of Jackson's takedown of GrayStar would be pushed from hundreds of news outlets in Latin and South America, and more than two dozen in Europe, Asia, and Africa.

Even so, Jackson knew it was very possible David and Hannah would miss the news, would question it, would be hesitant. He had some Plan B's percolating in his brain for just such an occasion, but he knew he had to give it time.

Friday night after the last interview, Jackson and Maggie got in the Granada and cruised up the PCH. Reggie had not souped up the A/C in the forty-year-old car, so they drove with windows down, the balmy evening air rushing over them as the sun dipped into the hazy horizon. They got ice cream at a place by the marina in Santa Barbara, then went for a walk on the beach as the moon rose over the mountains to the east. They talked about little things—not strategy and contingencies and who to trust or not trust and how far was too far. The evening was magical, and Jackson felt like life was returning to normal.

Now, to make it all the way back . . .

*   *   *

Sunday, June 8
2:19 p.m.

GRANT WAS picking up some overtime, so it was just Jackson and Leroy sitting on the upper deck of his houseboat on a beautiful afternoon. Jackson had gone to his old church that morning, for the first time in ages, taped a quick hit to air on several news stations the following morning, then grabbed a late lunch for the two of them—subs from Jersey Mike's.

There had been no word from David or Hannah yet, but it had only been a couple days. Jackson tried to console himself with reasons why they might not have seen his ads and interviews or would have taken their time to reach out. He refused to panic that they were dead for at least two weeks. One minimum.

"Something on your mind, bud?" Leroy asked, having finished his sub, while Jackson nibbled at his.

"Yeah, kind of."

"That's what I'm here for."

Jackson put down the last quarter of his sub. "Something's been kind of bugging me for a while, and one of the songs in church drove it home. When I was a kid, the Rams were playing the Falcons, in the Deion years."

"You all sang a song about Deion Sanders in church, did you?"

Jackson leveled a gaze at his grandpa. "I'm going somewhere with this."

"Just making sure."

"The Rams were down like seventeen or twenty-one points in the third quarter, and pubescent Jackson was having a fit. Jim Everett threw a pick-six to Deion, and he high-stepped into the end zone, and I was in a terrible mood. Dad gave me a little talking to, but I was still in a funk. And then the Rams got hot. Rolled off three touchdowns in a span of about five minutes and went on to win by ten or fourteen or something. And I was on cloud nine the rest of the day."

Leroy leaned back a little in his lawn chair and nodded, waiting.

"My attitude changed because my circumstances changed. Dad said something to me afterward—I didn't put that together as a nine year-old. He said I hadn't so much addressed my bad attitude as gotten lucky. And now, thinking back to where I was a year ago—even six months ago—I was mad at God that my life had turned out the way it had, that He'd taken Mom and Dad and Grant from us, and wondering why He wasn't comforting me and why all those Bible verses and songs and sermons about God always being there and seeing you through and giving you all-sufficient grace didn't seem to be true in my life."

He looked at his Grandpa.

"And then my circumstances changed. Maggie showed up, and we had a talk, and she got me back to reading the Bible and praying. And then we rounded out our idea to take down GrayStar, and then we got the money and the island and the house, and then everything somehow worked out despite not working out, and we took them out. And now . . . I'm not mad at God anymore, but it's because we scored a bunch of touchdowns, not because I fixed my attitude."

"And you're feeling guilty?" Leroy said.

"And a little worried, because if something has happened to Mom and Dad and all this was for naught and they don't come back . . . if my circumstances change again, what's to keep me from going back into Job's wife's territory?"

Leroy pursed his lips. Then stroked his jaw. "You say Maggie got you back to reading the Word and praying?"

"I wasn't exactly monastic in either practice, but yeah."

"How?"

"She reminded me that my anchor is in the next life, not this one, and that while I didn't have all the answers here and now, God did."

"Good advice."

"It was. And she said in the meantime, she wasn't letting me slack. It was the kick in the pants I needed."

Leroy nodded. "And?"

"A few nights later we were talking, specifically about why God wasn't helping. And she said maybe He was, but that I didn't see it. I had you, Reggie, her. She pointed at all the good I'd done, most notably witnessing to her, leading her to Jesus, so she could one day corral me."

Leroy nodded again. "That's a smart woman."

"Yeah."

Leroy slowly stood and paced to the railing, then turned back. "A number of years ago, I was preaching through the Gospel of John, and when I came to chapter eleven—you know, Lazarus?"

Jackson nodded.

"I didn't know what to do. Seems all the obvious points had been made before. So I looked at it from the perspective of Mary and Martha, looked at their suffering and compared it to our suffering. You ever look at it from their point of view?"

Jackson shook his head.

"They called out to Jesus for help, to save Lazarus from death, and He did nothing. Could have come, and didn't. He let them suffer, with no explanation. Even though, just verses before that it says that Jesus loved Mary and Martha. Think about that, bud. He loved them, and He let them suffer. Doesn't seem to fit. You'd think those two things would be mutually exclusive."

Jackson nodded.

"He also told the disciples He was glad He wasn't there, '*so that you may believe*.' Mary and Martha's anguish was, at least in part, so that the disciples might believe." He squinted at Jackson. "Sound familiar?"

"If I hadn't gone through all that, Maggie and I might never have had the relationship we do." He thought back to the hotel after the family's visitation, where he had cried himself out on Maggie's shoulder. That moment of vulnerability and intimacy—while almost undoing them a few times—had forged a bond that had grown from casual friendship to romance, with Maggie's conversion somewhere along the way.

Leroy nodded. "Now, of course, eventually Jesus did raise Lazarus—He made everything better, just like one day He'll make all our problems better. But that doesn't mean we won't suffer along the way, and that sometimes He won't let us suffer. But it does mean that, even then, He still loves us and is still at work, whether we see it or not."

Jackson thought for a moment. "So you're saying my realization of this now makes up for my mood change only being because of my circumstance change?"

"I'm saying everything in life can be a lesson, can serve to make you more aware of who God is and what He's doing. No, you didn't handle your adversity as well as you could have. But you're learning. God's working on you. And even if you're faithless at times, He's always faithful."

Jackson grinned. "I could have used your wisdom over the last year."

"I didn't go anywhere."

"I know, Grandpa."

Leroy stroked his jaw again. "What song was it that got you thinking?"

"'The Days of Elijah.'"

His grandpa frowned. "What's that got to do with any of this?"

"Nothing. You know how my mind works."

"That I do," Leroy said, retaking his seat. He sat back, looking off toward the horizon. "I never did figure out what that song was about."

Chapter One Hundred Fifty-Seven

Thursday, June 12
8:19 p.m.

THE CALL CAME just before the scene where Matt Damon ran into Franka Potente after climbing down the embassy walls. Late enough that they were into the movie, but early enough that Maggie hadn't gotten too cozy on Jackson's arm.

It had been a week since they'd started their efforts to reach out to David and Hannah, and not a word had come back. Jackson had done several more interviews that week, talked to Cathy DeVane again, and increased his ad buy. He'd also been seriously kicking around additional ideas and trying to figure out when to implement them. Everyone—from the White House Press Secretary to his own brother—had told him it was too early to panic, that this might take time. But he couldn't stand it, couldn't fight off the myriad reasons why David and Hannah might be dead after all. So Maggie had suggested a movie marathon, something to take his mind off it. Since he'd just played Jason Bourne, they'd opted for the trilogy (*The Bourne Legacy* was optional if things really got dicey).

Jackson reached for his phone while Maggie paused the DVD. It was a familiar number, although he couldn't place it. But he answered anyhow. "This is Jackson."

"Jackson, it's Francis Sullivan."

He almost seemed out of breath, and Jackson leaned forward. "Yes, sir, Admiral."

"They're alive, Jackson. I just got off the phone with your father. He and your mother are alive."

Jackson froze. He didn't jump up and celebrate. He didn't break down in tears. He didn't turn to Maggie with a smile or a thumbs up. He merely stared into space—or, more technically—into Franka Potente's eyes as she looked at Matt Damon leaning into her car window.

He couldn't believe it. His hunch, confirmed by DNA, was true. His efforts, his do or die plan had worked, and it had *worked*. He'd so long believed his parents were dead, that he'd never see them again this side of eternity, that even though he'd never come to terms with it, he'd started to acclimate to it. And now they were alive!

He thought of Mary and Martha, who'd thought Lazarus was dead and buried and never coming back. They'd given up, even on Jesus. He could relate. They'd had to wait four days for their miracle. His had taken just over three years. But it had happened.

He really couldn't believe it. His brain tried to pick apart Sullivan's words, to find an alternate meaning, to explain the inexplicable. They couldn't really be alive, and in touch. His one-in-a-million long shot couldn't have come home. Could it?

Sullivan and Maggie both said his name at the same time. She put a hand on his back. "Jack? Jack, what is it?"

"They're alive," he gulped.

She buried her head in his shoulder, wrapping him in a squeeze that almost knocked him over.

"Yes, they are," Sullivan said.

Suddenly a million questions came to Jackson's mind. Where are they? Where were they? How did they find out? Are they okay? When can I see them? Sullivan, the wise old veteran that he was, apparently sensed the questions.

"Your father said he and your mother are fine. They've been in Belize for the last eight or nine months, on a little island off the mainland."

"Belize?"

"They have satellite there, and he said your mother saw your interview on *Fox & Friends* with Tucker Carlson."

"That was Saturday."

Maggie had sat up and leaned in close, trying to hear. Jackson wasn't thinking clearly enough to put the phone on speaker.

"Your father was dubious, wanted to check some things out. He finally called me, using a code we'd worked out for such a . . . well, not this circumstance, but a situation like this. I gave him the all clear. Jackson, he and your mother will be arriving at NAS North Island Saturday morning."

Jackson realized he hadn't breathed in a while. So he did.

"We're working out some of the details, and I'll be in touch in the morning. But I wanted to let you know right away. I'll let you tell your brother and other family members."

"Thank you. Yeah, I'll do that."

"I'm very happy for you, Jackson. I'll call you tomorrow."

"Yes, sir. Thank you, Admiral."

The phone clicked, and Jackson turned to Maggie. Neither spoke, instead embracing each other in the tightest hug of their lives.

It lasted for just a few seconds. "I need to tell Grant. I need to . . . I should drive over there. He's with Grandpa, still." He stood, and paced. "He's going to . . . This might kill him," he said, looking back at Maggie. "Grandpa, I mean. It's about killing me. Can you believe this?"

She shook her head.

"Maggie, you've never met them. You haven't met my parents. You have no idea who's to blame for this." He ran his hand through his hair. "I need to tell Grant and Grandpa. Maybe you'd better drive me. And don't let me be a smart-aleck about this, making jokes about orphans or quoting from *The Count of Monte Cristo* or something." He stopped pacing. "Shouldn't I be jumping up and down? I nearly tore out stitches for a touchdown in the Rose Bowl."

"I think you're in shock."

"You had better drive me."

"You want to go, or you want to pace and babble some more?"

"Let's go."

They headed out to her car, and Jackson couldn't sit still in the passenger seat as they headed toward Leroy's houseboat in Marina del Rey. Surreal didn't begin to describe the feeling, but it was starting to hit him that it was indeed true. And that brought with it a host of other feelings. Or rather, forebears of other feelings, announcements that they would be there soon.

When they arrived at the end of Bora Bora Way, Jackson threw open his door almost before Maggie had parked. Then he stopped and turned back. "What'd you say?"

"I'll wait here," Maggie repeated.

"What?"

"This should be a family moment. Just the three of you."

"Maggie, you don't have to do that."

"I know."

"It could be a while. This isn't the sort of news you just drop on somebody and then leave."

"Take all the time you need, Jack. You've earned it, I'd say."

He leaned in to give her a quick kiss, then backed out and closed the door. He took a deep breath, then headed for the houseboat to tell his brother and grandfather the best news he'd ever given anybody.

*　　　　　*　　　　　*

Saturday, June 14
11:09 a.m.
Naval Air Station North Island

A COOL, northerly breeze dried Jackson's eyes as he watched the Lockheed C-130 Hercules bank to its right several miles over the Pacific, then begin its final descent to Runway 36 at Naval Air Station North Island. The sun was shining brightly, the American flag held by the Navy Color Guard to Jackson's right was flapping with extra patriotism, and all was right in his world.

Unless some green pilot on a milk run missed the runway and ditched the C-130 in San Diego Bay.

For the last thirty-six hours, since leaving Leroy's houseboat, Jackson's brain had been running wild with horrible scenarios. The plane crashed. A hurricane hit Belize and David and Hannah drowned. GrayStar had a second cell that had gotten to Sullivan, faked the call, and was lying in wait to kill anyone ever associated with the name Douglas. Joaquín Padilla had crawled out of some sewer and chosen this moment to enact his revenge on Jackson for beating the tar out of him or the Navy for setting him up. Oddest of all, the fear that the reunion wouldn't be as magical and spectacular as he dreamed.

That would not be Admiral Sullivan's fault. David Douglas's former C.O. had arranged quite a welcome party for the once and now—technically—

again Navy Captain and his wife. In addition to the Color Guard there was the Navy Band Southwest, the Mayor of San Diego and the Lieutenant Governor of California, and a red carpet and banner. It was just like a TV show where the small-town hero returned from the war.

Sullivan, of course, was decked in his Navy service dress blues, every metal polished to gleam in the sun. The rest of the military personnel were also nattily attired. Grant wore a dress shirt and tie, and Hillary a lovely summer dress with loose little ties on the sleeves and hems to catch the breeze. She had given Jackson something of a frown when they'd picked him up early that morning and he'd been in jeans and a Dodgers T-shirt. But, he'd argued with himself while dressing and with Hillary despite her actually not making an argument, David and Hannah would want to see Jackson as he was, as they'd known him. She'd raised an eyebrow to that, but said nothing else.

Leroy wore a polo shirt with jeans, which was the only step below his Sunday go-to-church-meetin' duds. No other family was present, yet. Jackson and Grant had made phone calls the day before, letting siblings, aunts and uncles, nieces and nephews, even some cousins know that David and Hannah were alive. A big reunion would be planned somewhere down the line, on the *Pórtico Dorado* Cartel's dime, technically. Speaking of, Jackson spent a few minutes worrying they would somehow resurface and come calling for their money.

Maggie was not there. She had declined Jackson's invite, saying he should be with family. He'd argued that Hillary would be there, and she'd said that Hillary was family. Not for a couple more months, at least. She wouldn't be dissuaded, telling Jackson he needed the time with just family first. This wasn't the time to introduce her and, while he'd pushed back on the idea, he sort of agreed.

So it was just the four of them, along with Sullivan's retinue, watching as landing gear appeared beneath the plane, then its quadruple turboprop engines became visible on the wings. The breeze kept the sound of the engines away until the plane touched down at the end of the runway, then raced to a stop to their right. Jackson's whole body tingled as he watched the plane slowly turn, then taxi back toward them and just a little past them. Then the propellers wound down, the engines ceasing with a whine. Leroy, on

Jackson's right, put a hand on his shoulder as the rear hatch door cracked and began to open.

Friday had been busy, what with phone calls to relatives, talking to Sullivan, making plans with Grant, Hillary, and Leroy. Then dinner with Maggie and Leroy while Grant finished up some paperwork at the precinct and Hillary had dinner with a client. Finally, Jackson had returned home and, after as brief as possible of a chat with Connie, had a few minutes alone.

He'd prayed. Thanking God that He had made everything right again. Apologizing for not trusting Him when things were wrong, and for not trusting Him to leave things wrong—for needing them to be made right. Thanking God that he would get to see his parents again, and asking for help cherishing every minute with them, because he knew—like a killer encore from a rock and roll band—it wouldn't last forever.

He'd also spent a few minutes marveling—and thanking God again—that he'd actually succeeded in his crazy plan to take out GrayStar. He had no idea if God had played a role, sparing him from bullets and giving him extra strength and brainpower and luck. He still didn't know if his had been a righteous cause—bringing terrorists to justice and saving the world from their atrocities—or merely a secular one. But it had all worked out, and now was the moment of payoff.

Hillary grasped his hand. He remembered standing beside her three years ago, in a smoke-filled parking lot, when they'd gotten word that David, Hannah, and Grant had died in an explosion. In that moment, an agonizing, soul-crushing, poison of a pain had invaded his heart—a pain that was about to be excised once and for all.

The rear hatch hit the pavement with a soft clang. Jackson's eyes probed the plane's dark interior. He saw movement, and then glimpsed his father's head for just a moment. It disappeared back into the darkness and was replaced by Hannah Douglas.

She stepped out onto the ramp, into the sunlight. She wore a flared, blue, knee-length sundress with a thin white sweater open over it. Her brown hair was a shade lighter than he remembered, and he wasn't sure if that was due to graying or Belizean sun. She stood at the end of the fuselage for a moment, scanning the tarmac. Her eyes settled on the foursome waiting at the end of the carpet, and her hand went to her mouth.

Jackson could see her body shaking from where he stood, and then saw his father's arms embrace her shoulders from behind. David Douglas stood a half-foot taller than his wife, and his hair had definitely grayed over the last three years. He wore a peach button-down shirt and light slacks, and in his typical style, looked up with a half-smile and a simple little wave.

In seeming slow motion, Jackson's parents' descended the ramp arm-in-arm, Hannah dabbing her eyes with a kerchief and David still grinning crookedly. The band played *Stars and Stripes Forever*, and every member of the Navy offered David a sharp salute, including Admiral Sullivan. He released Hannah long enough to return it, then shake Sullivan's hand. Then he and Hannah paused at the end of the red carpet, looking at their sons, father, and future daughter-in-law.

Sullivan made a slashing motion, and the band trailed off. Close-up now, Jackson could see David's face had aged, far more than three years. The same lines were there, but deeper. Hannah too. But they both looked strong—not malnourished or worn down. Knowing them both, that was no surprise. Jackson could just see his father rigging a homemade fishing net, wading into the Straits of Belize to catch dinner, then lounging in the sand with a cockeyed look at Hannah as she fileted and cooked his afternoon catch. Maybe with fresh fruit she'd picked on an afternoon walk.

When they were only a few paces away, Grant broke forward and enveloped them in a hug. Hillary dropped Jackson's hand, but he stood where he was, watching as Grant embraced his mother, then reached for David as well. The lump in Jackson's throat was too big to swallow, and so was Leroy's, judging by the way he squeezed Jackson's shoulder.

The trio finally broke their hug, and David was the first to make eye contact with Jackson. His lips pinched tightly together, Jackson stepped forward. Both men extended a hand at the same time, and shook firmly. David spoke first, merely uttering his son's name.

"Jackson."

"Dad."

It was all either of them could get out before they embraced. And then, Jackson could control himself no more. Wrapped in his father's arms—the same arms that had rocked him to sleep as a baby, sat him on a knee to hear stories of the American Revolution as a child, tossed him baseballs and footballs on sun-splashed afternoons, and draped over his shoulder in casual, tender moments on vacations—wrapped in those arms, he released the pain and suffering of three years and the ardor and adversity of the last nine months.

Finally he lifted his head from his dad's shoulder and hugged him tightly once more, cheek to cheek. Then he turned, wiping away the tears, and enveloped Hannah. He inhaled the same scent he remembered from his youth—not her perfume or shampoo, but her. He felt her face pressed tightly against his, just like when he'd skinned his knee and needed comforting or had been about to go off into the wilds of college for the first time. He heard her voice, a voice he thought he'd never hear again, telling him how much she loved him and missed him and loved him some more.

At some point, they separated, and Jackson reached for Grant, pulling him into the circle. Before beckoning to Leroy and Hillary to join them, the four members of the Douglas family shared the first of many hugs. The tears and the smiles were mixed, the firsts of many as well.

Jackson was the first to step back, blinking away tears as he looked at Hannah kissing Grant's cheek and David holding her waist tightly to him. It was a mental snapshot that Jackson knew would, like this moment, never fade.

After three years and one month, David and Hannah Douglas were home.

And so was Jackson.

Chapter One Hundred Fifty-Eight

Three weeks later . . .
Thursday, July 3
7:20 p.m.
Pacific Palisades, California

RAIN HAD STARTED falling somewhere around Irvine, and had been steady all the way home. Jackson had dropped Grant at Leroy's, paused to say hi to his grandpa, and driven home through the heaviest rain yet. He parked in the garage, threw his two bags into the house, then walked out to get the mail, which had been held until that day. After two weeks, there was quite a stack, and Jackson shielded it with his body as he hurried back into the house through the garage.

He thought about unpacking, but was bushed from a long day of travel, and merely kicked his bags toward the steps, followed them with his shoes, and crashed on the couch to sort through his mail, which included a small brown package.

David and Hannah had spent the better part of a week coming back to life. There had been tons of paperwork, the purchase of their old house—which the Navy had been holding onto, more or less—and a couple cars, setting up various utilities and insurance and so forth. The Navy handled most of the expenses, and Jackson assured his parents that he was now flush and could cover anything else that was needed.

They had also made plans to get away with their two boys to reconnect. They'd had some initial time on Saturday afternoon at the 19th Hole Restaurant & Lounge on the base, but they needed more than a couple of afternoons or meals. So after Grant's workweek ended, he and Jackson drove down to San Diego. The following morning, the four members of the Douglas family flew to Denver, rented a car, and drove north to Estes Park, to a cabin on the edge of Rocky Mountain National Park.

For two weeks, interspersed with hiking and sightseeing and consuming metric tons of fudge and saltwater taffy, the family had reconnected. They'd recapped their time apart, with David explaining his thinking in arranging the original disappearance, continuing it without Jackson and Hillary and Leroy, and apologizing for pain he'd caused. He also recounted how he and Hannah had come under attack on their way back to Marcus Chase's safe house from dinner in Bariloche, how Hannah had returned fire while David careened into the garage, and how they'd somehow made it to the panic room shortly before the house exploded, likely from a stray bullet hitting a gas line. Then they'd hidden in the tunnel under the house for four days before setting out on foot for a village twenty kilometers south of Bariloche. From there, they'd used David's well-honed skills to make their way into Chile, then north to Central America, and ultimately to Belize. Hannah softened his stories of tradecraft with accounts of making a life on the island a few miles from the mainland and about their preparations to possibly make it permanent.

Jackson had been open about his pain, his use of marijuana as an attempt to numb the pain, and his subsequent arrest and therapy. He regaled them with stories about his career as a private investigator, and recounted the efforts he had taken to bring them home. They'd hugged a lot, shared memories from the past and discussed possibilities for the future. It was a wonderful two weeks, and while things weren't back to normal by the time it was over, they were close. In some ways, they were better than normal.

Most of Jackson's mail was the usual—a combination of junk and bills. He had Reggie to thank for those—he'd taken care of Jackson's utilities while he was gone, keeping everything hooked up and up to date. He set aside a notice for the renewal of his P.I. license, then reached for the package. Before he could look at it, the phone rang.

"Hey, Hoss," he said, recognizing Reggie's number. He hadn't gotten around to programming this phone with ringtones.

"How were the mountains, J?"

"Snowless. Must have been an early thaw."

"Good time?"

"The best."

"You all still up for tomorrow?"

"Tomorrow?" Jackson asked, glancing at the package. Had his name and address in hand-written block letters. No return address.

"Fourth of July," Reggie said. "We were going to have a little bash here."

"That's tomorrow?" Jackson asked, looking up. "I thought it was Saturday."

"Tomorrow."

"That's right. Friday the fourth. Yeah, we're planning on it."

"Gonna bring Maggie?"

"Yeah, and that reminds me, I have to call her."

"She met your folks yet?"

"Nope."

Jackson could hear Reggie's grin. "They'll love her, J."

"I know," he said, again looking away from the package. It was postmarked in Denver. Had they left something behind at the cabin?

"J?"

"Yeah, sorry. What were we talking about?"

"Maggie meeting your folks."

"Oh yeah. It's still a little weird."

"What is?"

"Merging these two spheres."

"Ah, it'll be fine."

Somebody hollered in the background.

"I gotta go, J. See you tomorrow."

"What time?"

"Afternoon. Whenever."

"All right, see you."

Jackson tossed the phone on the couch, and studied the package for a moment. Then, since there was no other way to find out, he tore it open. Several layers of thick brown paper enclosed a shrink-wrapped book. He leaned over to flick on the light so as to better see where to unwind the wrapping and, as he did, spotted the book's title: *The Holy Bible*.

He tore off the rest of the wrapping, then held the Bible in his hands. King James Version, leather bound, not cheap. Onion-skin pages, he noted, flipping through it. Then he closed it and held it in his hands, wondering. Denver . . .

He opened it again and this time looked at the flyleaf and saw a handwritten note etched on it.

Jackson,

I ran not to save my own skin, but because I figured I could be of more help from behind the scenes. Turns out, you didn't need it. I should have known. You have more lives than a cat.

In case you're wondering, I'm fine—just may not be making another trip to Moscow anytime soon. I think that's where our neighbors picked up my scent. Still upset about that Bible I pilfered from under your nose. There might be something to those CIA secrets hidden in the pages after all, but I've got people working to clean that up.

Anyhow, I'm glad everything turned out okay. I never doubted it would. Well, maybe for a minute. But, Jack, you're something else, you know that? Maggie got herself a catch. Just make sure you hold on tight.

If you ever need me, you know where to find me. Well, at least you do if you can figure out the code in this Bible too. You're pretty good at that sort of thing, from what I hear. ☺ And if you don't need me, don't be a stranger anyhow. We should get together and share war stories. Maybe all of us have a five-year reunion in St. Charles—not in hurricane season.

Take care of yourself. And I mean it, take care of that woman too.

-Robbie, et al.

Jackson grinned as he finished reading, knowing the name that was coming. He read it again, then set it aside to decipher later. But first, he had to call "that woman" to check in after two weeks away.

*　　　*　　　*

Friday, July 4
11:09 a.m.

VACATIONS WERE meant for relaxing, and the Douglas family had done plenty of that. And yet, there had been so many late-night talks and early-morning coffees that Jackson hadn't gotten any extra sleep. So he didn't set an alarm for America's 238th birthday. He woke late to find the rain gone and bright sunlight replacing it. He had coffee on his deck, drinking in the view of the Pacific Ocean less than a mile away, then—with nothing else to do before Maggie came by later—fired up his Xbox. It had been months and months since he'd led his virtual Trojans onto the field, but it came back to him.

Midway through the third quarter, his doorbell rang. He was roasting Cal, and paused the game, glad for a distraction, quite frankly. It was too early to be Maggie, so he debated between Connie with more treats and the Ghost of Peter Lance.

It was Sam.

Correct that. Any woman who looked that good had to be called Samantha.

She was the very definition of femininity in a white, knee-length, fit-and-flare sundress. A lacey blue ribbon was threaded through blond hair that was long and curled, rolling down her bare shoulders. A trace of makeup highlighted a beaming face, sparkling white teeth framed by lipstick red as the flag. And the scent of citrus wafted through the open door. She had never looked more beautiful.

"Sam. Hi."

"Jackson, how are you?" She stepped into the doorway and wrapped her slender arms around him to give him a tight, face-to-face hug. He remembered her touch, the softness of her skin, the blend of her perfume and shampoo, the way her hair felt when it brushed against him.

"Uh, you want to come in?" he said, stepping back and out of the way.

Sam breezed through the doorway and into the living room, stopping and looking at the TV with a smile. "Some things never change, huh?"

He grinned sheepishly.

"Is this a bad time?"

"No, it's fine. Something on your mind?"

"I heard about your parents, Jackson, about everything you did. I can't believe it. We thought you were in Mexico, in that prison forever . . ."

"Sorry about that."

"Reggie explained it."

"You talked to Reggie?"

"Last week. He told me briefly what had happened and where you were. Like I said, I can't believe it. And yet, knowing you, I kind of can. I'm so glad you're okay." She grabbed him and hugged him again. "But oh, Jackson, I am so happy for you," she said as they parted.

"Thanks, Sam. I'm pretty happy myself these days."

"Happy looks good on you."

He smiled, and she smiled back, a look they'd shared many times before.

"Um, can I get you something to drink? Or you want to sit down?"

"Jackson, you don't have to be formal."

"Sorry. It's, uh—"

"Reggie told me about you and Maggie."

"He did?"

Sam nodded. "That's why I'm here."

"It is?"

She nodded again.

So did he, just once, wondering where this was going.

"We talked about you, down in Mexico, you know."

"I would imagine."

"I mean, about dating you—or about whatever we did."

"Busted."

"Um-hmm," she said with that perfect smile.

"I never meant to hurt either of you."

"I know." She turned and took a few steps toward the dining room, then turned back. "When we were looking for you, before we knew how bad it was, Maggie and I were talking, like I said, about our relationships with you. We were both a little confused then, about what we felt and what we wanted. It sounds like she figured it out now."

He nodded.

"Thing is," she said, taking a step closer, "so have I."

"You have?"

Sam nodded, biting her lower lip. "And, Jackson, I don't want to come between you and Maggie; I don't want to break you up. This is so not me. But . . ." She took another step, now just a few feet from him. "Before things got too serious, or before you made a commitment, I wanted to let you know how I feel."

He swallowed. "How do you feel?"

She stepped forward, grabbed his face with both hands, and kissed him. Immediately, he flashed back to a couple Christmases ago, when they'd shared a long, slow, soft kiss in a gazebo during a rainstorm. That moment had felt so wonderful, so perfect. Now, this didn't feel too bad either.

Sam stopped and stepped back, just before the point where Jackson would have had to figure out if he was kissing back or merely receiving a kiss. She looked him in the eye, her sapphire blues radiating with intensity. "I'm sorry if that was too forward," she said, then shook her head slightly, causing curls of hair to dance back and forth, "but I wanted to throw my hat into the ring. Because I've come to realize—and I admit it took me a while—that I love you, Jackson. I love you as a friend, as someone I'll always care for no matter what you say, but also in a way so much more than that—in a way that says I could make a life with you—that I *want* to make a life with you."

He nodded, tried to find his voice, tried to remember what time Maggie was stopping by. And if it was too late to go back and hand Hayes the gun at the lookout point on the east side of St. Charles.

"Sam . . ."

"It's okay," she said, her face falling at his expression.

"No, let me say this."

She swallowed.

"You and Maggie are two very different, but two very wonderful people. And I could see you and I making a life together, I really could. And I do care about you, very much. But Maggie and I are . . . Sam, it's like we're made for each other, like hand and glove. We fit perfectly, as if we were meant to be. And I don't know if I believe God creates people for each other or not, but she and I . . ." He shrugged. "We fit."

Sam nodded slowly.

"I'm telling you that because I want you to know it's not you—it's not that I don't feel the same way, or wouldn't under different circumstances. But Maggie . . . she's the one."

Sam formed a thin smile. "I understand. Thank you for being honest."

He nodded.

She reached a hand up and traced his cheek. "I withdraw my hat," she said as she lowered her hand. "I won't interfere, and I wish you both the best. I really mean that."

"I know you do, Sam. I wish it for you too."

She smiled one more time, the sweetest, most angelic smile he knew, then turned and walked for the door. He followed her there and stood in the doorway as she walked to her car. She paused once, turned around, and offered a still-handed wave. He returned it, then watched her go, her cascading blond hair catching the sunlight as it trailed her pure white dress.

Dang, if George Strait couldn't write a chart-topper about that.

Chapter One Hundred Fifty-Nine

1:42 p.m.

MAGGIE WORE BLUE jeans with holes in the knees and a white tank top with a washed out American flag on it. Her hair was loose, but restrained in part by sunglasses propped in her hair. She wore no makeup, no perfume that Jackson could detect as she brushed past him into the living room with a smirk. She looked like a million bucks, natural and casual as could be, beautiful in her simplicity. Jackson couldn't deny the attraction he felt for Sam, but he knew he'd made the right choice.

"You somewhere else?" she asked as he closed the door.

"No, not really. What's with the smirk?"

"Nothing. Just riding the high, still." She gave him a hug and a quick peck. "How was Colorado?"

"Good. Really good. We cleared the air on a few things, cried and forgave each other, caught up on life—the ups, the downs, the stretches flat as a Nebraska highway."

She nodded.

"I told them I had a girlfriend they'd be meeting today."

"What'd they say?"

"Dad smirked, Mom teared up. She does that a lot these days."

Maggie stuck her arms out. "I look okay to meet the parents?"

"Wouldn't change a thing, Mags."

She put her hands on her hips. "Okay, something's on your mind."

"What?"

"You just started staring off into space."

He sighed. "I guess I should tell you."

"Uh-oh."

"It's not an uh-oh. I don't think so anyhow."

"Uh-oh. Maybe I should sit down."

243

"Sam stopped by."

"When?"

"Mid-third quarter. Late morning sometime."

Maggie nodded.

"She said she wanted to throw her hat into the ring, vie for my affections."

"She use those words?"

"Not the vying part, no, but the hat in the ring, yes."

Maggie nodded again.

"And she kissed me, Maggie, and it was a very nice kiss, and she looked beautiful and everything. And she left with her hat," he added quickly.

Maggie frowned.

"I told her basically what I've told you, that under different circumstances, sure, I could see myself with her. But you and I were . . . like that old pair of jeans."

"*You* use those words?"

"I believe I said 'hand and glove.' The point is, I won't deny she was tempting, but she also kind of wasn't, because you're the one for me, Maggie."

"You trying to convince me or yourself?"

"You. I am convinced," he said, making sure to look her in the gray-blue eyes. "Like I said, she left with her hat. Her metaphorical hat. She was actually wearing a ribbon, kind of—"

"Jack."

He flashed her his very best Hawkeye Pierce smile, and she couldn't help cracking one in return.

"I mean it, Maggie, it was that scene where Cate Blanchett looked into Frodo's eyes and didn't kill him for the ring."

"If you don't stop with these nerd references, I'm going to call her and tell her to come back."

He reached out for her hand, then pulled her to him. "Maggie, you know me well enough to know I wouldn't lie to you. If there was a danger here, I'd tell you. I'd say I'm torn between the two of you and need to figure things out and . . . that's not the case. I am sold."

"I don't know, Jack, you did date us both for a while."

He narrowed one eye.

She smirked. "I'm kidding. I trust you."

"Good."

"You ready to head out?"

"I need my hat first."

She nodded, and he climbed the stairs to get his new Dodgers baseball cap. The old one now belonged to Manny, the poolside bartender at Tijuana's *El Hotel Pacifico*.

"How long did she kiss you?" Maggie asked playfully when he got to the bottom of the steps.

"I don't know, time sort of stopped."

She whacked his arm.

"Then it took a little while for her to get her tongue out."

She punched him hard enough to leave a mark. But the look on her face told him she wasn't worried or mad, so he grinned and complained about the punch on the way out to her car.

*   *   *

2:13 p.m.

WITH TEMPS in the mid-80s and the sun unhindered by any clouds, Santa Monica State Beach and the pier in the distance were crowded to capacity. Cameron's, being right on the beach and not that far from the famed pier, was bustling too. But Reggie had reserved half a dozen tables in the sand for his private party, consisting of Jackson's family and friends. A steady supply of cool beverages, an all-you-can-eat, on-the-house menu, and a small stereo setup playing patriotic hits awaited them.

Jackson and Maggie were the first to arrive. Reggie greeted them, wearing a blue T-shirt with a flexing cartoon eagle on the front, under the words "Back to Back World War Champs." That would probably trigger half of California, but Reggie apparently wasn't concerned about the potential hit to business. Especially the way he was doling out free food.

They grabbed drinks and sat down in the shade of an umbrella. The distant waves, the chatter of hundreds of people on the beach, and the traffic just up the way on the PCH made for a background din that was easy to block out. They talked about Reggie's business plans and the transition to

Katie being the manager of all three Cameron's restaurants, about several favorable conversations Maggie had had about a potential line of work, and about what to do with their ten million dollars (each) and the ninety million in change that was sitting in a bank account in St. Charles but was designated for charity.

"Hey, man," Reggie said with a nod toward the parking lot. "Mouse is here."

"You invited Mouse?"

"Of course, man. Where else he gonna go on the Fourth?"

"That's decent, Reg," Jackson said, getting up and turning toward the parking lot. Mouse was getting out of the passenger side of a blue coupe. The driver was an unfamiliar woman, but even from the backside, Jackson could tell she was out of Mouse's league. Tallish, made more so by heels. She wore a white mini-skirt, emphasis on the mini, and a pink blouse. Her hair was long, luxurious, and blond. Almost as good as Sam's.

"Who's the—excuse me, Maggie—knockout with him?"

Reggie shrugged. "I said plus one."

"Wipe the spit off your chin before you go over," Maggie said.

He winked at her and trudged through the sand toward the parking lot. "Mouse!" he said with a grin as his friend looked up.

"Jack," he said, also beaming. "I thought you were dead."

"I almost was." They slapped hands, then engaged in an awkward man hug. "It's good to see you, man," Jackson said. "How you been?"

"The usual. Word is you've had an interesting year."

"You can say that again." He nodded toward the woman, who had trailed a few paces behind. "Who's your fr . . ."

Mouse raised an eyebrow.

"No way."

"Hello, Jackson," Pam said.

Fighting to keep his mouth from dropping open, Jackson surveyed Mouse's older sister from head to toe. It was borderline inappropriate, especially since "the one" was sitting fifty feet behind him nursing an Arnold Palmer, but he couldn't believe it was true. Pam had been a chunk, well over two bills, hips and arm flab and butt everywhere. Now she was toned. Her spray-tan was a real tan, and her stringy mess of brown/blond hair was now photoshoot blond. He failed, and his mouth drooped.

"Oh, grow up," Pam said, pushing past him.

He looked over his shoulder, then turned to Mouse. "She hasn't changed on the inside."

"Not a bit."

"What happened?"

"Joined a gym. I don't know what got into her, but it keeps her out of the house. Only thing is we eat like total crap now. Have you heard of something called kale?"

"She and Clark still together?"

"He's the one who got her into it. You should see him now. Looks like the gov-uh-nuh," he said in his best Schwarzenegger.

"Clark? The guy shaped like a potato?"

Mouse shrugged, and he and Jackson walked over to the table where Reggie and Maggie had been joined by a somewhat sullen Pam. The arrival of a Metropolitan a few minutes later mollified her, and Mouse didn't seem too intimidated by Reggie or Maggie. Then, for the next half hour, it was Mouse and Pam's mouths that were agape as Jackson recounted his adventures yet again. Mouse was briefly hurt that Jackson had gone over his head for a hacker, but it morphed to relief when he realized all he'd have had to do. And he did score points for recommending the Night Ram in the first place.

Tori Walker was next to arrive, while Reggie was gone getting a round of sliders and Pam was in the ladies' room. Tori wore a USA flag bikini top partially visible under a white button-down shirt and a pair of denim shorts, reasonable attire for a beach party, and practically prudish in SoCal. But with the breeze blowing her hair and tugging at the collar of the shirt, it wasn't prudish to Jackson.

"Kiss her and I kill you," Maggie whispered as he started to get up.

Mouse raised his eyebrows.

Jackson waved him off and went to give Tori a hug. "Walker, good to see you again."

"You too, Champ. You cut your hair."

"Technically a barber did."

"Still as hilarious as ever. That Navy lawyer took care of you, apparently?"

"Air Force, and yes. You spend your money yet?"

"I bought a new car."

"You got rid of the Saab?"

"Bought a pink Ferrari."

"Are you for real?"

"In the parking lot," she said. "Wanna see it?"

"Pink?"

"I wanted to stand out."

He turned and waved to Maggie that he would be right back, then followed Tori around the corner of the building. His eyes went up when he saw the hot pink paint job glistening in the sun. It was a newer model than Magnum's, obviously, but the resemblance was still there. He dislodged from his brain the idea of *Magnum, P.I.* spinoff featuring a flag-bikini-wearing lady P.I. driving a pink Ferrari and took a lap around the car. He stopped to look at the vanity license plate: Walker 1.

"Clever."

"I thought so."

"What'd it set you back?"

"Quarter of a million."

"Is that all?"

"Figure it will pay off in advertising. Wouldn't you want to hire a sexy female private eye who drove this?"

"I wouldn't even need a case."

She smirked.

"You hungry?"

"Starved," she said.

"Come on."

They returned to the beach, and the group shared some laughs and stories—and sliders. A little before four, Grant texted to let Jackson know they were just a few minutes out. Jackson nodded for Maggie's attention, and they excused themselves from the table and headed toward the parking lot. A small slat-wood fence, partially overgrown with shrubs, served as a barrier between the beach and the parking lot, and a wood trellis covered in clematis (it hadn't been Reggie's design) allowed access. Jackson and Maggie stopped just beyond the trellis, and he looked at her. Not wearing a fluttering sundress, nor a flag bikini, she was still stunning—even if she did seem a little nervous, which wasn't her at all.

David got out of the driver's seat of a Lincoln MKS, waited for the others to get out, then stopped in his tracks. Jackson smirked, realizing his dad was looking at the pink Ferrari. Grant made some comment, and David made a reply about the Lincoln handling differently than a golf cart. That had apparently been the mode of transportation on their Belizean island.

Both David and Hannah were dressed casually, her in a patriotic T-shirt and white shorts, he in a U.S. Navy polo shirt and khaki shorts. Grant too was decked in red, white, and blue, if his plaid shorts counted. Hillary broke the mold in an ankle-length, flowing sundress that was red with yellow accents. Unpatriotic, it was not unappealing. And Leroy, who ambled out of the passenger seat a little more slowly, technically only had blue jeans and a white shirt, but who was keeping score?

Jackson stepped forward for handshakes and hugs, and a frown at Hillary.

She raised an eyebrow.

"Only you would wear Soviet and Communist China colors on the Fourth."

"Really, Jack?" Grant asked.

He smirked and stepped back. "Mom, Dad, I would like you to meet Maggie," he said, stepping aside. "She was invaluable in taking down GrayStar, in keeping me sane and on the straight and narrow the last six months, and, more than that, I'm sweet on her. Mags, Mom and Dad. Grant, Grandpa, Hillary, you all are already acquainted."

Hannah was first forward to give Maggie a warm hug and a bright smile, then David and Grant offered handshakes and smiles just as convivial. "Jack speaks very highly of you, Maggie," David said.

"Thank you, sir."

"No 'sir's. I'm retired," he said with a wink.

"Again?" Jackson asked.

David nodded. "Officially as of this morning."

"For how long?"

"For good."

"Can I get that in writing, maybe signed in blood?"

David gave his son a bemused smile, then turned to Maggie. "Seriously, he bragged of your exploits in Mexico and the exposé you wrote, some of the other adventures you chronicled, your blossoming career as a correspondent."

"Hard work and some breaks," Maggie said. "And plenty of help," she said, nodding Jackson way.

"You two make quite a team, you're saying?"

"David, honey, knock it off," Hannah said.

"Yes, heaven forbid Jackson and his girlfriend take any ribbing," Grant said.

"Yeah, yeah, yeah. Shall we get something to eat, Officer, Chairwoman McKenzie?"

"Boy, I've missed the old gang," Leroy said.

The group headed down to the beach, where more intros were made. And then, for the next several hours, Jackson's family and closest friends enjoyed an afternoon and evening of food and drink, sunny weather, good stories and good laughs, and freedom on so many levels.

*   *   *

8:18 p.m.

AFTER A full meal, a swim in Grant, Hillary, and Walker's case, and some football tossing between Jackson, Reggie, Maggie, and David, the group settled down to more cool drinks as they watched the day fade into the Pacific. During a lull in the conversation, Grant motioned for Jackson to join him away from the tables.

"What's up?"

"Take a walk?"

"Something on your mind?"

Grant nodded. "Sort of."

"Okay. Be back in a few," Jackson called to Maggie, then he and Grant set off down the beach, toward the Santa Monica Pier. For a few minutes, Grant said nothing, and Jackson let him speak at his leisure. He just soaked in the ambiance, an ambiance that he'd experienced many times in recent years, but always with an aching hole in his heart. Now, that hole was gone, and every bit of the day—from the ambiance of the beach and colorful pier ahead of them to the laughs and conversations and bonding—was a joy he never thought he'd know again.

"Remember last Fourth of July," Grant said. He nodded toward the pier, its iconic Ferris wheel shining iridescently against the darkening blue sky.

"Yeah."

"You and I came to the Pier, trying to have a normal day. And you gave me that speech, about the Founding Fathers and risking everything on a long shot because they believed in it, and how you were going out in a blaze of glory."

"Yeah, I remember."

"And at the time, I thought you were crazy. I thought it was just that, a blaze of glory. And yet . . . somehow, deep down inside, I guess I always thought you might just somehow pull it off, because that's kind of who you are and what you do. I don't know how, but you do it."

"Mix of brilliance and determination, mostly."

"Uh-huh. Anyhow, Jack, I wanted to tell you that I'm proud of you. It was crazy, but you did what you felt was the right thing to do, and you were right. So I'm proud of you, and . . ." He stopped.

"Yeah?"

"Thank you, Jack. You saved our family."

Jackson looked down at the sand.

"And you saved mine."

He looked back up.

"If not for you pushing me and goading me and, quite frankly, pestering the heck out of me, Hillary and I . . . might not have gotten back together. We wouldn't have. We owe our future to you."

"Don't remind me."

"Come on, Jack. Deep down, I mean really deep, admit it, you like her."

Jackson winced.

Grant tipped his head to the side.

"Really deep, like Aaron Eckhart and Hilary Swank in *The Core* deep. Maybe."

Grant smiled and held up his hand, in front of his chest. Jackson somewhat reluctantly clasped it, and Grant pulled him into an embrace. "I love you, brother."

"I love you too, but can we not do this right now? I mean, two dudes hugging on a California beach . . ."

Grant let go and shook his head. "Come on," he said, turning and starting to walk back. "There is one other thing I wanted to tell you."

"You killed Brian and Mark Fuhrmaned the crime scene so no one will ever know?"

Grant shook his head again. "I wanted to tell you that, for all the times I bust your chops about your methods or your attitude, I really do respect you. And it is just teasing. It's our repartee," he added with a shrug.

"I know. And when I accuse your fiancée of being a Communist sympathizer . . . I only half mean it."

Grant exhaled a laugh.

"And if you ever tell her about *The Core* or half meaning my insults . . ."

"It stays on the beach, Jack."

"Good."

Fifty yards from the party, Grant stopped. "Oh, one other thing."

"Yeah, Colombo?"

"Will you be my best man?"

Jackson frowned. "I thought I was."

"That was the first wedding."

"And you were thinking of bumping me off now?"

"Not so much me as Hillary."

"Uh-huh."

"There was never anyone else, but I wanted to make it official."

"It's official," Jackson said. "I'll start working on my remarks immediately."

"I was afraid of that."

"Oh, and how do you feel about a private jet to St. Charles for the bachelor party?"

Chapter One Hundred Sixty

"I'M SORRY," GRANT said in reply to Jackson accusing him of being a frump. "I'm just not sure why you need me to tag along, and why today, a week before my wedding."

"I need you to tag along because I spent too much time alone," Jackson said, navigating Van Nuys traffic on the 405. "Eight hours by myself in the car each way?"

Grant sighed.

"Plus it wouldn't look proper, me going to visit another woman by myself."

"Since when has propriety been an issue?"

"Ouch. And, I want to talk to you about several things, man to man, brother to brother. This is our last chance as single dudes."

"And what, you're hoping we get stranded in some small California desert town, flirt with the local girl who works the family diner, maybe have a TGIF sort of adventure?"

"No. I mean, I'm not entirely opposed to the idea, but no. Think of this as a bachelor party."

"An eight-hour drive to Redding is my bachelor party?"

"Well, the best you're going to get. I'm not having all the precinct buddies to some sleazy joint where a lady can pop out of a cake, and I'm certainly not having you, Grandpa, Reggie, and Mouse over to watch *Magnum* and eat pizza."

"Really?"

"Now that you mention it, that isn't bad."

"Why Redding anyhow? What's the deal with this girl?"

"She was my friend. Is. She came looking for me in Mexico, put herself on the line countless other times. I owe her a visit, an explanation."

"A chance to throw *her* hat into the ring?"

"She's married, Grant, and it was never like that between us."

"She ugly?"

"She's cute as you please. And I resent the suggestion that I can't have a professional or friendly relationship with a good-looking woman."

"First time for everything."

Jackson harrumphed and sped around a slow-moving pickup. They'd rented a car, since the Granada still wasn't primed for long, interstate journeys. This had been sort of last minute, but Maggie was spending the day with an up-and-coming media mogul who wanted to hire her (for a six-figure salary) as his foreign correspondent, and while Jackson didn't think there was any risk of breaking up a marriage and another relationship if he went to see Ashley solo, it wouldn't look quite right. Besides, he did want some time with just Grant.

They cleared the city and entered the mountains, and Grant put some Matthew West on the CD player. Jackson tolerated it.

"So, what'd you want to talk about?" Grant asked.

"For starters, your honeymoon."

Grant raised an eyebrow.

"I haven't heard, you have anything planned?"

"Not right away. We'll take a few days off at the new house—we close Tuesday."

"That was fast."

"Tell me about it." He shrugged. "We've got some painting to take care of, a few very minor renovations we can do ourselves."

"How romantic."

"I've taken a lot of time off lately, and so has Hillary, so we decided to save the official honeymoon trip for a little bit down the road."

"Well, wherever you go, I'd like to pay for it."

"You would?"

"Yes."

"This so you can have naming rights on our firstborn?"

"I thought that was pretty much a given anyhow."

"Jack."

"I've given you both a lot of grief, and as a means of burying the hatchet, I'd like that to be my wedding present. Besides, it is drug money anyhow."

"You're serious?"

"Deadly. Go wherever you want, spend whatever you want—it's on me."

"That's very generous. Thanks, Jack."

"Besides, I looked at your registry and none of it's really me."

"Considering I was expecting *The Dukes of Hazzard* box set, that's really nice."

"Grant, I wouldn't get you *The Dukes of Hazzard* for a wedding present. You can borrow mine."

They followed I-5 through the heart of California, talking about the wedding, about future plans, about the good old days. The trip reminded Jackson of the train trip he'd taken in pursuit of the Vanderbilt Bible, back when he and Robbie had been frenemies. He'd decoded her Bible code in recent weeks, which came out to a phone number and an e-mail address—just in case.

They stopped in Stockton for lunch, then cruised through Sacramento and north to Redding, as temperatures pushed one hundred outside. As they neared Northern California's most prominent city, with the distant Mount Shasta towering over the landscape in front of them, Grant asked, "You call ahead? She expecting you?"

"I called her husband. He knows we're coming and promised she'd be home."

"Tell me more about this lady cop who's just a friend."

With a sideways glare at his brother, Jackson explained how they'd met on his thirtieth birthday, how she'd been undercover and he'd saved her life—and that of her partner, Dylan. She'd been a resource on cases thereafter, and something of a confidant. Then her partner had proposed, out of the blue. She'd accepted and they'd moved to Redding, where he'd taken over the family lumber store and she'd continued as a detective.

"Well, I always like to meet a fellow cop," Grant said.

"Just beware, she doesn't look like a cop."

"Oh, what do cops look like?"

"I don't know. Not her. And if she strays into Valspeak, don't think anything of it."

Grant frowned.

"Here, read me these directions," Jackson said, handing Grant a slip of paper as he signaled to exit the interstate. Five minutes and a crossing of the Sacramento River later, they pulled up in front of a single-story cottage in a neighborhood that was neither new nor old. The house wasn't anything fancy, and the yard—like all those around it—appeared dead. But there were little touches of life—flowers in a planter, a welcome sign on the front door, an American flag on a mount beside the door.

Jackson and Grant got out and, having stopped just once during the 550-mile drive, took a moment to stretch. It was a little after four-thirty in the afternoon, and the summer sun was beating down on them. "Wow, it's hot," Jackson said.

"At least it's a dry heat."

"So's an oven."

"Thank you, Grandpa."

Jackson nodded at the front door, and they climbed onto a small wooden porch. Before Jackson could reach for the bell, the door swung open and Dylan O'Brien appeared behind the screen door. He extended it with a smile. "Jackson Douglas. Good to see you, man," he said, stepping aside to let him and Grant enter. They shook hands, and Jackson introduced his brother. Dylan announced that Ashley had a department softball game but should be back any time. He offered them drinks, and they sat down in the living room. It was on the back of the house, overlooking a small pool and garden. For twenty minutes, they talked about the trip up, the weather, Dylan's business—the normal chitchat for people who didn't really know each other that well.

Then the door leading from the kitchen to the carport opened. It slammed a minute later, punctuating a high-pitched, "I swear, some people are such wimps. Like I'm supposed to not slide because it's a friend . . ." Ashley stopped at the entrance to the living room, looking at the two visitors who, like her husband, had stood. She dropped a small backpack off her shoulder, then an aluminum bat and glove with a clunk. "Jackson!"

She ran and jumped into his arms, nearly knocking him over. He held her as she hugged him tight, shooting a glance at Dylan as he did.

"Babe, I'm right here."

"You're here all the time," she said without letting go. "I thought he was dead." She gave a final squeeze, then let go and dropped to the ground. She wore a white and blue raglan shirt, denim shorts, and kneepads. Maybe more of compression braces. Her blond hair was in a ponytail, damp with sweat. She turned to Grant. "Is this your brother?"

"Hitchhiker I picked up near Chino."

She slapped his arm.

"Ashley, Grant. Grant, Ashley Larson. Uh, that is, O'Brien."

She waved it off. "I still forget half the time." She shook Grant's hand. "What are you doing here?" she asked Jackson.

"I came to apologize for missing your wedding. Congrats," he said, looking first at her, then Dylan. "And to thank you for coming to look for me."

"You'd have done the same for me. You did the same for us—as good as."

He shrugged.

"You drove all the way to Redding for that?"

"I wanted to see you, after everything that happened. And I figured you'd want to hear the full story."

"Of course I do. You drove all the way today?"

"Yeah."

"You staying overnight?"

Jackson nodded.

"Then you have time to stay for dinner?"

"We don't want to impose," Grant said.

"Nonsense. Dylan, order something delicious. I'm going to shower and we can catch up. You *do* owe me an explanation," she said, jabbing a finger at Jackson. "And I want to know who you picked."

"Excuse me?"

"Maggie or Sam," she said with an eyebrow raised. "My money's on Maggie."

"Why's that?"

"Because she's the female version of you. I'm going to shower. Dylan, make sure they have enough to drink."

He saluted as she headed down the short hallway to the bedrooms. "So, what do you boys want for dinner?"

*   *   *

8:28 p.m.

BY THE time the sun set and shade covered Dylan and Ashley's backyard and pool, the temperature had dropped to a mere ninety degrees. Knowing Jackson well, Ashley kept the iced tea flowing, and it, along with a slight breeze, made the conditions tolerable. Once again, Jackson rehashed the last year of his life, explaining his "disappearance" in Mexico and his work to take down GrayStar. And he also briefly summed up his relationship with Maggie.

Dylan and Ashley talked about their wedding and first three-quarters of a year of marriage, as well as the difference between being a detective in Los Angeles and being one in Redding. All things considered, the newlyweds were happy with their life in the north.

"You guys up for ice cream?" Ashley asked.

Jackson shrugged.

"There's a great little local place just a short drive from here, by a park. What time do they close, Dylan?"

"Nine."

"We can make that, right?"

"If the guys want to."

"Let's do it," Grant said, and it was decided. They loaded into Jackson's rental car, and from the backseat, Ashley and Dylan argued over the best way to get to Judy's Drive-In. It was a slice of Americana, little more than an ice cream stand, offering over twenty flavors, a variety of cones, along with some basic fried foods and drinks. They all got cones and took them to a table under stringed-up lights. The too-loud conversation and laughs from a group of teenagers at the next table bubbled around them, as did traffic on a nearby street. It was perfectly summerish.

"So are you totally in the clear?" Ashley asked between licks of her chocolate chunk ice cream.

"As far as I know," Jackson said.

"No legal repercussions?" Dylan asked.

"Pardoned by the president, and he said they squared things with everyone else."

"I can't believe you met the president," Ashley said, then licked again.

Jackson caught a drip before answering. "Neither can I."

"I can't believe you didn't say something untoward," Grant teased.

"I can't believe you used the word 'untoward.'"

"What about GrayStar?" Ashley asked. "Are you sure they're gone?"

"I think so. Eli—the former Mossad guy—is keeping his ear to the ground, and so is my hacker. None of these guys had any family they can track down, so if there's somebody out there, we don't know who it would be."

"I still can't believe it all," Ashley said.

"She's turning into a skeptic," Dylan said.

She elbowed him, and as he reacted, one of his scoops of ice cream fell off the cone and into his lap. That started Ashley laughing to beat the high school kids at the next table. She finally controlled herself and reached for some napkins, but Dylan stopped her. "I'll take care of it."

"I'm sorry, honey."

He excused himself to use the restroom around the back of the building, leaving her to hold his dark chocolate cone.

"He's going to look like he filled his pants and then turned them backward," she said, then laughed some more. Jackson and Grant joined in, enjoying the festive mood. Ashley nursed both cones until Dylan returned. Sufficiently caught up, she tilted her head and looked at Jackson. "You ever wonder what would have happened if you'd have decided not to take the case of that dippy Valley Girl?"

"Been doing a lot of that lately, wondering what if. For years, it was always sad, wishing things had been different. Now . . . I'm haunted by what if things *had* gone differently."

"We probably wouldn't be together," Ashley said. "Who knows what would have happened to Dylan."

"I'd never have had a contact at LAPD, some of those other cases wouldn't have turned out the way they did . . ."

"I guess it's a good thing you found Shay cute enough or pathetic enough to help."

"Like, for sure."

Chapter One Hundred Sixty-One

Saturday, the Ninth of August, Two Thousand Fourteen
Five o'clock in the afternoon
Bel-Air Bay Club
Pacific Palisades, California

EVEN HAD JACKSON not made Grant rich with cartel money, his and Hillary's wedding would have been extravagant. Hillary's father had built a small aerospace empire, and he and Hillary's mother now spent their time traveling the world and "giving back." Jackson had no idea how much the McKenzie family was worth, but he knew they never lacked for money. Even so, he was a little surprised.

The Bel-Air Bay Club, perched on the side of the bluff overlooking the PCH and the California coast, was a 1920's Mediterranean-style event venue with several guest rooms. Thanks to a cancelation, it had become available on somewhat short notice for Grant and Hillary's weekend, and they had snatched it up. On an absolutely glorious afternoon, Jackson could understand why.

Standing literally in the shade of a palm tree, Jackson looked across the club's private lawn at hundreds of guests. They were seated on white chairs, fanned out around a pergola draped with peonies and split by a white runner dotted with rose petals. A row of hedges separated the lawn from the cliff side leading down to the road while preserving the view of the ocean, Catalina, and Santa Monica. On the other side, the stucco and stone exterior of the club glowed in the afternoon sunlight, the Spanish-style tower serving as the focal point. At least for the moment.

Beside Jackson, Grant looked dapper as ever in his tux. He also looked nervous as shep. To Jackson's left, one cousin, one old friend of Grant's, and one fellow policeman stood with a modicum of twitching and wincing in the heat of tuxedos. On the other side of the minister, Heather and Holly McKenzie were showstoppers in their peachy-pink gowns. Jackson still hadn't figured out the color. The other two bridesmaids, reasonable-looking California girls, were bland by comparison.

After several seconds of silence, the live string quartet off to the side resumed playing, this time Pachelbel's Canon. The guests rose in a wave, and all eyes turned to the base of the shrub-lined stairs leading down to the lawn. Escorted by her father, Hillary turned the corner and came into view. The earth nearly stopped spinning.

Catching every ray of sunshine, her dress was resplendent. Jackson had no idea what style of dress it was, the term for the neckline, or how to describe the train. He just knew it was magnificent, adorned with lace and little ruffles of fabric. He'd heard the word "thousands" used to describe its price, and something about being imported from Spain. He wouldn't doubt if it had been hand-sewn by seamstresses born and bred for that very purpose.

Hillary's hair was styled on top of her head, with only a few curls left to trace her face. It was, as always, beautiful, a design so exquisite it almost seemed unreal. A glittering tiara also served as a fount for a veil that trailed behind her like a misty island waterfall. And the bouquet she held as she advanced step by step by step was as vibrant as the San Diego Botanic Garden.

None of her accoutrements, however, could hold a candle to the splendor of her face as she maintained her focus on Grant. In that moment, for the first time, Jackson saw beauty besides the natural—a beauty rooted in her love for his brother. As she and her father stopped at the end of the aisle, she flitted a quick glance toward her sisters, and then the briefest of looks Jackson's way—perhaps with just the faintest upturn in an already smiling mouth. He couldn't help but return it.

The next twenty minutes were a blur to Jackson. There was the usual wedding yada-yada, a brief sermon from the minister, the pouring of unity sand or whatever they called it, and a solo by some woman with a hint of country twang. She couldn't hold a candle to Sawyer's voice. Then the vows and the rings, and before Jackson knew it the minister was citing the power vested in him.

"I now pronounce you husband and wife. You may kiss your bride."

While Grant went to town, Jackson thought back to that first day he'd met Hillary, through all their squabbles, to their adventure in Nevada, to the gradually forged respect, and to the simple note he'd written her the night before. He'd blocked out his smart-aleck nature entirely and simply and succinctly welcomed her to the family and told her to take good care of his brother. He was getting sappy in his old age, or maybe in his second take on life.

The guests applauded, the minister presented the couple, and they started down the aisle. Jackson watched them with a smile, and almost missed his cue to step forward and extend his arm to Heather. As the oldest sister, she had been placed closest to Hillary, despite being co-maids-of-honor with Holly. Given his druthers, Jackson preferred Holly, but it was a short walk. He caught Maggie's eye and gave her a wink. She was seated by Leroy, and looked stunning in her own right in her royal blue sheath dress.

After marching through the crowd, the wedding party ascended to the club's living room, which opened to a patio courtyard, complete with a fireplace and a fountain, beneath stringed lights. Grant and Hillary had eschewed the "don't see the bride before the wedding" rules and gotten pictures out of the way earlier, and were also bypassing a standard receiving line for a more casual cocktail hour before dinner. No longer tethered to Heather (his brain liked it), Jackson ambled around, looking for a non-alcoholic drink, then searched for Maggie. Seated with family, she should be one of the first to arrive.

He spotted her, being chatted up by Jackson's cousin Brook. The middle of five children of Hannah's sister Ruth, Brook was a decent guy but a bit of an oddball. Very talkative, very nerdy but about non-nerdy things. He could go for hours on baseball, science, and *Star Wars*. Okay, so maybe nerdy things. He'd also been girl crazy since puberty, which hadn't been that long ago—Brook was nine years Jackson's younger. He thought about going over to rescue Maggie, but then with a smirk decided to let her get the full Douglas/Goldman experience. So he took his Fresca onto the patio.

It was small and intimate, feeling very much like the courtyard in a Spanish mission. A little sunlight still found its way over the main building, but already the fire and the stringed lights were creating a dusky atmosphere, and the water fountain competed with piped in string music to enhance the cozy feel.

A hip gently bumped Jackson in the side, causing him to nearly spill his Fresca. As he flailed his arm away from his tux and managed to keep the contents in the glass, he didn't have to look to see who it was.

"Hi, Holly."

Hillary's youngest sister stepped into view. "Hi, yourself. Been a while."

"About three-thirty during the photo session, I think."

She gave him a playful scowl, then reached to hug him. "How are you?"

"I am great. How are you?"

"Mmm, a touch jealous. Makes me want a wedding of my own. You?"

"Someday."

"You seeing someone?"

"As a matter of fact, I am."

"Darn. I was hoping to steal you for a dance."

"We'll sneak one in. What about you? A Mr. Holly McKenzie in the picture?"

"Wouldn't that be very modern of us? No. Not for lack of trying." She leaned in close. "Heather keeps scaring them away."

"I don't doubt it."

He was gently cuffed in the back of the head.

"Oh good, another tag team," he said, turning to see Heather. She handed Holly a champagne glass, then the two of them stood on either side of Jackson, smirking. He looked back and forth between the two sisters. "What, don't either of you have dates tonight?"

"Technically, I believe you are my date," Heather said.

"He's seeing someone," Holly said.

"So I hear. Where is she?"

"Probably getting an in-depth breakdown of the hottest *Episode VII* rumors. Come on, I'll introduce you," he said, figuring he could kill two birds with one stone. And if he was really lucky, sic Brook on Heather and Holly and let them fend him off till dinner.

*   *   *

7:32 p.m.

THE COCKTAIL hour actually proved quite fun. David and Hannah were as much the focus as Grant and Hillary, with all their relatives celebrating their return and catching up. Jackson only had to tell his story in full a couple of times, and deflected as much as possible, catching up on his cousins' lives instead. When the chime sounded, everyone moved into the Bel-Air Bay Club's dining room, a spacious area made more so by numerous windows looking out at the ocean and by a high, open-rafter ceiling with wrought-iron chandeliers bathing the room in a soft white glow. Seating at the head table was by couple, so Jackson ended up between Heather and Hillary. The bride's focus, as expected, was on her new husband, and Heather seemed to hit it off with Stacey (Brook's brother—all five kids had names generally associated with the opposite gender) who was on her left. So Jackson concentrated on a delicious dinner of filet mignon, roasted potatoes, and tempura green beans.

When the bride and groom got up to cut the cake and take a few photos, Jackson pulled up a chair at the family table, where Maggie was getting along with David, Hannah, and Leroy. She seemed comfortable with them, which wasn't insignificant.

"You want a piece of cake?" Jackson asked her.

"Sure."

"Anyone else?"

"You're honestly asking that?" Leroy said.

"Well, I'd have asked how many but I didn't think you wanted to have a second heart attack on Grant's special day."

"My doctor cleared me for a normal diet."

"Normal for you or normal for normal eaters?" Maggie asked.

"Well, it's a special occasion."

"I'll find you a big one," Jackson said.

"You may have another matter to take care of first," David said, and nodded to where the deejay was calling for everyone's attention from a microphone stand at the end of the head table.

"Ladies and gentlemen, as the lovely couple makes their way back to the table, I understand the best man has a few words to say."

"David, honey, hold me," Hannah said as Jackson stood.

"There, there, dear, everyone knows he's been through a lot of trauma."

"Well, I should be able to exceed expectations. You want to make a crack before I go, Gramps?"

"No, just keep it short so I can get the cake."

Jackson walked to the mic with some awkward applause. He sent a small smirk toward Grant and Hillary, who had just taken their seats, then cleared his throat.

"Grant, you've always been my little big brother, always looking out for me. And if we're both honest, it was annoying at times, although not as annoying as I'm sure I made it out to be. I've come to realize that all that looking out for me, all that trying to make sure I turned out all right, came from a good place, came from love. And so I want you to know, little big brother, that I appreciate it."

Grant nodded slightly at him.

"But it's also time to stop. It's been touch-and-go at times, but I know now that I'm going to be all right. And you've got someone else to look after now, someone else to take care of. And I know you're going to do it well, because you do everything well, which is why I also know that you're going to be a great cop again now that you're back on the force, and a great dad someday—probably about nine months and six hours from now. (Sorry, Mom.)"

She winced as David smirked and a few others chuckled.

"Now, I would be remiss if I didn't say something about your bride. Hillary McKenzie is the most poised, stoic person I know, but if you look closely, you can see the terror in her eyes, wondering 'What is this fool going to say or do?'" He winked at her, then looked back out at the guests. "Fair disclosure, everybody, Hillary and I haven't always gotten along, which is an understatement akin to saying she's kind of sort of good-looking." He turned his eyes back to her. "We have fought way too much, said things we regret, been at each other's throats almost constantly, and I may or may not have spit back into your drink once. Okay, twice. Who's counting? The point is, I always found it easy to find fault with you, and keeping up this theme of honesty, I still do—just as I know you do with me. But, as Grant looks at me wondering if this is about to go off the rails and if I'm about to ruin everything . . . No, I'm not. Hillary, there is one quality you have that outweighs all others, and that is you make my brother happy. I don't mean happy like I'm happy when USC throttles UCLA every year or when a good steak comes off the grill, but I mean you fill him with joy in the deepest part of his soul—you complete him. And because of that, I say this quite sincerely, welcome to the family, Sis. As far as I'm concerned, all our fighting, all our disagreements and harsh words and everything else is water under the bridge."

She smiled sweetly as Grant put his arm around her.

"Now, like any river, the water is going to rise from time to time, and maybe overflow the bridge on occasion. We'll still not get along, still see things differently, I'll still be glib and you'll still be imperious. (Yes, I looked the word up.) And we'll fight and bicker, I'm sure. But we'll get through it, we'll make sure we get through it, we'll still love each other, because that's what families do. And you can believe me when I say, you do anything for family."

He had to swallow a lump in his throat, and surveying his various family members, gathered he wasn't alone. He looked over to his parents, David with a proud smile, his arm around Hannah as she dabbed her eyes with a tissue.

"Mom, was that everything you wanted me to say?"

"And he fumbles at the one-yard-line," David called out.

"Seriously, to the happy couple . . . I sincerely wish you all the best, and may God bless your marriage, your family, and your lives together . . ."

As everyone drank to his sentiment, then applauded, he returned to his place at the head table. Hillary gave him an embrace and a kiss on the cheek, tears in her eyes. Then Grant gave him a bear hug as well, with maybe just a little relief on his face that Jackson hadn't indeed gone off the rails. The hug ended in a handshake, then Jackson took his seat.

Just before Heather stood to offer her own toast, she leaned over and said, "You really are okay, you know that?"

"Sorry, taken," he said, then looked at Maggie and her remarkably contented smile.

Chapter One Hundred Sixty-Two

8:19 p.m.

SPACE WAS MADE in the dining room for a dance floor, and Jackson fulfilled his last obligation of being introduced with Heather, then stood by as the bride and groom had their first dance, to Etta James' "At Last." He then procured the long-awaited cake and took a seat at the family table while Grant danced with Hannah and Hillary with her father.

"You did well, Son," David said, putting his hand on Jackson's back.

"Seriously, everyone thought I was going to put it in the ditch?"

"Fifty-fifty," Leroy answered.

"Uh-huh."

Everyone was invited to the dance floor, and several couples made their way out, including David and Hannah. Jackson watched his parents for a few minutes, drinking in the festive atmosphere that a year ago had seemed like a pipe dream, and a year before that an impossibility. Grant and Hillary were swaying together, and Jackson even found himself happy for them. That had been about as big of a long shot as any at one time.

As the songs changed, Leroy leaned across the table. "Aren't you going to ask this pretty lady to dance?" he said to Jackson.

"This pretty lady doesn't like to dance."

"That true?" Leroy said, looking at Maggie.

She nodded.

"Makes us a good fit," Jackson said. "By the way, if you see Holly, shoot me a warning."

"He's getting better," Leroy said, stabbing a bite of cake.

"What's that?" Maggie asked.

"Pretending he doesn't like it when pretty girls give him attention."

"He must have been really bad before I knew him," she answered.

"Remind me not to let you two sit together often."

When Michael Bublé took over for John Legend, David and Hannah came back to the table. As Grant and Heather paired up, Jackson feared Holly was headed his way. Instead, Hillary approached the table and beckoned with her finger for Jackson to join her.

He shook his head.

"Jackson," she mouthed.

"I'll pass," he said, holding up his half plate of cake.

She pointed down at the floor. "Get out here."

"See what I mean?" Leroy said.

"Not bad," Maggie muttered.

Jackson sighed and stood, edging around the table. "Probably wants to turn me into an ice sculpture with her eyes," he said to Leroy, who shook his head with an eye roll.

He joined Hillary as they moved to the middle of the floor. He loosely wrapped his arms around her lower back.

"Don't worry, I'm not going to break," Hillary said as she rested her forearms on his shoulders.

"Not you I'm worried about."

She contained a smirk and they began very rudimentary dancing. After a few steps, she briefly touched the lapel of his tuxedo. "You clean up nice," she said, moving the arm back to his shoulder, clasping her hands behind his head.

"You've seen me in a tux before."

"I'm not talking about your clothes."

He raised an eyebrow.

"Your toast was very good."

"I meant it, Hill. Hillary."

A grin started to come out but didn't.

"Every word."

She nodded. "Well, for what it's worth, I'm sorry too . . . Bro."

He grinned.

They danced a few more steps, making a full revolution in the center of the dance floor.

"So I never did ask," he said, "how did Grant convince you to give him your rose?"

"Please tell me you don't watch *The Bachelorette*."

"Of course not. It's all dudes. I did watch a few seasons of *The Bachelor*."

"Are you serious?"

"I had a girlfriend who liked it, and, well . . ."

Hillary let a smirk fade. She cut her gaze to Maggie. "Speaking of girlfriends . . . are you in love with her?"

He too looked at Maggie for a moment, then back at Hillary. "Yeah."

"First time?"

He nodded. "Yeah."

"I thought I'd been in love before, but when I met Grant, got to know him—I realized he was the only man for me. Then, when I thought he was gone, I did fall for Brian. But when I saw Grant's face again, got over the shock and realized he was alive . . . there was never a decision to make."

"He wouldn't tell me, how'd he do it?"

"How'd he do what?"

"Re-insert himself into your life?"

"That will stay between us."

"He buried Brian in the desert, didn't he?"

Hillary shook her head in disbelief, and they danced some more.

"I think Maggie's good for you," she said a minute later.

"Good for me?"

"She complements you."

"Wit for snark and so forth?"

"That, but . . . I don't know how to say it."

"Hillary McKenzie at a loss for words?"

"Hillary Douglas now."

"You'll have to print up new stationary at CD&R."

"They can afford it."

He grinned.

"Maggie draws out the best in you. I've seen it in the few times you've been together and just in you in general. And I saw it down in Mexico, how you affected her. You're good for each other."

"Well, Mrs. Douglas, I appreciate that. Sincerely."

She smiled, then leaned in to give him a hug as the song drew to an end. "Don't blow it," she whispered.

He gave her a quick peck on the cheek. "I won't. Now go dance with somebody who knows what they're doing."

*   *   *

9:20 p.m.

THE DANCING had morphed from couples arm-in-arm to groups, and from slow ballads to pop hits and '80s classics. Jackson and Leroy were both contemplating third pieces of cake, while David and Hannah sat back with happy smiles, enjoying their family and the magical occasion. Jackson excused himself to the restroom, enjoyed the solitude of a handicapped stall for a couple minutes, and then returned to the table. Pharrell was making everyone "Happy," and he nudged Maggie's arm. "Take a walk?"

She nodded. "Sure."

They exited onto the patio, overlooking the ocean now reflecting back flickering beams of moonlight, framed by palm fronds lazily floating in a breeze that was still warm enough to be pleasant. They descended down to the lawn, now cleared of chairs with the ceremony long over.

"Where we going?" Maggie asked.

"The wedding coordinator told us there's a little lookout point down this way," he said, pointing across the lawn. Holding hands, which was unusual for them but seemed appropriate this night, they walked slowly through the grass, then down a sidewalk flanked by hedges on the right and a mown hillside on the left. When they reached the small lookout area, Jackson was relieved not to find one of the bridesmaids playing kissy-face with one of the groomsmen. Instead, they saw the curved coastline, with Santa Monica to the left and Malibu to the right.

"Beautiful, isn't it?" Maggie said, standing beside him and looking out at the expanse.

Jackson's eyes were on her. "Sure is."

She turned to face him with an incredulous face. "I meant the view, you dork."

"So did I. Maggie, you're a blue jeans and T-shirt kind of girl, but this works too."

"I think that was a compliment."

"It was. You look spectacular."

She beamed.

"Almost insulting to the bride."

"Okay, that's enough."

He grinned as she looked out at the ocean. He kept looking at her, waiting until she turned her head back to him.

"You remember that time we spent the day in Monterey?" he asked.

Maggie nodded as a whisper of breeze lifted a curl of hair off her shoulder.

"And I bought you that mood ring, then threw it off the cliff at Big Sur because I said you were turning it into a strobe light?"

"I remember."

"Well, I've been thinking," he said as he deftly reached into his pocket and pulled out a small, black box, "that I should get you a replacement."

Maggie swallowed hard. "Jack."

"Are you nervous because of what might be inside or because of what might not?"

"A little of both."

He nodded, lifting her hand and placing the box in it. "Well, you don't have to open it just yet," he said, folding her other hand over it and holding her hands between his. She took a deep breath as he started talking.

"Maggie, we've never had a normal romantic relationship. First just bantering and hanging out and neither of us committing, then breaking up or whatever that was, then starting to date for real while hunting terrorists. And even now, we're not the hand-holdy, cuddly, sweet-nothing whispering sort. This isn't what I pictured it would be someday, not what I thought falling in love would be like. And to be honest, that was a little concerning to me for a while. I was worried that because we didn't call each other punkin' or honeykins or stupid stuff like that and didn't have nervous first dates or spring picnics or moonlit walks on the beach that maybe ours wasn't the real thing. But, Mags," he said, gently shaking his head, "the more I've thought about it—and I've thought about it a lot—I've realized that you and I don't have to be that Hallmark-movie couple, because that's not who we are. We're banter and shoulder punches and pizza-and-a-movie or kick it at the arcade kind of people. And more than that, I know like I've never known anything, Maggie, that I love you like I've never loved anyone else. I want to spend the rest of my life with you, to know that wherever life takes us, you and I are home. I can't explain it other than to say it's obvious that you're the one for me. So this," he said, lifting his hand off hers and gently pulling her hand off the box, "is not a mood ring. It's a representation of the easiest decision I've ever made, and the most important question I've ever asked. Maggie, will you marry me?"

She exhaled slowly, then licked her lips. "Before I answer, I need to confess something to you."

"Okay."

"You remember when I came to Nebraska and told you I loved you?"

"That does ring a bell."

"And I told you that I needed to know how you felt, needed you to be honest, and that I was a big girl and if the answer was no, that was fine, I'd be okay? Well, I was lying through my teeth, Jackson. I knew then, and I know it even more now, that there is no way I would ever be okay without you. You are the only thing in this world I have that truly matters, and you mean the world to me. So yes, of course, I will marry you."

They both leaned into a kiss that turned into a hug, her clasping the back of his head and he tracing her cheek with his hand.

"That's two pretty good speeches in one night," she said as they separated.

"I'm rich enough to hire a speechwriter."

She exhaled a laugh, and he reached for the box, still in her hand, and opened it. He lifted out the ring he and Reggie—two jewelry knuckleheads—had picked out just two days ago, and slid it onto her finger. She extended a flat hand to look at it.

"It's beautiful, Jack."

"It's probably not quite up to snuff for a couple of our combined net-worth, but we didn't really get that honestly, and I figured you'd prefer something a little less ostentatious."

"It's beautiful," she said again.

"Well, then it fits."

She smiled brightly as another hint of breeze caught her hair. The smile slowly turned to a smirk. "Can I ask you something?"

"No takesy backsies."

"Did you propose tonight—even just in small part—so you could steal a little of Grant and Hillary's thunder?"

"Wow, it really is everyone coming for me."

"Come on, Jack, you have to admit that wouldn't be terribly out of line for your relationship with Hillary."

"I almost did *not* propose tonight for that very reason. But, even though I was pretty sure you would say yes, I couldn't wait to ask any longer. And even though we're both casual and carefree, I figured something like this deserved a little formality. And I didn't know when we'd ever get this sort of moment again."

"I'm sorry I doubted you."

"That said, if you want to keep wearing that the rest of the night and see who notices first . . ."

She had already draped her arms around his neck, and softly tapped the back of his head in reproach. Then she drew him in for another kiss. "I love you, Jack."

"I love you too, Maggie."

"You want to make this moment last a little longer?"

"Well, I don't want to miss the Cha Cha Slide."

"You are a dork," she said, then tipped her head and kissed him slow and soft and wonderful, like he'd never been kissed before.

Chapter One Hundred Sixty-Three

Sunday, August 10
10:40 a.m.

SOMEONE—PROBABLY THE mothers—had come up with the idea of having Grant and Hillary's immediate relatives get together for a post-wedding brunch the next morning. Jackson had brought Maggie and cajoled Leroy into coming, since he was the only living grandparent. He couldn't tell if Warren and Danae McKenzie had been displeased or if that's how their faces normally looked in the morning. But it didn't matter. He was being treated to brunch at one of Malibu's finest restaurants, seated between Maggie and Leroy, and he was sitting on a bombshell.

While the parents of the bride and groom talked and laughed at one end of the long table and Maggie kept up a conversation with Heather and Holly, Jackson and Leroy—who sat at the end of the table—engaged in a bacon-and egg-eating contest. A few hot donuts too.

As the meal wound down and the fathers sat back from the table, Jackson tinked his glass with his fork. Eight sets of eyes turned his way. One hand found his under the table.

"So I don't mean to steal the moment," Jackson said, "but I do have something to share with you all sooner than later."

"What, you and Maggie getting married?"

Jackson turned to Leroy, who'd lifted another piece of bacon. "Really, old man? Of all the thunder to steal?"

"Is he right?" Holly asked from across Jackson.

He dipped his chin. "Show them."

Having slipped her ring on, Maggie held up her left hand. "He proposed last night."

"Who's a thunder-stealer?" Heather asked.

"Is this a joke, Jackson?" Hannah asked. "I don't mean that the way it sounds, Maggie, but . . ."

"It is Jackson," David said.

"You'd have thought I proved myself with that toast. No, it is not a joke. I am in the tank for Maggie, and she said yes, so . . . we are getting married."

"Well, congratulations, Son," David said, standing at the end of the table. He came and placed a hand on each of their shoulders. "Maggie, it's obvious how happy you make Jackson, just from the short time we've known you. Welcome to the family."

"Thank you, David," she said, standing to give him a hug. Jackson and Hannah also stood, her dabbing her eyes.

"Pretty sure those are happy tears," Jackson said.

Hannah nodded, then embraced Maggie. It was hard to tell through the tears and hair, but it sounded like she said something echoing David's words. While they hugged and talked and looked at the ring, David offered his son a hearty handshake. And a restrained upturn in the corner of his mouth. Then Hannah came over to hug her son through the tears, telling him how happy she was for him. She might have even said relieved.

Eventually they all sat back down. Hannah and Maggie continued to chat. David and Warren went back to their conversation. The three McKenzie women all smiled, perfunctorily in Danae's case, sincerely with a wink in Holly's case. Jackson never had been able to get a solid read on Heather.

And at the end of the table, Leroy resumed eating bacon.

*   *   *

Thursday, August 14
7:20 p.m.

"HERE YOU go, dear." Connie set down a mug of coffee and a fresh-baked cinnamon roll. Jackson was stuffed from homemade ossobuco, but he couldn't pass up one of her cinnamon rolls, dripping as it was with melting icing.

"Thank you, Connie."

She sat down opposite him at the table on her deck. It was much larger than his, but the views over her shimmering pool were no more spectacular than those from his. He'd more or less invited himself over, bribing her with household chores and knowing she couldn't resist cooking for him—or anyone. He hadn't arranged to have Connie's Pomeranian, Fluffy, locked up for dinner, but Connie had suggested dining al fresco, which had alleviated that concern.

"So, what do you want to talk to me about anyhow?" Connie asked.

"Did I say that?"

"Feminine intuition," she said with a wink.

He nodded and took a drink of her gourmet coffee. Almost as good as the stuff in the Swiss airport shop.

"The lawn looks marvelous, by the way."

"Thanks," he added.

"You going to try your cinnamon roll?"

He cut into it with a fork and savored the doughy goodness, then licked frosting from his lip. He praised Connie for a moment, both for her ego and because it was true. Then he said, "I do have some news."

"Yes? Well, don't make me drag it out of you, Jackson."

"I'm getting married."

Connie sat back with wide eyes. "Land of Goshen. Is it Maggie?"

"I told you she and I were dating."

"Boy, the way you used to parade women through that house, how should I know?"

"I didn't parade women. But yes, it's Maggie."

"I like her."

"Me too," he said, cutting another bite of his cinnamon roll.

"I kind of liked Samantha better. Wasn't that the blond girl?"

"Yeah."

"But it is your choice. I'm happy for you, Jackson."

"Thanks, Connie."

"Have you set a date yet?"

"We're still looking, checking football schedules and things like that."

"You don't mean this fall, do you?"

"Why wait?"

Connie harrumphed. Jackson ate more cinnamon roll, giving her a few minutes before dropping the other shoe. "I'll probably be moving too."

"Moving?"

"House is kind of small for two."

"Just two?"

"Well, for starters." He quickly moved on before she questioned his and Maggie's reproductive plans. "Besides, we're both rich now, so we might as well move up in the world."

Connie tisked—the woman living off ex-husbands' money in a house full of knickknacks she'd purchased on her world travels—disapproving of luxurious living. She leaned back again with her cup of coffee and looked out toward the Pacific. "I sure do hate to see you leave."

Jackson grinned, knowing she was likely thinking of his free labor.

"You promise not to be a stranger, don't you?"

He grinned some more, thinking of his propensity for mooching snacks and desserts. "I do if you keep making cinnamon rolls like this."

*   *   *

Sunday, August 24
2:19 p.m.

"WHY ARE we watching this, again?" Maggie asked. She and Jackson sat side by side on his couch, slouched, their feet propped on the edge of his coffee table. It held the remnants of a takeout lunch from Chow Down, the best Chinese restaurant in Greater Los Angeles.

"Because we're good Americans," Jackson said.

"We go down with the ship, is that it?"

"There's still an inning and a half left. It's only nine to one."

Maggie nodded.

A short—even for a twelve-year-old—Taiwanese kid struck out a lanky kid from New Jersey, reducing the Americans' chances in the Championship Game of the Little League World Series by another out. They were down to four.

"So what's the limit?" Maggie asked.

"The limit?"

"I mean, what level of competition will you watch in the name of patriotism?"

"Maggie, if an immigrant from Canada challenged a natural-born American to a game of pinochle, I'm ready to wave the flag and chant 'U-S-A.'"

She looked at him with a grin. "You are a strange duck, you know that?"

"Besides, this has always served as something of a preamble to the college football season. You can almost feel the excitement."

The next U.S. batter popped up to second base to end the inning.

"It's palpable," she said.

He nudged her elbow. "Refill?"

She held up half a glass of lemonade. "I'm good."

Jackson went to the fridge to top off his glass, and was on his way back when the doorbell rang. He set the lemonade down and went to open the door. He was greeted by a swarthy but smiling Israeli. "Eli. What are you doing here?"

"I wanted to talk to you in person."

"Uh-oh. Bad news?"

"Just the opposite," Eli said. "Can I come in?"

Jackson admitted him as Maggie muted the TV and stood.

"You are watching children's baseball?" Eli asked.

Maggie shrugged.

"What's the word, Eli?" Jackson asked.

"I was in London on business last week, and I met up with Blackshear. We compared notes. We've confirmed no living blood relatives for any GrayStar members but one, the woman. She's an enigma."

"An enigma?"

"Chelsea Rayburn. May be a Courtney Rayburn who served in the Marines for four years at the right time, or Chelsea Ray, who briefly worked for the CIA after a stint in the U.S. Air Force, or somebody else entirely. We have no idea who she is—was—and Blackshear said we probably never would, with no body to work off."

"What about security camera footage at the estate?" Maggie asked.

"That's how we got as far we did, but it wasn't conclusive. Could be she was one of those women and had plastic surgery or matured enough that her face changed, or could be she's somebody else. He'll keep looking into it."

"How much you want to bet she has a cranky ex?"

"It's been three months," Eli said.

"Took me a lot longer than that."

"Jack, if it were me, I wouldn't be worried. My guess—and Blackshear's—is she's Chelsea Ray, and there's nobody in her life—I mean *nobody*."

"That would make her an ideal GrayStar candidate," Maggie said.

"It would," the Israeli agreed.

"How strong of a guess?" Jackson asked.

"Eighty percent."

He shrugged. "What about non-blood relatives?"

"Three ex-wives, none of whom are on the radar. And of course, there's always the chance of an illegitimate child somewhere, but they likely don't know it and might be liable to shake your hand more than come for revenge."

Jackson exhaled. "There's risks to everything, I guess. Thanks, Eli. You want to take a few more million out of petty cash?"

"I'm good. And one more piece of good news."

"What's that?"

"Blackshear found financial records, payments to a Collantes Investigations in Honolulu. Tens of thousands over the last several years. Looks like Mia was a private contractor."

"Eli, that's not good news. It means there could be any number—"

"He said it looks like she was the only one. And even if she wasn't, private contractors like contracts. If there's nobody to pay them . . ."

"Yeah."

"You're in the clear, Jack."

He nodded.

"I should be going."

"Nonsense," Maggie said. "You just got here."

"I wasn't being polite. I have another appointment across town."

"On a Sunday afternoon?" Jackson asked.

"We're both Jewish."

"Work or pleasure?" Maggie asked with a sideways grin.

"Work."

"Thought you'd retire for sure," Jackson said.

"It's in the interest of Israeli national security. Potentially. And I should go." He gave Maggie a hug, then pumped Jackson's hand. "I'll keep my ears to the ground, even once I retire for good. If anything should ever change, I'll let you know. But by all accounts, you're in the clear."

"Thanks, Eli. I appreciate all your help, you know that, right?"

"I do. *Shalom*, my friend."

"*Shalom*, Eli. *Shalom* at last."

Chapter One Hundred Sixty-Four

Monday, September 1
4:47 p.m.

SOUTHERN CALIFORNIA WAS experiencing a modern drought, which was bad news for farmers and presented a danger of forest fires, but made for outstanding picnic weather. The entire Douglas family (and their plus ones) had been invited to the McKenzie house outside Santa Barbara for a Labor Day soirée. They were not alone. Other family members, friends, probably some former business associates and the like were welcomed to the estate—really more of a hacienda—in the hills overlooking town and the ocean. Because he was doing his best to be a decent in-law—and because he and Maggie couldn't figure out anything better to do, and sitting around alone in his house or her apartment talking about marriage and all that went with it might be too tempting for them—Jackson had accepted the invite.

The party was typically Californian. Gals in skimpy swimsuits hung around a pool. Guys with bronzed backs played volleyball in the lawn. Festive music thumped through speakers. Warren McKenzie and his cronies sipped drinks and laughed at inside jokes. Grant (apparently it was a perk of the job) kept grilled meat in ready supply while several women managed the rest of the food—the usual picnic sides.

Jackson—his stint in Nebraska notwithstanding—hadn't ever become enamored with volleyball, and cavorting in a pool with a bunch of women still reminded him of Lisa, Brooke, and Kelly at *El Hotel Pacifico*. So he sat on the deck behind his shades, eating and drinking and trying to keep his eyes only on Maggie. Then again, the biblical warnings against lust didn't make dispensations for recently engaged people.

David took his mind off it by sitting down beside him. "Set a date yet?"

"October 11."

"That's soon."

Jackson looked at him. "You saying it's too soon?"

"Not mine to say, Son. You know if it's right or not."

"It's right, Dad."

"I believe you. And for what it's worth, your mother and I both approve of Maggie very much."

"Good."

"I have to say, we were a little surprised to get an announcement so soon."

"You saying it's too soon?" Jackson asked with a wink.

"Same answer as before."

Jackson downed some iced tea. "Dad, I'll be honest with you."

"Good policy."

"The best, I hear. There is no way I would get married if I wasn't a hundred percent sure. This is one area where I wouldn't fly by the seat of my pants."

"That's good to know."

"Mom okay with the soonness of it all?"

"I think having both her sons married off in a couple of months is a little much for her, but she has no qualms about you and Maggie."

Jackson nodded.

"And it will take time for her to get back in the groove of everyday life, having a church, getting involved in the community, going for groceries without looking over her shoulder."

"Having the groceries be dead when you go for them."

"That too."

"Seriously, Belize?"

"It was off the grid, Jack. We were starting to acclimate to the possibility of it being permanent—at least until something changed that made it possible for us to come back without endangering you all."

There was a shout from the volleyball game—a spike or a diving pancake or something.

"How's the home re-decorating coming?" Jackson asked. Hannah was in the process of restoring their old house to its old condition—with a few tweaks.

"Keeping her busy. And me," David said with a smile. "Busy is good right now, though. Too much thinking about everything at once might drive us crazy."

"Are you both okay?"

David looked at him. "We're good, Jack. Not perfect, but we're okay."

"If you're ever not . . ."

David placed a hand on his shoulder.

"Oh, I didn't mean me. I had this therapist."

"Yeah, you mentioned that. The whole toking thing."

Jackson frowned.

"That not the term the kids use?"

"Just never expected slang from you regarding my burning hash."

"Never expected said burning hash from you."

"Touché." Jackson took a drink. "You talked to Sullivan since the debrief?"

"About?"

"I assume he's recruiting you for another stint."

"I am absolutely done in the Navy, Jack. I'll wear a sweatshirt when we play Army, and that's it."

"What are you going to do then?"

"I'll figure something out."

"You always do."

"Douglas & Son Investigations or something. I'll be the Rocky to your Rockford."

"I could ask for nothing more in life."

David grinned. He looked away and exhaled as he turned back. "I don't think I ever got around to telling you, Jack, but I'm awful proud of you."

"For anything in particular?"

"Everything you did to save us, to take out GrayStar. There's something admirable about a man believing in something so firmly—even when others question him and even when he questions himself—that he sticks with it. Can be a dangerous thing too, but not when that man is a man of character and conviction."

"One-time toking aside."

David nodded. "Jack, I can see in your eyes even more than what you've told us that this took a toll on you. A lot of people would have backed down or quit, or maybe never started. So I'm proud of you."

"Thanks, Dad."

"And grateful."

"Well, in fair disclosure, I'm proud of you too. I admit, I had conflicting emotions about you leaving me behind, about you not coming back, about you getting involved with this whole thing in the first place. And I've always struggled with the idea of God, Country, Family. Shouldn't family be second? But somewhere along the line, it hit me, that sometimes truly loving your family or your spouse or your kids or whoever means putting the country in a higher position—that serving country ahead of your family is actually a way to love your family. I still can't quite quantify it," he said, then made eye contact with his dad, "but I get it. And I can tell from the lines around your eyes the toll it took on you. So . . . I'm proud of you too."

Jackson couldn't recall ever seeing his father cry, but he had seen his eyes wet a few times. And they were now too as he placed a hand on Jackson's arm.

Sloshing water ruined the moment, and then a shadow covered half of Jackson's body. The next thing he knew, water was dripping all over him. He jerked forward, then looked up and back to see Maggie wringing out her wet hair over him. "Agh, what are you doing?"

She grinned playfully.

"The McKenzies are rich—they have towels."

Maggie smirked for a moment more, flicking a little more water at him. "I'm not interrupting, am I?"

"As a mat—"

"Not at all," David said and started to get up. "Here, you want to sit down?"

"No, that's all right."

"I insist," he said. "Can I get you something to drink? Jack, a refresher?"

"I'm good."

"Me too," Maggie said. "You don't have to get up."

"I should find Jack's mother, see how she's doing." He winked and headed off.

Maggie waited a moment, then dropped into the chair. She soaked up the sun for a minute, then turned her head. "There more to that?"

"To what?"

"Seeing how your mom's doing? She okay?"

"She's a little concerned about her sons' choice in wives, I hear."

Maggie whacked his arm.

"She's okay," Jackson said. "Reentry can be a little rough is all."

"Yeah." She took a breath. "You want to take a walk?"

"Any place in particular?"

"Around."

"Okay."

They got up, and Maggie pulled a tank top and a pair of shorts on over her swimsuit, and they set out. The McKenzie property flowed down the hillside, first in several acres of mowed grass, then in yellow-brown native grass interspersed with a few bushes, to a fence-line and a grove of trees in the bottom of the ravine. A large oak tree was halfway down the hill, standing grandly if a little crooked as a sentinel over the property. From the edge of the lawn, a winding dirt trail cut through the grass to the oak, and Jackson and Maggie followed it.

"I've been meaning to talk to you about something," Maggie said when they were within a hundred feet of the oak, and twice that from the lawn.

"I've been meaning to talk to you too."

"You wanna go first?"

"No, go for it."

She took a breath.

"Something bad? You've reconsidered?"

"No."

"Should Jack stop being a smart-aleck?"

"For about five minutes."

He nodded.

She took a breath. "You remember when we had talks about sex, and you said it was supposed to be something shared by a couple in a lifelong, committed relationship and I said it was a way to show love or something fun to do?"

"I remember."

"Well, it just didn't make any sense to me, your way of looking at it. You seemed like a prude."

He looked at her.

"But now that I've changed the way I've looked at some things . . ." She stopped and pawed the dirt with the toe of her Sperry boat shoe. Then she lifted her head. "Jack, I feel bad that I can't give you the same thing you can give me—an . . . unwrapped gift."

Jackson took her hand. "Maggie, when I look at you, I don't think about who you were or what you did in the past. The Bible says you're a new creation, and that's what I see."

She squeezed his hand.

"We both have regrets, both have baggage," he said. "And some of those things might give us some trouble, might be things we have to work through together. But that's what a marriage is—working through things." He shook his head. "But I don't want you feeling bad about it. I don't want you regretting it. And I wouldn't change a thing about you or who you are."

She swallowed, and Jackson nearly smiled seeing the vulnerable side of Maggie.

"You're not just giving me a speech, are you?" she asked.

"No."

"Because you're good at giving speeches."

"I mean it, Mags."

She grinned beautifully and squeezed his hand again.

He smiled.

"What?" she asked.

"That was pretty much the scene where George Clooney called Julia Roberts a liar and she called him a thief."

"It was nothing like that. If it was, Reggie'd be here and we'd be talking about getting a date for him."

He conceded with a nod.

She pulled his hand to start walking again, then let go. "You wanted to talk to me about something?"

"I've been thinking about our wedding."

"*You* having second thoughts?"

"I'm just thinking about your family. I know where things stand with them, Maggie, but if there was ever a time to reach out with an olive branch one more time, this would be it. I don't want to try to talk you into anything, but I want to make sure you're giving this the consideration you'll wish you had one day."

They had reached the shade of the oak tree. An old wood swing was hanging by ropes from one of its branches, and Maggie wandered over to it and leaned into it. She wrapped her hands around the ropes, and Jackson couldn't help but smile as he looked at her there, backlit by the sun-splashed hillside.

"What?" she asked.

"You look like you're posing for a senior picture."

She looked at him under a raised eyebrow.

"It's a compliment, Mags."

Her feet still on the ground, she swung back and forth a few inches. "When I was a little girl, I used to dream about my dad walking me down the aisle. That is the way it's supposed to be, right, the dad gives his daughter away?"

He'd wandered over to lean against the trunk of the tree, and nodded.

"And my dad wasn't anything special, not the kind of guy you'd dream about, but I was a little girl," she said with a shrug. Then she swallowed. "That dream died a long time ago, Jack. My dad already gave me away. And before you say anything about your dad walking me down the aisle or Reggie or Admiral Sullivan or whoever you have in mind or think it would be if this was a TV show, forget it. I'd just as soon walk down the aisle alone, because that's how I'm coming to this marriage, alone."

"That's sad, Maggie."

"No it's not. Because I'm never going to be alone again, Jack. It's like I told you when you proposed, you're my world. And the icing on the cake is I get a family now too."

"Okay."

She smiled and let go of the swing. She walked over to him. "But you are sweet to think of it," she said, giving him a quick kiss and a pat on the chest as she passed.

He enjoyed it for just a moment, then caught up. "You know, speaking of the wedding, if your family isn't there, it might look kind of lopsided. So I'm thinking, since we just had a huge gathering of the Douglas clan, what if we had something really small and simple? We don't have time to plan it big anyhow."

"Small and simple?"

"You, me; Mom, Dad; Grant and Hillary, I guess. Grandpa can do the hitchin' as a retired minister. And Reggie will be my best man. You have a maid of honor?"

"Nope. I have female friends, but none that close, especially after disappearing for half a year. And I'm not having you ogling Walker all through our wedding, so don't say it."

"Never crossed my mind."

"Can you have a best man and no maid of honor?"

"It's California, Maggie. You can marry your mink stole if you want."

She stopped. "You're picking Reggie instead of Grant?"

"*'There is a friend who sticks closer than a brother.'* Reggie's my boy. Grant will get it."

"You haven't told him yet?"

"Waiting for the right time."

"Good luck."

"Yeah."

"Jack, I really don't care about a traditional wedding. Simple sounds great. Invite whoever you want, have just Reggie or whoever standing beside you. Just say 'I do' and I'll be happy."

"Okay. Wow, you're low maintenance."

She winked, and he draped his arm over her shoulder and pulled her close.

"You can make up for it by going extravagant on our honeymoon trip."

Chapter One Hundred Sixty-Five

"MAN, I STILL can't believe it," Reggie said.

"What, that Jackson shot Hayes?" Maggie asked.

"That he survived two hand-to-hand fights long enough to get the shot off?" Grant asked.

Hillary smirked. "That he didn't miss?"

"Naw," Reggie said, raising his cigar. "That he didn't ask him first if he'd seen the sunrise."

Sitting across a coffee table from Reggie, Jackson slapped his palm against his forehead. "Dangit. Moment of a lifetime, and I blew it. Must have been the concussion."

"Really, *Magnum, P.I.* at a time like that?" Grant asked.

"Is there ever a bad time?" He looked at Reggie. The five were seated in an alcove of the newly opened Cameron's Lounge. Filling two floors of a commercial building in downtown Santa Monica, the lounge was a cozy mix of living-room-like seating areas, booths and bistro tables, a couple private rooms, and a small stage for live music. Currently, it was a jazz pianist keeping it light and cheerful. "Why'd we invite them all anyhow?" Jackson asked. "This was supposed to be you and me lightin' up a couple celebratory cigars."

"It was your idea, J. Something about not getting a bachelor party."

"I offered to throw you one," Grant said.

"Yeah, a Grant Douglas party. I remember your twelfth birthday."

"What was his twelfth birthday?" Hillary asked, leaning into Grant on the loveseat they shared.

"It was a space theme. Everybody dressed up like astronauts and futuristic beings and planets."

"That was one kid," Grant said.

"And no girls," Jackson said.

Grant shrugged.

"See what I mean?" Jackson said.

"You should talk. My bachelor party was a drive upstate to visit one of your old girlfriends."

"She wasn't my girlfriend."

"Who, Ashley?" Hillary asked.

Grant nodded.

"To be fair," she said, "I think she was the one girl Jackson didn't have a thing for."

"You all know Maggie's sitting right here, don't you?"

"You shouldn't take secrets into your marriage," Grant said with a tip of his head.

"Oh, and did you tell Hillary about that time at camp when you asked that redheaded counselor on a date?"

"Like an actual date?" Maggie asked.

"Archery and snacks at the canteen," Grant said. He shrugged. "I was ten."

"Yeah, and she was twenty-six," Jackson said.

"She was twenty-one and a junior in college."

"That isn't much better, Grant," Hillary said.

"At least I wasn't trying to hide a crush on Alex Mack from my whole family."

"You knew?" Jackson asked.

"You bought the neighbor girl a beanie, Jack. Everybody knew."

"You had a thing for the neighbor girl?" Maggie asked.

"No, I had a thing for Alex Mack and she looked more like Harriet from *Small Wonder*."

"Craziest dang bachelor party I've ever been to," Reggie said, "and going back to my playing days, that's some crazy. You all want something more to eat?"

The bar and several waitresses at Cameron's Lounge served drinks, cigars, and a small selection of appetizers and desserts. The group was dining on an antipasti charcuterie board and a plate of steak bite and Portobello mushroom kebabs. At everyone's suggestion, Reggie got up to get more kebabs.

"Are you really going to be that flip about it?" Hillary asked when he was gone.

He looked at her, sitting with legs crossed in a lacey blouse and skirt combo, her hair brilliant as ever. There had already been one fight, when she'd made a comment about Jackson—who always got on her for drinking—smoking a cigar. He'd said it was just one, for a special occasion. She'd said that's what addicts always said. He'd said she should talk. Then the first round of kebabs had arrived to serve as an armistice.

"Flip about what? Bachelor parties?"

"No, about Hayes, about the way you shot him . . . in the back?"

"Back of the head, technically. Right at the base," he said, pointing to his own head.

"That doesn't bother you?"

"No, because one of the basic laws of the universe is that good guys stop bad guys."

"Laws of the universe?" Grant asked.

"Yeah. It's like all those Westerns where the marshal or sheriff is corrupt or derelict in his duties or just doesn't exist, and the only thing that will stop the bad guys is a good guy standing in the gap—taking the law into their own hands and doing what has to be done for the good of the town. In this case, the 'marshal' couldn't stop GrayStar, for whatever reason—couldn't stop these terrorists. So I did."

"I get that," Hillary said, "and I'm not challenging you on legal grounds. But . . ."

"Nobody in a Western ever shot anybody in the back," Grant said.

"Nobody ever turned their back in a Western either." Jackson took a puff on his cigar. "But that's not the point. I have no doubt if I had let Hayes walk away—or had I tried to stop him by less lethal means and failed—he would have come for me one day, and not just me but all of you. So I did the only thing I could do, and if I had to do it again, I would. Good guys stop bad guys—it's what makes them the good guys. And sometimes, when the bad guy is really, really bad, the good guy has to take a drastic step to stop him."

Reggie returned with a plate of sizzling kebabs. He sat down and picked up his cigar. "What we debating?"

"My ethics," Jackson said.

"Jack, I wasn't really questioning your ethics."

He reached for a skewer and looked at Hillary.

"I'm asking if you're okay with everything you've done and had to do?"

He took a bite and looked at her again.

"I'm serious."

He nodded. "I believe you. And I'm good."

"Okay," she said.

"Even talked to my therapist the other day."

"Your therapist? You have a therapist?"

"Yeah, an old converted hippie. A good guy. We hashed through a few things, and he thought I was doing quite well, cons . . . idering."

They all looked at him.

He sat back, smiling to himself.

"What is it, Jack?" Grant asked.

"Zach, my therapist, used the same expression a couple years ago, when we had our biggest breakthrough. He said I was doing quite well."

"Okay . . ." Hillary said.

"I went outside that day and prayed for rain. Metaphorically. We'd talked about how I was holding onto the pain of losing my family because I didn't want to let that connection go—let the water out of the dam, so to speak—but that it also rained from time to time to refill my reservoir."

"That's . . . deep," Grant said.

"Especially for me, right, Hill?"

"I didn't say it."

"No, I mean deep, water, a dam—a pun," Grant said.

"He writes his own stuff, believe it or not," Jackson said to Maggie.

"Oh, I believe it," she said before pulling a mushroom off her kebab.

"Anyhow, rain could be the family I still had, friends like you," he said with a look at Reggie, "my co-girlfriends. Sorry, Dear."

Maggie shrugged.

"So I prayed for rain, hoping that God would help heal the hurt, give me a way to go on."

"And he did," Grant said with a smile.

"Well, more than that. The only way we caught GrayStar, got Mom and Dad back, was because their plane couldn't take off in a hurricane. Because it rained."

"You think God sent a hurricane to St. Charles to reunite our family?"

Jackson shrugged. "I don't begin to know how God's sovereignty works over the weather, or to presume that He altered global weather patterns for little old me. I just know what I prayed for and what happened."

"And here we are," Grant said.

"Yeah. Anyhow, I'm good, Hillary. Honest."

"Okay."

"And thanks."

She smiled pleasantly.

"What about you, Maggie?" Reggie asked.

She had joined Jackson and Reggie in a celebratory cigar, and exhaled. "How so?"

"I haven't heard, how's your re-acclimation to normal society going?"

"Good."

"You figure out what you're going to do with the rest of your life?"

She looked at Jackson.

"Might as well tell them," he said.

"For starters, I'm writing a book about GrayStar—the rise and fall. More the fall, with an insider's perspective."

"For real?" Grant asked.

She nodded. "I've already contacted a publisher, and a couple people at Fox have talked about promotion opportunities. And I'll still be doing some contributing on a couple of Fox shows."

"Wow," Reggie said, then took a drag on the cigar. "That's great, Maggie."

Jackson looked at her. "Can you still go by Maggie in public?"

She frowned.

"Why couldn't she?" Hillary asked.

"Because her name's going to change when she marries me."

Hillary shook her head.

"You don't know?"

"Jack, I don't know," Grant said. "What are you talking about?"

"Maggie is a nickname," Jackson answered. "Her real name is Anne Magstadt. Get it, Magstadt, Maggie? But now she'll legally be Anne Josephine Douglas."

"I guess you could switch to Duggy," Grant said with a smirk.

"Digger, maybe," Reggie said.

"I think I'll stick with Maggie, thanks."

"It does fit you," Jackson said. Then he frowned.

"What?"

"Maggie Douglas."

She shook her head.

"I don't know. It sorta sounds like the name of a New England lobsterman's Boston Whaler. 'This is Captahn O'Connah of the *Maggie Douglas*, we're approachin' the hahbah, ovah.'"

"You know it's not too late to change your mind," Hillary said.

"I'll sleep on it," she said with a wink at Jackson.

"What about you, J? You figure out what you gonna do?"

"Well, I've won seven straight Rose Bowls and have a killer recruiting class coming in . . ."

"Are you going to let him sit around and play video games all day as a married man?" Hillary asked.

"It'll be a nice break from the '80s reruns."

"I don't know yet, Hoss. I'm mulling options. But we both agreed we shouldn't just sit back and live off our millions."

"Especially since we could live off the interest," Maggie said.

"So we're going to figure out something to do. She has her book for a while, and I'm still kicking around ideas."

"P.I. one of 'em?"

"Maybe in some form. I could put forward a pretty good résumé, then pick and choose my clients a little more carefully."

"Thirty-six, twenty-four, thirty-six?" Hillary asked.

"Or we might make a modern reboot of *Hart to Hart*."

"You could never pull off Robert Wagner," Grant said.

"Alex O'Loughlin's a far cry from Jack Lord, but it works."

"What other options?" Hillary asked.

"Admiral Sullivan and I had a meeting last month."

"Don't tell me you're enlisting in the Navy," Grant said.

"No. We didn't talk specifics, but he hinted at a possible position as a liaison or advisor, or something."

"You're gonna be advising our military?" Reggie asked.

"I don't know what it'd be. But Sullivan was impressed by my acumen," Jackson said, raising the cigar to his lips.

"He teach you that word?" Hillary asked.

Jackson stuck out his tongue, and she smiled back at him.

"Anything else on the radar?" Grant asked.

"We're talking about building a house and doing most of the work ourselves—at least what we can."

"Do you know how to build a house?"

"It's 2014; I'll YouTube it."

Grant rolled his eyes.

"I'm not talking about running electrical wires or hanging trusses, but what we can. That would take a while, however, so I may not have a career per se anytime soon."

"Where would you build?" Hillary asked. "In the area?"

"Don't worry, we won't move to Bel Air," Maggie said with a smirk.

"We're actually considering San Diego. Be a little closer to Mom and Dad, get out of the gridlock of L.A. Move to St. Charles?"

"You keeping the estate?" Grant asked.

He shrugged. "We might sell it, might keep it as a vacation home. TBD."

"And depends if he's allowed back on the island," Maggie said.

"True enough."

"Either way," she said, "we've had such an odd dating relationship and then a short engagement that we want to spend a little time just getting used to being married before we make any permanent decisions."

"That's smart," Hillary said. "We've been so busy with work and getting the house set up that we haven't had a lot of us time to adjust, and it's been a weird year for us too."

"Not a lot of us time. So no baby announcement?" Jackson asked.

Hillary shook her head in disbelief and took a drink of her red wine.

The lull in conversation lasted for several seconds, which prompted Maggie to check the time. "We should get going, Jack."

"You can tell we're almost married," he said. "We're already turning into fuddy-duddies."

She kicked his knee. "I've got to finish my vows."

"You're writing your own?" Grant asked.

"Yes, and just relax, both of you. I knocked out your toast, didn't I?"

"Yeah, but you know what they say about lightning striking twice," Hillary said.

"It's the journalist who writes for a living having trouble, not me."

"Not exactly a Tuesday morning column," Maggie said.

"I guess not," Grant said. "But before you go, we have gifts."

"Gifts?"

"Pre-wedding presents," Hillary said as Grant reached around the side of the loveseat and lifted a gift bag and a wrapped box. He handed the bag to Jackson and the box to Maggie. "Nothing much," Hillary said. "We didn't pay for your honeymoon or anything, but we thought we'd help make it a little more special."

Maggie raised an eyebrow.

"Nothing weird," Grant said.

"Uh-huh." She looked at Jackson. "You go first."

He reached into the bag and lifted out a wad of tissue paper. Wrapped inside were two satiny pieces of cloth. He held them up. "Scarves?"

"Ascots," Grant said.

Jackson shot him a cockeyed look.

"We figured you'd want to go out for some nice romantic dinners, and, well, Maggie, Jack isn't known for his formal wardrobe."

"And you picked ascots?" Jackson asked.

"We thought it fit," Hillary said, "since you see yourself as an international man of leisure."

"There's also a gift certificate to Men's Wearhouse," Grant said. "They've got a store in Honolulu in case you don't have anything appropriate packed."

"Thank you. Ascots," he said, looking at Maggie.

She began to tear the paper loose from her package. Then she lifted the lid off the box and pulled out a dark blue baseball cap. She held it up. "Detroit Tigers."

"We also figured Jack would want to take another stab at finding Robin's Nest, and this would authenticate the *Magnum, P.I.* experience."

"Shouldn't I have gotten the cap?" Jackson asked.

"Knowing you," Hillary said, "we thought you'd find it sexy if Maggie was wearing the hat."

He pursed his lips, thinking for a moment. She, meanwhile, put it on over her chestnut hair. "What do you think?"

"It works," he said.

"And, there's a gift card to a women's fashion store in Waikiki," Hillary said.

"Jack said you looked great in all the sundresses you wore on St. Charles but still haven't gotten all your possessions back," Grant said.

"And let's be honest," Hillary tag-teamed, "he'll surely enjoy tagging along while you try on dresses."

"Hat fetishes, male scarves, you wanting to shop with me . . ." Maggie said. "Let's get out of here before this gets really awkward."

"Agreed."

"But seriously, thank you," she said.

"You're welcome," the married couple said in unison.

Jackson looked at Grant. "You guys headed home now?"

"Yeah, why?"

"Would you mind giving Maggie a ride? I need to have a man-to-man with Reggie."

"Sure."

They all stood, thanking Reggie for his hospitality.

"I will see you tomorrow," Maggie said, giving Jackson a quick kiss.

"Tomorrow." He pointed at the box in her hand. "Make sure you pack that hat."

She shook her head, hiding a smile.

Jackson turned and gave Grant's hand a shake, then gave Hillary a hug. "Maybe you can condescendingly tell me how to wear an ascot sometime."

"After you master the collared shirt."

He grinned as she, Grant, and Maggie left. Reggie watched until they were headed down the stairs, then turned to Jackson. "Can't believe the two of you are frenemies now."

"I know, right?"

"So what do you want to talk about?"

Jackson nodded at his chair, and they both sat down. "So I've been thinking a lot lately about life, about the past. I was thinking of that day we first met—what was it—eight years ago, how we became friends, and how ever since you've been paying me back—serving as my wingman on cases, giving me free club sandwiches, risking your life to save my family. And I know what you've said, about how we aren't keeping score because friends don't owe friends. And what I've realized, Hoss, is that we aren't friends anymore. We're brothers. And I don't mean that like homeboy brothers or really good friends. I mean you are family, Reg." He shook his head. "Tomorrow it isn't going to be the Douglas seven and Reggie; it's going to be the Douglas eight. You're one of us. And wherever life leads us, whatever comes, you know I'm always here for you, man, because you do for family. And I just wanted to tell you that."

Reggie nodded. "That means more than I can say, J. And I feel the same way. You're family. And Maggie. I don't think Hollywood could have cast a better woman for you, man, and if you're my brother, she's my sister. And you know I'm always there for you."

"I do, Hoss."

The jazz pianist had stopped, and now Perry Como was crooning over the speakers. The upstairs portion of the lounge had only one other group, in a booth tucked in the far corner.

"How do you feel about one more?" Reggie asked, holding up his cigar stub.

"I don't know, man, sounds like a gateway to lung cancer."

"It's celebratory, man. One for the job we finished, one for your upcoming nuptials."

"All right, you talked me into it. But then I gotta go."

"Vows?"

"I figure I should reduce the *Magnum* references to one, two at most."

"How many you got now?"

He squinted. "Four? Maybe five."

"We'll smoke 'em quick," Reggie said, then got up to get a pair of cigars.

Jackson sat back and took a few final puffs on his first cigar, looking up at the ceiling and listening to old-guy music that had survived the test of time. He couldn't help smiling as he thought back on the train wreck his life had been a few years ago. Now, his parents were back, his brother was back, and he was down to hours left before Maggie would become his wife. He offered a short but very sincere thank you heavenward, then put his cigar in an ashtray as Reggie returned with another.

The big man tossed him a gold-plated, engraved guillotine cigar cutter from his pocket, and Jackson pinched off the end of the cigar, then drew on a lighter to ignite it. Reggie did likewise, then dropped into the chair where Maggie had been sitting. He took a puff, then removed his cigar. "Here's to the continuation of a beautiful friendship."

Chapter One Hundred Sixty-Six

Monday, October 13
5:33 p.m.
Santa Monica, California

"YOU NERVOUS, BRO?"

Jackson glanced at Reggie beside him. "No. I've never been more certain of anything in my life."

Plus, he'd worn out his nerves already.

The wedding had been scheduled for Saturday afternoon, just before sunset, on a cordoned off stretch of beach near Cameron's. Esteban, the bartender at Cameron's, occasional cigar aficionado at Cameron's Lounge, and part-time crooner at each, had agreed to serve as musician. A guy from church who ran a part-time photography business had agreed to come take some photos—nothing fancy or staged, but a few mementos of the day. Katie, the new manager of Cameron's, had overseen catering and decorating, including a flower-adorned archway for Maggie to walk through, a white runner lined by flickering torches, and several more standing flower displays to enhance the vibe and provide a small measure of privacy on what was otherwise a public beach. Both Jackson and Maggie were looking forward to a simple, intimate ceremony, then a relaxed and casual dinner on the beach with family.

The Santa Ana Winds had other ideas.

They kicked up overnight Friday and brought dry, hot, dusty conditions to the California coast, including gusts into the forties and fifties. Since it was such a small group, all of whom were local (David and Hannah were crashing at Grant and Hillary's place) and since the best man owned the venue and employed the wedding support "staff," they decided to postpone until Sunday. Jackson changed his and Maggie's airline tickets and honeymoon reservations, and instead of a wedding, they ordered pizza and watched "I

Do?" and "Resolutions: Parts I and II," wedding themed episodes of *Magnum, P.I.*

The winds died out by Sunday morning, but they had ushered in atmospheric instability that resulted in unexpected rain. Sunday afternoon, facing a washout, Jackson and Maggie had made the decision to postpone again. Grant and Hillary had rearranged their schedules, albeit with a few jabs from Hillary about Jackson's fear of commitment driving the postponements. David and Hannah had made themselves more at home at Grant and Hillary's house. Reggie and Katie and Esteban and the photographer had all made the necessary adjustments. Jackson had altered travel arrangements again. And he and Maggie had spent the evening on Leroy's houseboat, playing Monopoly and joking that maybe this was a sign.

Then Monday had dawned clear and calm. Jackson had checked forecasts every five minutes until he was sure the evening would be perfect. As of three o'clock, a few fair-weather clouds were the only impingement on an otherwise beautiful October day. He dressed in a white dinner jacket and jeans, no tie. Another churchgoer who was something of an amateur florist, had provided him a burgundy carnation boutonniere. He liked to think of it as USC cardinal red. Reggie, dressed likewise, had one too. Leroy, the minister, had donned a tie with his jacket and jeans. David and Grant both wore button-down shirts, no ties, no jackets. David even had the sleeves rolled to his elbow. Hannah wore a dress, not the mother-of-the-groom floor-length V-neck she'd sported at Grant's wedding, but something a little more beachy. And Hillary, as usual, would have stopped traffic with her short-sleeved, flowing midi dress, her hair styled as if this was a prom. Her beauty, which for years had left Jackson nearly speechless, barely registered.

Instead, his eyes were focused down the runner to the flower-decked archway. As the late afternoon sun draped the beach in a golden filter, and as Esteban coaxed U2's "Beautiful Day" out of his acoustic guitar, accompanied by the waves crashing onshore a hundred yards west, Jackson waited for his bride to appear.

It was hard to believe. A year ago, he'd thought Maggie was out of his life forever. Marriage had been the farthest thing from his mind. He'd been alone, traveling the world, driven by a quest to reunite his family. Now, here he was, surrounded by the people who mattered most—the only ones who *really* mattered. The reality of what he'd accomplished, the miracle that he'd actually been successful, hadn't hit him at one particular moment, but had dawned on him more and more over the days and weeks. But this, right here and now, cemented it.

Beyond the ordeal with GrayStar, it was hard to believe he was getting married. Everything with Maggie had been so casual. Everything with everyone had been so casual. He'd never really thought—not with any specificity—about getting that serious, about getting married. Yet as he'd just told Reggie, he'd never been more sure of anything. That certainty had only grown on him in the two months since he'd proposed. And he, Mr. Casual, Mr. Laidback, Mr. Indifferent, was waiting with bated breath.

Maggie appeared in the arch. She wore a white, modified A-line dress with a portrait neckline. No flowing train. No puffs or lace or bows. Jackson wasn't even sure it was technically a wedding dress, but in its simplicity, it was perfectly her. She wore no veil or tiara, and her hair was styled beyond its natural wave, but nothing fancy. Its chestnut curls draped over her bare shoulders, catching glints of light as she began a slow, deliberate walk down the runner.

She was barefoot, wearing only a trace of makeup if any. Jackson had bought her a matching diamond pendant and teardrop earrings, which made up her only jewelry. The same florist had arranged for her a simple bouquet of carnations and dahlias, which she clutched before her as she approached. Jackson had always loved how good Maggie looked without the effort, without going through a ton of work to primp and prep, how simplicity worked for her, and he drank in her beauty now as she approached. Or tried to. Instead, he found his eyes glued to her radiant smile. It was the smile of someone perfectly content, perfectly satisfied, perfectly at home—and more than that, someone who was content and satisfied and home for the first time.

"You look spectacular," Jackson whispered as he stepped to her side and they interlocked arms.

"I thought you'd be wearing your ascot."

He grinned as they turned their attention to Leroy.

He cleared his throat. "Dearly beloved—and I say that not for the sake of tradition but because it's true—we are gathered here this beautiful day to celebrate the union of Jackson and Maggie. We've all shared a few laughs over the last couple of months about prayers being answered for Jack and wondering if he'd ever settle down, but I never had my doubts," he said, looking at Jackson directly. "I knew when the time was right, you'd choose wisely. And, Maggie," he said, turning her way, "I've had the pleasure of getting to know you over the years, and my grandson has chosen very well. To put it in football terms, he outkicked his coverage."

Maggie squeezed Jackson's arm with her own.

"Now, nobody likes a long wedding, and none of you all here need a whole lot of preaching to, and I get tired of standing too long, so I'll keep this brief. Jack, Maggie, I want to challenge you on three things that, if you do them, will guarantee you a long, happy marriage."

Leroy cleared his throat again. "First, you determine that failure is not an option. The Lord said '*they become one flesh.*' You have forever changed your status. You're no longer Jackson . . . and Maggie, you're Jackson and Maggie. In the Lord's eyes, that's an irreversible bond. And if it's one in your eyes as well, then you have a firm, secure foundation on which to face anything.

"Second, you choose to love each other every day. It may not feel like it now, when you're all young and in love and full of excitement, but take it from me—take it from anyone who's been married—the days will come when the feelings aren't there and you have to choose to love each other. Keep making that choice. Society tells us marriages last as long as two parties feel like making them last. But your marriage will last as long as you choose to make it last.

"First you need the right attitude. Second, you need to put that attitude into action. And third, you need to ask for help. Pray every day for each other and for your marriage. Ask for advice when you face new things. Ask for guidance if you're struggling. You've got people here who love you more than anything, and will do anything for you, who have faced challenges in life and in marriage and can show you the way through."

He cleared his throat again. "Now, I know that didn't sound all frilly and happy. But if you set your minds that failure is not an option, if you choose to love each other every day, and if you pray and ask for help—well, you'll find that the happiness kind of takes care of itself. Sure, you'll still have problems and hard times—you won't be floating on a cloud every day. But you will find strength to sustain you through the hard times and pave a foundation for plenty of good times. And, you know I'll be praying for you. In fact, let me start right now."

They all bowed their heads, Jackson and Maggie still clutching arms.

"Father," Leroy prayed, "we are so grateful to all be here today, in the middle of Your wonderful creation, surrounded by those we love and who love us. Personally, I'm so thankful You let me see both of my grandsons find godly women who love them and will partner with them in this covenant of marriage. Thank You for Jackson and Maggie, for their love for You, for each other, and for all of us. Guide them now on this path of marriage. I want to pray that You'll spare them hardships and difficulty, but I know that's not how life goes. I know that You use those challenges to make us stronger. So make them strong. Help them to love each other every day, through the good and the bad, to never lose sight of You, and to cherish each other as a priceless gift from on high. Bless their marriage—bless it abundantly—and bless others through them. We pray in Jesus' holy name, amen."

Several others echoed the amen, and Jackson mouthed a, "Thanks, Grandpa," as Leroy lifted his head.

"Now, the bride and groom have written their own vows. This should be good," Leory muttered.

Jackson and Maggie unlocked arms and turned to face each other. She held up her bouquet. "Um . . ."

Jackson looked over his shoulder. "Hoss, you mind?"

"You do for family," he said, then reached and took the bouquet from Maggie, who winked at him. Then she clutched Jackson's hands.

"Jackson," Leroy said.

"Maggie, I wish I could promise you today that my eyes will never wander, that I'll never utter a harsh word to you, never take you for granted, never be selfish or stubborn, never ignore you because I'm in the middle of a really good episode of *Magnum*. I wish I could promise to be the perfect husband, but you're not naïve enough to believe me anyhow. I know I'll fail and do all of those things, because I'm only human. And that's not to make excuses—which I will do plenty of too—but to be honest with you. We could spend hours listing my faults and outlining the ways I'll fail you or the ways you'll fail me. But instead, I want to focus on the thing that will never fail—love. I will always love you, Maggie. I promise you, no matter what happens, no matter what we say or do, no matter what we feel, that I will love you for as long as I live. I promise that I will always pray for you, and pray that God will help me to love you the way that I should. I promise to always be there for you, to always protect you—whether it's from two-bit critics who don't like your article or descendants of GrayStar with a vendetta—as long as I have breath in me. I promise to be your best friend—sorry, Reg—and your closest confidant. I promise to tenderly guide you through your failures and to allow you to guide me through mine, so help me God. Maggie, I love you, and more than anything, I promise that you and I—like Grandpa said—are irreversibly united. Through all the ups and downs, the good times and the bad ones, through our successes and failures, we will always be together, and we will face everything together."

Maggie's eyes were wet, but her voice was strong as she took her turn.

"Jack, when we met three and a half years ago, I thought you were a good-looking guy who might be fun to hang around with. I had no idea that you were also a man of strong faith and conviction, or that your faith and conviction would lead me to a faith of my own. I had no idea that you were brave, funny, caring, dedicated, clever, forgiving, and sometimes a loveable dork. More than anything, I had no idea . . ." she swallowed hard. "I had no idea that you would one day be home. Jack, you are the place where I feel right, where my world can be falling apart, but your smile, your embrace, your presence can make it all okay—just being with you makes it all okay. Until I met you, I could never envision settling down, couldn't see myself giving all of myself so freely to one person and only one person, couldn't see a lifetime commitment. But you make it easy. Jackson Lee Douglas, I promise to be faithful to you as long as we live, to love you and cherish you above all others, to encourage you when you're down and champion you when you succeed. I will be your lover, your partner, your wingman, and your friend. I will do all that I can to point you to Christ, and to follow you as you point me. And as life changes and life changes us, as we see our share of heartache and have our hearts warmed, I promise to be by your side always, because together is where we belong."

Leroy, his own eyes damp, turned to Reggie. "You have the rings?"

The big man fished into his pocket and handed Leroy a pair of rings. He handed Maggie's to Jackson, who slipped it on her finger after repeating Leroy's words: "Maggie, with this ring, I thee wed."

She then eased Jackson's ring onto his finger. "Jackson, with this ring, I thee wed." Her smile was as bright as the setting sun, and Jackson imprinted it on his mind as they turned to face Leroy. He gave Jackson a slightly sideways glance, and Jackson gave him a barely perceptible nod.

Leroy cleared his throat. "If there are any here who know any reason why these two should not be joined together in holy matrimony, let them speak now or forever hold their peace."

On cue, both Jackson and Maggie turned over their shoulders to look at Hillary.

Tongue in cheek, she gave them something between a smirk and a glare. Jackson winked at her, then turned back to Leroy.

"Um-hmm," he said. "Then, by the power vested in me by the State of California—and far more importantly by Almighty God—I now pronounce you man and wife. Jackson, you may kiss your bride."

*　　　　　*　　　　　*

6:23 p.m.

THE PHOTOGRAPHER snapped a few shots as the sun sank into the ocean. Then the Douglas Family sat down to an outdoor dinner. More torches and candles on the table lit their meal, and portable heaters kept away the evening chill. In keeping with the casual theme, dinner consisted of club sandwiches or burgers from the kitchen at Cameron's, with chocolate lava cake for dessert.

Several hours passed in laughter and stories and the pleasure of being with family. Hannah made almost everyone cry when she talked about how she had prayed nightly for her two little boys to grow up and meet godly women to be their wives, and how now, two very different but close brothers had found two very different but wonderful wives. Those whose eyes had somehow remained dry met their match in David, when he chokingly stated that for three years while he and Hannah and Grant had been on the run, he hadn't dared to dream—but hadn't been able to keep the dreams at bay—that someday his family would be united. And now, the last couple months and two weddings had made his dream complete.

Even Hillary took a turn praising the couple, sincerely, and Jackson refrained from any wisecracks. Leroy said he could die happy knowing that his grandsons were taken care of, and Reggie pledged his loyalty to the

Douglas Family. It was the sappiest moment of Jackson's life, and yet one of the best.

As the evening dwindled, he sat back, Maggie leaning against his shoulder, his arm around her. It was like a dream, the way his life had turned out. And he thought back to their conversations during "apartment life." What if he hadn't been taken with her and made time to send her a gift card, thus delaying him and Hillary from making it to San Diego in time for the dinner/evacuation/fake explosion? He and Hillary would have been in Argentina too, leaving Leroy all alone. Jackson and Maggie never would have gotten together. Jackson may not have survived GrayStar's attack on the safe house. Grant—if he had survived it—wouldn't have had anyone to run to, and there would have been no one to go after GrayStar. That one decision that had made him late had been a decision he had rued for years. Now, in retrospect, it was one of the best he'd ever made, even before considering the relationship it had launched.

He squeezed Maggie's shoulder, causing her to turn her head his way. "You want to head out?" she asked. "It's getting late."

He shook his head slightly, then dropped a kiss on her forehead. "We've got all the time in the world."

Chapter One-Hundred Sixty-Seven

Two and a half years ago . . .
Monday, May 14, 2012
7:27 a.m.

JACKSON AWOKE WITH a start when his cell phone began playing Kiss's "Shout it Out Loud." He lifted his head off the pillow and squinted against the light streaming in through the blinds. It was morning already?

He reached for the nightstand and grabbed his phone, then rolled onto his back, bringing the tangled sheets with him. Even in his condition, he recognized the ringtone he had set for his neighbor Connie. He glanced at the clock and stifled a sigh. It figured.

"Yeah?" he said, his throat dry.

"Oh, good, you're awake," Connie said in a sing-song voice. "I made sticky buns."

He blinked a few times, wondering if he was missing the obvious.

"For your birthday, dear." She lowered her voice, even though it was just her and Fluffy in the house. "I took a peek at the DMV."

"If you made coffee, you're forgiven."

"I'm insulted that you'd even question that."

"I'll be over in half an hour."

She clicked off and Jackson sat up with a smile. While there were other women—or at least one—he'd rather spend his birthday breakfast with, he couldn't deny how delicious Connie's cooking was. And about time all his favors and lawn-mowing paid off.

He had a quick shower, then ran a razor over his face and a brush across his teeth. He'd just poked his head through a Switchfoot *Vice Verses* T-shirt when his phone rang again, this time playing Green Day's cover of "I Fought the Law." He scooped it off the bed. "Yello?"

"Happy birthday, Jack."

"Thanks, Grant."

"You and Mom figure out where we're having dinner?"

"No. Sounds like she and Dad are way behind on stuff since getting back from D.C."

"Yeah, well, you provide the intel to take out an Al-Qaeda reboot, you have to take a few victory laps."

"I wouldn't know."

"So we going down there again?"

"No, Mom said they'd come up here since we went down to San Diego last year for my birthday. But we haven't figured out where."

"Okay. Let me know when you do. I'm planning to invite Maria, if that's okay?"

"Do I know her?"

"We just started dating a few weeks ago."

"She like the others?"

"Like the others?" Grant asked.

"Well, since you and Hillary broke up, it's been a string of dark-haired women who are very pleasant, and none of them exactly a stunner."

"You should talk, dating a teenager."

"Hailey's almost twenty-five, Grant, and we aren't dating; we're engaged."

"I'm just busting your chops, Jack."

"Let's save it for tonight. I've got sticky buns waiting for me."

"Okay. You'll call me?"

"I will call you. Man, if Maria doesn't work out as a girlfriend, maybe she can be a secretary."

"I'm sorry," Grant said through a yawn. "Night shifts are getting to me."

"Yeah. Hang in there, bro. I'll call you after I talk to Mom."

"After your sticky buns."

"Right."

"Later, Jack."

"Later." Jackson closed his phone, saw that he had a text from Hailey, and stopped at the top of the stairs to smile and send her one back. Technically, their first "date" had been his last birthday dinner, so this was their one-year anniversary. They were grabbing lunch and heading to the beach later. So for now, he focused on sticky buns and coffee he could almost smell.

His phone dinged, representing another text, and he glanced down to see Hailey had replied with a simple "X" and "O." He grinned as he tucked the phone in his pocket and reached for the last step. He missed and stumbled, and his effort to grab the railing caused him to spin around and bang his head on the wall. As his body sagged to the floor, his vision faded to black . . .

He woke groggily in a dark room, then blinked a few more times before realizing he was on the couch. The TV was off, and the clock on the cable box beneath it showed 11:58.

Jackson sat up slightly and surveyed the coffee table. The final quarter of a frozen pizza had congealed on a paper plate. It sat next to a closed photo album, itself beside a bottle of Glenmorangie scotch. The evening was coming back to him. He'd gotten the scotch as a gift from a client, and pulled it out the night before, maybe with intent and maybe to prove he could overcome temptation. He looked at the foil seal and saw that, intent aside, he'd passed the test.

Then his eyes drifted back to the cable box as the clock flicked to 12:00. That meant it was technically his birthday. The big Three-Oh. One year to the day since his world had been torn apart. Sticky buns, lunch beach dates, dinner plans, his family being alive—all a dream, one that was already fading from his mind.

His throat dry, he stood, a hunk of pepperoni falling off his shirt. He left the slice of pizza, the album, and the bottle on the coffee table and trooped up the steps. Without undressing, he crashed into his bed and flopped over onto his back. He stared up at the ceiling, resisting the urge to break into tears. He tried to pray, tried to ask for help, tried to ask for some way out of this mess. But he'd run out of ways to ask, and almost out of faith that God could ever make it better.

With a groaning sigh, he closed his eyes, hoping for sleep and maybe another dream that would serve as a brief respite from the nightmare his life had become—and was likely always to be.

*　　　　*　　　　*

Wednesday, October 15, 2014
7:20 p.m. (Hawaii Standard Time)
Honolulu, Hawaii

THE SUN had set, but the evening was still balmy. Trade winds stirred palm fronds overhead, caused the candles on the table to flicker, and lifted wisps of Maggie's hair off her shoulders. She looked even more casual and carefree than usual, in part because of the blue floral maxi sundress and in part because of the contented smile that had graced her face for the last two days.

They'd arrived in Hawaii the previous afternoon, and spent the first full day of their honeymoon lounging around the resort pool, taking a walk on the beach, and fighting off jetlag in a hammock in the shade. Their resort featured several restaurants, and in keeping with the day's theme of staying in, they'd chosen the Sunset Grille on a patio just yards from the surf. While leisurely dining on filet mignon and lobster tails, they'd discussed plans for the next two weeks—lots of sightseeing, including a helicopter tour, a trip to the Ko'olaus, the USS *Arizona* Memorial, and Diamond Head; plenty of time at the beach; sampling the island's best cuisine; and maybe a *Magnum, P.I.* reenactment or two. Maggie did have that cap, after all.

As Jackson drained the last of his iced tea, Maggie leaned toward him. "You want dessert here . . . or later?"

"Are they mutually exclusive?"

"Yes, because it's ten-thirty in my head, and a nap in the hammock aside, I'm tired."

He bit his lip.

"Jack, we're married now. You don't have to fight off my temptations any longer."

"Perish the thought, Mags, but the guava chiffon cake looks awfully inviting."

She slowly ran her tongue over her bottom lip. "Well . . . how about you get your guava chiffon cake and I'll head back to the room to wait?"

He grinned. "I was sure you were going to say 'slip into something more comfortable,' and I just know you, Maggie, that would be a Rangers hoodie."

"You are killing the mood."

He smirked. "I'll eat fast."

Maggie leaned in and gave him a slow kiss on the jaw. "I'll see you soon."

He smiled as he watched her exit the patio, taking a torch-lit, wood-plank path through the "jungle" back toward the resort's villas. As she disappeared into the darkness, he turned and signaled for the passing waiter. He ordered cake and a cup of coffee, then sat back and enjoyed the warm breeze and the strains of soft, unannoying ukulele music playing softly in the background.

The guava cake came quickly and was delicious. He was halfway through it when he sensed a presence beside him and turned, ready to ask Maggie if she'd changed her mind.

It was not Maggie, however, but a man in a stylish sport jacket over a bright white shirt, opened a button extra. He was young, handsome, his dark, short hair intentionally disheveled. He stood behind Maggie's chair and smiled with a closed mouth, his hands clasped in front of him.

Jackson took a sip of coffee as he looked up at him.

"Sorry to interrupt," the man said in a smooth voice, "but I noticed it was just you. Mind if I sit down for a minute?"

"All right," Jackson said, trying to place the guy from the patio. Normally he was pretty good at identifying people around him, but he'd been focused on Maggie.

"I'll be brief," the man said. "My name's Carmichael, and I'm what you might call a headhunter. I work for an organization that specializes in finding and recovering missing objects."

"Not the Osborne Corporation, is it?"

Carmichael grinned. "I should have known you'd know."

"Robbie give you my name?"

"She did. She said you were the best. And we'd like to hire you. An exclusive contract, working the cases you want, when you want. Full right of refusal. From what Robbie tells us and from our very thorough research, we're convinced you'd be a huge asset for our company, do a lot of good. And you won't find a more competitive salary or benefits package. Osco takes care of its people."

Jackson nodded and deliberately took a bite of his guava cake.

"I don't expect you to answer now, but I wanted to reach out to you privately—and secretly—and give you a chance to think about it."

Jackson nodded and took another sip of coffee. When it was clear Carmichael's pitch was over, he said, "Thanks, but no thanks. I've had enough. Enough killing, enough dodging bullets, enough with this life, and I don't need the money. I've got my family back. I've got a beautiful new wife waiting for me in our villa. I'm going to get a nice house in San Diego, find something with no stress to occupy my days, and come home to my wife every night . . . visit my parents on the weekends, maybe give them some grandchildren. And the closest I ever want to come to this sort of cloak-and-dagger life is watching *Colombo* reruns on a rainy Sunday night."

Carmichael smiled. "I understand." He reached into his jacket and pulled out a business card. "If you change your mind," he said, handing it to Jackson, "the offer stands." He stood and extended his hand. "Thanks for your time. Enjoy your honeymoon."

Jackson watched the man walk away, then studied the card. Just a phone number, toll free. Nothing more. Jackson took a final bite of his guava cake, thinking. He washed it down with a gulp of coffee, then reached for his wallet. He stopped. He remembered the explosion that had rocked his world and the feeling when he thought his family was gone forever. He remembered what it felt like to take a life . . . the first time, the second, the third, and the last. He remembered embracing his parents after three-plus years apart.

And he remembered Maggie and her floral sundress, her brilliant smile, her beguiling eyes.

He tore the card into several pieces and dropped them into the inch of watered down tea at the bottom of his glass.

Then he stood and, without looking back, smiled as he headed back to the villa and his waiting wife.

The End?

Author's Note

TWELVE YEARS AGO, I was watching an episode of *Magnum, P.I.* (I bet you couldn't tell I was a fan) when the idea hit me to write a series of books all revolving around the same set of characters. As with most of my inspiration, this idea grabbed me suddenly and started running. I was only too happy to try to keep up, and before I knew it, *The Douglas Files* had been conceived.

I began fashioning characters and searching for a home for them, collecting plots and subplots, and drafting a master plan for *the* story. Jackson is a hodgepodge of my favorite fictional detectives and adventurers, everybody from "Hannibal" on *The A-Team* to Shawn Spencer, Psychic Detective. (You're picturing him with his finger to his temple, aren't you?) There's a little bit of me in there too, as some of you have noticed, and some of the me I wish there was or am glad there isn't. Jackson can say and do things I never would (like date multiple women at the same time) and have adventures I'd never have the courage to undertake. Some of those adventures got a little carried away, admittedly, but I tried to keep them as realistic as possible—with the understanding that if Jackson was a regular guy, there wouldn't be much to write about.

I also lived vicariously through Jackson. I've never shot a gangster with a Glock, played high-stakes poker in Vegas, rubbed elbows with Hollywood starlets, survived a shootout atop Masada, skin-dived off the Keys, or enlisted the aid of a former Mossad agent. (Okay, scratch that "realistic as possible" bit in the previous paragraph.) Vicarious living went beyond being an action hero. Jackson Douglas gave me a chance to see the world (mostly through Google Street View), to be a smart-aleck with no reprisal, to once more feel the searing leather seats of Grandpa's candy-apple red 1976 Ford Granada, to take chances I otherwise wouldn't dare, and to tip my (Detroit Tigers) cap to Thomas Magnum as often as possible. (I, like Jackson, am a dork.)

As for those aforementioned women, the original plan was to have Jackson date both Maggie and Sam but end up with neither. I was going to have him fall for another woman in the end, but as I tried to design the ideal girl for Jackson, I realized she already existed. Like he told Maggie, they were made for each other (although Sawyer tried awfully hard to get in the way in *Golden Key*).

I made Jackson a protagonist with a heavy burden, and I couldn't tell you exactly why. From day one, the plan was for him to ultimately have that burden lifted (my sister can swear to that, as I laid out the "aha!" end-game on her old deck in the summer of 2010), but to have him just about broken before that. Some of you can relate to that. In my own way, over these last dozen years, so can I. Some of that struggle came out in Jackson's—it was the truest and purest writing I've ever done, albeit fiction. Much more of it was just imagination and letting the character take over.

Speaking of that imagination, it never stops. People ask where I get ideas, and I tell them they come from everywhere—a newspaper headline, a subplot of a movie or TV show, or long walks around the neighborhood to stir them up. I imagined plenty of fictional locations too (there is no Dutch island of St. Charles, for example) while blending in plenty of real ones. Sometimes across the street from each other. I did as much research as I could stomach, and excused the rest to "artistic license."

Throughout the years, I've been indebted to numerous people for their encouragement and kind words. I am especially grateful to Sierra, Mom, Dad, Mark, and Tiffani. They have proofed almost all if not every book, listened to countless ideas, answered questions, and provided a morale boost when it was needed. There have been others too, who have been named before, but the five above have been my rocks. Over the last ten years, our group of six has grown to eleven with the addition of five nieces and nephews. They know next to nothing about Jackson Douglas, and I don't know if they've ever *attempted* to boost my spirits, but Caleb, Gabey, Chloe, Sophie, and Laynie mean the world to me, and have been invaluable to my psyche over the life of *The Douglas Files*.

I would be remiss if I didn't also thank God for all He has blessed me with. There are plenty of hardships in life, as Jackson can attest to, but plenty of highlights too. And ultimately, there is life everlasting through Jesus Christ. No words of thanks in an "acknowledgments" section can ever be sufficient for His grace and mercy, but here they are anyhow. I'm also grateful that God has given me the ability to write. The name Birr may not be bandied about with the likes of Cussler and Grisham just yet, but this labor of love/hobby is one of those highlights—one of the things that truly brings me joy in this world. If you've stuck with me through all ten books in this series—or, for that matter, if *Nine Lives* was your first foray into *The Douglas Files*—I hope that in some way Jackson's story has brought a little joy to you as well. (If it hasn't, that old smart-aleck side might have caused some harm after all.)

One more thing, as my late detective friend Columbo would often say, some of you may wonder about the way this novel ended, with a question mark. Is this really The End for Jackson Douglas? I'll say this—*The Douglas Files* are closed. But Jackson and Maggie—and the entire Douglas family—have their whole lives in front of them. Who knows what sort of adventures and mysteries might ensue?